Stay With Me

Single Dads of Meadowbrook Book 2

ROSE FRESQUEZ

Paperback ISBN: 978-1-961159-25-9

ACKNOWLEDGEMENTS

I want to thank the Lord, my Savior. Without you, Father, there's no point in trying to do anything at all. It's my prayer that I can honor you with my words. I thank you for connecting me with an amazing group of people who helped support me in accomplishing this novel.

To my husband Joel, who works so hard to provide for our family, so that I can stay home and take care of the kids. I'm so blessed that we get to journey through life together.

To my children Isaiah, Caleb, Abigail and Micah, you fill my heart with joy. Thanks for the giggles, laughter and encouragement.

To my editor, Deirdre Lockhart. You're a true blessing from God. Your insights and wisdom have helped shape this story. To my friend Trudy Cordle, Thanks for re-reading the manuscript to clear out any slip throughs. To my Beta Team, Thanks for willing to answer any questions I have during the early stages of my manuscript.

To my insider team, thanks for always suggesting the coolest ideas.

And to my Street Team. Thank you from the bottom of my heart for helping spread the word about my book.

CHAPTER 1

Ethan

I doubt I'll ever forget the girl who made me believe in forever—or stop wondering what might've been if things hadn't ended so badly between us.

Days like today, mentoring a couple on their way to marriage, make the ache unbearable. This time, it's Jason Sterling, my best friend, walking ahead of me with his fiancée. His arm drapes over Valentina's shoulders as he guides her along the narrow path by the well-lit pool. They lean close, lost in their own world, his whisper drawing out her laughter. The sound stirs a longing for the kind of love I once had. Young, hopeful, and full of possibilities. A love I threw away.

"My office here is more spacious than the one at the church." I adjust the folder under my arm. "Better acoustics too."

They don't respond. Jason traces lazy circles on Valentina's shoulder while she points out the fountain. I might as well be invisible.

As a pastor, I've officiated many weddings, and while each is special, Jason's in four days has me thrilled like I'm the groom. He was so confident he'd never marry again. Then Valentina stormed into his life. If he'd surrender to marital bliss, there's hope for everyone to find their one and only. Except for me, I found—and lost—mine.

Their laughter blends with distant music from the restoration center's main room. Glowing lamps line the walkways, haloing manicured gardens and sitting areas. The last of the evening light fades, its reflection shimmering on the pool's still surface.

It's quieter in the gardens tonight, due to the event in the clubroom. I wave at familiar residents along Skypoint's winding pathways, though I try to keep a low profile. My role here extends beyond founding this center. Warmth settles in my chest as laughter drifts from the tables edging the pool. Every time I walk these grounds, I savor the same assurance I experienced when I signed the papers. It's a place for soldiers and anyone who needs a temporary home to heal wounds, both seen and unseen. Tonight, it's also pulling double duty as an impromptu counseling center, since teenagers took over the church for their annual October slumber party.

Please, God, keep sending generous donors so we can continue to run Skypoint at its full potential.

The air shifts when a slender woman emerges from a powder room beyond the pool. Her heels click against the courtyard tiles, her focus on the main four-story stone building.

Something about her tugs at my memory, and my pulse quickens. I don't make a habit of noticing women, but a daunting familiarity compels my gaze.

She rounds the bend, and my breath catches. Flawless brown skin. Pixie hair. Taller than I remember, or maybe it's the poise she now carries herself with. Striking enough to pin me in place.

No. It can't be.

But even with her hair cropped close, I know that jawline. That stride. Every part of me remembers. The last time I saw her, her hair spilled over her shoulders. Twelve aching years ago.

I blink hard, take another look. It's her.

"Ruby?" Her name slips from my lips. I step forward. "Ruby!"

"Should I know Ruby?" Jason glances over his shoulder.

I lengthen my stride, squeezing past the couple. "Ruby."

"Ethan?" Valentina's voice floats behind me as I pull ahead. Ruby stops.

The world blurs. My foot catches something, a side table, sending bottles clattering across the tiles. My hands flail as momentum carries me forward. Warm water swallows me whole, the sting of chlorine in my nose. I push up through the surface, sputtering, water streaming down my face.

Gasps and laughter burst around the pool deck.

"Sorry!" I call to the amused bystanders as I swipe water from my face and wade to the edge.

She's closer now, right at the edge. Those brown eyes lock on me. But the spark I remember is dimmed, replaced by something... guarded? Her lips twitch into a half smile, and I'm fourteen or fifteen again and the rest of my teenage years narrow into a single blur—Brooklyn summers, her laugh bouncing off alleyways, her bravado daring me to keep up. Oh, how many times did we climb fire escapes to watch the sunset from the rooftops?

"Ruby?" I breathe her name, needing confirmation.

She's still there, eyes narrowing as if trying to make sense of me. I cling to the cool tile wall and take her in. Those eyes gleam in the light. Her disbelief mirrors my feelings, but we just stare without moving. I'm dizzy in a way I haven't been in years. I'm not the pastor or single dad with responsibilities pressing in from all sides—I'm a teenager deeply in love with the most beautiful and adventurous girl, the one who held every dream I thought I had at the time.

"Ethan?" The *V* between her brows deepens. "Is it really you?"

Every word I've rehearsed in imaginary conversations over twelve years sticks in my throat. With my heart pounding so hard, I can barely think straight. But I manage a nod.

"You always did know how to make a scene."

"Only you... could make me forget how to walk straight."

Her gaze dips to my left hand. I follow it to where I'm gripping the pool's edge. The gold band catches the lamplight.

When I look back at her, her smile is already slipping.

Why haven't I taken it off? Maddie's been gone almost seven years. Okay, I know why I kept the ring on, but right now, it feels trivial.

Ruby crouches, one hand braced on the deck ledge, the other resting on her knee. No ring, but that doesn't mean anything. She's thirty-two and beautiful. Could be dating or married and forgot to wear her ring today.

My stomach coils at that. But I have no right to be jealous.

"It's... really good to see you."

"I'm..." Her voice trembles. "So glad to see you too. I can't believe it's you."

A microphone squeals its sound test from the main building, and something shadows her features.

She stands and steps back. "It's unfortunate I have to be on stage in five minutes."

"Of course."

But what I want to say is: "I'm sorry for breaking your heart. Sorry for disappearing. Sorry for every word I should have said and didn't."

Instead, I watch her go, heels clicking against stone tiles like a countdown.

"Ethan." Jason extends a hand to pull me out of the pool.

I shake my head, and reality crashes down. His grip is firm, a jolt back to the present, to Mrs. McBride, the punctual seventy-nine-year-old babysitter waiting at home, and the Sunday sermon I haven't started working on. Not to mention, it's a school night for the kids.

Otherwise, I'd stay. I'd wait for Ruby to finish—what, exactly? Performing?

"Care to explain, Pastor?" Jason tosses over a towel. "Who is she?"

I catch it, rub the water from my face, then drag it across my drenched shirt. "Someone... my past."

Grinning, Valentina nudges Jason. "Sounds interesting."

"It's a long story. For another time." I scrub the towel through my hair, but my gaze and mind drift toward the building Ruby entered. "Someone important."

"Clearly." Valentina exchanges a knowing look with Jason.

"Looks like our pastor has a few stories of his own." He smirks.

"It's complicated," I say.

"Love usually is." Valentina's smile holds the wisdom of someone who's fought for her happy ending. "Perhaps he can fill us in on those details during tonight's counseling session."

They linger, warmth evident in the way he holds her close and whispers something that makes her smile. My chest tightens with longing, not just for Ruby but also for that sure comfort shared between them.

"You two are going to be just fine." I slip back into counselor mode and look around for my folder. But where is it among the mess of scattered bottles and cans? Guess we didn't need the last session after all. "Just put God first, keep talking to each other. Remain open and forgiving—"

"And avoid pools," Jason quips. "You'd better not pull this stunt on Saturday."

"No promises." Even as I joke, my gaze strays again to that empty doorway.

Music now floats out.

After my friends leave, my feet carry me to the lobby. Cool air bites against my drippy clothes as I wrap my arms around myself. A wall-mounted screen streams the live performance from the clubroom.

I nearly swallow my tongue.

Seated before the piano, eyes closed, Ruby glides her fingers over the keys. With the melody so achingly haunting, the entire room's transfixed.

She always had a captivating voice when she sang in the school choir, but playing the piano?

What else has she learned in our years apart?

From time to time, I come to the restoration center events. Most performers are volunteers, drawn by Skypoint's healing mission. Is that why Ruby's here? Or is this just another stop on a tour?

A deep longing grips my chest. Every instinct urges me to stay, to wait and talk, to perhaps close the twelve-year gap between us.

But I need to sort through my thoughts, figure out where to start. I spent years wishing I'd see her again. And now that she's here? I'm terrified it won't be enough.

The reflective song ends and flows into another, and her fingers glide with ease. After a lingering look at her beautiful face, her eyes now open, I turn away and carry unfinished business into the night.

It was I, after all, who ended it. And it's my greatest regret.

But how did Ruby end up here? Will she stay on schedule? Might I see her again? Maybe some prayers get answered in ways you never expect.

Her appearance today is an answer to prayer. One way or another, I'll contact her through our event coordinator. If I get a second chance with her, I won't take it for granted.

The wedding band feels heavy on my finger. Time to take it off, let go of what's gone, and fight for what's still here. Now I just need to pray she's still single and willing to talk to me again.

CHAPTER 2

Ruby

"If you close your eyes, you'll realize you only get one life to live." Emotion clogs my throat as words spill from my lips. My fingers glide across the piano keys, anchoring me with the familiar melody. I pray these words, composed during one of my darkest hours, will encourage someone tonight. "Live each day as your last and embrace those around you."

My life veered off course twelve years ago. Scattered thoughts spiral into dead ends, shadows flicker at the edge of my vision, and sometimes I see things that aren't there. Too much medication can twist a mind that way. But it's been six months since I've touched anything, not even for a headache. Still, my history makes me question what I saw by the pool: water dripping from his dark hair, that impossible dimple where I remembered it.

I keep my eyes closed. Then, opening them, I make a quick sweep of the audience. I don't need to look at the sheet music. My voice dips to a whisper, threading through the air.

"Every day is a gift...."

Like today for me. I just saw Ethan. My heart is still racing. It's irrational, probably, but I feel him out there—watching me. He always had that magnetic pull, awakening a sixth sense. I'd told myself I was over him. But the second I saw him... well, my heart forgot the memo.

Besides taking me off medication, my shrink, Brenda Calderon, ended my therapy sessions. If I sense old patterns threatening to break through, then I must call her. But I'm now in a good place and should start living again. After seeing Ethan—even if I just imagined him?—that's a dream I'd willingly lose myself in. And a reason I might have to call Brenda again.

The final notes fade into applause. I open my eyes, nod, then transition into the next two songs as scheduled, muscle memory guiding me, even as my thoughts drift.

When the guitarist steps onto the stage, I slip away from the piano bench, clutch my purse tight, and exit the back side door. Willow and I agreed to meet at her car after my performance, but I need clarity, proof tonight's vision wasn't another cruel trick of my mind.

My feet hurry toward the courtyard, to the place where I could've sworn I interacted with Ethan.

There's no sign he's been here, though. Except for the pool he was seemingly in, the water now catching the reflection of string lights, the surface disturbed by the evening breeze. Even the people laughing under the yellow umbrellas earlier are nowhere in sight.

But if it was Ethan, wouldn't he have wanted to wait and talk to me? Regardless of the way things ended between us? I shake my head, my heels clicking against the tile as I swing open the back door from the pool area. Then I make my way to the lot.

Clearly, I imagined the encounter. Why would Ethan be at a restoration center? It's for people to find their footing again after battling addiction, anxiety, depression, or trauma. Unless he's a pastor here to counsel the residents?

The blue Forte is right where we left it, parked under the streetlamp near the back row.

Willow's head bobs behind the wheel, engine running. She's my closest friend, my only confidant. We're the same age, thirty-two, but she carries a confidence I lost somewhere along the way. I swing open the door and slide into the passenger seat. Willow hums "One Life to Live," a melody I sang tonight, fingers tapping the steering wheel like she doesn't see me.

I set my purse at my feet. "Sorry if I kept you waiting."

"You were incredible tonight." She pivots toward me. "I knew you'd be a blessing to the residents here."

"You only say that because you think flattery will guilt me into staying in Meadowbrook." I fasten my seat belt, grateful for the transition, my mind still reeling.

"Dare I remind you that you moved in last night?" Willow shifts in her seat and backs out of the lot. "The librarian is expecting us on Friday when the new printer comes in. We're getting flyers printed and handing them out right after. This town's always been your dream. Now that you're here, I'll make you stay and take root."

One step to beating anxiety is taking root. Not exactly Brenda's words, but something I've underlined more than once in the book, *Anxiety Shadows*, I've been reading these past months. "Thank you for telling me about Skypoint. Performing for an audience with little to no expectations felt good. And yes, Meadowbrook was once my dream." With Ethan. Back when we pictured a future here before it all fell apart.

She pats my arm. "Like you wrote in 'One Life to Live,' you gotta live each day like it's your last. And that starts with letting people in."

Or so Brenda advises. I just grunt my response.

I spent years dodging real friendships, fearful of anyone knowing what went on at home. Once Ethan came into my life, I didn't need anyone else.

I let out a breath. "Thanks, girl. If it weren't for you always checking in, I doubt I'd be in town now."

She doesn't respond. Doesn't have to. We met six years ago at a restoration center—me trying to claw my way out of another relapse, her speaking about the power of connection. About how easy it is to lose hope when no one reminds you that you matter. She didn't ask why I was there, and I didn't divulge it.

She talked me into teaching piano lessons after hearing me play one evening. We even shared a booth fee at the Park Fest in Ridgewood, her recording interviews for her relationship podcast, me handing out flyers, desperate for students to cover rent for a studio I couldn't afford. I thought I was ready for routine back then. I wasn't. I ended up working for an established studio instead.

"Now that you're in Meadowbrook, you can sign up anytime to sing and play at Skypoint." Her voice pulls me out of my thoughts. "They might even start paying if you're consistent."

"Seeing their faces light up—that's payment enough."

Music's been my therapy, the only thing that reached me when nothing else could.

Her kind eyes catch the dashboard light as she glances my way. "Sunday's a long way off, but in case you need to plan, I usually close the shop and go to church."

I fold my hands in my lap. "I was hoping you could join me for a drive. Hudson Valley and the nearby towns? Foliage should be at its peak right now."

It's fantastic to be here. I already had good memories of Meadowbrook, but knowing Willow lives here makes me feel less like a stranger. When I admitted I'd visited and loved it, she jumped straight into convincing me to move here. She might have backed off if I hadn't left out the part about discovering this place with my ex. The love of my life, though, apparently, the feeling wasn't mutual.

"Maybe we can go after church..." She hesitates. "I mean, when I get back from church."

I prefer online services. I've never explained why I dread stepping inside a church. It might stir up memories I'd rather leave undisturbed.

Streetlights flash across her honey-brown hair as we drive, and soft shadows move over her neutral expression. Good. She's not upset I turned her down. God understands my history with church and why I talk to Him on my own. For now, that's enough.

"If memory serves, you don't have any pumpkins yet. We need some to set the tone for the season."

"That's another reason I wanted a roommate." She adjusts the heater before returning her hand to the steering wheel. "Mom decorates her place like it's a magazine spread. After seeing hers, I get my fill."

"I appreciate you letting me stay with you."

"Happy to have you. It can get lonely sometimes."

I can attest to that.

Beyond the window, shadowy trees blur past. Maybe this time I'll let my roots settle. "How'd you get connected with Skypoint?" And what was Ethan doing there?

"One of my friends coordinates events." She navigates a hairpin turn on the winding road. "The founder is my pastor, which makes it easy to root for the place."

What I want to ask is whether she knows Ethan Bishop. Did I really see him?

If so, why didn't he stay for the entertainment and wait to talk to me? After all, we haven't seen each other all these years. Maybe he stayed, and I left too soon? I hope so. Yet, I know better. If what I saw was real, Ethan was wearing a wedding ring, which means his brother was telling the truth all those years ago, when he found me and apologized for whatever role he played in ending things between us.

I was never worth fighting for. My chest tightens, squeezing with the weight of that day—Ethan walking away, my mom passing, the cruel storm that followed. My breathing turns shallow, and my ribs ache. I press a hand to my sternum and force a slow inhale, then another, like they taught me after my last episode. Of course, I don't get any more of those.

"You okay?" Willow asks.

I nod too quickly. "Just tired."

Leaning my head against the window, I let the darkness blur by. When I arrived earlier, the hills were brushed in autumn gold and ruby red, and the place seemed to promise fresh starts. Now, with night closing in, it all feels so far away.

I hate being bad company. I straighten up, figuratively and literally. "Can we listen to your radio station?"

"If you're hoping for *Heartline with Willow*, it's not on at this hour."

"But the station still plays decent music." I tinker with the knob, and I'm met with static.

"Around this curve, the radio station gets messed up, but we're almost home." A softness enters her tone now, like she's caught on to my earlier panic. "You can spend tomorrow resting. The apartment isn't big, as you've noticed, but I'll stay out of your space."

"It's your place. I should be the one saying that."

"If we hand out flyers on Friday or Saturday, you can begin building your student list."

"I'll start at the coffee shop on Monday, then. Enough time for me to get trained—"

"Why not take the rest of this week and next off? You still need to unpack."

"Wow, unpacking two suitcases, even at a tortoise's pace, won't take that many days." I give her a look that says I'm meeting her halfway. "I'll start Monday. Deal?"

She laughs. "Bossy. Landon will cover the afternoons starting on Monday, then."

"You're so kind to let me move in."

"You insisted on earning your keep. I don't feel like I've given you anything to thank me for."

I would've worried I was taking Landon's job, but he can only work half days anyway.

We turn onto Main Street. String lights loop between vintage lampposts, hand-painted signs line brick sidewalks, and shop windows glow with Closed signs. At the end of the block, Willow turns down a narrow alley and parks behind a brick building. "Each resident is assigned to two spots in this lot, by the way."

"Great. If I get a car soon, I'll have a place to park." There's no bus service, so in the meantime, I'll take a taxi to places I can't walk.

We head to one of the metal staircases, all with balconies. Hers, strung with lights, leads to the private rear entrance above her family's café/bookshop.

"I can't wait to check out the shop." My shoes clatter up the steps. "Didn't have time to explore it last night."

"And the best surprise?" She pauses at the door, grinning. "Someone was giving away a piano."

My eyes widen. "No way."

"Way. Guess where it ended up?"

"In the bookshop?"

"Bingo. Play whenever you want. It's all yours."

"Wow." My hand presses against my chest as my heart warms. My shoulders loosen, my bag nearly sliding off. "I'd planned to travel to students' homes for lessons, but this changes everything. I can't believe you were able to find a free one."

"I promised, didn't I?" She unlocks the door and motions for me to go in first.

"Yes, but you did it so soon. Thank you!" I step into the warm apartment. Amber and cream walls, earth-toned furnishings, and exposed brick further cozy the atmosphere. As does the faint scent of cinnamon and coffee drifting from below. "I just love this place."

"I try to keep life simple." Willow hangs her bag on a wall hook and kicks off her shoes.

I do the same, sliding mine onto the mat beneath the bench. "Simple? That's impressive for someone who hosts a relationship-advice show."

She laughs. "Talking about love and actually living it? Two very different skills." Waving me along, she walks to the kitchen and opens the fridge. "I've got leftovers if you're hungry."

"They fed me before the performance." Though my stomach was still too tight after the Ethan encounter.

"I'll let you settle in. If you want, we can sit on the balcony later. The view overlooking the town at night is stunning. Not Brooklyn kind of magic, but it's still something."

"Let me shower and change first." I'm already anticipating my cozy sweats and sweatshirt, both the same shade of green as the top she's wearing.

She nods and disappears into her room while I step into mine. With my candles lit and a photo of my mom and aunt on the nightstand, the space already feels like home—the start of something new.

Ruby

The rest of the week, Willow insists I relax and settle in. Not that I need much time, after unpacking two bags in two hours. But I savor the stillness and catch up on sleep. *And* I think about Ethan way more than before Skypoint. Still, I do my best to shove him aside.

When Willow goes to work at the radio station, I read and dust the bookstore section of her coffee shop while Landon runs the shop. I don't play the piano when people show up for a book club, but each evening after the store closes at four, I head downstairs to play and sing while no one other than Willow is around to listen.

Now, I need to pick up the coffee-shop basics.

"The espresso machine looks intimidating, but it's pretty straightforward." Willow tells me while Landon tends to customers. She flips switches and presses buttons with ease. "You'll mostly be making basic drinks, nothing fancy."

I trail her through the café space, meeting some usual customers and trying to commit their names to memory. She points out the menu's most popular items. Most are named after literary couples, of course.

"The *Romeo and Juliet* is our sweet vanilla latte. *Elizabeth and Darcy* is strong coffee with a hint of bergamot. And *Gatsby and Daisy*?" She smirks. "Champagne-colored tea. Looks romantic—tastes bitter."

"I've never worked as a barista, but I'll do whatever it takes to earn my keep until I can start booking piano students."

"Smoothies are easy enough."

"Says you." I tap anxiety out through my toe. "The blender's many buttons and settings leave me second-guessing myself. I'll have to shadow Landon again one evening."

She shrugs. "That's easy enough. And you met our baker during this morning's delivery." She then gives the rundown on how she handles payments through Sips and Scripts to pay the supplier.

It's Sunday before long, and I sleep in, waking at a knock on my door. I rub my eyes as the door creaks open.

"Just checking to see if you're okay." Willow peeks through the doorway, her brown hair catching the light streaming in from the window. She's wearing a brown floral dress with leggings underneath. Either she's going to church, or she's just coming back.

"What time is it?" I yawn, sitting up.

"Only twelve." She winks.

"Twelve!" I leap out of bed. "Let me make lunch."

I've not been into breakfast for a long time, not since rehab. After we eat a prepackaged roast I microwave, I shower and change. Then we drive around Meadowbrook's outskirts, meandering along country roads with the windows down, music low. My heart soars as I take in the town I fell in love with. During those last three years with Ethan, we read about the best fall destinations, and Meadowbrook, lined with gold and ruby trees, was in the top ten. I told Ethan we had to check it out since it was just a train ride away. After that, we visited each fall until our breakup.

We extend our drive to Hudson Valley, its historic downtown and the surrounding hills stunning. My breath catches again as memories resurface. Ethan and I ventured here before. Fall was a favorite time for us.

We drive fifteen minutes to Catskill, right across the river from Hudson, and wander one of the riverfront parks, following trails through ruby red and gold leaves. It's as beautiful as Meadowbrook, but I'll save exploring my new town for tomorrow.

From there, we head another thirty minutes to Rhinebeck. Maples and old brick storefronts line the postcardlike historic downtown, where I treat us to ice cream and steaming apple cider.

Our last stop is Sunvalley. There, a fall festival spills across the town square, and the air smells of cinnamon, sugar and woodsmoke. We pass hay bales stacked into a photo backdrop, a row of carved pumpkin displays, and tents where kids bob for apples, families compete in pie-eating contests, and teams race to build the tallest scarecrow. I buy us each a pumpkin, already picturing them against the balcony railing. And a small pumpkin for the coffee table next to the lantern with a flameless candle.

By the time we return, most shops are closing.

"Sundays, shops close a lot earlier," Willow says as we walk down Main Street.

A few people greet her by name, others wave or smile, and she pauses to introduce me when we stop to chat. I return their polite smiles, but it's clear Willow belongs here. Maybe I'll get comfortable around this new community someday.

We grab dinner at Brook's Diner with some regulars, Willow pausing midbite to introduce me to the people who stop by to say hello.

Back at the coffee shop, we lug two large pumpkins up the stairs, and somehow, in this town, I feel closer to Ethan than I have in years. Maybe it's just the place. Or maybe it's the memories I've spent years trying to bury, the ones I rerouted every time they clawed their way up... until five days ago. I healed without him. But seeing him again stirs the ache of remembering how we used to be.

Surely, it was just someone who looked like Ethan. I'm not letting him take over my head again. I came to Meadowbrook to start over. And that means... without him.

CHAPTER 3

Ethan

"Daddy, don't go!" Poppy's arms wrap around my neck. Cloud, the stuffed unicorn, presses between us. Now seven, she's mastered the art of turning a goodbye into a guilt trip.

"For only three hours." I kiss her forehead, breathing in that familiar soft shampoo scent. A stray curl sticks to her skin. I brush it back. "Mrs. Chen is going to take good care of you and Asher." I nod to my son, who's got a new tower to show off. "Right, buddy?"

Asher, thirteen months older than Poppy, is knee-deep in Lego bricks, narrating his latest invention to Fei Chen, who watches with an indulgent grin. One minute, he's lost in the still focus of building. The next, he's all energy and motion, chasing down any sport that involves running.

Poppy isn't up for that kind of chaos, but Asher will slow his stride to match hers.

"Go say goodbye to your father, Asher." Fei calls him over, her voice warm as she sits on the ABC-print rubber mat.

"Bye, Daddy!" he calls without looking up, stacking another set of blocks.

I shift Poppy's weight and lower her to the mat.

"Come here, sweetheart." Fei pats the space beside her, her rough hands brushing mine as she gathers Poppy close. She's older than my mother. But her glossy dark bob catches the morning light streaming through the window, and her gray strands remain barely visible despite her seventy-three years.

"She'll be okay, Pastor. Don't worry." Fei lifts one finger. "Yī." Then a second. "Èr."

When she holds up the third, Poppy's voice stirs beside her. "Sān."

The rhythm's a little different from the other caretakers. But that's what I want—my kids being open to different cultures, different people, and experiencing care from our community. Perhaps the variety helps them feel safe with more than just me.

"Thank you."

"I like babies any time."

Poppy isn't a baby, but to someone with grown kids, she still counts.

I crouch and brush my thumb over Poppy's cheek one last time. She leans into the touch, but her lower lip quivers. That look always creeps in—quiet sorrow, like a shadow for the mother she's never known.

"Where's that smile, Peanut?" I tickle under her chin, coaxing a flicker of a grin. "That's not enough." I find the soft spot behind her ear, and her laughter bursts out—shoulders shaking, eyes crinkling. The sound wraps around me and eases the tightness in my chest.

Fei laughs too and rises as she clasps Poppy's hand and gathers stuffed animals. "Time to take our animals to the vet. And guess what? We've got real cookies to bake, to reward ourselves for the hard work."

"Cookies?" Poppy's voice lifts. It's a fragile lightness in her storm.

I catch myself before tripping over a Nerf gun. I should've had the kids pick up the playroom last night. But there's always a reason this room ends up forgotten by bedtime.

I ruffle Asher's rumpled hair, and he launches into my arms. His grip tightens. "Have fun at work, Daddy!"

"You too, bud." I hold him for a beat longer than usual before he wriggles free and heads back to his Lego masterpiece. I'd thought a no-school day might buy me extra minutes of sleep this morning, but school or not, these two always wake early. No alarms needed.

"Can Mrs. Chen and I build the airplane?" he asks without looking up.

"We'll work on it together. Deal?"

"Okay."

The one-thousand-piece engineering nightmare my parents gifted him will have to wait. Fei would give it her best shot, but I'm not subjecting my volunteer caretaker to such challenges.

Leaving the playroom, I check my watch. It's only eight, but not enough time to make coffee. It'll be easier if I make a stop at Sips and Scripts. As long as Mary Beth doesn't drag out the staff meeting with unnecessary updates, it should only take half an hour. I'll have plenty of time for my planned stop and shut-in visits before heading home.

I've never needed to hire a nanny. My job lets me be a constant in my kids' lives, and I'm blessed with my best friends on the lane. We help each other out. Then my congregation's elderly members are always eager for a "grandbaby fix" and happy to watch the kids. I'm still careful about who spends time with them, but the church community has embraced us since we arrived in Meadowbrook six years ago.

When Maddie died a month after Poppy was born, I stepped back from ministry to raise my kids, an infant and a barely walking toddler. Then the Meadowbrook church was searching for a pastor, in a town I'd once loved, and it seemed divine timing. I sold the Manhattan condo and bought a modest two-story farmhouse. Shortly later, I learned about the sale of Skypoint, a former assisted living facility, now the perfect memorial for Isaac and Maddie.

Leaving Manhattan was the right move. The kids love it here and have made more friends than they would have in the condo.

Meadowbrook was supposed to be about starting over, catching up to unfinished dreams, even without Ruby. She was my past, the memory I buried. But since I saw her again last week, every heartbeat reminds me she was never really gone. It's like she's reawakened something in me that I'd long thought dormant.

I imagined her when I was officiating Jason and Valentina's wedding two days ago. I pictured her yesterday, sitting in the audience while I preached, as if she belonged *here*. In my life again.

Even now, the memory jabs through my chest, and my pulse kicks up.

I need to see her again. That much is certain.

Ethan

Main Street on a Monday moves smoothly, with random cars passing by. Now that the last of the tourists are clearing out as October winds down, parking is a breeze. I pull the 4Runner into an open spot before Sips and Scripts and head toward the shop. The rustic wooden sign swinging above the door displays a steaming mug on an open book.

The bell chimes when I push my way in, and the scent of coffee, cinnamon, and paperbacks wraps around me.

"Good morning, Pastor," two voices call from the right. Doris and Shirley, devout church members and regulars here, sit tucked by the bookshelf with steaming mugs in hand.

"I thought I beat you here this time." I smile, shaking my head.

"You'll have to show up thirty minutes earlier," Doris teases.

I pivot toward the counter, and my feet freeze. My heart slams against my ribs, the beat echoing in my throat.

Behind the counter, in an apricot-orange apron, is Ruby. A midnight-blue blouse sways over the floral leggings hugging her slender calves. Her back is angled just enough for me to catch the curve of her profile as she watches Willow work the espresso machine.

Morning light streams through the window, gilding her flawless brown skin. Is she real, or is my memory playing tricks?

Then she turns.

Her gaze finds mine, and her name slips from my lips like a prayer I never thought would be answered.

"Ruby?"

Her deep brown eyes squint. They're still flecked with amber, familiar, but guarded now. And shadowed with a faint bruised hue, like sleep hasn't visited her in days.

She was delightful at fourteen with her spunky, carefree attitude. She grew into her beauty by twenty with long hair and a radiant smile. Now, hair short and edges sharper, she's still breathtaking. But I missed every moment of watching her grow into the woman she's become. Grief that wraps black mourners' bands tight around my lungs.

Her gaze sweeps over my face, lowers, then climbs back up.

When our eyes lock again, recognition flickers, then fades. Her brows pinch, her eyes soften even as her shoulders draw tight as if she's holding back twelve years of hurt I left behind. I'm a stranger now. But I still remember the way she whispered my name, like it was a vow, when she loved me.

Even the vanilla and coffee can't sweeten the charge between us. It hums like a live wire stretched too thin.

"You two know each other?"

I shake my head, glance at Willow, then back at Ruby just to make sure I'm not daydreaming. She gives a slow nod, and I approach the counter.

She edges to the left, gripping the bare counter. Her perfume wafts toward me, not the orange blossom from our past, but something softer now, peppermint and vanilla warmed by her skin. And I'm seventeen again, walking her home through dark alleys, breathing her in, my mouth lingering on her lips for a goodnight kiss.

"Great that you know Ruby, Pastor." Willow's voice snaps me back from unholy thoughts. She hands me a flyer I barely glance at. "Ruby's looking for students. Maybe your kids would be interested in learning piano."

"You live here?" Ruby's cautious question draws my full attention to her, in case I hadn't already been obsessing. Her wary gaze holds mine as if searching for the boy she loved who broke her heart.

"Like... you." My voice sounds foreign. I shift my weight.

The flyer shakes in my hand as I scan the wavering print long enough to sight her name and number printed on the bottom. She always had a beautiful voice, but hearing her at Skypoint proved how remarkable she's become.

I lower it. "You're teaching piano now?"

She shrugs. "I'm not great—"

"She's wonderful, talented," Willow interrupts, waving a spoon.

"My kids will love it." Whether they want to advance past the keyboard and toy piano or not, they just got a new hobby.

Ruby's lips part, close, then part again. "How many kids do you have?"

"Two."

The golden glow in her eyes dims. Her shoulders pull tighter, and her hands twist together, drawing my attention to her left hand. No, I didn't miss a ring last time, but I did miss that unfamiliar scar on her wrist.

My stomach knots. What happened to her in those twelve years?

"Morning, Rick." Willow greets someone behind me.

Ruby steps back, clearly transitioning into work mode. "Um, Eth—Pastor." She then raises her chin and recovers. "What can I get you?"

"Call me Ethan. Regular coffee. Medium. Black."

Willow rings me up, and I add a generous tip, though not overwhelming enough to raise suspicion. Ruby returns with my coffee, and our fingers brush during the exchange. The brief contact sends sparks racing up my arm, blood rushing to my ears until it's like a tidal wave crashing inside my head.

She jerks her hand back as if burned, a quick breath escaping, so she felt it too. Her eyes stay shuttered.

"Thank you, Ruby." I fight to force out my voice, so I have to clear my throat. "I'm glad you're here."

Her lips press into a thin line, revealing too much—mostly that she might leave town now that she knows I live here. Did she assume I'm married just because I mentioned children? Well, none of that matters right now.

"Bye, Ethan." She speaks with a finality I can't accept.

"I'll see you around." It's a promise to her and to myself now that I have her number.

I knew I still loved her, but I didn't expect the pain in her eyes to strike sharper than the ache in my chest.

***

Ethan

"We need real volunteers for the fall fest this year." Mary Beth Moore taps her pen against her planner like a gavel. As one of the church matriarchs, she's on every committee, keeps the books, and never holds back her unsolicited advice. "Not just your friends, Pastor, but people who'll keep their hairnets on while running the grill."

I'd defend my buddies, but my mind's too wound up to come up with anything worth saying.

"We should still be grateful for those dads who are always willing to help." Across from us, our hospitality coordinator, Nessa Dawson, folds her hands on the tabletop, her brown skin glowing beneath the harsh fluorescent lights. "That said,

I doubt kids will care about food when they're getting that much candy."

Nessa keeps in the background. But she knows every detail about everyone, and the church would unravel without her.

"We're still short on volunteers for the booths, and we could use every trunk full of treats we can squeeze into the library lot. Sign-up sheets are already with all the Sunday school groups."

Mary Beth nods, satisfied for now.

"I encouraged the youth group to put together care packages again for those in need." Krish Mahato's Indian accent comes out soft beside Nessa's voice. He's been our youth pastor since moving to the US three years ago. "But this time with notes or verses inside. Something personal."

"I like that." I sink back in my chair. His point is simple enough to grasp, and he's looking at me for confirmation. "Outreach beyond just kids, but families too."

"Last year, the band at the park was a hit." My assistant, Diana Moore, pauses from scribbling with her blue pen and glances up at me through her lashes. In her early thirties, she's hardworking. But now and then, her mother's influence slips through. Her voice softens. "It was your idea, Ethan, and we should add it back."

"It's not in the budget to hire an electrician just for the fall fest." Mary Beth narrows her gaze at her daughter. "The wiring in that park is a mess."

"It's too last-minute to get the sound set up there, but..."

As the worship director continues, I try to stay present, as in really try. But my mind keeps drifting back to Ruby in that coffee shop, her hands gripping the counter, her eyes flaring with something like memory and heartbreak woven together.

Focus.

The meeting rolls on to budgets, new shut-ins, hospital updates, Thanksgiving prep, Sunday volunteers, rotations, but it all hangs behind me like mist.

Ruby's in Meadowbrook.

After twelve years of separation, she's less than three miles down the road, handing out coffee and piano flyers like a local.

"Ethan?" Mary Beth's voice slices through the fog. "Skypoint Christmas?"

I blink. "Sorry, what?"

"The Christmas carols," she repeats, slower now. "Are we still hosting that this year? I'd like to know where I need to adjust the budget for food."

"Yes." I scoot my chair closer to the table after a beat. "The residents look forward to it."

"Good. That's settled." She jots something down in bold strokes.

Nessa unfolds her hands and raises one. "I thought this year the church could provide food, not just cookies."

"Of course." The table cuts into my midsection. I've scooted too close as if it can keep me pinned in place and focused. "Sound, seating, and parking volunteers—Skypoint's coordinator already has that arranged."

Our generous donors and volunteers believe in Skypoint's cause, but I keep paid staff to make donor calls. Most are willing to give without needing my pitch. Having the right people in place keeps me from stressing. But with the holiday season kicking off and Ruby in town, how am I going to keep my focus?

My heart is once again back at Sips and Scripts with the woman I never stopped wondering about. I'd say never stopped loving, but for a time, I had to shove Ruby aside. I got married and moved into ministry as my parents had always hoped and encouraged. I have no regret now, but that doesn't mean I didn't wonder, especially after Maddie's death, what life would've been like if I hadn't gone to seminary.

The leadership meeting blurs through budget updates, the fall fest, holiday outreach, volunteer needs, and everything else piling up. Yeah, there's work to do. Our busiest outreach season begins now and lasts through Christmas.

And Ruby's here.

My mission too, I guess.

After twelve years of me wondering what happened to her or if I'd ever see her again, she's in town. The place we dreamed about but never reached. Together.

I see it in her eyes—she's afraid to trust me again. But I'll wait. I'll fight with everything in me to prove how much I've missed her, how much I still need her. I don't know how to fix what's broken between us... but I'm going to try.

With Your help, God. Please.

CHAPTER 4

Ruby

"I love how our pumpkins turned out." Running my fork through the steaming quinoa, I scoot my chair to face the pumpkins lined along the railing.

"Thanks to you, my place feels like autumn." Willow salutes me with her water glass. "I didn't even correct Mom when I sent her a photo. I let her think it was my idea."

Her words warm me, but they also stir something else, an ache I can't quite name. It's hard to comprehend what home feels like when you dreaded returning there after school. Most days, I braced for whatever waited behind those walls. When something set Papa off, Mama took the worst of it.

No wonder my stepsister bolted the day she turned eighteen, not bothering to call or come back. My advice to Mama to leave too bounced off those walls Papa sometimes pushed her against. "You can't walk away from a marriage over something small," she'd say, even as I dabbed at her split lip or wiped the blood from her chin after his latest outburst. The next day, she'd trudge on like Papa's anger hadn't marked her.

When his heart gave out from too much drinking, things seemed light around the house. But peace didn't pay bills. It meant Mama worked two jobs to keep the lights on.

I started pitching in at fifteen, working part-time at Aunt Shania's flower shop. By the time I was full-time, trying to give Mama a financial break, she didn't live long enough to enjoy it.

Maybe that's why I've never known what home is, except for when Ethan stumbled into my life at fourteen. Back then, home became something simple in my mind. A place you craved, with someone you loved and felt safe with. Somewhere you could stand in the kitchen without feeling in the way. Somewhere quiet enough to breathe.

I'm trying to build something like that here in Willow's place. Hence, instead of grabbing a microwave dinner, I stopped at the Corner Crate after my shift and picked up ingredients for a simple chicken salad—just to pretend I had that kind of place waiting.

With Ethan in town, though, can I make Meadowbrook my home? The friendly faces in the coffee shop and the grocery store make me want to believe I can. Even sitting here on the balcony now, wrapped in my hoodie against the chill, I can imagine this feels close to home.

"So..." Her brown hair lifts in the breeze. Willow stirs quinoa into her avocado, spinach, and chicken. "Want to tell me about this morning's emotional earthquake?"

I adjust in my seat, balance my fork on the untouched food, and tilt my face to the string lights overhead. While most nearby shops use their upstairs for offices or storage, Willow lives here, and for now, so do I.

"How about we talk about that last caller on *Heartline with Willow*?" Her show's always a safe diversion. "He wants to take you on a date?"

"No way are you going to use my show as a diversion." She wiggles her empty fork at me. "You and the pastor might become my next topic if you don't start talking."

She doesn't mean that, but she might give me some practical advice. "We go way back."

"Let me guess." She leans back and snuggles deeper into the blanket draped over her lap. "It's no coincidence Meadowbrook is your dream town, just like it's Ethan's dream place since he moved here about six or seven years ago?"

Heat rises in my cheeks. Of course, she figured it out—psychology major and love specialist. "My first love, my biggest what-if, and all." And my last, as it seems I can't ever love anyone but him. "I cried for days when his brother told me Ethan got married. Probably worse than when he broke up with me." That was when my aunt died, and I fell into a relapse.

Willow's eyes widen, the fork clinking against porcelain when she drops it. "You both had plans to build your home in Meadowbrook then?"

"I didn't realize he moved here with his wife."

"He was already single when he moved here."

Single? Does that mean he's not married? And he never lived here with someone else? That small relief settles within me, though curiosity nags about his wife's whereabouts. I brush it aside. "I never imagined he'd be here."

"From the way he took you in, he obviously imagined he'd say the same about you." Her grin knowing, she tucks wind-blown hair behind her ears. "Whatever happened between you two, the chemistry is still cracking. Spill."

I wanted to scream at him, hate him. But when he looked at me like I was still his... I forgot how to breathe.

Cool air seeps through my sweater, so I wrap my arms around myself. "We met at fourteen." The confession feels raw. My gaze wanders to the enclosed gas firepit flickering nearby. "He's the only man I've ever loved."

"Now your whole staying-single-forever slogan makes sense."

"It still stands."

She rolls her eyes, not believing me now. "What drove you two apart?"

Sadness takes over. "His parents never warmed up to me. He was seminary-bound, and I was supposed to work in a flower shop after graduation." Rehashing it is easier this time, despite the lingering pain. "We met at a basketball game in freshman year." Man, he was sweet and gorgeous. "We became inseparable, but his parents blamed me for his hesitance in pursuing their career choice. See, he wanted to rush into the fire academy so he could stay near me."

They'd added many other accusations. Eventually, Ethan made it to seminary from what Harvey shared.

Heat burns behind my eyes. Why is it still so hard to remember?

"Everything changed within a few weeks. *He* changed, became distant, and ignored my calls as if he didn't want to hang out anymore. It all ended when his brother..."

A tremor runs through me, and dizziness overtakes me as the image returns. I went looking for Ethan at their house. I found his brother, Harvey, bleeding. On instinct, I hurried to him and pressed a clean cloth to the gash to stop the flow. Then everything fell apart from his stupid act of lust—one I had nothing to do with. Still, it fueled Ethan's and his parents' distrust of me.

Why is it so cold? I'm chilled to the bone, trembling.

Willow's gentle hand touches my shoulder.

Oh, she's now squatting beside me. "You don't have to explain everything."

"I'm fine." A calming breath helps me still myself. "He's built a good life here, a beloved pastor."

"And single." Willow slides back into her seat. "Now, let's finish this delicious food."

"Right." I force myself to eat, allowing my heartbeat to steady. He hurt me, yes. But loving him was the most real thing I ever felt. Still, if he wouldn't love me then, when I hadn't done anything wrong, how could he love me now, when I've been far from doing anything right? After a few bites, I sit up straighter. "Any dating updates from you since six months ago?"

Her laugh light, she points her loaded fork at me. "Trust me, you'll be the first to know if anything changes."

Dinner ends, and we head inside to watch a rom-com. The romance part stirs up feelings I'd rather ignore, but the comedy helps. I've got this habit of pausing movies whenever someone looks familiar, pulling out my phone to look up what else I've seen them in. Willow complains I'm distracting her, but Ethan just used to laugh, already accustomed to my quirks. For now, I can laugh too, forget, and fall asleep without overthinking.

By morning, I'm energized and confident I can handle the coffee shop without Willow's guidance. I mix and serve drinks and pastries. Customers grab flyers from the counter and ask about borrowing or donating books. And me? I fixate on the entrance. Each time the chime announces someone entering, I'm hoping Ethan might come back.

And fearing I might be tempted to ask him what still haunts me.

Why wasn't I worth fighting for? Why did my side of the story never matter?

Landon arrives at noon after the morning rush quiets, so I focus on the bookstore area, checking on the customers chatting or reading on sofas. Soon, I gravitate toward the children's area with its untouched blocks and Legos and the piano beside it—ready for future students who might not own one.

My fingers trail over the keys, careful not to inflict any noise on those lost in literary worlds. Then I start reorganizing shelves. My phone buzzes. An unknown local number.

"Hello?" I whisper so I don't distract those reading.

"Ruby? It's Ethan."

My heart pounds. I nearly drop *Pride and Prejudice*. "Hi."

"I hope it's okay I called. Your number was on the flyer."

"Right." My voice shakes as much as my hands. I leave the book on the empty table, move to the piano, and perch on the bench, leg bouncing.

"Would you consider giving my kids piano lessons? Poppy's seven. Asher's eight. Poppy's worn out the toy keyboard. It's about time she graduated to the real thing." His soft laugh, albeit nervous, sends familiar sensations through me. "After hearing you play at Skypoint, I know I couldn't ask for a better teacher."

So, he was there that night but chose to leave rather than wait to talk to me? "Ethan, I don't think—"

"Please." His voice dips into intimate tones. "Pretend I'm just a local needing an excellent piano teacher. You're talented, Ruby."

No simple local would be sounding so warm, familiar. Still, his praise has my chest expanding. I close my eyes, fingers pressing my forehead. My savings are dwindling. Teaching piano is my primary income now, but I quit teaching at the Brooklyn studio a month ago. Ethan's call is the first I've received since distributing flyers, including the ones Willow took to the local shops and put up at the library.

But can I handle seeing him regularly? While he moved on, I'm still fragile and confused, regardless of the heartache. I could leave town again, but my former roommate found someone to replace me the moment I told her I was moving out.

Even if the studio could take me back, renting solo and coming up with an advance will leave me broke.

"Are you still there?" Ethan's almost pleading now.

"Are you planning to bring them here?" I already regret the words. I've always been too weak where he's concerned, and he knows it.

"Will my house be all right?"

"I don't have a car." I didn't need a car in Brooklyn, but I'll buy a bargain now if it shows up.

"I can pick you up. Do you have time today?"

"*Today*?" He can't be serious.

"It'd be a good day for you to meet the kids. See if they're a great fit? No need to start right away. We have a piano and—"

"A guitar."

"Yes." He sounds pleased that I remember he always played the guitar. He taught me to play too.

"I assume your kids are in school, right?"

"Yes. They'll be home after three."

My leg bounces faster. Say no. Say no. Say—

"Five o'clock okay, then?" The wrong response slips out.

"Really?" Relief floods his voice, sending a dangerous warmth through my chest. "Thank you, Ruby. I'll be there."

"I'll be ready."

The call ends, and I gape at my phone. The three women discussing a book nearby glance my way, and I stride back to the shelves. What did I just agree to? I hadn't planned on seeing him so soon after yesterday. But the way he looked at me with questions and all sorts of emotions... Does *he* have regrets?

Now, I need to figure out what to wear this afternoon.

No, it doesn't matter what I wear.

Ugh. I thought time would change things. Instead, it's only made me miss him more... want him again.

CHAPTER 5

Ruby

At five o'clock, a text buzzes my phone.

Ethan: I'm here.

My hands tremble as I reread his text, second-guessing my outfit—a navy top and ankle boots, mustard cardigan, and brown leggings. I've been ready for an hour, but nerves push me back into the tiny bathroom.

I meet my reflection in the half mirror, drawing a shaky breath.

"You'll never belong to Ethan," whispers the voice I fight to ignore.

My gloss is still intact, a faint pink—not for him, just a habit. I forgot my earrings, but I'll wear them next time. My fingers fluff my short pixie cut, which demands more upkeep than I'd imagined. With another breath to steady myself, I step out and head for the door.

I pat my leggings pocket to check my phone, ID, and house key. No need for a purse as this meeting should be brief. I still don't understand why it has to be at their house when he could've brought them here.

The brown bag with its Sips and Scripts logo feels light in my hand. I bought chocolate croissants for the kids, using Ethan's generous tip from yesterday. Hopefully, they like sweets.

I'd texted him to pick me up out back, avoiding the afternoon parking chaos on Main. Now, a white SUV parks in one of Willow's designated spots. Definitely Ethan.

Every step down the stairs clangs louder. My pulse quickens as he emerges from the driver's side and rounds the vehicle. My mouth goes dry. His unbuttoned red flannel hangs loose over the white T-shirt stretched across his broad chest. I don't linger on how perfectly his jeans fit. Instead, I lift my gaze to those brown eyes. Focused on me the way they used to when we were in love, they're impossibly vivid. My footing falters, and he's no longer Pastor Ethan. He's the boy who once owned my heart. Maybe still does, in a different way.

Then he strides closer and wraps me in an embrace so secure it feels like a protective cocoon. Startled, I somehow still grip the croissant bag as my hands slide up his back, feeling the solid warmth beneath the flannel. He smells like sunshine and fresh soap, laced with something spicy and new. Our hearts beat in sync.

"I had to be sure I'm not dreaming." His voice is a low rumble, warm against my ear, deep and textured, and a thrill tingles down my spine. "You're actually here."

My eyes close, absorbing the moment as I breathe out. "I'm here."

Ethan eases back, hands lingering on my shoulders. His gaze searches my face, disbelief and wonder brightening his eyes. My lips curve into a smile, and I manage a hi.

His lopsided grin returns, the dimple denting his cheek—a smile I've never been able to resist. New lines at the corners of his eyes and a shadow of stubble enhance his grown-up charm, making him even more attractive than my memories allowed. He's dangerously real and heartbreakingly handsome.

"I'm glad you're here, Ruby."

At the way he says my name, heat rushes through my veins and rekindles dormant desires and countless memories I'd fought so hard to stomp out.

"Daddy!" A small voice breaks the quiet, jolting us apart. A boy bounds toward us, waving a toy in his hand. "Are you my new piano teacher?"

The innocent question snaps me back to reality. I'm the piano teacher, nothing more to Ethan. I nod.

"Yes." Ethan steps back. "Miss, um, Mrs.—"

"Just Ruby." I crouch to meet the boy's gaze. Dark hair, wide brown eyes, and round cheeks, he's a replica of Ethan's childhood pictures. I offer my hand. "You must be Asher."

"You know my name?" He beams, then tucks the toy—Legos, maybe—into the crook of an arm to shake my hand. His tiny grip is warm and trusting, and his smile shows front teeth too big for his face.

"Your daddy told me how talented you and your sister are."

"Here!" He thrusts a colorful Lego creation forward. The tiny figurine has brown skin, black hair, and sits at a crafted piano. "I made this for you."

I accept it. "What did you make?"

"That's you, playing the piano."

Warmth spreads through me.

Ethan's smile reveals the unforgettable dimple that makes me want to forget how everything went down between us. "I told them they'd be learning from one of the best piano teachers."

The warmth tingles up my neck. I refocus on Asher. "You're talented too. This is amazing." The miniature piano has a tiny black-and-white keyboard and a bench where the figure is perched. Fascinating that an eight-year-old could put together something like this.

"Asher loves Legos." Ethan ruffles the boy's hair.

I tap the figure. "How did you know what I look like?"

"Daddy showed me a picture!"

Ethan's cheeks blotch a deep crimson. "Your choir banquet."

We attended different high schools, but Ethan came to my choir and basketball banquets whenever he could. Family complications got in our way, and I couldn't attend when his parents were there. But, despite the obstacles, he kept a photo all these years?

"You like it?" Asher's hopeful voice interrupts my thoughts.

"It's incredible." I hand the creation back.

"It's for you. Keep it."

"Thank you." I rise, still holding the bag in my other hand, and press the small gift to my chest. "I love it."

"Daddy, Daddy, are we going yet?" a girl calls from inside the car.

"Okay, Asher, hop back in before your sister unbuckles." With a hand on the boy's shoulder, Ethan guides him toward the vehicle.

I follow them to the open back door.

Inside sits a girl with soft brown curls and wide, curious eyes. She reaches for her car seat harness, but Ethan's voice turns tender as he tells her to stay put. "We're leaving soon, Peanut."

When he steps back, I lean in and offer a small wave. "Hello, Poppy."

She smiles shyly, wiggling fingers with chipped nail polish.

Ethan chuckles. "She gets shy sometimes."

"She gets that from her daddy."

"Is that so?" His sheepish smile sends warmth through me—misleading warmth, I should say.

Ethan was shy when we met. Confident, yes, but still reserved... until a month into our relationship.

After ensuring both kids are buckled, he closes the back door and opens the front passenger side for me. His gaze lingers long enough to stir the rush I used to feel when he looked at me like I was his whole world. I'm not sure what he sees now. My pulse trips over itself all the same.

His scent hits me again as I pass, pulling me into a different headspace.

When I settle and Ethan gets in, I buckle up and lift my bag, and the subtle scent of chocolate lingers. "I brought pastries for the kids. Is that okay?"

"Of course." He starts the engine.

"Is it chocolate cake?" Asher chirps.

I turn, but with him directly behind me, I can only see his sister in the middle seat. "Chocolate croissants."

"That's their favorite from Sips and Scripts." Ethan backs out of the lot. "Thanks, Ruby."

"Can I have one now?" Asher asks.

"Me too, Daddy," Poppy chimes in. "Chocolate, please."

"After dinner, kids."

The drive is quiet at first, not surprising after our reunion. Ethan waves at passing cars, each greeting returned with the easy familiarity of someone who belongs here. The evening light cuts across his sharp jawline, and something tightens in my chest.

So I break the silence and ask Asher about his Lego creations. He launches into an animated description—airplanes, towers, shapes I can't picture but pretend I can. I nod and smile, but my focus keeps drifting. To Ethan's hands steady on the wheel. To the faint draw of his cologne mingling with the warm scent of chocolate croissants. To the subtle shift of his gaze, once, twice, like he's checking on me.

When I glance toward the windshield, our eyes meet in the rearview mirror. It's only a second, maybe less, but the recognition there makes my pulse stumble. I look away first, pretending to focus on Asher's story, though my mind's already ages back in time, back when I was the only one Ethan looked at like that.

We turn onto a wide, bumpy road. My hands vibrate on my lap as gravel crunches under the tires. I take in the expansive land and aged trees, their branches tinged with fiery colors. A breeze sends leaves falling into the open space. The cattle and horses in the fields are refreshing. There's a sense of calm here, a slower pace than Brooklyn, where I spent my whole life.

Soon, we turn onto another road. I read the street sign. "Renewed Lane?"

"My buddies and I came up with our street name."

Of course, Ethan and his pastor friends chose a redemptive name like that. With the road now smooth pavement, I don't bounce anymore. It's well-maintained, the homes spread far apart. To the right stands a modern yet rugged two-story stone house with play swings in the yard.

"This seems new."

"My friends built homes here recently," he explains. "When I moved here, I talked them into coming too."

"They must be good friends."

"They are."

"We have bonfires on Sundays!" Asher exclaims. "Daddy and his friends play basketball, and we swim with my friends at Mr. Sterling's house." He then names whose house has which activities and how they all take turns gathering.

Further down the road is another two-story home. The road then meanders through swatches of land boasting yellow or brown leaves, where patches of fallen leaves catch in the tall grass. Then he pulls around the curve and into a charming two-story white farmhouse, the kind of house I dreamed of whenever Mama talked about someday living in the country. Of course, Mama left that desire for me too.

Across from here, a sprawling single-story stone house blends in with the earth.

"Welcome home." Ethan's voice has me refocusing. He's parked the car. Home. Wherever Ethan is has always been home to me. A safe place. That's what I always dreamed of with him, but it'd only been a dream.

"Thanks for the ride." I keep from looking at him and steer my gaze to the house, a classic modern beauty with white siding, black shutters, and a wraparound porch framed by white columns and matching railings.

Orange and yellow flowers spill from hanging baskets, a homey sight. My heart squeezes, but I hold myself together. A tire swing dangles from the oak tree, bikes abandoned in the golden-tinged grass.

"It's beautiful," I murmur, startled as my door swings open. When did he get out?

"The kids love the space."

A crisp breeze lifts, carrying his scent as I step past him.

"Thanks."

"Of course."

Asher bursts from the car, bouncing ahead. "Can I eat the chocolate now?"

"After dinner," Ethan calls. The boy takes off toward the swing set.

I wait while Ethan's daughter unbuckles from her booster seat.

Then she hops out. Bouncy curls frame big, brown, and innocent eyes. A purple dress with unicorn print fluffs over mismatched socks shoved into rainbow boots.

"Hello, Poppy." I offer my hand. "Nice to meet you."

She lifts her tiny fingers, and I shake them.

"Are you going to teach me piano?"

The drive must've shaken off her shyness.

"If that's all right with you."

Poppy nods. "I can already play 'Twinkle, Twinkle, Little Star' with one finger."

She demonstrates in the air. My chest tightens at the cuteness. Is that a dimple in her left cheek?

"That's a great start."

"You and Miss Ruby are going to make music magic." He winks at me and mouths *toy piano* behind his daughter's back. Then he takes her hand and guides us up the stone path.

"Are we having mac and cheese for dinner, Daddy?"

"Pizza today."

"But we eat pizza on Fridays."

He swings her arm. "I thought today was a good day to switch things. Tomorrow, maybe we can eat mac and cheese."

His tenderness squeezes something in my chest. I always knew he'd be an amazing father.

Ethan's voice bellows when he calls Asher over. I wait alongside a welcome mat as he unlocks the door. Then he reaches for my bag. Our hands brush, and electricity jolts up my arm. The flush that creeps up his face assures me he felt it too.

"Welcome."

"Thanks."

Asher darts inside. His sister chases him, giggling.

A lemony cleaner scent greets me as my shoes meet hardwood. Backpacks hang on wall hooks, a wooden bench beneath them.

"Shoes," Ethan calls after the kids.

Framed family photos on cream-colored walls line the entry—snapshots of the kids at different ages, and a woman holding a newborn and a smiling toddler in one beside them.

I don't study her face. I don't need to. It's their mother.

"You hungry?"

His voice beside me makes me jump.

Not expecting dinner, I nod or maybe shake my head. I'm not even sure which as I slip off my shoes and set them on the bench. Then my socked feet pad after him into the living room. Brown leather sofas face a stone fireplace. The kitchen opens to the left. The kids' laughter echoes from another room.

And then nostalgia hits hard. A gut punch. This could've been us. This life. A family. Together.

But I was never good enough for him. Not then. Still not now. What was I thinking coming here?

CHAPTER 6

Ethan

Ruby was the best part of me. And without her, I'm still trying to find my way back to the man she once believed in. I'm relearning how to get there.

"Water, Coke, or Sprite?" I swing open the stainless steel fridge and scan the shelves for anything she might want.

"Water is fine. I can get it from the tap."

She reaches toward the glasses on their floating shelf, then stops short, and leans against the counter instead. Twelve years ago, she would've grabbed a glass and raided the fridge without hesitation. Back then, she belonged with me, regardless of how unwelcome my parents made her feel.

We're not there anymore. Slow steps to make our way back.

I close the fridge, slide a glass from the shelf, and fill it from the tap.

Pizza beckons us to the table, delivered minutes after we walked in. The timing couldn't have been better. Otherwise,

I'd be fumbling whether to give her a house tour or fill the dead air. Still, a heavy silence presses in.

She's looking around, taking it all in. Her gaze lingered in the entryway—on the photos. The kids. Maddie. Her mouth tightened into that same guarded sadness I used to see when someone made her feel small.

The scent of pizza blends with lemon cleaner as I clear the table. I move Asher's half-finished math sheet to the counter along with Poppy's crayon masterpiece that could pass for a horse, though she called it a unicorn. Hyperaware of Ruby behind me, I let my gaze stray to her. Dark tights, crossed arms, the faintest clean shampoo scent. Her presence once again shifts the air, commanding my attention in a way I haven't felt in years.

"Sorry about the mess." I grab paper plates from the bottom cabinet. "We try to stay on top of it, but—"

"I don't mind." Her whispery voice underplays the kids' laughter from the playroom. "It's a home. Lived-in."

Something wistful softens her tone, like she's holding onto it too tightly. And still, just having her here stirs things I'd buried alongside everything we used to be. I broke her heart. Now I want to live every day trying to earn the right to hold it again.

"Asher, Poppy, come wash your hands." I set plates on the table.

They thunder in, already arguing over who gets the step stool.

"I had it first!"

"No, you didn't!"

I referee before voices climb to full-on war. Ruby lingers near the counter, her hand on the white marble. The white cabinets beneath it and white tiled walls stand stark around her. Her quiet smile tugs at me as she watches my duo with unmistakable tenderness.

Then she crosses over, takes the kitchen towel, and hands it to Asher once he hops off the stool, fingers dripping. She stays beside Poppy, squirting a small line of soap into her hands. "Be sure to scrub between your fingers."

Her hip braces against the farmhouse sink's apron front. It all seems natural, like she's done this before. Belongs here. My chest tightens.

Does she remember wanting a farmhouse kitchen like this? All open and airy, nothing crammed in, nothing cluttered, she said. The upper walls free of cabinets. The few floating shelves waiting to display the kitchen's treasures.

With the kids seated in their designated chairs across from each other—far enough apart to keep the peace—I pull out the seat beside Poppy for Ruby, the legs scraping against the hardwood. "You're welcome to sit."

"Thanks." She barely glances at me before she slides into place.

"Fair warning," I add, "dinner conversation's loud and unfiltered."

She grins. "I'll survive."

"Ew, Daddy. What is that pizza?" Asher's nose scrunches as he peers into the box topped with chicken and basil.

"It's high time Daddy ate something beyond cheese pizza." I laugh and nudge it aside, opening the other box. "There's cheese for you and your sister. But let's first thank God."

I slide into my seat beside Asher, across from Ruby, more aware of her than I should be.

"Who wants to pray for us today?" I look between the kids.

"It's my turn." Poppy's hand shoots up.

"Jesus," she begins, eyes squeezed shut and hands folded tight. "I'm happy for the cheese pizza. I'm happy Miss Ruby's going to teach me piano. She's very pretty. And nice too. She brought us chocolate treats."

Ruby lets out a cackle, and mine slips free as Poppy finishes with a firm amen. We echo it together.

Asher reaches for a slice but can't separate it. I grab the butter knife, free his slice, then do the same for Poppy. I slide the cheese pizza over to them, replacing it with the chicken-basil box. Ruby's now watching Poppy, who's peeling the cheese off her slice to eat it first. It's an odd way to eat pizza. I can't blame Ruby for being taken by it. My little one's quirks draw people in.

I place a slice on the plate for Ruby and pass it over. Our fingers brush in the transfer. There's that static jolt like a memory fused into one.

Her gaze flicks to mine, then drops to the plate.

"Chicken basil," she whispers.

"I hope it's still a favorite."

"Haven't had it in a while." She lifts the slice and takes a bite, muffling her words. "But it's still a favorite. Thank you."

"Do you like unicorns?" Poppy stretches cheese from her slice to her mouth.

"I do." Warmth threads through Ruby's voice. "Is that your favorite animal?"

"Yes! And elephants. And dolphins. Daddy says we can go see dolphins at the beach someday."

"Next summer, we're going to SeaWorld," Asher adds like it's already set in stone.

"God willing." It had been a maybe in my mind when we talked about it during our bedtime story, but my kids are professionals at turning maybes into promises.

"Have you been to SeaWorld?" Poppy leans toward Ruby, her face tilted up.

"I never have."

"You should come with us," Asher blurts.

"Well, uh—"

"Miss Ruby has her own plans." No need to make her more uncomfortable than she already is. "She's just here to teach you piano." The kids have already invited half of my friends and their families, so it's shaping up to be a big friends' trip.

Something flickers across her face, unreliable, but it could be relief or disappointment. This whole reunion must feel like emotional whiplash for her. For me, on the other hand, I've prayed for this day, hoped and dreamed God would somehow bring her back. And now, here she is.

If only things were different. If only we could pick up where we left off twelve years ago.

But it all came crashing down for a reason. Much later, I realized it wasn't as big a deal as I'd thought. By then, I couldn't undo it. I hate how I handled it.

"I built a Lego airport yesterday." Asher speaks around a mouthful. "It has a control tower and everything. Want to see it, Miss Ruby?"

"I'd love to."

"After dinner, okay?" I add.

He nods, grinning.

Ruby asks the kids about their favorite colors and school subjects... maybe to avoid talking to me, or maybe because she enjoys hearing them.

They talk over each other, bouncing between stories about friends on the block and the rugby lessons my buddy Liam started teaching the kids on our lane. "He wants to start a team in our town."

She holds up a hand. "I'm not so familiar with rugby."

"Rugby's a cool sport." Asher sits straighter as he says it.

"I don't play rugby." Poppy shudders.

Leaning down, Ruby cups a hand beside her own mouth and stage-whispers. "So what do *you* like?"

That does it. Now Poppy's off in dreamworld.

When my daughter winds down, Ruby asks if they enjoy music.

"Daddy sings and plays guitar for us every night." Asher puffs out his chest.

"And prays with us," Poppy adds.

Ruby's wistful smile lingers—soft, but unreadable. She keeps the conversation going, but her gaze drifts to the refrigerator now and then, toward the photo of my babies with Maddie, tucked between coloring pages and gold-star charts. Questions simmer beneath the surface.

When dinner winds down, Asher's already tearing open the pastry box. "Can we have one now?"

"Just one each." I hold up one finger and wiggle it. "Then you can play before bath time." Maybe I'll show Ruby our piano too.

The kids scramble off with sticky fingers, and I remind them to grab the disinfectant wipes from the counter. They oblige before disappearing into the next room, voices fading as they go.

The sugar rush will burn out before bedtime.

Suddenly, the kitchen feels too quiet.

Ruby pushes her crust around the plate, her lowered eyes avoiding mine.

"So." I lean back in my chair and wipe my mouth with a napkin. I've eaten more than I realized, though every bite was tasteless with all the tension coiled in my stomach. "What have you been up to? I mean, besides teaching piano?"

"You mean the last twelve years minus two months?"

Exactly. She's not the only one who's been counting.

She looks up, shoulders straightening like she's bracing for something. "That's pretty much it." Her lips part, then close again, then open. Her eyes look bigger with her hair shorter.

"I've taught at schools, done private lessons. Helped at music camps when I wasn't busy doing nothing."

"You stayed in Brooklyn all that time?"

"Took the train whenever I had students in other parts of New York."

"When did you move here?"

"The day before I ran into you at Skypoint." After a beat of silence, she asks, "What inspired you to start a restoration center?"

Willow must have told her. "Maddie." I tip my chin toward the fridge. "The kids' mom. And my friend, Isaac. I'm not sure if you remember him?"

"The one who joined the army."

"And became an engineer. He died." My throat closes.

"I'm so sorry for your loss." Her brows furrow, her voice tight.

"He struggled with PTSD... and a traumatic brain injury. It wore him down." My thumb rubs at a purple smudge on the tabletop left over from Poppy's coloring. "Two years in the army was all it took to break him. The tech we built sold, but the money never felt like mine to spend."

And yet, I knew what I wanted to do the moment I sold our drone camouflage technology to the military. Technically, Isaac was the brains behind the invention. I merely helped refine, test, and pitch it.

"You remember how we started out building it as a side project in Isaac's garage? An adaptive surface coating for small drones, allowing them to blend into their surroundings?"

"Yes, you thought it might be useful for wildlife research or search and rescue when you were considering joining the fire academy."

"Right. That changed when we got a booth at the National Innovation and Technology Expo." A great convention where inventors showcase prototypes to potential investors and government agencies. For some reason, I keep rambling. "We demoed our drone for fun, but halfway through the day, a Defense Department rep stopped by, questioned us, and left with our contact information. Months after Isaac passed, I got a call and found myself sitting across from a military procurement team, hearing numbers I'd never dreamed possible. After that, I invested some of the money in the tech start-up, saved the rest until I knew how to use it. It wasn't my money, and I was glad I waited years to spend it, because that deal funded Skypoint."

"You're a good man, Ethan. One in a billion, I always thought."

I gulp as her praise leaves me speechless. But the last part? Did she ever find another one in another billion? Not that today is about me. It's about mending what I broke, even if I'm fumbling through it.

"I'm sorry about your mom."

She blinks. "How did you—?"

"The landlord. What happened?"

"She was crossing the street." Her voice dips. "A motorcycle." She exhales, and under the recessed kitchen lighting, her eyes gleam.

I fight the urge to reach out, just one touch, but I keep my hand flat on the table instead.

"You came looking for me?" Her surprise slices into me.

"I wish I'd come back a year earlier, before I convinced myself letting you go was the right thing." Now that she's here again, life without her will never feel right. "Your aunt's flower shop was already an antique store by the time I made it back. The new renters didn't even know her."

She closes her eyes, lashes trembling, and her throat works as if she's swallowing something jagged. The quiet ache in her face lands as a jab to my chest, twisting deep until I can't breathe. My hands itch to pull her close, anchor her against me, but she won't trust me to be that safe harbor anymore. I rub my achy chest.

A thin, uneven plink of notes drifts from the other room, a sound like raindrops hitting an empty can. Poppy's new "song," no doubt.

If Asher's quiet through all that racket, he's knee-deep in building something... or dismantling it.

"Where's your wife?" Ruby asks, lips pressed tight.

"Maddie died... drowned."

Her eyes flicker, but I look away, my jaw locking until it aches. I mourned Maddie, but I never truly understood her. She kept to herself, disappearing for days on retreats, hours for needed alone time. I spent years walking on eggshells just to see her smile.

I'd rather not think about how we came to terms for a marriage, how I ignored every warning my gut had given me. I won't unload all that now.

"Unfortunately, she never really recovered from what she'd been through."

"I'm so sorry, Ethan." Her eyes carry recognition of someone who's lived through loss. "Are the kids…? How are they handling it?"

"Poppy was a month old. Asher, fourteen months."

She glances at the fridge—at the photo of Maddie with the babies.

"I keep her pictures up." She hadn't wanted a funeral, only her ashes scattered on the lake—right where her former boyfriend's ashes had been released. "It's nice for them to know they had a mother once."

Ruby's hands rise to her chest as she lets out a jagged breath. Her eyes turn glassy, like she's fighting tears that refuse to fall.

"Are you okay?" I ask.

"It's… I should probably go." She stands, the chair scraping the hardwood floor. "It's getting late."

I stand too, moving around the table. "Wait. I'm sorry if this feels… weird. Having you here, I mean. I know it's complicated." Maybe it was all the talk about death, too close to what she went through losing her mom. I wanted to ask more about when and how it happened, but she seemed set on moving to the next question.

She hugs her arms tight across her chest. A silent "don't touch me." "It's just..."

"Just what?"

She glances at the fridge again, at that photo. Out comes a flicker of pain, longing, or hurt.

"This is... I don't know." Her voice cracks on the last word.

"Daddy!" Poppy's cry rings out from the playroom, a welcome interruption. "Asher won't share the good crayons!"

"Miss Ruby!" Asher barrels into the kitchen. "Come see my building!"

"Yes, of course." Ruby sniffles, her smile flickers for Asher, not quite reaching her eyes. But she lowers herself to his level and touches his shoulder. Maybe, by the time she leaves, whatever sadness emerged will have faded. "Let me clean up the table first, okay?"

"Actually, Asher and Poppy should clean up after themselves." My daughter has returned to the playroom, so I raise my voice. "Poppy, come help."

After the kids throw their paper plates in the trash, I slip leftover pizza into zip-top bags.

Once we move into the playroom, Asher launches into an excited explanation of his creation. Ruby listens, crouching beside him, and her fingers graze the Lego pieces like fragile art. "I'll keep the one you gave me on my nightstand."

"Oh." Asher's eyes light up as she nods.

Poppy tugs at her hand, holding out two dolls. "Come have tea with me and my friends?"

"How about next time?" I ruffle her soft curls beneath my palm.

"I could use some tea." Ruby smiles, then peeps at me as if asking for permission.

I nod.

Poppy then summons Asher and me to join her and Ruby at the mini table. My bottom barely fits on the small chair as we lift the dirty pink cups for tea and plastic scones. But her happiness melts my heart. How kind of Ruby to stay, regardless of the mishap.

After the tea party, we venture to the living room to show Ruby the piano. I plant my palm on it. "Will this work?"

"I like the bay window." She waves to the piano's back-drop.

"It's already too dark to see anything outside." I should probably turn on the porch light soon.

Ruby slides onto the piano bench and pats the seat beside her. "Poppy, come sit here. Asher, on the other side."

They scramble into place.

"Okay, first things first." Ruby flexes her fingers. "We're going to learn what the piano can do. These white keys? That's our musical alphabet—A through G. Let's find middle C. It's right under this lock here."

Tiny fingers tap eagerly. She shows them how to press gently and how the pitch changes depending on where they sit.

"Can you find two black keys?"

Asher points. "Here!"

"Perfect. We'll use those to help us locate our notes."

After playful exploration, Poppy tilts her head. "Can you play 'Old MacDonald'?"

Ruby grins, looks at me. "Are nonreligious songs okay?"

"Of course."

Thanks to my father's ways, Ruby must think I'm legalistic.

She plays the tune, and the kids belt the lyrics, off-key but joyous.

When the song ends, Asher bolts toward my guitar leaning against the wall. He hauls it over with two hands. "Daddy, can you play 'Little David'?"

I take it from him before he trips over the coffee table.

"Let's hear from Miss Ruby again. She's our special guest."

Ruby glances over her shoulder, her gaze catching mine. In that heartbeat, dizziness hits. Perhaps it's the softness in her eyes or the old memories it stirs—I can't tell.

"Can you play a goodnight song?" Poppy asks.

Ruby tilts her head. "Depends on whether I know the one you want."

"Play any song."

Ruby smiles. "I'll play something you might recognize."

She starts with "Twinkle, Twinkle, Little Star," then lets the notes melt into a quiet, unfamiliar lullaby. The melody stills my kids.

My feet move, carrying me closer until I'm hovering behind her. She's not looking at the music. Impressive. The faint scent of mint and something uniquely her drifts back to me.

I hum along with the chorus, and the kids join in, chasing the tune until the room feels lighter.

Ruby sings Asher's name, telling him good night. Then Poppy's.

As the final notes fade, Poppy throws her hand in the air. "Sing Daddy's name!"

"Good night, Ethan," Ruby sings.

"Good night," the kids chime in, not quite in unison. "We'll see you next time."

Almost forty minutes later, I fall into step beside Ruby in the lit parking lot where we picked her up. The kids have already said their goodbyes, eager to know when she'll be back. I'd told them to stay buckled while I walked her only as far as the base of the stairs, close enough to still see the SUV. We linger there at the steps leading to her balcony.

"Thanks for coming, Ruby." I shove my hands deep in my pockets to keep from doing anything I shouldn't. Like pulling her into my arms from an old habit.

"Your kids are wonderful." Her soft eyes are luminous beneath the overhead string lights. "I always knew you'd be a great dad someday."

I shift the weight of my foot, her words hitting somewhere I don't know what to do with. I don't deserve her kindness.

"I'm not so sure I'm getting it right." That's just what it is.

Then, drawing out a breath, I push through the hesitation clogging my chest. "I know it's a lot to ask, but... would you—could we maybe meet on Saturday? Just us. To talk? I mean, about what days you'll teach piano and all."

She tilts her chin. "I'm sure your kids are too young to stay home alone."

"They'll be gone for the day." Harvey promised them uncle time at the amusement park, but summer went fast. This is the last weekend it's open. "We could go to Sunvalley." Ruby and I stumbled upon it back in the day. "Close enough to Meadowbrook. I just... I think we need to talk. About everything. I'm not saying we can go back or fix things, but..."

She keeps a hand on the railing. With one foot on the bottom step, she's ready to take off.

Then she shakes her head. "Ethan, you know this isn't a good—"

"Please. Just think about it?"

Silly to have pretended we're just going to talk about the kids' piano schedule, but I had to try.

"I'll text you," she concedes. Then she starts up the stairs, her clanging footsteps putting space between us, the distance settling heavier than I expected. But she'll text me.

I just need to have Sunday's lesson ready before Saturday, in case she says yes. I pray she does, and I pray I'll have the chance to tell her everything I've wanted to whenever I thought about her through the years.

CHAPTER 7

Ruby

This is not a date. Or so I tell myself for the hundredth time as Ethan's hand finds the small of my back, his palm warm even through my cable-knit sweater. The early afternoon breeze slips under the hem, brushing against my jeans, and the sun, bright but cold, reflects off the cracked sidewalk. Sunvalley is smaller than Meadowbrook, quieter. We ventured here once before.

"Careful." Ethan's breath caresses my ear, and a tingle spirals down my spine. He draws me to his side as a scraggly man barrels out of Hello Burgers, the hand-painted sign above the door swings in the breeze, letters faded more now than they were thirteen years ago when we visited.

I feel the loss of his warmth like a draft as he steps ahead to open the door.

Hello Burgers stands right next to Sunvalley Hardware, its dusty windows crammed with fishing gear and chipped paint cans.

"After you." Ethan holds the door.

Inside, the scent of grilled onions and melted cheese engulfs me, and my stomach growls.

"Welcome to Hello Burgers," chirps a brunette at the hostess stand, ponytail bouncing as she hands us two laminated menus. "Sit wherever you like."

A slow country song drifts from the overhead speakers. Only two booths are occupied—one by a man hidden behind a newspaper, the other by a couple eating in silence. Red-and-white checkered tablecloths drape each table, and framed black-and-white photos line the walls, displaying faded storefronts, kids in overalls, fishing boats, and a diner.

Ethan didn't bring me here to stroll down memory lane, but to avoid the Meadowbrook locals—his congregation.

We slide into a corner booth. The red vinyl squeaks when I scoot further.

The waitress returns, two waters balanced on a tray. Ice clinks as she sets them down. "Anything else to drink?"

"Water's fine." I fiddle with the menu just to have something to do.

She rattles off the day's special—beef stew.

"I'll have what she's having," Ethan repeats the words he used the last time we were here.

"Two peach shakes and two cheeseburgers, it seems." If we're going for last time's order.

"And chili cheese fries." He hands the waitress his menu. "We'll share."

As she walks away, I can't stop the intruding smile. "You always ordered enough food for three people."

"Hey, you always stole my fries."

"The scraps, you mean?"

"Correction, I had to eat them fast to protect you from cholesterol."

I used to tease him for ordering chili cheese fries with his burger, even though I always ended up eating most of them.

"Good to see you still have some of your old self in there." He smirks. And for a heartbeat, everything feels... easy.

"I'm still me." Sort of.

The truth? Anything tied to him I locked away for a reason. I trusted Ethan, and he broke me. Yet somehow, he's still the only man I want to run to. Which explains why I'm sitting across from him, despite having sworn I'd keep him at a distance. But no need to second-guess myself. I might as well enjoy the meal and the place I never thought I'd step into again.

"We weren't supposed to meet again. But God doesn't seem to ask for our permission." Ethan's finger traces a line of checks on the tablecloth before he leans in, forearms on the table, fingers laced. His yellow-and-brown plaid makes his dark hair look even darker, the short sides neat against the slight curl on top. "I want to clear the air. We're going to be seeing more of each other. I don't want it awkward... or to sabotage the kids' piano lessons."

On the drive over, we'd nailed down the schedule to Wednesday and Friday evenings. Besides his kids, I have three other families. One mom even asked for an early morning session before school since her son's brain works better then.

"There's no need—"

"Really?" His voice stays low as his gaze rises to mine, capturing me. Those soft brown eyes full of love were always my downfall. "I never meant to hurt you, Ruby."

"It's okay." I shrug like the last years apart weren't grueling. But what else am I supposed to say? He made his choice.

"I don't know what got into me." His jaw flexes. He glances past me, out the window, then back to the table like it might hold the answer. "I always respected my parents, and their decisions mattered. Probably too much. That's no excuse. When Harvey... after that incident... I felt like maybe God wanted something else for me. But I didn't even pray about it."

Uncomfortable warmth seeps under my skin. How easily our relationship ended. Brenda wouldn't be proud of me for letting myself sink into the past. She said it could trigger a panic spiral.

I draw a slow, measured breath to steady the churn in my chest. I've fisted the corner of the tablecloth. I work on smoothing it out.

"Siding with your family makes sense." My voice comes out flatter than the creases in the cloth. "Besides, I didn't have the strong religious background your folks wanted."

He was the reason I understood the concept of God. The reason I saw any light. The reason...

I press a hand to my cheek, elbow on the table, lips clamped shut to keep the lump in my throat from rising. I will not cry here.

"I was young and stupid." His somber voice echoes in my head.

Young. Yet, he married someone else the second he couldn't find me.

"You said you came looking for me a year later?"

He nods, and the sadness in his eyes puts an end to all the questions brewing in my mind.

A full year.

The throbbing ache in my chest settles. It was probably for the best that he didn't find me then. I was a wreck.

The server returns and sets down our shakes, each crowned with whipped cream and a cherry.

We just stare at them.

I'm not hungry. But the ache of what never happened, the life we never had, gnaws at me. I shove a straw into the glass and stir, needing to do something, anything.

The black-and-white photo beyond his shoulder displays beaming boys holding up the fish they've caught. Too bad life's not like that, nothing but joy and triumph.

The grief—his kids losing their mom, my own losses, and the thought that maybe some of it could've been prevented—nearly crushed me at his house. I'd wanted to leave. But his kids' playroom diversion eased the tension enough for me to play the piano.

"How long did you date Maddie... before you married?"

His hand clenches his shake. "Her family was in ministry with mine for a while. Old friends. Good people."

Our parents never moved in the same circles.

"She was in seminary as a children's minister. I was missing you and thought maybe dating someone in ministry would give me... perspective. While we connected so well as helpers, I didn't feel we loved each other... like the kind of love I'd expected. After about nine months, I planned to end things but..."

His Adam's apple bobs. The steel guitar on the radio drones like heartbreak itself.

"Her dad was dying. He wanted to walk his daughter down the aisle."

A knot clogs my chest.

"It's all in the past." My tongue trips in my hurry to get the words out, my heart racing just as fast. We can't undo what happened. "You don't have to explain."

"But... can you forgive me?"

His rawness makes me look at him. And there he is. Not just the boy I once loved, but the man he's become—lines etching his brow, sorrow chiseling his expression, regret shadowing his eyes... and yet, hope.

Hope, as he waits for *my* answer.

"Why not?" I bob my straw. "Isn't that what God wants?"

Something shifts in his face, an emotion I can't name.

The waitress returns with our food, ending our moment. Plates clink as she lifts them from the serving tray to the table.

"Let me know if you need anything." She smiles before moving on.

Ethan clears his throat. "Is it all right if I pray?"

When I nod, he pushes his plate aside and offers his hands.

My hesitation lasts half a second before I take them. Warm. Solid. Familiar. The kind of touch that once made me feel safe. Still does now.

He bows his head, eyes closed, so I do the same. "Father... thank You." His steady voice cracks. "For second chances. For Your mercy... for keeping Ruby safe... for bringing her back into my life."

My throat locks, a weight pressing against my chest, unsure which part of that he means.

"I'm grateful for the forgiveness she's given me, even though I don't deserve it."

By the time he says his amen—his voice frayed and thick with emotion—I can barely whisper mine. I blink back the tears burning behind my eyes and pick at the chili cheese fries. The burger can wait. I need safer ground.

"You have a big responsibility." I focus on the light, anything to keep from spilling the darkest parts of the years we were apart. "What's it like being a pastor?"

He takes a long pull with a straw from his shake, nodding, then meets my gaze. "Some days I think I've got it together. Other days, I remember I'm human. You can't really fall when you're a pastor... but you do. Quietly. And it hurts more because no one's supposed to notice."

We eat in silence, sip our shakes. I finish mine and edge it aside. "What brought you to Meadowbrook?"

"Unfinished dreams." He raises his hamburger as if giving a toast.

So his reason for coming mirrors mine.

"And being a single dad? How's that going?"

"It's better now. Those early days after Maddie died... the ache of watching our babies grow up without a mom." He shrugs. "I joined a support group during the year I stepped away from ministry. That's where I met the friends, before accepting the pastor role here in Meadowbrook. Of course I convinced them to buy the land here so we could be neighbors."

"That's amazing, having friends who'd follow you anywhere. Willow's like that. We met—" Nope. Not gonna tell him I met her when I was a guest at a restoration center. "When we met, I challenged her on her personal experience with relationships, rather than her degree. Through one park walk after another, service projects, and endless conversations about what it meant to show up for people, we became friends. I later learned she drove over an hour to meet me in Brooklyn each time."

"That's friendship." He wipes ketchup from his lips. "My friends' kids became my kids' friends too. Such support—all of them having also lost their mothers helps."

I swallow down the lump in my chest at the thought of his pain, his kids' pain... and his friends who were hurting then, maybe still are.

"But God carried us through it all."

I don't realize I'm crying until a warm trail slips from the corner of my eye and pools at my jaw. I duck my head and busy myself with our fries.

But Ethan's hand comes to rest on my wrist. It's warm and steady. "I didn't mean to make you cry."

"I'm... sorry." I grab the napkin off my lap and blow my nose.

"Your mom died too."

"And my aunt."

I swallow down fresh tears, blowing my nose again, even though I don't need to. Ethan's pain was always mine too. Some things haven't changed.

"I'm so sorry about your aunt. You want to talk about it?"

I shake my head. "Enough sadness for one day."

"Let's talk music." His dimple flashes, that familiar disarming grin.

"That guitar of yours." I lift my burger halfway to my mouth. "You're the one who introduced me to music."

"You already knew how to sing."

"For fun. Forget the school choir."

It was so romantic whenever he'd lug his guitar to the park just to play for me. "Do you remember the first time we sang together?"

"You made fun of me for being off-key."

"You were off-key." I stuff a wayward pickle further into my burger.

His lip curls sideways, the dimple deepening. "I was distracted."

Warmth runs through me, but I arch a brow. "By what?"

"You." His gaze locks on mine.

The burger trembles in my hand until I set it down so how much I'm shaking isn't obvious.

"You were always my distraction."

I'm holding my breath, but I can't hold his gaze too long.

As though aware of that, he clears his throat. "How did you learn piano?"

"I had an opportunity to learn for free." At rehab, when they gave us things to do. "Later, I took lessons online. In my first job, I taught kids in exchange for training. After that, they kept me on."

"When did the florist dream die?"

The day you walked away. "I got older. Plans change." Still avoiding his gaze, I dip a fry in the gooey chili sauce. I barely taste the usually luscious cheese. I'm not ready to tell him my music and piano took precedence in my life over flowers. I'd have to talk about rehab, and now isn't the time.

"You still go to music festivals?" he asks.

"Uh, hello?" I grin, although I only started back this summer. "Wouldn't be New York in summer without those concerts in the park."

"I went to a couple, hoping I'd run into you, but..." He waves my way. "You're here now."

We slip into easy conversation and laughter, reminiscing about the time he got into his first fistfight in a Brooklyn alley.

A man had stepped out of the shadows and demanded his wallet.

"Who do you think you are?" I'd asked first.

He called me something I won't repeat, and Ethan fired back. The guy swung. Before I knew it, we were both throwing punches, then sprinting for our lives.

"You were always trouble." Ethan points a fry at me. Chili cheese plops from it to the platter between us.

I laugh, but part of me stiffens. Maybe that's why he gave up on us.

"In the best way," he adds. He must've caught my expression. "The best adventures I've had in life were with you."

"Me too." And not just the adventures. He'd been my best friend. Starting to date in freshman year made it hard to prioritize other friends, at least for me. I hadn't had steady ones to begin with, and once Ethan came into my life, I didn't need to spend time with anyone else.

"I want to show you something."

I blink. "Here?"

"Something we missed last time we came."

He's taking me somewhere unknown? My heart kicks up, sending a flutter through my chest.

When we finish eating, he pays and stands. The weight between us feels lighter.

"Where are we going?" I ask as he holds the door. Barely paying attention, I trip on the entrance rug.

Ethan's arm shoots out, and he steadies me against his chest.

His warmth and the weight of his arm around my waist turn my legs to mush, and I don't dare move, especially with the pull of his warm brown eyes inches from mine, the familiar scent of him wrapping around me like home.

"Careful." His gruff voice rumbles in his chest. His breath brushes my lips. "I can't have you tripping in front of me."

"Says... the man who tumbled into the pool." Horrible that I'm so breathless.

His mouth curves. "I figured if I was going to see you after twelve years, I might as well dive in headfirst."

He lets go, and we step onto the sidewalk. "There's an arcade two blocks from here."

I'll follow him anywhere.

The afternoon sun dips lower, a breeze picking up as we stroll. I might as well be floating on it. Being with Ethan has always felt like this.

A man approaches from the opposite direction, two kids skipping at his sides. He lifts one, then the other, swinging them in turn, both clutching his hands, their faces alight.

"Harvey?" Ethan says.

The man looks up.

The kids rush toward us—Ethan's kids. "Daddy!"

As Ethan hugs his kids and they chatter about the rides, my gaze locks on Harvey. My mind goes blank, though. What do you say to the guy who kissed you behind his brother's back and lied about it? Yes, he apologized, but did he ever tell Ethan the truth?

CHAPTER 8

Ruby

Harvey's older now, still handsome in that boyish-rebel way, and carries an easy confidence. Two years older than Ethan, he always did things his own way. He'd slip out of church before his father's sermons ended, refuse the tie his dad insisted on for Sundays, keep his eyes open during grace, and never once join Ethan in skipping meals when their father declared a family fast. By his family's standards, that was rebellion. Maybe that's why he felt more at ease with me than with relatives who took their faith so seriously.

And yet... It was never a secret to him or his family that I was head over heels for Ethan.

"Ruby! What a sight for sore eyes." Harvey grins and reaches for me the way he always did when we were only friends, before the lie wrecked what we had. He's relaxed, like nothing ever weighed him down.

I keep it to a quick side hug. He smells faintly of cedar and coffee.

Small arms wrap around my waist.

"Miss Ruby!"

Poppy.

I bend to hug her, grateful for the distraction. "I hear you went to the amusement park."

"I was scared of the roller coaster." She steps out of the hug, brushing loose hair from her face. "But the merry-go-round was fun."

"Did you and Dad come here to meet us?" Asher gives me a side hug.

"We were talking about your lessons." I pat his back. It's not a lie. It was sort of our reason for meeting. "How was your time at the park?"

"The roller coaster was awesome. You and Daddy should come next time."

"Today was the last day." Harvey crosses his arms, having stopped right before Ethan. He recaps what the kids did and didn't like.

"What brings you to Sunvalley?" Ethan's tone is edgy, his eyes guarded.

"We're here to eat." Asher grins, flashing those too-big-for-him front teeth. "Uncle Harvey promised to take us to the arcade if we finish our dinner."

Poppy darts toward the steps by the railing, calling for her brother to join her.

Harvey's gaze settles on me. "You look good, Ruby." His smile is genuine as he nods. "I was worried when I ran into you... Ever end up finishing those piano lessons?"

"I did."

"I didn't realize you and Harvey…" Ethan's shoulders edge up. "You run in the same circles?"

"We crossed paths a few years back." Harvey shoves his hands into his khakis, not elaborating.

"I was taking piano lessons in the same building as—"

Ethan's gaze narrows as he looks between us. Clearly, Harvey never mentioned the encounter to his brother.

"We're adults, Ruby." Harvey shrugs, meeting his brother's stare head-on. "No need to explain anything."

He makes it sound like we had a thing, rewriting the past without apology.

"I'm glad you reunited with my brother." He pats my arm, his smile soft with sadness. "Good to see you. Gotta get the kids some food."

I nod. We've cleared the air, but old wounds are close to reopening.

"I'll take my kids home," Ethan says.

"You be the one to tell them it's your idea they're not going to the arcade."

Ethan glances at the kids hopping around the railing, then back to Harvey. He pinches the bridge of his nose. His gaze shifts to me—laced with the same betrayal I saw twelve years ago. Maybe worse.

"All right, troops." Harvey claps his hands. "Couple more hours together—ice cream, then the arcade."

The kids cheer and surge toward him.

"Food first," Ethan bellows.

"Oops, my bad." An incorrigible Harvey raises both palms in surrender. "Food first, kids. Then ice cream. Now, say bye to your dad."

"Bye, Daddy!" They charge back and throw their arms around Ethan.

Poppy rushes to me, curling her small hands around my waist. I bend to hug her, her curls brushing my chin. "When will we see you again for piano?"

My heart squeezes. I'm not sure this piano lesson setup will work anymore. "Soon, I hope."

"We'll see you soon." Asher waves as he bounces backward.

I nod, even though this reunion with Ethan just ended.

As they disappear down the sidewalk, Ethan's silence beside me holds me mute. It trails us like a storm cloud while we walk in the opposite direction, away from the kids.

"I should head back." It's not urgent, but I have things to do. Things like calling a parent to confirm Monday's lesson.

"I'll drive you home."

He doesn't look at me, doesn't ask another question about my run-in with Harvey.

Why do I even let him drive me home? I could've called an Uber. Maybe I'm hoping we can talk, get back to where we were minutes before running into Harvey.

Unlike the easy chatter on the way here, the drive back is silent. My fingers twitch to turn on the radio.

"Why didn't you mention you'd run into Harvey?"

"At least now we know New York isn't that big," I snap. Beyond the window, the open fields blur. "You didn't bother to look back when you walked away, Ethan. You never paused to wonder if I was hurting. I didn't have any choices like you did."

My muscles tense, and I lift a hand to steady myself, not for emphasis. "I loved you. But you walked away, never fought for us. How could I not wonder if you ever loved me at all?"

"You know that's not true. I just meant... You could've—"

"Again." The breakup replays in my mind, so vivid. "You're doing it again—judging me as the guilty one because I'm not religious enough. Why don't you ask your brother why he didn't tell you? You see *him* all the time. You've only seen me for less than two weeks—*three* conversations—and you expect me to dump twelve years of history on you like it's nothing?"

Tears sting my eyes. I fiddle with my seatbelt strap, yanking it further from my neck. My thick sweater's now too heavy, the collar too tight. In the flash of passing streetlamps, I catch him clenching his grip on the wheel, knuckles white.

"I'm sure Harvey never told you he kissed me. Or that I didn't kiss him back. I didn't tell you because I didn't want to be the reason you stopped speaking to your brother."

"He told me the truth. Later."

The seat belt snaps back into place. Its slap against my chest jars me. "And I'm guessing that's when you *finally* came looking for me?"

"I came looking before he told me."

It should make me feel better. It doesn't erase what happened.

"You were my best friend, and I'd tell you anything. The one thing I chose not to tell you was to protect your family... but my mistake." My voice cracks, the lump in my throat making it hard to go on. "I just... I need to leave. I thought moving here was a good idea."

His silence says he'd rather I go. But leaving means breaking my commitment to the families who signed up for lessons. It means calling Brenda and explaining why I didn't give the place the year she suggested, unless I had a good reason to uproot again.

One of the steps I've read in my books on battling shadows is to build consistent habits. Find purpose. Wake up with something to look forward to.

My mind is so busy weighing what I should and shouldn't do that I don't notice we've arrived until Ethan pulls into the lot beside Willow's Forte. The engine idles, the silence between us heavier than before.

"See you at—"

I swing the door open and step out, not letting myself hear the rest.

I pivot, glancing back through the open door. The overhead lamp lights his face—grim and shadowed. Not the man who picked me up earlier, holding the door with the dimpled smile that gave me flutters.

"I'm not looking for complications, Ethan." My voice shakes. "Please. It'd be best if I didn't teach your kids. Really."

"Ruby—"

I slam the door and stride across the lot to the back steps, keeping my head down, afraid I might turn around and look at his SUV.

Tears blur my vision. My chest tightens, lungs burning, and my heartbeat drowns out everything else.

I stop midclimb, grip the railing, and press a hand to my chest. *Breathe in... Hold... Breathe out.* Again. Slower.

Things haven't changed between us. Twelve years ago, he took Harvey's words over mine.

My breathing steadier, I climb the remaining steps. It's only a dozen or so, though each feels heavier than the last.

I fumble for the key in my phone case, the metal jingling as moths flutter overhead. My vision stays tear-hazy.

The door jerks open, and I step back as Willow appears. Her brows draw together the moment she sees me.

"Oh, Ruby."

She hauls me into her arms, and the key falls from my hand as my arms wrap around her. I hold on longer than usual. When I step back, her hand stays on my back. She guides me inside and closes the door behind us. We head to the tan corduroy love seat, and she doesn't ask what happened, just tugs a tissue from the box and hands it over.

I wipe my eyes and blow my nose. "Thanks."

"Take a slow breath."

I do. Then again.

When my breathing evens out, she slips away. The microwave beeps.

Moments later, she's back with two mugs. "Chamomile. It'll help."

She sips hers in silence beside me, steam curling between us. I blow across my mug, then test a sip. And another.

"What happened?"

She already knows I was with Ethan, so I don't bother with that part.

"We ran into Harvey." Just saying his name should trigger another spiral. "Ethan got upset. I never told him I ran into his brother years ago."

"He should be mad at his brother, not you."

"I don't want to talk about Ethan."

Willow watches me over the rim of her mug. "Then don't talk. Show him."

I blink. "What?"

"Your first instinct right now is to leave Meadowbrook. Instead, you're going to stay, and you're coming to church with me tomorrow. The church where Ethan is the pastor."

"Are you insane?" I even manage a laugh.

"The best way to get over someone is to live like you've moved on. Come to church and show him you're not the same girl he left behind. Don't get me wrong. I love my pastor, but *you're* my best friend, and I'm not letting him run you out of town."

"I'm not sure that's great advice."

"Trust me." She smirks, full of the confidence that makes people listen to her radio show. "Just come to church with me."

"Does it have to be Ethan's church?"

"Where else are you going to show him you're the new-and-improved Ruby?"

"If, and when, he shows up at your shop?"

"He's going to avoid coming over now." She lifts her mug. "The longer you wait, the more your heart builds it up into something it's not. You need to remind Ethan you moved to Meadowbrook for yourself, not for him."

I sip the tea. She's right—it's calming. My muscles loosen.

This is my new beginning. If Ethan always chooses his family first, maybe it's time I choose mine, even if it's just Willow for now.

"For the record," I mumble into my mug, "I'm only going if I can sit in the back row."

"Perfect." She clinks her mug against mine.

But when we go to bed and the only sound is crickets, reality crashes in.

Going to church? It doesn't just mean seeing Ethan, but... memories I'd rather forget. No, Ethan wouldn't turn me into a sermon like his dad did—preaching about dating dress codes while staring at my skirt that hit above the knee, about ripped jeans being "a sign of shaky faith," about how a believer should never date a nonbeliever. Maybe it wasn't aimed at me, but it felt personal, especially since he'd already said those things to my face to keep me from "interfering with God's plans" for his son's ministry.

No, Ethan wouldn't do that. Still, I can't face him tomorrow.

I throw back the covers, pull on a robe, and head to the kitchen. I flick on the light.

The knife glints on the counter.

I edge closer. If I were hurt, I could stay in bed all day and not go.

No. I don't do that anymore.

I push out the back door. Cool air cuts through my robe, my bare feet freezing against the rough boards, splinters pricking my skin. Dumb. I cross to the railing and look down. The drop isn't far, just far enough for a broken arm, maybe a leg. Just far enough to disappear from everyone for a while.

Go back inside now.

The gentle voice stops me. I shake my head. The song "Live Like You're Loved" comes to mind. One of the gospel choruses that's carried me through darker nights.

I step away from the edge and rush inside, back to my room. Under the covers where it's warm, my heart still races at what I almost entertained.

My gaze falls to the photo on my nightstand, one like it used to have Ethan in it, and then to the Lego figurine Asher gave me. *Battling Shadows: Finding God in the Panic* lies beside it.

A wobbly smile finds me. I have a purpose.

I close my eyes. *Lord, I know You didn't bring me this far to let me waste my life.*

I pray. I sing songs of hope. And before I know it, sleep claims me. *I've got this.*

CHAPTER 9

Ethan

A mental battle rages as I back out of the parking space, gripping the wheel. Her raw words about forgiving my brother and judging her echo in my ears.

The way she stumbled out of the passenger seat and staggered across the lot, gasping like she was drowning... I should've gone after her. But it's best I leave her alone.

My heart slams my ribs. Why did Harvey have to ruin what could've been a good day? Ninety steps forward, and now, I've stumbled twice as far back.

I jab the radio to drown out my thoughts. But even the music mocks me, something about never judging others lest you be judged.

I should avoid the gospel channels. I switch stations. A talk show. Another click. A song I don't even know, but the lyrics still land. Something about climbing mountains, taking leaps, fixing what's broken.

"Can't a man get a break, even on a random channel?"

Great. This conviction is not what I need the day before I'm supposed to preach on living in God's grace—the beginning of *God's Masterpiece* series.

The fifteen-minute drive back to Renewed Lane drags. I make it home before Harvey and the kids. I need space to work through this.

I pace the main floor, stopping at the wall of family photos in the entryway.

Maddie's smile beams back at me, but I know now what hid beneath it. Guilt presses down as I remember her sister at the funeral confessing Maddie's lifelong battle with depression—worsened after her high school boyfriend's tragic death.

"Why didn't you tell me?" I whisper to the photo, though I know. I should've seen it in the way she wandered off to the hills alone or retreated to her late boyfriend's family cabin whenever they offered it. In the first years of our marriage, I buried myself in learning my role as a student pastor. Then came Asher, sleepless nights, distractions. I missed it all.

I climb the stairs, Ruby still tugging at my thoughts. *You didn't give her the chance to explain back then, you idiot.* Too afraid Harvey might be right.

Besides preparing sermons here, I use my office for my prayer room. Here, my mind gets in the right space and prayer form. I avoid the desk against the wall with my laptop closed and sermon notes scattered beside an open Bible. A sofa across from it beckons. I lower myself there and reach beneath the side table for the worn brown shoebox hidden in the storage shelf.

I retrieved the box from Mom and Dad's house after moving to Meadowbrook. Back then, it was safer out of sight, where I wouldn't look while I tried to move on with Maddie. But after her death and in those dark nights when I feared Ruby might be gone too, I needed every piece of her I could still find.

I flip the flap open and lift the top photo, a group shot from her high school choir banquet. The one I showed the kids when I told them about their talented piano teacher.

"Why do you have Miss Ruby's photo?" Asher asked after I gave him the simple version, that our schools played against each other and that's how we met.

I smile now, eyes tracing her in the picture—a wealth of dark hair falling over her shoulders, a black dress I can still picture vividly, a radiant smile that warms my heart.

I rummage through the stack of our few photos together, the folded letters she slipped me on birthdays, and other reminders of the night we met. My chest tightens, cutting off air, and I drop to my knees. The rug is soft against them, my sermon study guides spread nearby. I brace my hands on the table.

"God... I need Your guidance. Peace for Ruby. Forgiveness for not living up to the role model I should've been, the only Christian she knew, the one she trusted when I told her about Your love, Your mercy. Even now, I'm not sure I'm the pastor I should be."

The doorbell cuts through my prayer. I push up and head downstairs.

"Daddy!" Poppy launches herself at me.

"Did you eat your mac and cheese for dinner?" I scoop her up and kiss her forehead. Her hands curl around my neck, and my chest takes on the familiar ache of love for my two biggest blessings.

"I had *two* scoops of ice cream with sprinkles!"

"Did you eat dinner first?"

"Uncle said I only had to take a few bites of mac and cheese if I wanted."

Behind her, Asher trudges in. Sticky fingers try to hide a yawn, but can't cover the chocolate smeared on his chin. The kids chatter about the amusement park and their favorite rides as cool night air seeps through the open door. I usher them inside and shut it behind us.

Harvey follows, studying me. "You want to talk about it?"

One look at his compassionate expression tells me we will. "Let me get the kids settled first."

He nods. We go through the routine—bath time, tooth-brushing, bedtime hugs, and prayers. I promise to play three songs on the guitar tomorrow if we skip tonight.

"But, Daddy, we always sing." Asher yawns, his protest soft as he sinks into his pillow.

"Tomorrow, buddy." I press a kiss to his forehead. A song tonight would feel hollow. "Promise."

Harvey says good night to Asher. Then I take Poppy's hand, her unicorn tucked in her arm, and walk her to her room. I tuck her in, kiss her forehead, and with Harvey's quiet good night, we step out.

"They seem tired enough not to argue long." He follows, and our steps thump down the stairs.

"Good thing you wore them out enough to overcome the sugar rush."

In the kitchen, he swings open the fridge and scans the shelves. "What happened to all the casseroles your church people used to send?"

"My assistant gives them to those who need them."

He grabs a can of Coke. "Care for a drink?"

I decline and pull out a chair. He still sets a water bottle in front of me before sitting across the table.

"Thanks for helping with the kids today." I twist the cap. My throat is dry, so I take a sip.

"No thanks needed." He cracks his Coke with a pop and fizz. "I'm their uncle."

"You've been going to Alyssa's church lately?"

"Yep." He avoids my gaze. "Mom and Dad are still laying on the guilt. They want us married already. Want us closer to home while Dad finishes up his last years in Albany."

Our hometown—where Dad chose to close out his ministry.

Harvey talks about Alyssa's job prospects. I nod, and we drift into Thanksgiving plans. Safe topics. But the elephant's still here.

"You sure you still want to host Thanksgiving this year?" Harvey asks like I've given reason to doubt it.

"Yep." Another sip. Cool water slides down my throat.

"We both know you don't want to talk about Thanksgiving or Alyssa right now." His chair scrapes as he leans back and crosses one leg over the other. He pins me with the calculating look that's made him a good medical sales rep. "Let's talk about Ruby."

I pinch the bridge of my nose, pressure building behind my eyes. "Why didn't you tell me you'd seen her all this time?"

"You were married. Why would it matter?"

"You know it mattered." My voice emerges too loud, so I breathe out, steadying. "I thought she was dead. Or worse."

"I know you followed Dad's footsteps." He narrows his eyes. "But I never took you for someone who'd fake righteousness."

"Dad never fakes righteousness." I understand his interpretation of our family dynamics, but I can't side with him in questioning how Dad leads his spiritual life.

"You gonna tell me I was the only one watching? Mom and Dad yelled all the way to church, then plastered on perfect smiles the second we hit the parking lot. Dad preached alcohol is a sin, yet he cracked a beer every night with supper. Don't tell me you didn't know. The first alcohol I ever tasted was from Dad's stash in the garage behind his tackle box."

I swallow hard. "I saw." But I respected my parents. The Bible says to honor your father and mother. That doesn't mean Dad didn't love God. I just never wanted to be that way. My voice dips low. "It doesn't make him much different from us."

"Right. Of course. I'm talking to the golden boy. Always got good grades, did whatever Mom and Dad asked, followed every commandment like you were God's gift to the world."

I clench my jaw. "Is that what you think of me?"

He tilts his head. "You ever think people lie because they're scared of what the truth will do?"

"I don't see how you keeping mum on meeting up with Ruby helped anything."

"It took you five years to speak to me after I told you the truth." He means the kiss. The one he swore was the other way around. "I didn't want to lose another five—or forever. Running into her wasn't planned. I was meeting a client in the building. She was walking out of her piano class. She obviously didn't want to see me, but I asked—*pleaded* for—a minute to say I was sorry."

He twists the Coke can between his hands, smearing condensation on the tabletop. "I lied about the kiss because I'd just earned back Dad and Mom's trust after wrecking Dad's prized Mustang. I was already the black sheep. I couldn't risk another strike, another sin pinned on me." He drags a hand down his face. "If I'd told you then… that I saw her… what were you going to do about it?"

I stare at the table, at the purple and green smudges from the kids' markers I'll never scrub out.

What would I have done? Probably gone looking. A temptation I couldn't afford when I was married. How many times did I ask myself why I agreed to marry Maddie? A thousand, maybe? I wondered if it was God's plan to reroute my life or my own stupid choice. The only confidence I had later came from the kids. They're not mistakes. They're worth the detour.

"She looked tired," Harvey says. "Worn down. Like she was carrying something heavy. But today? She looked better. Relaxed."

"What do you mean she didn't look good?" My chest clenches. Had I done that to her?

"You can't live in the past." He lifts his soda, takes a sip. "She's here now. I won't ask how it happened, but I will ask what you're going to do about it."

I shake my head. "Nothing."

"Sure." Harvey's chuckle is dry. "Aren't you the one always preaching about second chances? God's grace bigger than our worst mistakes?"

"She's not staying after the way I acted today."

"Then it's time you take your own advice." He raises his fingers in air quotes. "'Repent, even when we're not wrong, just to be at peace with thy neighbor.' Sound familiar?"

"I already apologized. Earlier. Then I ran into you, and... it all spiraled."

"Apologize again." He exhales. "You loved her. Judging by your real smile when I saw you with her, the anger when you realized I'd run into her, and the fear in your eyes now, you never stopped. You preach to almost three hundred people every Sunday. Surely, you can figure out how to get to the one woman who used to be your best friend."

He's right. The moment Ruby came into my life, she became my priority. I had friends, but I was only in as long as their plans with me included Ruby coming along.

Harvey stands, crushes his empty can, and tosses it in the recycling bin. "Give her space to cool down after tonight." He wipes his hands on his jeans. "But don't wait too long. We both know she's the one who got away. Don't let it happen again."

I rub my jaw, the scruff rough against my fingers.

When he leaves, silence settles heavily. His words echo louder than the stillness.

How foolish to think twelve years of damage could be fixed over burgers and milkshakes. "Smooth, Ethan. Real smooth."

I'll give her a couple of days to cool off. If she hasn't already packed up and left town.

CHAPTER 10

Ruby

"It's freezing." I rub my free hand up and down my arm, the chill seeping straight through my jean jacket. Each breath leaves a puff of white mist.

Despite the air biting my ears, my palm is damp on my purse handle. My nerves, of course, have nothing to do with the possibility of running into Ethan. Or so I've been telling myself all morning.

"November's here." Willow tucks her plaid scarf into her charcoal peacoat. "Means more cold days."

Our shoes click across the crowded lot. Cars slide into their spots, engines cutting off, doors slamming. Willow waves at folks as we pass, calling some by name.

A middle-aged man approaches with a bag of candy.

Oops. "I forgot to pick up candy for tomorrow." I slap my forehead. I'd assumed Ethan and I would stop at the store together. Foolish assumption.

"We still have the afternoon. And with all the fall fest activities at the park, half the kids won't even bother going to doorsteps anyway."

"I can't believe tomorrow's the last day of October."

"You've been busy. Easy to lose track." Willow tips her chin in greeting to a couple who stride past us.

The church's dress code is all over the place—a man in a suit, a woman in jeans and a sweater, a couple in business casual. Meadowbrook doesn't care what you wear. Unlike Ethan's parents' church. There, appearances were gospel. I'd played it safe today, choosing a sunshiny maxi dress that skims over my ankle boots, just in case.

The church looms ahead, a modern brick building with a steel cross anchored to the facade. "The building looks different from the picture I carried in my head. Not a quaint white chapel with a steeple."

"It used to be a community center. The church bought it and expanded." She shifts her purse, then nods toward the far end of the yard. "The kids have their church there now."

Beneath a canopy of golden oak and maple trees, a tiny steeple tops an older chapel. Leaves swirl and scatter around it like children playing tag.

Warmth envelops me once we step into the lobby. Big windows flood the space with light, and the air carries the cozy mix of coffee, cinnamon, baked goods, and a trace of wood polish. Conversations hum, voices rising over the instrumental music drifting from hidden speakers.

A cluster forms near the center, eight or maybe ten people. Women my age, some older. A couple of men. But the women stand out—hovering, leaning in, laughing too high, Bibles tucked under their arms. And there is their center of gravity. Ethan.

My chest tightens, and my pulse skips. Before I realize it, I've spun too fast and shouldered into Willow. She steadies me.

"Want some coffee?" Her brows lift like she knows what's happening under my skin.

"I don't drink coffee." My doctor's advice, though I don't need to explain that.

"Right. How can I forget?" She shakes her head. "Not that anyone ever says, 'Let's grab tea sometime.'" Her light tone should ease my stiff shoulders.

It doesn't.

Pastor Bishop Sr.'s church was all strict code and starched collars. Here, people tip their heads back, laughing, as they sip coffee or tea in the lobby. A few men sport suits, but plenty are in khakis or jeans and flannels. Women in slacks, jeans, or knee-length dresses and boots all chat easily. Still, the ease does nothing to calm me. Not when Ethan is right there, drawing smiles like moths to flame.

"Let's just go sit down." I clutch Willow's arm and scan for a back entrance.

She winces. "That's the only way inside."

Of course, she knows my fear.

"Maybe we can get some tea," I say. Anything to stall until Ethan disappears into the sanctuary.

We drift toward the self-serve coffee counter. Willow starts introductions as a couple restocks trays of home-baked muffins, cinnamon and bananas scenting the air.

"Tonya, Peter, this is Ruby. She's new in town, staying with me."

"The piano teacher." Tonya's smile is warm, her Jersey accent making it sound like a declaration. "Linda signed her kids up, and I wanted to call about group classes. I've got four grandkids, so it'd be easier for their parents if they all came together."

"Of course." My voice steadies as I lean into familiar ground. "We can work something out."

She prefers the coffee shop to home lessons, so we set a time to talk later.

I hadn't considered group lessons, but it's a great idea. My heart softens as I pour my tea while Willow fixes her coffee. Then, almost against my will, my gaze strays to Ethan's circle.

He shakes hands and accepts yet another basket of brownies.

A few women linger close—beautiful, polished. Their flirtatious smiles come easily, their playful touches even easier. One stands shoulder to shoulder with him as if they're a couple. Her smile lights up each time Ethan speaks, and her hand taps his shoulder. My chest knots.

"Don't mind Pastor's admirers." Willow's voice is for my ears alone.

I lift my tea, hoping the rim hides my sullen face. "Who's the woman in green?"

"Diana. His assistant." Willow waves it off. "She takes all the food people hand him, passes it to Nessa, our host coordinator, who donates it where it's needed." Her gaze flicks to the cart near Ethan, where a middle-aged woman with brown skin laughs with three elderly folks. "Pastor's nice to everybody. Some swooners mistake that for interest."

With that dimple, I can see how they would.

"Now's a good time to head in while he's busy. He won't see you."

I toss my cup in the trash with half its contents and follow her as we circle the group.

"Willow!" the woman by the cart calls.

"Oh, Nessa." Willow detours to hug her and squeezes her tight.

Nessa steps over and hugs me too. She smells of lemons and something homey. She pats my hand as she releases me. "I love the yellow pattern in your dress."

"Thank you." My smile slips free. "I love that red sweater. Reminds me of the autumn leaves that stand out from all the others. Bright and unforgettable."

"I like her already." Nessa's kind eyes meet mine, her dark hair streaked with gray. "I'm Nessa, my darling. Don't think we've met."

"Ruby. I'm staying with Willow."

"She's my bestie, and teaches piano if you hear of kids or even adults interested." Willow winks at Nessa, then glances at me. "Mostly kids, but she could be open to adults once she sorts out her schedule."

Nessa nods. "I'll let you know. And if you need anything at all, whatever answers Willow doesn't have, I'm here."

"Thank you. I'll remember that." Warmth spreads in my chest, loosening the anxious knot I've carried all morning.

We head on.

Ethan's now talking with an older couple. His assistant hovers close by like a permanent shadow. Then his gaze snags mine like he's known I was here all along.

A jolt shoots down my spine. I tear my focus away and push forward, heat crawling up my neck.

Inside the sanctuary, the air feels stifling. I want to shrug off my jacket, but my dress's spaghetti straps would expose my shoulders. Not appropriate for church.

I remind Willow where I plan to sit, and we slide into the back row of a repurposed room more like a carpeted auditorium than a sanctuary, me at the end near the exit and her to my left. Drapes block the wide windows, and banners bring down the high ceilings.

Still shifting in my chair, I set my purse down when a man with green eyes walks up, smiling like he knows us.

Willow stiffens beside me. "Liam," she breathes.

"Hello, Willow." His voice is low, vowels rolling with a lilt that isn't American. He crouches to wave.

"Haven't seen you at the shop this week."

"Been out of town for work."

"Oh." She brushes her hair behind her ear. "You took the kids along?"

"Jason's parents were in town this week. They helped."

"Honeymoon… I mean, they're coming back tomorrow."

"Correct."

Willow nods too fast, a flush rising to her cheeks. This Liam fella has her all flustered. Then the man turns to me.

"I'm Liam White." He extends a hand. "I doubt we've met yet."

I take it. "Ruby Morrison."

Willow blinks. "Oh, right. I forgot my manners."

"Nice to meet you, Ruby." Liam then bends to Willow with a soft smile. "You look dashing, by the way."

"And you…" She stumbles through a reply. "Um, yes. Thanks."

He heads for a seat near the middle. Willow peels off her jacket and scarf, maybe suddenly warm. Funny, she tells every parent in town to enroll their kids in my piano classes, yet she didn't ask Liam. If he's close to Ethan's age, his kids must still be little.

"Liam, huh?" I lean toward her, whispering. "He's handsome."

"Seen better." She flicks her hand, eyes fixed straight ahead.

Microphones crackle as someone tests the sound.

People keep filing in—couples, families, singles—every age and style. The rustle of coats, low greetings, and steady swell of voices enlivens the room.

"How do you know Liam?"

"One of the locals." She nods toward the screen as another Bible verse fades from view.

"Doesn't sound like just a local to you."

She rolls her eyes. "He caught me off guard. That's all."

The twitch at her mouth gives her away, but I let it drop.

By now, the sanctuary is nearly full, voices humming. Then the music begins.

Everyone rises, a soft shuffle of movement. I stand too, peering through the rows, searching without meaning to—for him. From the back, all I catch are silhouettes and raised hands.

It's better this way. Not seeing him this early into the service.

Willow's earnest voice pulls me back, off-key but full of conviction. I blink, fixing on the lyrics rolling across the screen.

The first song is an anthem I don't know.

The second is upbeat, one from my playlist. Its truth about praising God in all circumstances presses against my ribs, quieting the noise inside me. Music tends to do that, and songs about God relax me the most.

The pianist sways with each chord, the drummer's steady beat thrums through the floor. They're not performing, but soaking in every word from the song. And I am too. Air reaches deeper into my lungs.

I haven't stepped into a church in years.

Yet, everything feels right, except for one problem. It's Ethan's church.

It shouldn't matter. Should it?

Then a slower song rises—surrender, hope, release. Midverse, the worship leader falters, voice thick with emotion. He breaks into a heartfelt prayer that stills the room.

When he gestures for us to sit, announcements follow. Fall fest. Thanksgiving outreach. Christmas service. An event at Skypoint.

I'd thought about volunteering before I knew Ethan was the founder. He doesn't handle events, but he's probably there at each one. Worse, what if I run into his kids? I hate breaking my word about lessons.

And then, he steps up to the pulpit. His fingers fumble with the wireless mic at his collar, settling it in place. A navy flannel hangs loose over khaki chinos—far more casual than anything his father would've allowed in church. His gaze finds mine. How did he spot me all the way back here?

My heart misfires, thundering in my throat. Everything I told myself this morning—that I wouldn't care, wouldn't flinch, wouldn't let him see—is gone. Like it never existed.

CHAPTER 11

"Who's excited for the new series?" Ethan's voice booms through the sanctuary.

A few people call out, and applause ripples.

He smiles, waiting for the excitement to settle.

"You know, when we planned this series months ago, I had no idea how much I'd need it myself." He flips open the Bible on the podium and steps aside, one hand in his pocket. "But God has a funny way of lining things up."

Gentle laughter ripples through the crowd.

"Just the other day, I was cleaning out my garage. Man, you should've seen the junk I'd been holding onto." He rolls his eyes, eliciting more commiserating laughs. "I opened an old box of photos from when I was a teenager. As I flipped through, I realized how much life has changed. Some changes were great, some... not so much. A lot of those old dreams and mistakes—all that *old stuff*—I've been carrying around like the junk in my garage. As I reviewed my notes for today's message, it hit me: God set me up."

He grins and spreads his hands. "Of course, God is full of surprises and miracles. The last two weeks have been nothing short of miraculous in my life, and I suspect He's got something special in store for all of us with this series."

He returns to the podium and gestures toward an overhead screen. *God's Masterpiece* is written in elegant lettering. The subtitle beneath it declares: "Welcome Home."

"Today, we're kicking off our five-week series with 'Welcome Home—Leaving the Old Behind.'"

The title is relatable, not just to me, as the enthusiastic clapping indicates.

Ethan holds up a hand, silencing us. "How many of you are familiar with the story of the prodigal son?"

Several hands go up. I raise mine halfway. I've heard of it, but I'm not as versed as these people who seem *so* close to God. Even Willow has hers in the air. I slink back against the chair and tinker with the silver stud on my left ear, self-conscious.

"Great." Ethan nods. "It's a powerful parable. For those who aren't familiar, don't worry. We're going to read part of it. Let's all open our Bibles to Luke chapter fifteen, verse twenty."

I fumble my phone from my purse's side pocket, heart thumping. Luke 15:20, Luke 15:20... I swipe through my apps and tap the Bible app. Around me, Bible pages rustle, including Willow's as she opens her pocket-size Bible. My screen loads. With my hands unsteady, I barely make it to the verse.

"'While he was still a long way off, his father saw him and was filled with compassion for him'..." Ethan stops reading there. But my gaze skims ahead to where the father runs to his returning wayward son, throws his arms around him, and kisses him.

Ethan gazes out at the congregation. "Coming home isn't just closing miles. It's closing the distance between our hearts and the Father's. The prodigal son thought he was returning to a place. In reality, he was running to his father's embrace, where he'd always belonged." He paces the stage. "That's compassion. The moment we turn back, God runs to us—no judgment, no 'I told you so,' just open arms."

He pauses, then resumes softer now. "Last night, I was up praying for this message, and God reminded me how far from perfect I am. Being a pastor doesn't mean I don't stumble. I need His grace every day."

His humility and vulnerability grip me. I sit straighter, unable to look away.

"So many of us have walked with Christ our whole lives." His voice regains its strength. "Some of us grew up in Christian homes and know all the Sunday school answers. Even so, some of us still haven't truly *come home*. We're not home yet if we're held captive by guilt or by shame or by feeling we have to earn our place. We think we have to fix ourselves before God will accept us. But that's a lie."

He plants himself center stage, his gaze roving as if he's looking at each person individually. "For the person who feels like they don't belong anywhere"—his gaze drifts over and locks with mine—"for the wanderer who believes God stopped waiting for you..."

My breath catches. I duck my head, but I can still hear him.

"It doesn't matter what everyone else is saying about you." He enunciates each word with gentle force. "You are a child of God. Chosen, loved... Never let anyone make you think they are more righteous than you, never let their judgment get to you."

My throat tightens. Heat prickles behind my eyes. It's like he's speaking to me and the ache in my being. I'm not righteous enough. That I know. I feel forgotten by God sometimes, judged even. Memories of his dad's church misfire. People looking at me during his sermon about dress codes—me, the undeserving wannabe girlfriend for the pastor's son. I blink and swipe at a threatening tear. How did he know?

His earnestness carries as he speaks of God's life-altering grace—grace that overshadows everything we've done, where even our sins pale in its light.

I hadn't overdosed on medicine the last time I prayed for forgiveness. I hadn't slipped into darkness, trying to let go of my life as if it were mine to end. Can God still welcome me home? After everything I've done?

Emotion surges through my chest.

"Your history is not your destiny." A tremor wobbles his voice. "I had my life all mapped out at seventeen, but it didn't turn out the way young Ethan thought."

A quiet chuckling rumbles around me.

Through tears, I lift my chin. Wow. His eyes are glassy now.

"Maybe that's a good thing in some ways, but in other ways, I've had regrets, moments I wanted to go back and change." He presses a hand to his chest. "But I can't keep asking God why things went 'wrong.'" His focus sweeps along us, encompassing everyone. "You see, we all have a story, and the good news is that God's still writing our redemption story."

He smiles through the tears that have now escaped and shine on his cheeks. Ethan's crying openly up there? My tough, confident Ethan showing this much emotion?

Now, the room's so quiet I can hear sniffles. I'm not the only one crying.

"God says, 'Welcome home,'" he repeats a whisper into the mic. "'Come home, child.'"

A sob catches in my throat. Tears slip down my face now. I feel those words in the depths of my soul. My shoulders tremble as I cry.

Again, his attention settles me. My vision blurs through my tears, but he's looking right at me, gaze steady and intense. To those sitting up front, it must look like he's looking toward the back wall. "You're safe. God will never let you down. I might have let you down. Everyone around you might let you down at some point. But God... God will..."

Is he...? He's acknowledging the hurt between us, even if no one but Willow knows about it. He's not just talking about last night but also twelve years ago when everything ended. Suddenly, the snowstorm, Mama's death, the downward spiral that followed, the addiction, the darkest times of my life—it all presses on me like a weight. I feel dizzy.

Lord, can You rewrite my story with Ethan in it?

But I'm still not pastor's wife material. All the beautiful single women in church who carry their Bibles and hover around him are what he's looking for in a wife.

I'm a recovering addict who almost gave up on life more than once. I'll never be free of my past.

No, Ethan's words about grace and healing are out of reach for someone like me.

My chest constricts. A familiar dark panic crawls up from my stomach and claws at my lungs.

Oh no. Not now.

Shame's voice, so loud in my head, drowns out everything else: "You don't belong here. You will never belong. Look at you, falling apart."

I can't breathe.

The sanctuary tilts and fuzzes at the edges of my vision. My heart races so fast it might burst. Each thud pulses against my temples, against every pore on my skin.

Am I dying? This is it. I'm dying right here in church.

I remember my breathing exercise from the last hospital visit.

One... ten. Breathe in through the nose, out through the mouth.

But the air hitches in my throat in a shallow wheeze. The lights overhead blur into halos. I sway.

A high-pitched ringing assaults my ears. I double over in my seat, trying to gasp in a breath. My hands are shaking.

"Are you okay?" Willow whispers. Her hand presses against my back.

I either nod or shake my head, my vision tunneling. Then I'm slipping from the chair, landing on my hands and knees. The carpet scrapes my palms. My chest heaves, but I can't get enough air.

A thud, perhaps Willow's Bible, drops on the floor as she slides down beside me.

Somewhere above, someone shouts my name. Ethan. His raw voice cracks through the roar in my ears.

Footsteps pound. Chairs scrape. The mic shrieks with feedback before cutting out. Hands grip my shoulders, steadying.

Willow's voice is close, urgent. "Ruby, I'm here. Just breathe, sweetie."

But I can't. My arms are so weak, giving out, and I slump onto the carpet. My head thumps the floor.

Distantly, I register someone shouting, "Call 9-1-1!" Ethan?

Another voice responds, "We have a medic—Josh, over here!"

Everything muffles like I'm trapped underwater in a rushing, icy river. Blackness edges in, merciless. My body jerks as someone rolls me onto my side. My eyelids flutter, but I can't force them open.

"Ruby? Ruby, stay with me!" The trembling deep voice slices through the fog. Ethan. That's Ethan. My Ethan. "Stay with me. Please."

CHAPTER 12

Ruby

"Stay with me." A warm hand cups my cheek. "Ruby, can you hear me?"

Ethan's fearful voice thrums through me. I try to answer, to ease him, but I'm locked inside my body, my lungs struggling for air. A ragged, wheezing sound scrapes my throat, foreign even to me.

"Easy, easy," another voice sounds. Fingers press my wrist, then my shoulders. "She's having a panic attack. Give her some space."

"I'll just hold her hand." Ethan's voice rumbles low. His grip slides around my left hand.

Warmth shoots up my arm. I'm safe.

"Ruby, I'm Josh." The new voice is calm near my ear. "I'm a medic. You're gonna be okay. We're going to breathe together. Ready? One... two... three... four..." His voice is a rope tossed into my darkness. I cling to it. "That's it. Nice and slow. Five... six... seven... eight..."

I drag my lungs to obey, fighting the chaos inside me. My chest loosens. Oxygen slides back in. The sharp ringing fades from my ears.

Something is beneath my head now, and Ethan's familiar scent surrounds me. His hand still locked with mine offers the comfort I need.

"...nine... ten. Good, Ruby," Josh murmurs. "Keep breathing just like that."

I do, each inhale steadier than the last. My heart, once a hammering storm, begins to slow.

The world comes back into focus. I blink open my eyes against harsh fluorescent light, vision swimming until shapes sharpen. I'm not in the sanctuary anymore.

A small couch, pastel walls, and a rocking chair in the corner. This must be the mother's nursing room.

Near the closed door, Liam, Willow, and Josh now hover, their shapes tense. Willow catches my eye. Her smile wavers, and her pinched brow betrays the fear she must've felt as I collapsed. Does this entrance lead to the sanctuary? Faint voices drift beyond the door. Josh tells Liam he's canceled the ambulance.

Good. I have no idea how ambulance rides work here. My health insurance coverage ended last month.

"Hey." Ethan's voice draws my gaze to his. He's kneeling beside me, pale and shaken, his eyes rimmed red. A long, breathy sound leaves him, and his relief nearly undoes me. He lifts our joined hands and presses them to his chest, against the frantic thud of his heartbeat.

"Ruby." My name seems almost like a plea. His free hand brushes hair off my clammy forehead. "You are still with me."

I manage a nod.

He presses his lips tight. Then he leans in and rests his forehead against mine, his skin damp with sweat. Is he... shaking? His shoulders tremble. Was he that scared *for me*?

He draws a ragged breath and pulls back enough to meet my eyes. "I'm not sure I'd have survived if anything happened to you." His thumb strokes my cheek, and heat floods through me, chasing out the last of my dizziness. My chest aches. Maybe he still loves me.

"Of course I'm okay." I huff a laugh to shove that last thought out of my head. "T–takes more than that to get rid of me."

Ethan exhales a sound that might be a laugh or just relief. The tension on his face eases. The room is quiet now, just the humming air conditioner and a muffled voice or two in the hallway.

His thumb rubs over my cheek. His touch is so familiar, so comforting that I have to close my eyes.

I can almost pretend we're back in time, the last years didn't happen, and we're just Ethan and Ruby, young and in love. He's here taking care of me like he used to when I had the flu or stubbed my toe or any of the million things he fussed over. A tear slips free at the bittersweet memory.

His thumb wipes it away. "You're still the most beautiful woman I've ever known." The words rasp from somewhere deep.

My eyelids fly open. Did I—did I imagine those words? I stare at him, and he stares right back, that familiar dimple denting his cheek as he wobbles up a tremulous smile. His tender expression is how I remember him looking at me all those years ago. My breath catches. Neither of us moves or speaks. But my heart might burst, torn between joy and the fear I'm dreaming, misunderstanding, something.

"I'm going to take care of you." His intensity leaves no room for argument, like a vow.

"You look more beat than me." I have to lighten things. "I should be the one taking care of you."

"If you're volunteering, I won't argue. But don't expect me to lift a finger."

My cheeks bunch into a smile. Time to reclaim a little dignity. "Really, I'm fine now." I wipe at my face and sit up straighter. My body still trembles with aftershocks, my head foggy and aching from the fall, but I'd better switch positions lest I start melting into his arms. And that is *not* a good idea.

He helps me to my feet. With my legs still unsteady, he guides me to the couch before settling beside me. Willow steps in front of us, holding two purses. I'd even forgotten my purse.

Liam strolls over with a water bottle. "How ya holdin' up, Ruby?"

"Besides making a scene in church?"

He chuckles and tips the bottle toward Ethan, then me. "Not sure which of you needs this more, hey?"

"Ethan."

"Ruby."

We answer at the same time, and Willow bursts out laughing.

Heat creeps up my neck. "If I wanted attention, I would've just hit the wrong note. Fainting was overkill."

Liam winks. "Reckon that's one way to liven up a Sunday service."

"You shouldn't be embarrassed, Ruby." Willow rubs my arm.

"No need to be embarrassed." Josh steps over, grabs the bag from the table, and returns to my side. "Panic attacks can feel like heart attacks. It must've been terrifying." He checks my pulse again and nods, satisfied. "Your pulse is nearly back to normal. You'll be okay, but you should rest for the next day or so. Panic attacks can knock the wind out of you, and you don't want another one triggered by stress or exhaustion."

I nod. "Yes, sir. Thank you for your help."

He smiles, then wishes everyone a good afternoon as he leaves, calling over his shoulder that he'll let the others know I'm fine.

Ethan takes the water, twists off the cap, and offers the bottle to me. "Here, drink."

I accept and down a sip, the cool water soothing my dry throat.

Ethan watches as if I'm made of porcelain and might shatter. "I still can't believe you had a panic attack." The crease remains between his brows. He's still worried. "Do you get them often?"

"This... this was the first in a while."

"When did they start?"

My lips twitch into something I can't call a smile. I know when. "About twelve years ago." I peek up at him through my lashes. And I catch something shadowing his face. So I touch his arm. "You have a church to take care of and your kids. No need to hover over me."

"Ruby's right." Willow drops to the cushion on my other side. "I'll take her home and make sure she gets plenty of rest."

Ethan starts to protest, but Liam tips his head toward the door. "You should go greet the visitors."

"Right." Ethan exhales and stands, but his gaze lingers.

"I'm okay."

Liam checks his watch. "I told Russ to grab my kids and yours from the kids' church. I'd better catch up. I can take them all home if you'd like."

"Thanks. I'll be there as soon as I can."

Liam slips out, and Ethan turns back, still hovering.

"I'll be okay," I repeat.

Willow loops her arm through mine, sealing the promise with action.

At last, he nods. "All right." His hand drags down to squeeze my fingers one more time. "But I'm coming to check on you this afternoon."

"Please do," Willow answers.

As she and I cross the sparse lobby minutes later, people gather around Ethan, chatting. He catches me looking, and I glance away. Still, a few who know what happened stop us to ask if I'm all right, and I thank them for their concern.

"First time I've seen Pastor Ethan stop a sermon like that," one woman says. She introduced herself as Mary Beth. A smile softens her stiff tone. "Glad you're okay. You gave us all a scare."

Heat rushes to my cheeks. "I'm so sorry."

"No apology needed." An older man holds up a liver-spotted hand, his orange tie patterned with fall leaves. "The moment you went down, I thought we'd have to catch him next. He looked panic-stricken."

My neck burns.

Willow steps in to explain that I need to get home and rest.

On the drive home, I sink back and close my eyes. I'm drained—emotionally and physically. Yet beneath the exhaustion, a quiet warmth glows.

Ethan's reaction, his words, keep replaying in my mind. *"You're still the most beautiful woman I've ever known…. I'm going to take care of you."*

And the way he looked at me? Like I was so precious and important to him.

When we pull into the parking lot, Willow shifts into park and lets the engine idle. I unbuckle, and she pats my arm, her eyes aglow. "Well, if you still had doubts, today sure proved something."

"Proved what?"

Her smile widens. "Our pastor is *not* over you."

I bite my lip and glance out the window at the lot already full of cars from the shops next to ours. "He was just scared, Willow. Anybody would be. He probably thought I was having a stroke or something. Pastors care about their congregation."

Yes, I'm downplaying what we saw. But it's safer to hide behind excuses. Because the alternative to hope feels far too dangerous.

"I've seen Pastor Ethan concerned before, like when Mr. Lee had that heart scare last year. But I've never seen him look like *that.* That man was ready to carry you in his arms all the way to the hospital if needed."

Was he? I arch a brow at her.

She deadpans me. "And if you didn't notice, he kept looking your way while preaching. That's how he saw you start to collapse even before I did. He *never* took his focus off you for long."

"I... I don't know what to think." My head ducks, and my fingers straighten my dress over my lap, uncrinkling the yellow pattern. "This is all... so confusing."

"It's not confusing. The man still cares for you—a lot."

"I just..." I draw in a shaky breath. "Even if he does still care, look at me." I motion to myself. "I'm a mess. Ethan has no idea I was a wreck who ended up in rehab for years. His parents told him I wasn't good enough back then—and now? If they ever find out what I did? His congregation is full of the right women... unblemished, godly, put-together. Not me."

Willow's eyes soften. Her touch warms my shoulder. Then she rubs my back. "We might have to replay his message because someone wasn't listening."

I heard his message, loud and clear. But after that fiasco, it'll be a while before I show my face at his church again.

Still, no matter how today began, there's that unquenchable thirst for hope. And right now, I can live with that.

CHAPTER 13

Ethan

"How are you feeling today, Amber?" I set the vase of yellow mums on her bedside table, their brightness no match for the sharp disinfectant scenting the air.

Amber Patterson, eighty-six, usually carries an enviable energy. But her sweet tooth often outpaces her insulin. When her sugar spikes too high for her pills to manage, the hospital staff step in with fluids and fast-acting insulin. Today, though, she watches me with a telltale glint in her eye.

"Better, Pastor. Much better now that you're here." Mischief crinkles her face as her lips twitch. "I heard about your... almost fainting from the altar today. Something about the lovely new piano teacher's emergency?"

I chuckle. "Word travels fast."

"I got visitors right after service."

Of course, she'd had visitors from church today. I'd barely left, just long enough to stop at Liam's and linger with the kids. He tried to corner me about Ruby, but I ducked out and swung by the Corner Crate for flowers before coming here. Gossip moves faster than the Spirit around here.

"Ruby will be teaching my children piano. That's all."

Amber hums like she's heard a sermon she doesn't quite grasp. An IV snakes into the back of her hand, but the fluid dripping from the bag hasn't dulled her eyes. "Funny how the Lord works, isn't it? Bringing people into our lives just when we need them most."

I shift in the padded chair. The cushion squeaks every time I move. "Amber—"

"I lost my Harold when I was forty-five." She barrels through my warning, her oxygen clip glowing faintly red on her fingertip. "Thought my life was over. But God had other plans."

"You never remarried."

"No. But I learned something important."

Beneath the natural light streaming through the window, her veined hand reaches out, and I let mine rest in hers—warm, steady, even with the IV taped in place.

"Love isn't a limited resource, Pastor." Her eyes search mine. "I noticed you're not wearing the ring you've kept on since you moved here. Not one of the beautiful women in church compelled you to take it off. And then Ruby shows up..." Her smile flickers. "Less than two weeks, is it? And the ring is gone. *That* means something."

I can't deny her words.

She falls quiet, as though she knows I need space to wrestle with them.

After Ruby, I married Maddie. A decent marriage on paper. She was kind, steady, and supportive in my ministry. She gave me two incredible children. I have no regrets. But even in our best moments, it was never what I felt with Ruby. Maddie and I knew we only truly shared the kids and our faith in God. She kept grieving her late boyfriend, and whenever she needed space, I—well, my thoughts would drift, grieving Ruby. Those wounds left a hollow in our marriage that no sermons or Sunday smiles could fill. We were partners, but never that soul-deep, laughter-and-shared-secrets, set-your-heart-on-fire kind of love.

Only God knew that. The guilt I carried. The imperfection I lived with. And yet, as Scripture reminds me over and over, He always used imperfect people, perhaps because imperfection breeds compassion for those who stumble in their faith.

"Sometimes God gives us second chances." Amber's voice, softer now, coaxes me back. "The question is whether we're brave enough to take them."

I squeeze her hand, her callused fingers rough against mine. Through the window, leaves in gold and fiery-red spiral in the breeze, each fall a reminder more'll be back on trees come spring. Like second chances.

I doubt I deserve one. But God's given me one.

"I came here to pray for you, and instead, you're—"

"Maybe God sent you here so I could be the one praying." Mischief curves her gummy smile, and she could be right. My lips lift, my chest loosens, and I close my eyes. I pray for her health, for strength, and for a quick recovery. She whispers amen with me, then continues—her prayer washing over me, asking God to give me wisdom and clarity to step back into the light of His grace.

Then she pats my hand. "It's a good sign that the old ring is gone."

I chuckle, keeping my eyes closed, and let her amen become mine.

Still, her words resound in my head as I exit the hospital and enter the crowded parking lot.

Second chances.... Love isn't a limited resource. Step into the light of His grace.

The autumn air bites crisp against my skin as I stride toward my truck. I left the SUV in the garage since I didn't need to drive the kids. Sliding inside, I pull out my phone and scroll through Brook's Diner app. I place a to-go order—chicken noodle soup, sandwiches, and apple pie—for Ruby and Willow.

My thumb hovers over Ruby's number. Call or text? I could have the food delivered, but I need to see her, need to know she's okay. My stomach twists over her collapsing, panic tearing through me so fast I nearly pitched forward, tripping over the steps in my lunge toward her.

Twelve years ago... her first panic attack. Was it *that* day? The day I told her it was over?

My lungs shudder, and I lean against the driver's seat. Today fades. My mind wanders where it always does when I let my guard down. To Ruby.

Freshman year.

The gym at Trinity Academy smelled like popcorn and hot dogs from the snack stand, layered over the tang of sweat. On the court, sneakers squeaked, and basketballs thudded as the team ran drills.

Meanwhile, I was half watching from the bleachers and half memorizing the Krebs cycle to keep tomorrow's quiz from eating me alive.

I'd come early to save seats for Isaac and me. The back row made the most sense, safe from stray balls that always flew over the front rows, and nobody fought for it anyway. I still had a decent view and space to spread out my homework. But I wasn't holding my breath. His aunt and uncle, the ones covering his tuition, were in town, so he'd ditch.

Dad didn't make much as a pastor, but we were fine because of Mom's parents. They owned old brownstones in Brooklyn Heights and Park Slope and raked in rent. With only two grandkids, private school wasn't a stretch. Dad's church, though, was still small. He'd moved us from Albany to Brooklyn five years earlier to start the church, which meant not enough people—or offerings—yet for a full salary.

"Is this seat taken?"

A girl about my age stood there. Bright, mischievous eyes. Brown skin. Midriff top. Unzipped jacket. Ripped jeans. A fruity shampoo scent. Redwood High, no doubt—the team playing us that night.

"Hello?" Her brows lifted.

I jumped to my feet, spilling my notebook and study guide across the floor. My heart thundered as if we were the only ones occupying the bleachers.

She pointed to the spot beside me, currently occupied by my jacket.

"Oh. It's yours." I bent to grab my stuff.

She crouched to help and handed me the scattered pages. "You must be smart, studying with all the distractions."

"Um, not really." She wouldn't have been the first to call me a geek. At least she didn't say it. I shoved the book under my feet.

I heard myself ask anyway. "You go here?"

"Obviously, you do." Her brows arched, lips curling. "Gonna have a problem if I cheer for my team?"

"No problem." I couldn't look away from her lighthearted ease. Most girls at school were serious, and the pretty ones only bothered with football stars like my brother, Harvey. "I'm Ethan."

Her face lit up like she'd just won a prize. "Meet your future wife."

I froze, eyes widening. I couldn't help it. I liked her humor.

"Kidding." She laughed, and the sound loosened something in my chest. "I'm Ruby."

"Well, meet your future husband."

Her smile deepened like we'd shared a secret.

"You play?" She had to raise her voice over the announcer.

"Yeah. Hoping to make varsity next year. You?"

"I just like watching. Mostly neighborhood games, but I had to support my school."

Redwood's record was awful, but tradition meant we played them every year.

The anthem started, and the players lined up.

As the game progressed, she proved she knew more about basketball than half the guys on our team. She called plays before they happened, critiqued the ref, and laughed when the visiting coach nearly blew a gasket.

"Your point guard's terrible at defense." She leaned in over the noise, her breath warm against my ear.

"He's just saving energy."

"For what, halftime snacks?" She smirked.

When her team missed another layup, I bumped her elbow. "Wow. Do they practice missing on purpose?"

She shot me a glare, but her mouth twitched upward. "At least we don't recruit half the neighborhood just to win."

Somewhere between arguing about free throws, mocking each other's teams, and groaning at the ref, it all felt... easy. Like we'd known each other for years.

By the final buzzer—our team took it—she didn't look bothered, just winced once. "Good game. I'd hoped today was the day for a win."

I high-fived her. I knew more about her already than I'd ever known about any girl.

"Guess I'll see you next time we play your school?" I asked.

"Is that your way of asking to hang out again?"

"Would that be bad?"

"Not if you come with me to this thing tomorrow. After school."

I had to figure out what to tell my parents to ditch the Bible study we hosted every Thursday.

"There's free food."

"Count me in."

"School gets out at two thirty for us. What side of town's yours on?"

"East of Flatbush."

She must have noticed I had no clue, because she had mercy on me and cuffed my arm. "I'll meet you at your school gate. Two thirty."

When I told Harvey after school the next day, he slapped my back and promised to cover me. I didn't ask what story he'd spin—less guilt if I didn't know. He even walked me over just to make sure I wasn't lying.

"Wow." He shook her hand and grinned. "My brother's actually hanging out with a real girl."

That's when I found out her school didn't get out till three. She didn't mind cutting class.

"You'll get in trouble," I fretted as we boarded the train and took an empty bench.

"I don't get in trouble as much as you probably do."

Her yellow crop top showed her stomach, and her jacket slipped off her left shoulder. With those hoop earrings so big, they could've fit a wrist. At church, no girl would've been allowed out in something that flashy—and ripped jeans? Forget it. Most of us wouldn't have even made it past the front door. She was out of my league and so intriguing.

"Where are we going?" I leaned into the sidewall and stretched my arm across our seatbacks, going for cool and relaxed even while my insides were anything but.

"A party. But we need to pick someone up first."

When we hopped off the train, Ruby led me through narrow alleys, the stink of cigarettes and beer bottles crunching underfoot. Shady guys lounged against brick walls, muttering low. I shivered, half afraid of what would happen if we got caught there after dark.

We stopped at a run-down apartment on the second floor. Ruby knocked. No answer. Knocked again. Still nothing. Then she slipped a pin from her jacket pocket and picked the lock like she'd done it a hundred times.

I gulped. "You carry pins all the time?"

"Always be prepared for emergencies."

Inside, the air reeked of stale grease and mildew. A heavyset woman lay on the floor, struggling. Ruby didn't panic. She just grabbed my phone and called a fire station like she'd grown up knowing every corner of this neighborhood. We stayed until firefighters arrived and lifted the woman safely.

"I'll sit this one out, sweetie," the woman said, breathless. "Go on without me."

The "party" Ruby had promised turned out to be a volunteer event at a homeless shelter. "We work first. Then we eat." She dragged me toward a woman named Patty.

Patty sent us to scrub trays and pots while the cooks dished food. Later, we ate shoulder to shoulder with strangers—rice, beans, bread rolls, pie slices that had seen better days—and somehow, it tasted better than any meal I'd eaten.

Her food finished, Ruby grinned. "Told you there'd be free food."

She walked me back toward my neighborhood.

"How about you?" I asked on the train. "Want me to make sure you get home safe?"

"Next time, you can escort me," she teased. "Not today."

She didn't need anyone protecting her. She was way more on top of her surroundings than I'd ever be. She knew the city—free events, hidden corners, shortcuts. That night was the beginning. From then on, we were inseparable. Sure, we went to different schools, but as soon as school was out, we spent each waking moment together.

My phone rings, jarring me from my reverie. Liam's name flashes on the screen while I swipe to answer.

"That was intense today. So, you gonna tell me about her, mate?"

I rock my head back on the headrest, eyes closed. "So many years to share." He might as well ask me to tell him who I am—we were *that* intertwined. "I wouldn't know where to begin."

"Yeah, the history was obvious. She's the one who got away, right?"

"Ruby was always *that* girl. The one you could never forget, the one you wanted with you forever." Our first summer together, she taught me how to lash rafts together and float downstream. I showed her knots from scouting and used Grandpa's old compass to lead us geocaching without a phone. She showed me the other side of adventure—jumping from piers into the river, climbing fire escapes to rooftops, sneaking into abandoned warehouses she swore were haunted.

"We were just kids, but my heart was always in my throat, following her. She didn't believe in rules—at least not the way I did. She'd push, daring me to break them. I pushed back, keeping us from crossing too far."

When she wanted to sneak into R-rated movies, I told her no—*"God wouldn't want us watching that."*

Isaac and Harvey were all in, but Ruby stuck by me—*"If Ethan doesn't want to go, I don't want to go either."*

I smile, sinking into the past. "Still, I gave in sometimes. We climbed rooftops to watch city lights, even snuck through the back of a theater for a PG flick. Ruby laughed like the whole world was ours." Some things, though, I couldn't let her risk. "Skipping school? I tried once—got grounded, never again. Playing near storm drains or daring thin ice on a pond? I yanked her arm away before she stepped on." I chuckle. "Man, that girl lived on the edge."

Over time, I understood why. Home wasn't safe. She admitted her dad was abusive—sometimes to her, always to her mom. She swore me to secrecy, terrified she'd end up on the streets if anyone knew. Sometimes she stayed at her aunt's place, where she felt safe.

"You should hear your tone, Ethan." Liam intrudes on the memories. "I never hear you like this."

"I think about her all the time, but I never talk about her, never share her." I rub my temples. I couldn't keep her to myself back then, though. "Eventually, I had to bring her home to my parents. Mom's lips pressed into a thin line at her ripped jeans. Dad stayed polite but stiff. Only Harvey welcomed her—too much, sometimes. 'Not only is your girlfriend hot,' he said once, half joking, 'but she's also fun. Way better than the geeky kids Mom makes us hang out with.'"

Liam clears his throat. "Do I detect some sibling tension there?"

More than that. "Sometimes I worried Harvey and Ruby were better suited than she and I were—both so daring and larger-than-life, while I was the boring rulekeeper holding them back." Always keeping her from trouble. "Like Harvey, she pushed the limit. I remember she smoked once or twice, cigarettes stolen from her dad's stash and brought to share. Harvey lit up like he'd done it before. I tried, coughed, and gagged."

Watching them like that... It was always there—the fear that they were the destined match, the perfect pairing, and I was the odd man out.

Liam snorts. "That sounds like you, Pastor."

"After that, I begged her not to follow that road, told her she was better than that. Different. She listened. She always listened to me."

Liam lets me fall silent.

Nostalgia holds me tighter than I can hold the phone. I lower it to my lap, my elbow braced against the truck console.

She was wild, yes, but she was also beautiful in ways that had nothing to do with looks. She knew no strangers and carried laughter into every room. After three years of joining me at church camps, she started asking questions about God and the Bible verses we read together. She began coming to church consistently.

"At eighteen, she gave her life to Christ. It should've been enough. But my parents thought otherwise. Her dreams didn't fit their mold."

"Somehow…" Liam's voice comes through thoughtful, his Australian accent softer. "I don't see you as the type to let that stop you."

"It didn't." I trace the phone's hard edge. "The more my parents frowned at her, the deeper I fell. Mom only saw her ripped jeans and wild streak. Dad stayed quiet but stiff, never encouraging. But I saw the girl who lit up a homeless shelter with her laugh, who made a crowd of strangers feel like family."

By the time I graduated high school, I was head over heels. With Isaac leaving for the army, I was ready to step into real life too. I didn't need a college degree to become a firefighter, so I enrolled in the academy, all the while planning my future with Ruby.

"We'd talked about starting a family someday. She dreamed of a farmhouse in the country like my grandparents, the Bishops, had. I didn't care where we lived, as long as she was with me. With my mom's parents owning old brownstones, I figured we could rent one cheap to start—something small, a place to build from."

Marrying her thrilled me as much as it terrified me. Not because I doubted her but because I wanted the moment to be right. I was only twenty, nervous and inexperienced, but certain she was the one.

"So what happened, what stopped you?"

I snort. "Harvey blindsided me."

Maybe *blindsided* wasn't the right word. "I'd long tried to ignore his interest in her. He was always looking at her, always angling himself into her way. I even confronted him once, but he laughed it off."

He'd sneered at me. *"Golden Boy always wants to be the center of attention around here."*

"So I let it go, tried to ignore the signs. Then he found me in the kitchen one night, hands shoved deep in his pockets. He wouldn't meet my eyes."

I hear him again: *"I need to tell you something. Last Friday, Ruby kissed me. She was helping me wrap up my arm. And next thing... she pulled away, said it was a mistake. But I thought you should know."*

I press against my stomach as the sucker punch of those long-ago words hits me anew. "He said Ruby went after him."

"Oh, mate... What did she say?"

Had I said that aloud? I pick up the phone, finger hovering over the End Call.

"Look. I can't talk right now." I cut the call, no further explanation. The void that was that time of my life sucks me in again.

What did she say? Liam's question haunts me. One I can't answer because...

Gutted, I avoided her calls for two days, too tangled in betrayal and the fear that my parents had been right all along. When I couldn't hold it anymore, I texted her to meet me at the bakery we favored halfway between our places.

Snow swirled in when she entered wearing the red coat I loved. Her eyes shimmered the moment she saw me.

"What's wrong?"

I couldn't even sit. "I know what happened with Harvey. We're done."

Her lips parted. Her hands flew to her head. Her obvious guilt tore me apart.

"You kissed him." My voice cracked.

"Ethan, wait. It wasn't—"

"I can't be with someone who doesn't know where her heart belongs."

When she reached for me, I stepped back.

Tears streaked down her cheeks. "Please. Just let me explain."

But I didn't. I walked into the snow, the ring I'd been saving still buried in my drawer at home.

By the time I realized I might have made the biggest mistake of my life, it was too late.

But today, I've been given a second chance. Or maybe a third.

When she collapsed in church, a part of my world crumbled in front of everyone. I still don't know what's behind her panic attacks, and the way she didn't look surprised by it unsettles me. But I do know this: I have a chance, and this time, I'm going to take it.

CHAPTER 14

Ethan

I pop the tab on a can of Sprite and slide it across the scarred coffee table.

Ruby's fingers brush the aluminum as she accepts it. "You didn't have to bring us food."

The living room is small but cozy. A knit throw hangs over the love seat where I sink down beside her, the cushion giving under my weight. Across from us, a navy armchair is angled toward the coffee table, but distance isn't what I need right now.

Vanilla lingers from a candle between a pair of mini pumpkins and a ceramic vase on the coffee table—a touch that feels like Ruby. A short bookshelf holds novels and more mini pumpkins. She always bought pumpkins in the fall.

From the kitchen, light spills across buttery-yellow walls, catching on the empty to-go bag I brought in earlier. Willow tucked the food into the fridge before grabbing her purse and her coat from the armchair. "I'll let you two talk," she called over her shoulder, crossing the room before the door clicked shut and enclosed us in silence.

"You sure you're not hungry yet?" I ask.

Ruby lifts the can, takes a sip, then sets it down. "Thanks for the soda. And for dinner. I'll eat when Willow comes back." She folds her arms over her oversized sweater, curling into the love seat's far corner. The gray knit slips off one shoulder, revealing smooth skin. In sweatpants and fuzzy socks, she looks comfortable, but she's holding herself tight, wary.

"I won't stay long." It's a school night for my kids, and I should be back before the bonfire at Jason's.

"You didn't have to come." She tugs at her sweater cuff.

My pulse stutters. Where do I even start? The fridge hums from the kitchen. The wall clock ticks above the TV. My fingers feel clumsy, and I reach for the blanket draped over the armrest. A hangnail catches on a loose thread. "I'm sorry about yesterday."

Her head tilts, and that pixie cut frames wary eyes. "What part exactly?"

Fair. She deserves specifics. "I'm sorry for a lot of things between us. But yesterday, running into Harvey? I shouldn't have shut down like that." My gut twists, the jealousy, fear, and old patterns clawing back.

Ruby studies me, her silence heavy, before she gives the smallest nod. "Your sermon today..." A hint of a smile ghosts her lips. "The part about not living in the past once you've come home."

She was paying attention. I huff out a breath. "Yeah."

She rolls her exposed shoulder. "Then maybe we can start over, leave the past where it belongs."

Something in my chest loosens. "Whew." I lean back, and the cushion sags beneath me. The room's suddenly cozier, just the love seat and an old armchair flanking the coffee table. A TV stand opposite. Photos atop the bookshelf—Willow and perhaps her family, plus one of her and Ruby, not teenager Ruby.

Hmm. How long have the two known each other?

My gaze skitters to the kitchen, to the plant in an orange pot on the counter.

"I'll take this as the first time you've been here?"

Her voice draws me back, and I grip the back of my neck. "That's true."

I turn toward Ruby, elbows braced on my knees. I came to take care of her, but how can I when I don't know where to start? "Do you know what triggered the panic attack?"

Her arms loosen. One hand rubs the other. "Um. Your message."

"My message?" I chuckle to ease the weight in her voice. "I don't think I've ever preached a sermon that caused a panic attack before. That's a first."

Her lips twitch, just a little more of a smile this time. "You're a good teacher, Ethan. It... hit a nerve."

I drag a hand down my face. Practice what you preach, right? Don't live in the past. And here I am digging it all back up. "Did your mom's death cause the first one?"

She nods, eyes shimmering. "It was the same day you and I... ended."

The words land like a blow. Two losses, the same day. And I wasn't there. My chest tightens, and my hand rises to cover my mouth before the sound of regret slips out.

Ruby... My heart pounds so loud it fills my ears. I want to speak, to say something, anything. But my throat feels torn as if I've swallowed glass.

Silence stretches. She trembles, holding in pain I caused.

"Ruby, I—" I manage a rough whisper, but the rest won't come.

We stare at each other, all the unsaid things burning between us. I try to clear my throat, to force words past the lump. "I wish I could turn back the clock."

Do I mean that? If I hadn't left, I wouldn't have my kids. But if I hadn't left, I wouldn't have lost her.

I gulp. "If I hadn't walked away from you..."

"No looking back. No what-ifs." Her voice cracks, fragile as static. She swipes her sleeve across her nose. "Your sermon—you need to own that, take your advice too." Her luminous eyes catch mine, a lifeline when I threaten to sink.

I nod, swallowing hard. She's right. Living in the past will ruin us both. But the truth claws its way out anyway. "With my parents against us, then Harvey... His confession hit when I was already questioning if the timing was right to propose."

She gasps out a choking sound. "Propose?"

"I'd bought a ring." My throat dries as I admit it. "I had this plan to rent my grandparents' place, starting fresh. But I kept worrying you'd think I was rushing things. I know I'd begun acting strange, but I was so nervous and afraid to be around you as I planned."

"You... were going to ask me to marry you around that time?" Her voice trembles, and her eyes go glassy before she ducks her head. Once upon a time, glossy hair would slip around her cheeks to coil down her chest. She has nothing to hide behind now. I never imagined her so vulnerable.

"You go after that girl again, it'll always be complicated." My mother's voice echoes even now. She said those words when, two miserable days later, I considered talking it out with Ruby. *"Do you really want to marry a woman your brother covets? A woman who's already had an affair with him?"*

I squeeze my eyes shut, sickened by how I let their judgment twist everything. "I should've fought for you, should've looked for you. Never should've given up."

"We can't go there now." Her whisper pulls my eyes open. She brushes at a tear, trying to hide it.

I inch closer and reach out before stopping short. My hand fists on the love seat's rough fabric between us. "You need to know," I confess. "Walking away from you is the biggest regret of my life. Losing you was my greatest mistake."

Ruby lets out a broken laugh and wipes her cheek with the back of her hand. "We were just kids, Ethan. And your family... The thing I admired most? They loved you so fiercely. They fought to protect you, always wanted to know where you were. That's why I never told you about your brother. Why I kept quiet when your parents summoned me, questioning my motives, reminding me of your calling in ministry."

They did what? My stomach drops. "They spoke to you in my absence?"

She waves it off. "Honestly, they weren't wrong. I had no plan, no direction. And I dragged you into things you never would've touched in your sheltered life." She rubs her eyes, voice low and raw. "I was trouble, Ethan. Always chasing escape. Attention. Anything."

"Trouble? You were the best part of my world, Ruby." I unravel my fist and touch her arm, her skin warm through her sweater sleeve. "Yeah, you made some bad choices, but you always knew how to turn back when it mattered. You weren't trouble. You were the one thing in my life that felt real."

Her fingers flinch away, and her head jerks up as if she doesn't quite believe me. Her nose scrunches before she forces out a shaky laugh. "Oh, sure. Smoking cigarettes behind the gym, sneaking out after curfew, exploring bad neighborhoods—real solid influences."

I chuckle. Sixteen-year-old me coughed my lungs out after she dared me to try my first and last cigarette. "Honestly? Teaching me to step outside the lines was what I needed. You showed me how to make my own choices, instead of just doing what everyone expected."

She bites her lip, quiet. Maybe she's listening. Will she believe me or protect herself from me?

"Remember that kid I rescued who lived next door?" I fiddle with her sleeve, tugging at knobby yarn. "The one who locked himself in the laundry room and started screaming his head off? I popped their kitchen window and climbed in, thanks to that trick you taught me."

A soft "oh" escapes, followed by her quiet laugh. "I forgot about that. I really was a bad influence."

"But you made me feel like a superhero." My mouth spreads wide. "All because of you. And those free summer concerts in Prospect Park you dragged me to? I'd never even heard of them before. You gave me music and nights under the stars I'll never forget." I can still hear that indie band's guitar twang into the humid July air, still see Ruby spinning barefoot on the grass.

"Let's not forget you taught me how to swim in the ocean. This finicky pastor had never swam beyond a pool until you pulled me into the waves at Coney Island." I chuckle at the memory of her grip on my hand, fearless. "Now I can let my kids play in the water without worrying because I can save them if I have to. Because of you."

She clamps a hand over her mouth. Still, a sound emerges, something caught between a laugh and a sob. Her eyes shine, locked on me.

"You showed me a world outside my little church bubble. That first 'hangout,' volunteering at the shelter? You made me see people I wouldn't have had a chance to see and know. You taught me love was more than a Sunday sermon."

Her other hand rests in her lap, trembling. I reach for it, and she lets me take it. Cold fingers slide against mine. "Ruby, you weren't trouble. You were a blessing. You made me a better man." My voice drops to a whisper, a vow. "I mean it."

Her lashes lower. "About that..." She slides her hand free, and the loss stings. She wraps her arms around herself, staring at the dark TV. "There's more you should know—what happened *after*."

After. What an ominous word. A chill uncoils in my gut. "Okay."

"I went under... hard... after everything." The words tumble out, jagged. "I didn't really have friends. Not outside of you. And that night—the storm..." Her voice catches. "Mama might not have been hit if I'd answered my phone."

Her face has twisted up with so much pain that my eyelids beg to shutter my vision. I hold them open. I deserve to see her pain now.

She swallows, breath unsteady. "After that, I... I could barely get out of bed. I was terrified of reality." A shaky exhale. "I just wanted to feel nothing. So I started using. Pills first. Then... other things."

My stomach lurches. Drugs. I hold my face still, scarcely daring to breathe as every part of me aches for her.

"Most of the time, I was high. Or drunk." Her voice wavers, bitter and broken. "It was the only way to sleep without nightmares. The only way to stop feeling. I... I nearly overdosed a couple times." A tear splashes her sleeve. "It got really bad."

I cover her trembling hand again, resisting the urge to pull her into my arms. Her body shakes beneath my touch. My chest pinches, and I picture her back then—alone, grief-stricken, drowning in pain while I was off with my life.

"My aunt stepped in. She sold the flower shop to take care of me, to get me into rehab—that's why she wasn't there when you went looking." She's rocking in her seat. "Dragged me to rehab kicking and screaming." A shaky laugh slips out. "I got back on my feet, even started business school. Two years in, my aunt died. She was the only family I had left. *After*"—again, the word has bite to it—"I couldn't keep going. I dropped out, relapsed. Ended up in a creek, nearly froze to death, and woke up in a hospital. That's when it hit me—all the sacrifices she made. I had to try again."

Tears streak her cheeks. "Therapy. Recovery centers. Ministers who stopped by to preach hope. I started clinging to verses. To anything. Willow... I met her the second time in rehab. She was the one good thing to come out of it."

I can barely breathe. "Oh, Ruby." I wipe her tears with my other thumb, my own eyes stinging. "I'm so sorry. You didn't deserve any of that."

She sobs, then turns her palm under mine, clutching like she's afraid I'll let go.

"I thought I was past all that. But the worst part is..." She's shaking, her voice quivering. "Just last night, I thought of pushing myself over the railing—just so I could use it as an excuse to skip Willow's invite and not come to church."

Her words punch through me, sharp. I'd assumed her old habit was buried, gone. Guess I was wrong. And now the gnawing thought takes root. What if I'm the reason she slipped back? She'd been fine before I showed up. Then she runs into me, and she's teetering on the edge again—panic attack, self-harm, spiraling. Am I the trigger that pulls her under?

"Thank you for telling me," I whisper, my throat tightening. "I know that wasn't easy."

She exhales, fragile but steady. "If anyone should know, it's you."

I squeeze her hand. "I'm here, Ruby. I'm not going anywhere this time. Whether or not we ever—" I can't say it. "No judgment. Do you think I can be your friend again?"

She snorts out a shaky laugh. "Funny. After everything, I never once thought of you as anything but my friend."

Her honesty sinks deep. "Here I thought you hated me."

"You're the pastor." She lifts her chin. "Aren't you supposed to be the good one?"

I can't help but laugh. "I'm just as messed up as anyone. Maybe more."

The tension thins, giving way to something warm and familiar. She gazes at me with a softness I haven't seen since we found each other again. I bask in imagined forgiveness.

I ache to hold her, but I stay still. The peace between us is too fragile to risk breaking. I was the reason she cried herself to sleep, the reason she reached for drugs to numb the pain. Now, I have to be the reason she smiles again.

"Tell me about your kids." She scoots against the armrest beside her, her back braced on it as she draws a knee to her chest. "What does Asher like, besides Legos? And Poppy, besides unicorns?"

I huff a laugh, lean forward to rest my elbows on my knees again, and brace my chin in my hands. "Asher's easygoing. He even puts up with Poppy bossing him around—probably because he never really knew life without her. He's used to sharing and adapting. And with so many of my buddies' kids around, he's always got a game to play—soccer in the fall, T-ball in the spring, something new every season."

"Tell me he's already playing basketball?"

I grin. "Yep. Just a rec league."

Her eyes glint. "Maybe he'll make it to the pros, since you never did."

Her teasing draws a low laugh out of me. For a moment, I just watch her. The curve of her smile, the light in her eyes when she's relaxed, the tilt to her head as she's thinking, it's all a gift I'd forgotten how to receive.

She wiggles her fingers, beckoning me back. "And Poppy?"

The kitchen light spills into the room. "Poppy. One day, the living room's her stage for a dance recital. The next, she's setting up tea for me and every doll and stuffed animal she owns. There's never a dull moment with her."

A tender smile parts her lips. She isn't just asking to be polite. She *cares.* The weight of it presses into me. "It means a lot that you want to know about them."

Her head tilts to one side. "Why wouldn't I?"

Why, indeed? We talked about a family of our own—dreams I let slip through my hands. I don't say it. Instead, I push a smile through the ache. "I'd like you to meet my friends sometime. Actually, you already know Liam. Russ saw you at church. And I suspect you'll end up teaching piano to all the kids on Renewed Lane."

She hugs that knee to her chest. "I'd love that."

"Jason's wife, Valentina—you'll like her. She's from Brooklyn too."

"That's what Willow said."

Her easy acceptance sparks something in my chest—hope, fragile but alive. I let myself picture her there, among my friends, at cookouts and birthdays, part of every moment I thought I'd never share with her again.

"Renewed Lane? You named it?"

"Sounds like me, doesn't it?" I chuckle. "But it was the guys. We wanted a reminder of a new beginning."

She bites her lower lip as if holding her smile in place. "I'm glad you had this place. And you brought friends along."

The pull between us hums like a live wire. I want to reach out, cup her face, thumb away the faint shimmer of tears threatening to rise. My fingers twitch against my jaw, but I hold them still.

"Thanks to you. I'd never have found this town on my own."

Ruby scrunches her nose, but a faint smile lingers. "We had such great times."

The front door swings open, and Willow steps in. "Hey, you guys."

Ruby and I both answer, a little too subdued.

I push to my feet and check the clock, almost five thirty. "Get some rest."

"I already did." Ruby stands as well. "Tell Asher and Poppy I'll be there on Wednesday for our first piano class. You didn't have to bribe me with dinner."

My mouth curves up. Her teasing hits something warm inside me. "Didn't want to take any chances."

She drifts toward the kitchen, where Willow opens the fridge.

I follow and call out to Willow. "What time do employees clock in at the shop?"

"Five minutes before seven. Why?"

"I'll be working Ruby's shift."

"No, sir." Ruby plants herself in front of me, chin tipped up. "I'm fine. If that's why—"

"Three days. Bed rest. Nonnegotiable."

Her eyes narrow. "You sound like a doctor."

"I've been a pastor long enough to know when someone's about to keel over. You're not fine."

"Listen to the pastor." Willow removes the clear plastic soup container. Chicken and herbs scent the space.

But my gaze stays on Ruby, her nearness tugging at every frayed edge of my restraint. I catch the faint trace of vanilla and peppermint clinging to her sweater, the kind of scent that makes me want to lean closer, breathe her in. My chest feels tight, my pulse hammering in my ears. "I meant what I said. I'm going to take care of you."

Her face softens, the protest caught in her throat. I see the flicker in her eyes. Is she remembering everything I blurted out during her panic attack?

I lean closer. "Every word I said at church earlier, I meant."

Her eyes close. I know her. She wants to say no but can't quite get the word out.

The urge to close the distance nearly undoes me, but I ease my weight back and force myself to speak to Willow instead. I give her a thumbs-up. "I'll be downstairs at six fifty. Make sure the shop's open for me."

She grins. "Word's gonna spread fast. People will think the pastor needs a raise if he's slinging lattes on the side."

I chuckle. "Could be a good thing."

"Whose side are you on?" Ruby clasps her hands and flashes her friend a mock glare.

Willow laughs, folding her arms. "I'm on his side, Ruby. He's my pastor. I gotta do what he says. Plus, this way the congregation might realize they should kick in a little more offering before he gets caught working the morning shift."

Ruby rolls her eyes. "Traitor."

"Mm-hmm." Willow smirks. "I'll still help with the pastry deliveries. You, missy, are staying put."

Ruby sighs, then shakes a finger at me. "You, buster, need training."

"Thanks to you pushing me at sixteen, my first job was where?"

She raises a hand like a student answering a question. "Coffee shop. I know."

The room hums with our playful banter, but everything unsaid lingers between us. I lean in, her subtle scent wrapping around me, and lower my voice so only she hears. "You being here... It's an answer to prayer. I've wanted to apologize for so long. To make things right."

She exhales, the sound trembling, a shudder running through her. When her gaze lifts, her eyes are soft, so soft it knocks something loose in me, makes me ache with the need to hold on.

I force myself to step back, giving us the space we both clearly need.

I don't push. Just lean in close enough that my breath stirs her short hair before I whisper, "Note that, Ruby."

Something ignites inside me—a rush of heat pounding through my chest. Hope surges like oxygen fueling a fire, and in this moment, it's everything.

CHAPTER 15

Ruby

The wooden stairs creak under our hurried steps as I trail Willow down from the apartment. My stomach knots tighter with each step. Ethan will be here in less than an hour.

We slip through the back door into the shop. Morning light spills through the tall windows, brightening the walls where black-and-white photos of Soda Creek's Main Street hang in frames. The place feels larger without customers.

The refrigerator steadily hums into the silence. Even though I don't drink coffee anymore, the smell still refreshes me, now mingling with the heavier scent of old books. I press a hand to my unsettled stomach, and my fingers catch on a loose thread from my sweater. "I can't believe he's doing this when he's got his kids to take care of."

"You should've seen him at church yesterday." Willow fumbles her keys into her pocket. "Looked like he'd been walloped by a two-by-four. Even the medic couldn't get him to back off. He's not letting this go, Ruby."

She flips the switch. More light floods the room. Then the heavy front door creaks as she twists the lock.

"Open sign yet?" I ask.

"Not yet. Give us a few minutes."

I move to the counter to make myself useful. The chalkboard menu has no smudges, so nothing to update there. The counter is already spotless. I make my way to the children's nook. A few blocks are scattered across the rug. I scoop them into the bin.

Hmm, now what? I tap my chin. The Lego table has no loose pieces either. Still, I need to keep busy.

I cross to the piano. My fingers skim the keys, releasing a soft, uneven chord. I straighten the beginner lesson book on the stand, its faded cover smudged with fingerprints from eager little hands.

The door jingles, and I jolt back as my gaze darts toward it. It's only Martha, bustling in with boxes of pastries. The aroma of warm bread and something savory drifts in with her.

"If I hadn't already eaten breakfast..." I hurry to slide on gloves and unload warm cinnamon rolls, blueberry scones, and chocolate croissants. The smell nearly undoes me.

"I'm eating one," Willow declares.

"You should always have room for treats." Martha winks at me, her round cheeks flushed from the brisk morning air.

With a wave, she's gone to deliver more pastries. Willow and I finish stocking the case. I toss the gloves into the trash, then adjust the two small pumpkins—one on each end of the counter—with bowls of candy set out just for today. Grabbing a cloth, I swipe away the stray crumbs.

The bell jangles again, and my heart lurches, already knowing who it is without looking.

"You kept your word, Pastor," Willow calls from behind the counter.

I wipe the wooden surface. My hand trembles, and the washcloth nearly slips from my grip. My eyes betray me and take him in as he approaches, each step slow and measured.

"I'm a man of my word." His gaze locks onto mine.

The room tilts, and my knees almost buckle.

Even casually dressed, he's striking. Dark jeans and a black hoodie, his hair wind-tousled, his face carrying an elusive familiarity. His brows lift like he already knows I'm checking him out.

Great. Now, the room's too warm. I duck my head. Fingers tightening around the washcloth, I scrub harder than the counter deserves.

The faint pull of his cologne reaches me, and I sense him beside me before his voice comes.

"You're supposed to be resting."

I force an inhale, steadying myself before I meet his eyes. "You've got a church fall-fest thing tonight. I'll be fine."

"The event doesn't matter if you keel over again." His mouth tilts, the dimple sinking into his cheek. "Kids coming for candy at your shop don't need that kind of scare."

"You're right." A smile pushes up my cheeks. "Nothing says spooky like the new piano teacher keeling over in the coffee shop."

"Exactly." His low murmur grazes my ear, and warmth trails across my skin until my resolve frays. The washcloth slips from my hand. I don't realize it until it's already in his. Of course. He never fights fair. "Behave. Please."

I can't help but smile.

"Ahem." Willow clears her throat, and reality rushes back. From behind the counter, she dangles a peach apron in his direction. "Pastor, coffee-shop duty. Here's your uniform."

After that, the morning blurs in mugs clinking, beans grinding, and customers streaming in through the jingling door. I weave between tables with a rag in one hand, scooping up abandoned napkins with the other. More than once, I balance a donation box against my hip while wiping crumbs off a chair, the scent of old paper clinging to the books left behind. Behind the counter, Ethan and Willow barely lift their heads—steam hissing and the register opening and closing nonstop.

Every so often, he looks my way and gives me a slow head-shaking, mouthing, "Go rest."

But bed is the last place I need to be.

At last, the line thins out, chairs scrape against the floor, and voices drop to low conversation. Even the espresso machine hums instead of roars. It's almost eleven. I slip away to the apartment and throw together turkey, avocado, and tomato sandwiches. I squeeze mustard into Ethan's sandwich. I hope he still likes mustard. I slide each sandwich into a separate sandwich bag. When I return, I hand one to him, then pass another to Willow.

"Lunch break. Doctor's orders." Or so he'd say to me.

"I should be the one making you lunch."

I roll my eyes, and his mouth quirks before he gestures to the counter. "Willow, you and Ruby should sit and eat. I've got this."

Her lips part, probably to argue. Then she checks the clock on the wall. "I've got to leave in an hour for work. Your shift ends at one, Ethan."

He nods and waves us off as a young man walks in, a bag slung over his shoulder.

Willow nudges me toward an empty table near the regulars holding down their corner. The trio of women trades paperbacks over half-drained mugs.

Mr. Jenkins hides behind his newspaper. The pages rustle, though his coffee sits untouched.

I slide into the chair and set down the sandwiches, while Willow lays out napkins. "I'll grab us drinks." She slips away.

Ethan's behind the counter now, moving with ease, though his grip on the espresso wand falters. I press a hand to my mouth to hide a smile.

He unwraps his sandwich, faces me, and lifts it in salute. The silent thank you stretches across the space between us.

"You're welcome," I mouth back.

"I'm not sure which of you is more smitten." Willow slides back into her seat.

I press my lips together, but the smile wins anyway.

"I was just..." My gaze flicks toward the café's far end, where two people, focused on their laptops, sit on the sofas.

"Is it okay if I pray for us?" Willow asks. When I nod, she begins, so I fold my hands as she prays. Her amen pulls mine in a quiet echo. Then she tears open a chip bag, setting it between us.

I sip my water, sensing Ethan's gaze. Sure enough, he's watching me over the rim of his water glass. Heat crawls up my neck. Grinning, I set the water down and scoot my chair closer to the table to put my back toward him.

At the next table, Doris lowers her book, glasses sliding to the tip of her nose. "Ruby, that pastor of ours keeps looking at you like you're the answer to his altar call."

My face flames. I nearly choke on my saliva. "Doris!"

"Don't play coy." Shirley fans herself with her weathered paperback. "We've lived long enough to spot a man in love."

"Told you so." Willow's mouthful of chips muffles her words.

"Whose side are you on?" I mutter.

Across from them, Mrs. Jenkins leans in and taps the closed book in front of her. "Speaking of love"—she elbows her husband—"Scott didn't carry me across town when we were courting, but he walked me home after choir practice every week. Rain or shine."

"That was two blocks," he mutters without lowering the paper.

"Romance is romance." She pats his shoulder.

"It's why you come to our book club every time," Willow teases.

"He thinks romance books are cliché," Mrs. Jenkins insists.

"I'm only here for the coffee." Scott Jenkins grumbles, and the table erupts in laughter.

I scoop up a smear of avocado. "I'd better eat so I can relieve Ethan of his duties."

"Unless you plan to keep him company, he's not leaving before one." Willow bites into her sandwich. "He's got that determined look I haven't seen in him before."

Clearly, my episode gave him a scare. "I hope he's not planning to do this again tomorrow."

"Actually, he is."

"No way."

"Oh, honey." Mrs. Jenkins's voice floats over. Both of us turn. "Men like him? They live for someone to take care of. He's a pastor, so it comes naturally."

"I've never seen a pastor date before," Shirley chimes in.

"Then just come here." Mrs. Jenkins smirks. "You'll see it."

The women cackle in unison.

At a hiss from the counter, we all turn. Ethan's laughter bursts out, broad shoulders shaking. Filling out the apron like it belongs to him, he looks at ease behind the counter. I can almost picture him here, week after week, as if Sips and Scripts is his second home.

"Feel free to call in to my show today." Willow dabs her mouth with a napkin. "If you need love advice for an ex."

"He and I are..." I grab a napkin and wipe at a crumb on the table. He and I are *just friends.*

"Anyway, I wasn't planning on going to the fall fest at the park, but—"

"The church thing?" I raise the napkin to interrupt, but something tells me it might as well have been a white flag of surrender. "After making a scene there? Not happening."

"Valentina's back in town, and I want her to meet you." Willow shrugs. "So does Ethan. We don't have to stay more than ten minutes."

"Do I get to wear a mask for a disguise?" Seriously, I don't want to let Willow down. Or Ethan. Maybe I don't want to let myself down either. I need to live again.

"Nonsense. It's not like everyone saw you at church," Willow adds.

Maybe. But those who didn't see me saw an emergency that had their pastor shouting my name and running from the altar. Word will get to everyone soon.

"What about the candy we got?" I divert us from *that* memory.

"We'll leave it at the door for the kids who don't go to the park."

Maybe I can pull it off. If not, the park isn't far. I could always walk back. Maybe Ethan will walk me back. Heat floods my veins before I can dam it up.

CHAPTER 16

The washing machine hums in the background while I scroll through my Bible app. I pause at Psalm 77:11: "I will remember the deeds of the Lord; yes, I will remember your miracles of long ago."

Corduroy rasps at my pants as I shift against the love seat, and the verse settles deep.

On the table, *Anxiety Shadows* is closed, a bookmark wedged in to hold the chapter about remembering and the Scripture reference. That book always walks me back to Scripture. The remembering chapter is about writing down victories, no matter how small. I should grab a pen and jot down last night's full stretch of sleep, something I haven't known in a long time.

I left the shop after lunch, claiming I had work. Technically true. But every time Ethan's gaze snagged mine across the counter, heat pumped through my silly, traitorous heart.

I frown at the wicker basket on the kitchen counter. I should pour the candy in it before the kids start knocking. I'm not sure how early they show, but I have two hours until I meet with the grandmother about the group lesson.

A knock startles me from my thoughts. I set my phone atop the book, nerves lifting. It has to be Ethan, if the butterflies in my stomach are any indication.

I swing the door open.

"Ruby." The tender way my name leaves his lips steals the breath straight from my chest. He rocks back on his heels, hands tucked in his pockets. A brisk breeze slips through my sweater, and I brace against the doorframe. His eyes search me like he's waiting for me to say something.

"You want to come in?"

He grimaces. "It's best I don't."

Right. Willow's gone, and no one knows he's here except the two of us.

"I just wanted to say—" He exhales, glancing past the parking lot and the apartments beyond. "My shift's over. Get some rest."

"Thank you."

"Dinner will be delivered at five. Brook's Diner."

I fold my arms. "You don't have to—"

"Consider it a bribe." He winks. "To get you to the fall fest."

"I already gave you your scare yesterday." A laugh escapes me unbidden. "I don't need a repeat at your church event."

"It's not my event. It's a community event we put up." He shrugs. "Come meet Valentina. And my friend Jason. Russ saw you but didn't get an intro yet."

"Guess I'll be there."

His grin deepens as he steps back. "See you tonight."

My lips part, but the words dissolve, caught somewhere between his smile and my racing pulse.

The anticipation clings to me all afternoon.

Ruby

Main Street glows with the string lights I remember from when we'd visited all those years ago. Tonight, every shop window flickers with pumpkins, paper decorations, and decorative lanterns. Children rush past us, probably heading toward the park, as their parents attempt to catch up.

We cross Main. Down two blocks, the park comes into view. Cars crowd the curb and line the lot, trunks popped open and dressed in straw sheafs, harvest bounty, and twinkle lights. Pumpkins spill from crates, candy bowls gleam, and laughter ricochets from every corner. Buttered popcorn and cinnamon spice scent the air, tangling with the sharper bite of cider.

"Care for some cider, or whatever they are serving over there?" Willow tips her chin to the tent in the park.

"I'm stuffed." I pat the jacket over my stomach.

"This way." She steers us toward another tent wedged between SUVs decked in orange string lights. Someone calls her, and we stop as Willow answers her questions.

While there's murmurs and activity as she waves to those she recognizes, Ethan's laugh catches my attention. I tilt my head to the side. He's talking with a couple of men, both unfamiliar.

As if aware of my attention, he nudges up his cap and catches me staring. His mouth quirks, pushing the dimple into view, and I think I smile or try to look away. Or not, since he waves to the men with him, and they start walking toward us.

My stomach lurches, and even though my eyes beg me to look away, I can't. He's in a red vest and a hoodie stamped with the logo from the church coffee counter, every inch of him looking prepared, confident, as if he belongs to this place—or maybe it belongs to him.

"Where are we going again?" one of the men asks. He's taller than Ethan, his jaw sharp, eyes icy blue.

"Willow." Ethan's voice cuts through, calling as she finishes her chat with the woman.

"We made it," Willow says.

"Glad you could come." Ethan lingers mere feet away, close enough that I catch the curve of his smile, just for me. "Ruby." My name rolls off his tongue in a personal way.

"Ruby." Another voice claims my attention. A man with piercing blue eyes steps forward, smiling like he knows something I don't. He extends his hand, and I take it. His grip is firm, steady.

"I'm Jason. Any friend of Ethan's is family."

"So true." Another man joins in, shaking my hand. "I'm Russ." Grinning, he towers over Ethan, Jason, Liam, and everyone else in the park so far.

"Nice to meet you." I manage, his warm handshake settling against my palm like we're old friends. He probably knows who I am. Word travels fast, especially after yesterday at church.

"Pastor!" someone calls, and Ethan gives us a quick salute. "I'll be back."

In an instant, a tide of kids tugging at his arms whisks him away.

More children spill into the park—painted faces blurring past, sneakers thudding against asphalt, shrieks riding the crisp air. Toddlers weave between legs while parents wrestle decorative totes from car trunks. Chaos and laughter abound.

"We'd better meet Valentina before you change your mind and bolt." Willow nudges me toward the tent.

Inside, a woman with tan skin and a sleek ponytail leans over the booth, passing a caramel apple to a child. Beside her, Nessa mans the popcorn machine, steam curling into the cold evening air. The buttery-sweet scent stirs memories of fall carnivals with Ethan, and my stomach aches.

Nessa's eyes brighten when she spots us. "Hello, sweeties."

"You scored the best booth in the whole park." I trade a quick greeting while Willow does the same.

"Willow, you made it!" The other woman turns, her gloved fingers sticky with caramel.

"Val!" Willow beams as the woman steps out from behind the booth. She leans in and kisses Willow's cheek.

"You're glowing." Willow beams. "How was the honeymoon?"

Valentina laughs, her smile easy. "Wonderful. But if you can believe it, we spent the last two days counting down. We missed the kids."

"Not a good sign for a newlywed couple." Willow smirks, then gestures to me. "Meet Ruby."

Valentina faces me with a daunting familiarity. "Ruby... You wouldn't happen to be the Ruby who had Pastor falling into the pool during our marriage counseling session, would you?"

Heat shoots up my cheeks. Of all the memories she could've dragged out, why that one? "I was there when he fell in the pool." Truth is, I barely remembered anyone else from that night. Just Ethan.

Valentina smiles, eyes glinting. She reaches for my hand, then stops when she looks at her caramel-smeared one. Instead, she leans in and brushes a kiss against my cheek. "I can't wait to hear everything you know about our pastor."

She seems easygoing. Being friends with her could come naturally.

Popcorn bags crinkle as kids and adults weave in and out of the tent, laughter rising with the chilly steam. Someone calls for a caramel apple, and Valentina ushers us to the stand. "Here, stand beside me."

Then we're recruited to pass out church pamphlets from the bucket, along with candy stacked across the tables. Willow keeps Valentina talking, asking about Venezuela and the honeymoon, while I slip candy bars into eager hands and half-full bags. Willow slides church flyers across the table with practiced ease.

Daylight thins, shadows stretch, and the air carries an intense chill. I'm not even looking for him, but my gaze zips right to Ethan. He strides between cars, stooping to adjust a boy's scarf, pausing to greet parents. His smile glows in the fading light, so alive I find myself grinning.

Then his gaze lifts and collides with mine. Hope bursts in my chest, fierce and foolish, as he lifts a hand and waves.

I'm barely able to raise my hand before a woman steps into the space between us. Diane—brown hoodie, jeans—leans too close to whisper in his ear. Maybe church business. Maybe nothing. Still, it knots something low in my stomach when her hand slides over his wrist. It could be casual, but it lingers like she has more to say than the words reaching his ear.

"Can I have some candy, please?" A girl with a butterfly painted on her face smiles at me.

"You look all glittery, pretty as a fantasy."

She beams. "My mama's doing the face painting."

"I'm a piano teacher. I might have to drop by that booth and get her to put some musical notes on my face." I wink, then drop candy from the bowl into the kid's bag.

Willow chats with parents hovering nearby, explaining the content on the flyers for upcoming church events to those who barely know Meadowbrook.

As daylight fades, the park glows under strings of lights. Headlights shine on open trunks, and lanterns sway above booths. The crowd has thinned, which might explain why the tent feels colder without all the earlier bodies packed inside. I hug myself against the chill, toes numb in my worn All Stars. Maybe it's time I bought a real coat.

"How are you guys doing?" Ethan's voice sends butter-flies through me, and his face seems to add warmth to the tent—achingly familiar.

"Popcorn was a hit." Nessa waves toward the stand.

"We still have loads of apples left." Valentina grins.

Willow stretches her back. "I told as many people as I could about the church Christmas events."

"I see the girls got you to work." Ethan gestures to me. "So how was your night?"

"Um…" I lift the half-empty candy bowl. "Not many can-dy fans at this tent."

He crowds in closer, head tilted, like we're the only two around. Then he pulls the knit cap from his head, his hair sticking up, and slides the cap down over mine. "You're cold."

My breath snags.

His fingers linger against my nape, and I savor the caress before he shoves his hands into his vest pockets and shrugs. The wool is still warm from him, still carries a scent of cedar and fall.

I tug the cap lower, struggling to find composure. "And now you'll freeze." Great. My voice emerges as a squeak.

The dimple flashes. "I'll manage."

"Ruby and I will head home now." Willow winks with a knowing smile.

Ethan nods, his smile so bright it follows me into the wee hours, keeping me awake or dreaming of long summer nights, tender kisses, and whispered words.

Then he shows up at the shop the next morning when Willow and I are setting up to open.

"Reporting for duty." His dimple digs deep as he rubs his hands together, and Willow opens the door wider to let him in.

I slide open the cash register drawer, tossing the dust cloth across it, but my fingers twitch. Self-conscious, I tap my hair. I barely combed it this morning, didn't I?

"I didn't realize you were coming today." Willow rounds the counter.

"I'm a man of my word." Ethan steps up to me, cutting off my air circulation with his intoxicating scent.

Glad to be standing behind the counter, I need something solid, so I grip the smooth edge. The polished wood cools my palms.

"I'll be here tomorrow as well." His gaze finds mine, a secret smile quirking his mouth. "Ruby needs an extra day to rest."

"I'm tougher than I look."

"I promised the medic I'd take care of you." He winks. "Three days, minimum."

God, what am I supposed to do with him? His smile shines like sunlight after years of shadow.

The older woman's words ring in my mind. *"Men like him... they live for someone to take care of."*

I'm not a damsel in distress. But I like it when he fusses over me. Maybe more than I did back then.

True to his word, he's back on Wednesday. Willow isn't downstairs yet. And just Ethan and me now? His presence fills the room, swallowing air and space.

"I'll leave you to it." I shove the apron into his hands.

But he catches my wrist, his touch gentle, electric.

"What?" The word slips out ragged, like I've run a marathon.

"Come an hour early this evening." His low rumble travels up my arm, every syllable a vibration under my skin. "Have dinner with us."

And I'm held captive by the brown of his eyes. My breath catches, leaving me in no position to give any other response but a nod.

"I bought music books for the kids. No need to bring yours."

"Okay." The whisper barely escapes my lips.

He keeps his gaze on me, and I can't retreat even as he takes the apron. He finally releases my hand, but the heat between us simmers through his gaze. It's enough to spark the next Meadowbrook fire.

I pivot and force one step forward. Every nerve begs me to turn around, to linger and bask in his presence. Instead, his gaze burns hot against my spine, searing me as I flee.

CHAPTER 17

Ruby

I steady the tote handle in my grip, but my off-shoulder bag strap almost tangles with my unzipped jacket as I climb Ethan's front steps.

I'd told him not to pick me up, claiming I had a ride. I honestly wanted to walk. On Monday, Willow pointed out a trail that cut from the library straight to Renewed Lane. Today, I couldn't resist checking it out.

The porch swing by the garden sways in the evening breeze, and I catch whiffs of cinnamon, grilled meat, and melted cheese.

My gaze flicks to the front window, and my heart stumbles.

The kitchen lights highlight Ethan's profile, gilding his hair. His arm flexes as he stirs something on the stove. Beside him, Poppy, no doubt standing on her little step stool, waves a purple stick like she's conducting an orchestra. Asher bolts past behind them and launches a paper plate like a Frisbee.

It's so painfully domestic I nearly miss the last step. I steady myself, then climb to the porch. My finger hovers before I press the doorbell.

In the flower garden beside the porch, robust shrubs stand amidst dead stalks that must've bloomed in the summer. Impressive, he's kept a garden alive.

A clatter rises beyond the door.

"It's Miss Ruby!" Poppy's voice rings out.

A beat later, Asher calls, "I'll get the door!"

Soon, the door swings open wide, and skinny arms noodle around my waist.

"Thanks for the hug." I scoop my free arm around her back. Warmth expands inside me. She's only met me twice, but she's handing me such generous hugs.

"How was school?" I ruffle her messy curls.

"Good."

Sticky fingers clamp onto my other wrist, and I let go of Poppy to pat Asher's shoulder.

"Did you bring us chocolate croissants?" His eyes gleam.

I'd have loved to, but I knew better. I tsk. "Don't tell me you ate all the candy from two days ago."

"Daddy says we can only eat them after dinner."

"Your daddy is right. You don't want to spoil your dinner appetite." I heft my bag. "I brought broccoli and carrots, though."

"Nah." In stage-worthy dramatics, he tosses his head back, groaning.

"I also brought you something else." I lower the bag onto the floor as a draft slips past me. With a nudge, I close the door.

"What's that?" Poppy leans forward.

So does Asher, their shadows blocking out the hallway light.

I crouch, the paper bag crunching as I pull out the flower and set it aside. Not exactly the kind of gift kids get excited about. I'd grabbed them something else earlier. I even added something for Ethan. But his is buried in my shoulder bag, in case I chicken out.

I retrieve a medium-sized box and pass it to Asher. "A hoop for your bedroom door."

"Awesome." He snatches the box from me.

I reach for the other box and hand it to Poppy. "Here's a cash register for your grocery shop."

She hugs it close. "It's a My Little Pony register. I love My Little Pony!"

But I have something else for her. I pick up the flower from the floor and hold it out. "This one's for you, Miss Poppy. I wanted to bring you a poppy, but they're hard to find this time of year. Then I spotted this sunflower and thought—wait."

Her eager eyes widen, her smile already glowing.

I tap her nose. "Poppy's smile is sunshine. And there's only one sunflower in the world as special as you."

She takes the flower and lifts it to her nose, sniffing. "It smells like sunshine."

A low voice rumbles from the hallway. "Sometimes it could be a rose."

My head snaps up, and I stand.

Ethan saunters toward us, dish towel slung over his shoulder, broad shoulders stretching out his white T-shirt. His gaze locks with mine, and that teasing dimple denting his cheek has me grinning like I'm sixteen again.

"One rose, for the one and only." His voice is a low timbre, every word vibrating through me.

Warmth blooms in my chest. He remembers. Those words I whispered at my aunt's flower shop when I handed him a rose. He surprised me with the same line more than once afterward, showing up with a single rose—always with that crooked smile—just because I'd been on his mind. *"You are my one and only... like a rose standing out from the whole bouquet."*

"Hi." I breathe.

"Hi, yourself."

We just stand there, suspended in a silence that says everything and nothing at once.

"Can I open this now?" Asher's voice yanks me back. He's already working the corner of the box, teeth marks pressed into the cardboard.

"Great chompers there." I tug at his sleeve.

"Did you say thanks to Miss Ruby?" Ethan asks.

Asher pops up and loops his arm awkwardly around my waist. "Thank you, Miss Ruby!"

"We'll set up the hoop after dinner. Deal?" Ethan pats the boy's shoulder.

Asher nods. Then, with the box clutched to his chest, he bolts down the hall.

"Thanks for my flower." Poppy beams and waves it with one hand. She's already got the purple cash register out of the box. "I'm taking this to my shop."

"Flower goes on the counter first." Ethan cups her cheek, his tone gentle.

She nods, and her hair bounces over her shoulders as she dashes after her brother.

"Come in, Ruby." Ethan's smile hooks me, and I bite down on mine, lips folding to keep it from spilling out.

I slip my bag into the tote and shrug out of my coat.

Ethan is at my side already. His hand brushes mine as he frees my coat. He then steps behind me and slides it off the other arm.

When his fingers graze my neck, I suck in air. The clean scent of soap and cedar wraps around me, stealing my sanity and leaving me dizzy with remembered longing. I didn't realize how badly I've missed him, missed having someone fuss over me and make my heart trip.

He hangs my coat on the empty hook next to the pink backpack. "Thanks again for the kids' presents."

"I should've asked if the hoop was okay." Does he even want balls flying around his house? "I shouldn't have imposed—"

"It's perfect." His hand finds my shoulder. The gentle squeeze sends warmth straight down my arm, and sparks sizzle beneath my skin. His gaze holds mine, and his lips part. "Thank you."

His touch has left me breathless, but I have to pretend he doesn't affect me. My chest rises as I exhale, then force a smile. "Careful, Pastor. You'll make me think you like my surprises."

His eyes crinkle at the corners, but in those dark depths is a tenderness that strips me bare. What if I give him my heart again? What if I can't survive when he breaks it?

Dinner is simple—mac and cheese with grilled chicken for him and me, while the kids are content with the pasta. But it's delicious being surrounded by chatter and laughter as Poppy elaborates about her unicorn's glitter-kingdom friends and tea parties. The kids seem more relaxed around me today.

"Her friends are imaginary." Asher's voice rises over Poppy's.

"No, they're not."

"Yes."

"Asher." Ethan turns to his son seated beside him, eyebrow raised.

"All right." The boy ducks his head and scoops a heaping spoonful of half-eaten mac and cheese. Elbow noodles tumble on their way to his mouth. "Real friends."

I ache as Ethan handles his kids—listening, answering, settling little battles with patience. He's a natural at this.

During the chatter, Asher's glass tips over. We mop up the spill and sit again.

"This is delicious." I turn to Poppy as she forks her pasta. "Did you help make it?"

"I did." She beams.

"I helped Daddy grill the chicken," Asher adds.

Ethan gives me an apologetic look. "Sorry, it's cold. Should've cooked it later."

"I never liked hot food."

He arches a brow. "Since when?"

"Shelter dinners." I shrug. "Everything was cold by the time we sat."

He nods like he remembers. "Builds resilience."

"Or ruins taste buds." I point my fork at my plate. "This mac and cheese is good, not soggy."

"Because I stirred it with my wand." Poppy brandishes the purple tool.

"And I taste-tested." A mouthful of pasta muffles Asher's declaration.

Once they finish eating, the kids squirm in their chairs.

"Daddy, can we have our festival candy now?"

"What's the rule?" Ethan asks.

"We only eat six today," Poppy says.

"Six?" I ask.

"Yes, you can have your candy." Ethan excuses the kids.

They bolt, trading pieces from their stash, and he faces me. "Eight the first day, seven the next. Today six, and when it's down to one, the rest goes to donation."

I laugh. "Smart. Self-control by numbers."

"Or survival." He grins.

The kids dash off to the playroom, and we clear the table, loading the dishwasher.

"You run a tight operation, Pastor Ethan Bishop."

He passes me a dripping plate, which I slide into the dishwasher. "I always meet them halfway, rather than shut things down completely."

"I like that." I take another plate from him. Unlike last time, when we used disposables, tonight it's real dishes. I don't ask why, just note the difference. "You've done a great job. They look happy. I loved hearing their chatter."

His gaze softens, sinking into me. "We don't usually have a beautiful woman"—he clears his throat, fumbling—"I mean, a woman—at the table."

My lips twitch. "Is that your subtle way of saying I'm the first woman you've had around since...?"

Oh! If only I could take the question back!

I duck my head, pretending to fuss with a plate in the rack, then snap the dishwasher shut. I can't look at him, and it's so awkward that he's not saying anything now.

"I have something for you." I wipe my wet hands on my leggings, then hurry back to the hallway. I retrieve the candy from my bag. I probably shouldn't be giving it to him now, but I needed a brief escape for composure.

He's drying his hands with a towel when I return.

"I didn't want to pull this out when the kids were around, in case you didn't want them having candy."

"Don't tell me it's candy corn." His eyes brighten under the lighting as he takes the bag from me.

"I'm going to assume it's still a favorite fall treat."

"Haven't had it in ages." He crosses the kitchen to the table, and the chair scrapes the hardwood floor when he sits. "I'm not sharing, in case you'd hoped I would."

"It's a gift." I follow and sit across from him. I'd have given him a serious gift, but I didn't want to seem like things are back to normal between us. "Thanks for taking care of me."

"Thank you." He yanks open the bag too fast, and the candy scatters across the table. I cover my mouth to laugh as he tosses a few into his mouth. They muffle his words. "For bringing this. For coming."

"I knew you didn't have any candy at the fall festival."

"Haven't had this in twelve years." He passes the bag to me. I reach for one and toss it into my mouth.

"Not since you and I... that last fall." His tone turns so somber that I go still in the chair. "And to answer your earlier question... since Maddie, I haven't. Couldn't—"

He's probably still guilty about moving on after his wife's passing, even if their marriage stemmed from partnership, not passion.

"Is that why you were still wearing a ring?"

"Huh?" His brows scrunch.

The kids' happy voices chirp through an open door not far from the kitchen.

"At the pool, I thought I saw a ring."

"You did. I used to wear it all the time, out of habit, mostly because I didn't want anyone assuming I was searching. Of course, when I ran into you, I realized it was time to take it off."

I snatch a few candies and pop one into my mouth. Needing clarity, but also distraction. Why, after seeing me, did he take it off?

When I look at him, he seems to know my questions.

"Are you seeing... dating anyone?" He's bolder than I remember.

"Why do you care?"

"I've always cared." Something rough edges his steady response. "Don't get me wrong. Maddie was wonderful. A great mom. Supportive. Quiet. We never even argued. Her personality was closer to mine, meaning she internalized emotions inside instead of talking them out. Whereas you called me out. We argued. We worked things through. What Maddie and I had was different."

The candy forgotten, he knots his hands together. "I switched my number when I married Maddie—afraid I'd be tempted to call you. Before that, I tried several times to reach you. But your number was always disconnected."

"A phone was the least of my problems after that day." Sadness presses at the edges of my mind. I block it. "When I left for the hospital, I'm not even sure what happened to it. The last call I had on it was about... Mama."

My eyes sting, and I reach for another candy. Only for his hand to catch mine.

"What about you?" His thumb rubs soft circles across my skin. "Date anyone?"

"I tried going out with a nice guy five years ago—dimples, dark hair, faith like yours. But he wasn't you. By the end of our first date, I knew there had been and would be only you."

His damp hand slides to my wrist, and my gaze braves his. His Adam's apple bobs. "No amount of apologies will ever justify—"

"Daddy! Daddy!"

I jerk my hand back as Asher bounds in.

Clutching the box, he begs Ethan to hang his hoop.

"We'd better start our lesson." I shove my chair back, needing air.

"Right." His voice clears behind me, rougher now. "I'll set up Asher's hoop."

Ruby

The first lesson is anything but smooth. My plan to have one at a time on the bench with me backfires when Asher and Poppy start bickering over who gets to go first.

"I should, because I'm older." Asher plops down on the bench.

"But I want to go first!" Poppy stomps a foot.

"Easy fix." I pat the other side of the bench. "One on the left, one on the right. That way I've got both of you."

Once they squeeze in tight, I point to the music sheet and trace the notes with a finger.

"See this little oval? That's middle C. When you spot it on the page, your finger finds it here." I press the key on the piano so they can hear the sound. "Asher, you try first."

He leans over and taps it, his brow furrowed.

"Perfect. Now, Poppy, your turn."

She presses the same key, giggling at the echo.

"Good job, you guys."

We go back and forth like that, one playing, the other repeating, until their small fingers stumble into a rhythm.

"I got it."

"Me too."

Their excitement has my heart expanding.

By the time I call it a lesson, the window glass reveals the darkness outside. I glance at the clock next to the wall-mounted TV. Seven fifteen.

"I'd better get going. You guys have school tomorrow."

"Sing us a bedtime song, please." Poppy leans into me to keep me from standing.

"I have to walk home before it gets too dark."

"It's already dark." Asher scoots in my way when I stand. "Stay the night."

"No, sweetheart."

"We have a guest room." Poppy pops up, grabs my pinkie, then hauls me along. "Let me show you."

We start walking toward the hallway. "I can see it next time."

Ethan emerges from upstairs, and Asher remembers his project. "Did you hang it up, Daddy?"

"All ready to go."

Asher snags my other hand, urging me to see his hoop, while Poppy pulls on Ethan's sleeve. "Can Miss Ruby have a sleepover? We can't let her walk in the dark."

"You walked here?" Ethan crosses his arms.

"It's not that far."

"But it's dark out."

Has he already forgotten our long-ago late-night escapades? "This town is safer than Brooklyn to walk at night."

He holds up a hand. "I'll feel better if we take you home."

"I'll call an Uber if it puts you at ease."

But now he's waving both hands. "Nope. Let us give you a ride."

"But can you see my room first?" Poppy's got my pinkie again, tugging harder.

Something thumps a door upstairs. Ah, Asher's already left and is playing with his new toy.

"We haven't given you a tour of the house yet." Ethan tips his head toward the stairs.

"A tour would be nice."

We start in Poppy's room. Cartoonish elephants and unicorns prance and pirouette across her pink bedding, and she introduces me to Cloud, the main unicorn. "She and I explore the clouds at night when everyone is asleep."

"I'd better put her back right next to your pillow, then." I set the purple toy down, and we pass a dollhouse on our way from the room.

A glance into Asher's room reveals model airplanes dangling from the ceiling and baseball cards scattered across his desk. He challenges us to shoot hoops on his new door set. We humor him before Poppy loses interest and disappears back to her room.

Then Ethan ushers me toward the open door across the hall. "This is my office."

Asher's ball thumps the nearby door. The faint blend of coffee and lemon cleaner lingers. Photos with Bible verses line the wall. Each one draws me in, every verse chosen with care.

A gray rug softens the hardwood floor, while uneven stacks of open Bibles clutter the desk. A laptop rests on an antique oak table with X-shaped legs, a lower shelf cradling books, and a shoebox tethered beneath. "This room feels sacred."

"This is where I study and pray." He steps further inside and waves me in. "If you're ever here and need quiet, you're welcome."

The photo on the computer table draws me closer. My fingers tremble as I lift the faded choir picture.

"I can't believe you kept this." And brought it out to show the kids.

"Couldn't part with it." He saunters over and gestures to the bottom shelf. "All the photos of you. I brought them from my parents' house. I needed them close, so I can pray for you."

I blink away the sudden itchiness in my eyes. "You prayed for me?"

"That was the one thing I never stopped doing. It gave me hope you were alive."

"I prayed for you too." The confession emerges from somewhere deep inside. "My counselor told me to throw away your pictures, but I couldn't. I was so angry. Told myself I'd never speak to you again if I ever saw you. I went through pain, hate, and healing before I could see you in a whole new light."

My breath catches, and I touch my grin in the photo. That girl had no idea what lay ahead of her. She thought going home after school was as bad as it could get. If I could tell her not to go to that basketball game, not to sit by the overachiever in the bleachers, would I? "For a while, I'd wished I'd never met you. Then I realized my best memories were with you. And compassion came. I prayed you'd be okay. Happy."

"Thank you."

The silence stretches between us. I fight the urge to lift my hand and touch him, step into his warmth, or embrace him. But now is not the time. He thrusts his hands in his front pockets and edges back, and I put the photo on the table.

When we step out, I point to the open bedroom. "That's your room?"

"Yes." He walks to the doorway, so I follow, stopping beside him.

The big bedroom dwarfs the queen bed. The door off to the side must lead to the bathroom. The dove-gray walls are calming, and a reading nook curves into the wall, shelves framing it. A low lamp casts a soft glow over cushions that beg to be claimed.

I imagine curling into that nook, leaning against the pillows. A mug of tea in one hand, a book in the other. A candle flickering on the table, and the whole world falling away. Maybe even a fuzzy blanket wrapped around me if the fireplace doesn't offer enough heat. My chest squeezes at what isn't happening, at how easily I can picture it, yet how far it feels from reality.

"Don't tell me you stole my idea of a bedroom," I whisper.

"Guilty." His dimple flickers. "This house didn't have one. When Liam built the other homes on the lane, I had mine redone the way I wanted. Kept the basics, but made it mine."

"You did good."

I'm still baffled as Ethan and the kids drive me home, barely registering their chatter. My thoughts circle the truth I can't shake. There's so much of me in Ethan's house. He was always praying for me. Who knows? Maybe his prayers are the reason I survived those close brushes with death.

When he parks in the lot and starts to unbuckle, I lift a hand to stop him, already pushing my door open. "The kids have school tomorrow. I can handle this."

He nods, letting it go.

"Are you coming tomorrow?" Poppy asks.

"She comes on Friday," Asher reminds her.

"Good night, guys." I glance over my seat and wave at them through the dim light over the lot.

"Can you stay for movie night when you come on Friday?" Asher asks.

"And a sleepover?" Poppy adds.

Their hopeful faces make it hard to say no.

"Not a sleepover." I laugh. "But I'll talk to your dad about dinner."

"Yes," Ethan says. The light illuminates his gleaming eyes. "I'd love for you to join us for dinner any time your schedule allows it."

My lips curve. "Careful, Pastor Bishop. Keep saying things like that, and I might show up every night."

"I'm not opposed to that." He chuckles. "Any chance you can come at four or earlier?"

"That depends on whether I can pull off making dessert in time." I tap my chin. "On one condition, though."

"What's that?"

"You don't drive me home."

He beams. "Okay. Invite Willow too, if she wants to come."

I catch his reasoning. Willow has a car. "Will do."

CHAPTER 18

Ruby

The wind has that crisp bite of early November, but the sun's still warm enough that I don't mind.

"The castle is ours!" Poppy squeals, her hair bouncing against her shoulders while she dashes across the wilted leaves scattered on the grass toward the play structure. My cheeks ache from smiling as I stumble through their game. After scrambling up the plastic steps, she plants herself beside the crooked red flag. "You're my knight, Miss Ruby!"

"Right, I am." I climb after her and crouch at her side while Asher lurks behind the slide, a foam ball cocked in his hand. Wind chimes clink overhead, the sound threading through bare branches.

"I'm going to storm the castle and take that flag!" he hollers.

Poppy tugs at my sleeve. "He has to hit us both to win. If we stay up here, the castle's ours!"

"Got it." I hunker in and focus on his approach. "Defending Castle Poppy."

"It's serious business." Her solemn nod makes me bite down on a grin.

My gaze drifts toward the porch where Ethan leans against a post, smile broad, watching us. The black Henley stretched across his shoulders has seen better days, but he looks at ease, too at ease. When his eyes catch mine, heat prickles through me, and I snap my attention to the leafless maple just beyond the spruce.

We'd barely finished the pizza and the lemon squares I baked before the kids begged to show me king of the hill.

Ethan then waved me off. He'd already pushed his sleeves to his elbows. "Go on. I'll clean up."

Willow couldn't come—birthday thing with her studio friends.

"Charge!" Asher's war cry yanks me back. He barrels forward, ball raised high.

Poppy squeals and dives behind me.

So I step in front of her and brace like a shield, shoulders squared.

The ball whizzes past my shoulder. Poppy leaps to her feet, arms stretched high. "Castle Poppy wins!"

Asher groans, already scrambling for the foam ball. "Round two!"

Laughter bubbles up in my chest. How ordinary and sweet this is! Every smile and moment Ethan's kids give me feels like a blessing from him, letting me into their world one step at a time.

But the day is slipping through my fingers. I clear my throat, still smiling. "All right, you two. If we want time for a movie later, we'd better get those piano lessons started."

Asher groans but clambers down, muttering about unfinished battles.

We head toward the porch, and Poppy's fingers latch onto mine.

Deep in focus, Ethan straightens the deck chairs, then scoops an errant oak leaf away from the flower bed lining the deck. When we approach, he brushes his hands together, grinding away dirt.

I swing Poppy's hand between us. "The asters are lovely."

He shrugs. "I get help—perks of being a pastor."

Asher bolts ahead, but Ethan stops him at the steps. Mud streaks both kids' sweats.

I laugh. "Maybe start with a shower, then piano."

"Can I shower too?" Poppy swings our linked hands faster, her gaze on me.

"That's up to your dad, sweetie."

"Is it okay with you, Ruby? It'll push lessons back."

"It's fine." I let go of her hand and check the darkening sky as the kids bolt. It has to be almost six. I've been here more than two hours already. Time slips by fast.

The chime clinks, and I gesture to the tree. "I like the wind chime."

"They make the house alive, right?"

My throat tightens. "I did say that." Back when we were kids, dreaming about the porch swing we'd grow old in.

I can't meet his eyes, so I turn to the garden. A lone rosebush catches my eye. Its leaves are still green in the corner of a dead flower bed. Dusky red petals hang on at the edges, defiant but alive.

I turn, and he's focused on the flower I'd been staring at. "Why only one rosebush?"

He grips the back of his neck. "Planted it for someone..." His voice dips low as his gaze meets mine. "Someone I thought I'd never see again."

Somehow, a single wind chime and one tired rose undo me more than a thousand apologies ever could. Heat creeps up my neck. Maybe the denim jacket is too warm for today's temperature.

"I should get the lessons ready," I whisper, not knowing how else to react.

"Yes." He strides ahead and slides open the glass back door for me.

I climb the steps, legs unsteady, but make it to the door. As I pass him, I draw a slow breath of his scent, and an internal warmth threads with the heat spilling from the house.

Maybe the past really is behind us. Maybe we can start again, right where we left off.

Later, the lesson seems scattered, no matter how hard I try to focus. With Ethan's presence commanding the space in the room, it feels like he's pressed at my side instead of the kids. My fingers go still on the piano keys as my gaze slips to him again.

He's on the sofa, guitar in hand, a sheet of paper balanced on his knee. Every so often, when the kids chatter, he strums a chord like he can't help himself.

Both kids have showered and changed into their pajamas. Ethan changed too, now wearing a faded T-shirt with lettering I don't dare read. I'm too afraid to look at him that long. His hair still glistens, damp from a recent shower.

"Let's try some chords for 'Over the Rainbow.'" Might as well tackle this since we've covered the basics.

Poppy claps. "We're singing that for the Christmas concert at school! Can you come watch us?"

"I'd love to." I'll have to ensure it doesn't interfere with any lessons I've scheduled. "That should make it easier to learn, then." I should reach out to the coordinator and see if some of my students can play at Skypoint for the Christmas program.

We work through a few chords. I play the accompaniment and sing the melody, then let the kids join in, each taking turns on the easy C chord. Their voices tangle with mine until they break into giggles. I close the music with a smile. "That's enough for tonight."

"Daddy, play us a song," Asher pipes up, abandoning the bench to sit by his dad.

Ethan shifts the guitar onto his knee, fingers brushing the strings as he clears his throat. "Actually, I was hoping Miss Ruby and I could play one together."

"What song?"

He stands and gestures the kids over to the sofa. "You two get the audience seats. We'll give you a show."

"Yay!" Poppy leaps for the sofa, Asher claps as she joins him, while Ethan comes to stand beside me.

He's close enough for me to feel his warmth. "Asher, hand me the paper from the table, please."

Asher hops up and drops the sheet on the piano.

I frown at the title. "'You Are the Reason'? Never heard of it."

"Me neither, until recently." He leans in, voice low, and tingles race through me as his words land for my ears alone. "Funny. So many songs reminded me of you. But the day at Sunvalley, I heard this one after I dropped you off. When it played again, I knew we had to sing it together sometime."

My throat tightens. "Songs can grow on you." My voice softens as his gaze holds mine. "Every love song reminds me of you."

His focus stays locked on me, too long, too knowing. "Interesting." He winks before turning to the kids. "You ready for a concert?"

"Give me a minute to read through this." And to steady myself.

"How about I play the guitar first, and you sing? Then we'll switch. You play piano, and we'll sing together. Whichever fits better, we'll keep."

"You play both!" Asher shouts.

"Yes." Poppy snatches a throw and tucks it around her feet, kicking them up as she settles in. She already lined some of her stuffed animals along the hearth, and now they shine in the firelight.

But I shake my head. "Let's have Dad sing while I look at the lyrics."

I always prefer learning the words before I play. No way can I memorize them on a whim, though.

Ethan moves to the table and settles his guitar on his knee. The first chord hums through the room, and then his deep voice follows.

Forget the paper. My focus is on him now.

He sings to the kids, then faces me. By the chorus, every word seems meant for me alone.

Before he finishes, my throat burns. I swipe my sleeve across my face, but tears keep slipping free.

"Miss Ruby, are you okay?" Poppy scrambles over, clutching Cloud. She presses the unicorn stuffie toy into my lap. "Here. She makes me feel better when I'm sad."

A broken laugh escapes, and I hug the toy. "Thank you, sweetheart."

"Are you going to sing too?" Asher bounces on his cushion.

With a nod, I hand Cloud back to Poppy. "I'll try, but I doubt I can manage the lyrics like your dad."

"I'll sing with you." Ethan's voice is soft now, almost private, but his smile is steady.

My pulse kicks up. "You take the first part. I'll join the chorus?"

"Perfect."

He leaves the table to stand at my side, guitar strap sliding across his chest. With him so close, I can still feel his presence when I look at the sheet music.

I press the keys, the melody wobbling under my fingers, but the moment Ethan starts singing, everything steadies. His comforting voice settles my nerves. By the chorus, mine joins his, weaving in like it's natural and we've done this before. I carry the second verse, shaky at first, then stronger, and the kids hum along from the sofa. When we hit the last chorus, Ethan's voice trembles too.

The final chord fades. Silence stretches. Then the kids explode into clapping.

"Again!" Asher shouts.

"Please, again!" Poppy bounces, her blanket slipping off her lap.

Ethan laughs and sets the guitar aside. "If you want Miss Ruby to stay for a movie, we'd better get started."

"Popcorn!" Asher calls.

"Hot chocolate!" Poppy scrambles after her brother.

Just like that, the spell breaks into a rush of noise, kernels popping in the microwave, mugs clattering on the counter, bare feet slapping the hardwood. Butter and chocolate scent the kitchen until it smells like home.

From the fridge, Maddie's picture smiles back at me. The ache is still there, but it's less about my place, more about what these kids lost. Ethan did what he thought was right, honoring Maddie's father's wishes the only way he knew how. That was Ethan, always trying to do right by everyone.

And now here we are. He's parenting his kids full-time and shepherding a church, yet still managing to make me fit into his world.

CHAPTER 19

Ruby

We end up downstairs in the rec room. Kids' sleeping bags and pillows litter the carpet, a mess of blankets and stuffed animals strewn in between. In one section, extra padding layers the floor beneath the blanket. That's gotta be Ethan's spot.

The TV flickers with the opening credits of *Cars*, light dancing across the room. We sink into the long L-shaped sectional, the kids curling into the cushions. Poppy leans against my left shoulder, while Asher wedges himself to my right, snug between Ethan and me.

A popcorn bowl rests on my lap, our empty hot chocolate mugs and a half-finished bowl of gummy bears on the side table. Poppy drifts, her head heavy against me. Asher sneaks gummy bears one at a time, pretending he's not watching us, even though his gaze keeps darting over.

Halfway through the movie, I still haven't grasped the voice behind the main character. I tilt my head. "Why does McQueen sound so familiar?"

Ethan chuckles. "Let's see if we can finish the movie without you pulling out your phone to research. Old habits never die."

His fingertips brush the back of my neck, and I jolt at the spark that shoots through me. Poppy stirs against my side. I manage a sideways glance, catching Ethan's smile. His arm stretches across the back of the sofa and grazes mine. The lightest touch sends awareness skimming up my skin, leaving me aching for more.

He doesn't move it. And I don't dare look at him again, afraid he might move it.

By the time the closing credits roll, Poppy is asleep on my shoulder. Ethan lifts her and tucks her into her sleeping bag. Asher yawns wide, showing off those adult front teeth in his child's face. Then he drags his blanket and curls into his own spot on the floor. "'Night, Daddy. 'Night, Ruby."

"'Night, Asher," I whisper as Ethan kisses his son's forehead, then his daughter's.

"Please, Miss Ruby," she mumbles, eyes closed. "Can you stay the night?"

"Sometime, I will." My chest tightens. I want to believe things between Ethan and me can grow into something lasting. My gaze flicks toward the open door across the hall, another spare bedroom, and one next to it.

"You can sleep in the guest room upstairs," Ethan offers as if reading my thoughts.

Yes, upstairs keeps us on separate levels. Still, his parents would never think it proper.

Either way, I stand. "I should go. I had a great time."

"I'll walk you out."

I glance back once more. The kids are breathing evenly, their shadows soft in the lamplight.

"You wore them out with that king-of-the-hill game," he says, voice low.

"More like they wore me out. But finishing up a long week with school on their schedule, no wonder they're beat."

In the hallway, I grab my coat and bag. Keys jingle as Ethan plucks them from the hook above the kids' coats.

"Take my truck." He folds my fingers around the keys, pressing them into my palm.

I blink. I'd forgotten I still needed to call an Uber. "We agreed I'd—"

"I only agreed not to drive you. I never said I'd let you walk home in the dark." His hand stays over mine, heat pulsing through me. "Even in a small town, anything can happen after dark."

"If I wreck your truck, I'm not insured."

"It's seen better days. Nothing worse can happen to it."

My brows lift. "Do you ever play fair?"

"Always." He leads me back through the kitchen to a side door, flicks on the light, and steps aside.

I enter the garage. "You still have Greta?"

"Not a lot of driving in Brooklyn." He forks his fingers through his hair, then rubs the back of his neck. "In Manhattan, I barely drove at all."

I trail a hand over the red Chevy's hood. "First driving lessons."

"Lots of memories." He nods.

So many days strung together like beads. Days of grinding gears and jerking stops, of him gripping the dash and snapping when I drifted too close to a tree, of me snapping right back that he was a terrible teacher. Some drives ended in laughter, some in silence, some in arguments.

And more than once, I yanked the truck to the roadside, furious—only for his words to die when our mouths crashed together. Anger gave way, the fight forgotten in the taste of him, in the way his hand curled behind my neck like he couldn't let go.

Heat floods my skin, races up my neck, and steals my breath.

"Be good to Greta," he says.

I blink, catching the curve of his lips in a secretive smile. Yep, he knows where my mind went. Maybe because his did too.

"I will." I follow him to the driver's door.

He swings it open and tugs a hoodie from the passenger seat. The T-shirt stretches across his back as he moves, and my gaze betrays me and snags on the elastic band of his boxers peeking above the loose sweats at his hips.

I shouldn't notice. I look at the tools hanging on hooks instead.

When he steps back, I toss my bag and jacket onto the passenger seat.

"Thanks again." I straighten, only for him to block the space between me and the open door.

"Ruby…" His hand lifts, trembling, and brushes a curl from my cheek. His gaze flicks to my mouth, so of course, my breath hitches again. "I've heard time heals, but time only made me more certain I want you in my life."

I spent years building walls he used to walk through like air. And if I'm understanding, is he asking if I'll open the door?

"I never believed in second chances. Until you appeared in Meadowbrook."

His breath fogs out warm between us, igniting heat within me. He wants me back in his life. Does he know how much I long for that? My lips part to speak, but my gaze betrays me and dips to his mouth. I don't know if I move first or if he does.

"I missed you," he rasps.

A broken sound catches in my throat, spilling into the space between us, half sob, half confession. Then his mouth is on mine. His kiss crashes into me like a wave. My hand curls around the back of his neck, clinging as though I might drown without him. His fingers slide into my hair, and the reverence of his touch on my skin undoes me. I melt into him. Years of aching and longing spill free while his passion sends my heart racing and my stomach tightening.

I fist his shirt, the cotton straining in my grip. He tastes like pizza and chocolate, smells of cedarwood and soap, and for a dizzy heartbeat, it's as if we never lost each other.

But we did.

The reminder slams through me. I tear back, still clutching his shirt.

Our breaths tangle, ragged. His forehead rests against mine, his fingers splayed beneath my chin.

"I loved you," I whisper.

"I know that." His grip firms, pulling me closer. "Our love story never ended. I thought I'd never see you again, but now that you're here, it feels like no time passed at all."

"But time passed—"

"It just paused in the middle of the heartbreak."

Losing him once nearly destroyed me. "I won't survive if I lose you again."

"You won't lose me." His voice hoarse, he cups his palms to my cheeks. His fingers ease into my hair, steady but trembling. "I don't deserve a second chance. But if you let me love you again, I'll spend forever proving I won't waste it."

His conviction brands me. My throat burns. "Ethan—"

He shakes his head. One finger presses onto my lips. "If our time apart taught me anything, it's that there's only one you. Everyone needs the chance to make their own mistakes, so they know how to fix what went wrong when they come back. My years with Maddie taught me patience. Taught me I can't run from problems." His voice drops lower. "With God as my witness, I can't undo the past. But I can learn from it, rewrite our love song with a better ending."

His thumbs brush my cheekbones, his raw sincerity underplaying every word. "I want to be the best version of me for you, Ruby."

Heat stings my eyes. And now the lump in my throat won't let me speak. All I can do is nod.

His dimple dents his cheek, and relief whooshes the air from his lungs. "Thank you."

Then his lips brush mine again. His kiss is softer this time, tender, every unspoken vow pressed into it until my toes curl inside my shoes.

"Good night, Ruby," he whispers against one last kiss. He steps back, waiting until I climb into the seat. Then he eases the door closed with a gentleness that makes it feel like I'm something fragile.

While I back out, he stands in the garage light, one hand raised in a wave. His smile, so wide and unguarded, leaves me glowing, shaken, and aching.

He just handed me my heart back.

Now, I'm terrified to trust it in his hands again.

Ruby

I'm not as late as I thought. The salt lamp on the bookshelf glows enough to guide me down the hall. Willow's bedroom light spills under her door, a podcast murmuring inside.

To reach my room, I have to pass hers.

The podcast cuts off. A second later, her door swings open, and light floods the hallway.

"Well, well." She leans against the frame, hair piled into a messy knot, pajamas covered in tiny cartoon coffee mugs. "And here I was worried you'd be late because the kids tied you up with duct tape or something."

I arch a brow. "Party go okay?"

"Great." She jitters from foot to foot. "But forget me. Aren't you glad I didn't tag along?"

I hitch my bag higher on my shoulder. "What's that supposed to mean?"

"You're glowing." She grabs my wrist and hauls me into her room. "Like, I-just-got-kissed-and-saw-fireworks glowing."

I roll my eyes, but she's already flopped onto her bed. When she pats the space beside her, I drop into place. "How do you even know?"

"Please. You can't hide this face." She crosses her legs, studying me like an English-lit professor who just opened *Great Expectations* and set her hopes just as high.

Her room smells like cinnamon and cedar from the candle burning on her desk, which might not be a good idea with all those notes and books around. Her laptop is still open from whatever blog or fan post she was working on.

"So." She taps my hand. "Did he kiss you in the parking lot? Or"—her grin widens—"was it in the truck?"

I drop my purse on the rug. "I drove his truck. And yes, we kissed."

"Excuse me?" She shoots upright and smacks my shoulder. "Details! Now!"

My smile breaks free.

She gasps. "You're smiling. You *never* smile after a date unless food's involved."

"It wasn't..." I can't even explain how it began, only the rush of it. "The second kiss—it was like every buried word we never said came spilling out."

Willow presses a pillow to her chest and squeals into it. "Ugh. Disgusting. Romantic. Keep talking."

I curl against the wall and hug my knees. I tell her about playing with the kids, giving a music lesson, singing alongside Ethan. "And he got a wind chime. And this rosebush. Just one."

"Oh no. Not a rosebush." She gasps in mock horror, one hand pressed over her heart. "Did he serenade it too?"

I swat the pillow out of her hands. "He planted it for someone he thought he'd never see again."

That shuts her up. For a second. Then... "You two are so dramatic. It's like living in a Hallmark movie."

"Shut up."

She laughs, but catches my hand, and threads our fingers. "Okay, but seriously. If he planted a rosebush and hung a wind chime with you in mind, Ruby... you'll regret it more if you don't give this another shot."

Her grin fades, her voice lowering. "He was the chapter you never got closure from. Now he wants to rewrite the ending. Why not let him write it with you? Together?"

Writing the ending together sounds comforting. I can already picture it—me on his porch, leaning against him while the kids play in the yard and the breeze carries lazy chimes. Is it possible?

CHAPTER 20

Ethan

The ball smacks against the blacktop, echoing inside the chain-link enclosure. Damp leaves cling to the edges of the court, and the crisp air stings my cheeks but doesn't slow my stride. At least, the game generates enough heat to balance it. Every breath puffs white as we push through the half-court set, two-on-two instead of the usual three-on-three.

Liam dribbles left, quick on his feet. "Oi, Ethan"—his Aussie accent carries heavy in his words—"you guarding me or daydreaming?"

I blink. He's wide open. "Shut up."

I lunge too late.

His shot swishes clean through the net.

A grinning Russ jogs past. "That's two in a row. Losing your edge, Preacher." His long strides eat up the court. He's built like the tech guy who somehow finds time for the gym between coding marathons.

Jason smirks. His blue eyes glint under the November sun. The guy's still glowing like a man three weeks' married. "Or maybe he's distracted. Piano lessons ran late last night." He drains a jumper that rattles in. "I never got the full story about the music teacher nearly giving our pastor a heart attack in church."

I snort and grab the rebound. "If you don't show up, you miss the deets."

But Jason only grins wider. "Funny, I still hear the details anyway."

The man runs a media company in Manhattan. Information is his currency.

Russ sets up on defense, eyes locked on me. "Overheard the coffee-shop gossip."

The ball thuds in my palms, leather warm from all our hands. I stare at it before passing it off. "Ruby and I have history. You know that." Pages of it. But I want more than memories. I want a future.

Liam raises a brow. "Let's say whenever she's around, our pastor forgets people are watching."

"First loves do that to you." Jason's far too smug. "Did he tell you he fell in the pool the first time he saw her again?"

Heat rises on my face. I cut past Liam and lay it in. "Too bad I let her go." The words taste bitter and sweet at once. That kiss flashes hot in my mind. "Seeing her again is like no time has passed. She's agreed to give us another shot. I just... hope I don't mess this up."

Russ huffs and leans in on his knees. "Sounds like you're falling all over again."

"I never stopped." I bounce-pass to Liam.

These guys never met Maddie, but they knew her through the nights I sat in the support group and admitted marrying for the wrong reasons, the element of love that lacked between us. They heard how her death left me battling guilt and fearing I could've changed the outcome for her. Yes, God determines those things, not me.

For a moment, only the ball's steady *thwunk* reverberates around us.

Jason breaks it with a low whistle. "You ready to blow up the small-town grapevine? Once Nessa hears this, she'll be planning your wedding by next Sunday."

I swipe sweat from my brow, laughing. For years, Nessa's been rooting for me to find love again. "Yeah, I'm aware."

"Bonfire tomorrow." Liam points at me.

"No snow yet." Russ tosses me a look. "Might as well enjoy it while the weather holds."

"Translation..." Jason snatches the rebound, spins, and drops in a layup. "Invite Ruby. If she's going to be part of the lane someday, we need to ease her in, get to know her."

I try to shake it off with another drive, but my focus slips. My body's on the court, but my mind's back home—her laughter filling my kitchen, her voice twining with mine at the piano, her warmth beside me on the sectional while the kids drifted to sleep.

But that goodnight kiss? It won't fade.

She kissed me like she trusted me with all of her. Her lips still linger on mine, tasting of popcorn and chocolate, reawakening every nerve and dormant ache only she can stir.

I *see* it. Ruby on my porch beside me, the breeze stirring the wind chimes while the kids run through the yard. Ruby in my kitchen, part of Saturday mornings with the guys while she and Valentina wrangle the kids at our place or Jason's. Ruby with me on the sofa during a Jets game, perhaps with our friends as she teases me for yelling at the TV. Ruby in my bed, her warmth and smile the first thing I wake to.

God, I want it all. The dream I thought I lost is now within my grasp.

Maybe I'll see her at church tomorrow. But she might not show, still embarrassed, convinced every eye will be talking about her after last week's slip.

When the game ends and the kids' laughter carries from Jason's yard, I don't stop for water, barely respond as they play with their friends. While I have a moment, I snag my phone and head back to the house.

I'm still hot from the game. The fridge hums behind me in the quiet kitchen. I scroll for Ruby's name, her last message warming my heart, the kind of normal I could get used to.

Me: Bonfire here after church tomorrow. Nothing big, just friends, kids, burgers, and s'mores.

I pause. Maybe I should invite Willow, in case she has no plans. One day soon, I want a date that's just Ruby and me. But I can't rush her. I type again.

Me: You and Willow are welcome.

My thumb hovers. Then I add what I really mean.

Me: Would be good to see you again.

I hit send.

The screen stays still. Maybe she's sleeping. My pulse drums against my ribs. Three little dots blink alive. Relief spreads through me like a tide.

Ruby: Making plans this early? No sleeping in?

A smile pulls at my mouth.

Me: Kids don't get the memo. Anyway, they had their basketball game at 8.

Ruby: I'll do virtual church. You livestream, right?

Me: Probably best. You'd be a distraction.

Speaking of which, I need to finish the sermon for tomorrow.

Ruby: If I don't go to church, can I still come to the bonfire?

Her words tug something deep inside me. My father had a stricter view of Sundays. If you couldn't make it to church, you didn't belong at the potluck. If your clothes weren't right, your faith was questioned. The list went on.

We never played in the backyard on Sunday afternoons, unless no one from church was expected to stop by. He'd just preached about keeping the Sabbath holy, so the last thing he wanted was his kids swinging a bat and knocking the message out of the air.

He's a godly man, and I respect him. But even as a kid, I knew I'd do things differently if I ever became a pastor. Faith shouldn't be about controlling what people can and can't do.

It should be about their relationship with the Lord—how God convicts them inside, not how their Sunday afternoons look from the outside.

Me: I'm looking forward to seeing you. The guys are too.

She sends a single smiley emoji. Simple, and yet it has me grinning like a teenager, heart hammering as if she just told me she still loves me.

God help me. I've missed this, missed *her*. And I'm not sure how long I can play it cool.

CHAPTER 21

Ruby

Willow parks her car in Ethan's driveway since he invited us.

"You're sure I didn't overbake those brownies?" I grab the glass container from the back.

Willow snatches it before I can close the door. "The kids already have marshmallows," she teases. "Your brownies might end up with Ethan alone."

"What do you mean 'Ethan alone'?" I close the door and fall into step with her.

"He'll be the most eager to eat whatever you bring." She elbows me, her voice light. "Especially if everyone else is stuffed with s'mores."

The fire's glow flickers through the bare trees between Jason's and Ethan's houses. Laughter floats on crisp air, and kids' squeals cut into the evening. Smoke, grilled meat, and autumn leaves mingle, grounding me in the freeing feeling of fall. Dry grass crunches underfoot as we head toward the blaze.

"I love how close these guys are." Willow's breath curls white. "According to Valentina, they play basketball here at Ethan's, have bonfires and swim at Jason's, Liam's got a Putt-Putt, and Russ—something else I can't remember."

"They've built their own small town." It's good that Ethan has this circle.

Jason mans the grill, spatula lifting as he flips burgers. Smoke curls up around him. Russ dumps ice and drinks into a cooler. Liam ties glow sticks around the kids' wrists and necks.

At the fire, Valentina crouches beside two children, sliding marshmallows onto sticks. Ethan stands nearby, steadying a younger one whose marshmallow threatens the flames. The glow flickers over his face, softening the weariness I know too well.

The whole scene hums, the fire popping, and the voices rise and fall. They're a family. A community. One I long to be part of. Ethan's world once again.

"Ruby!" Poppy squeals. A glow necklace bounces as she rushes me for a hug before darting to Willow.

"Miss Ruby made brownies, but you've already got s'mores. Guess I'll have to eat these alone." Willow waggles the container, but Poppy snags it.

Willow and I laugh.

"I'll take those to the table." Poppy nudges us toward the glow sticks. "You should get some too."

Soon, we're decked out with glowing bracelets.

"Ruby, Willow." Valentina hugs me, then Willow. "So glad you both came."

A neon glow follows my hand as I wave toward the roaring inferno. "Couldn't miss the famous bonfire."

"Willow's already bragged about your piano skills." She loops our arms together. "Okay, Ethan brags more. He says you've got his heart beating again."

Jason appears with a plate and hands it to me. "We'd like to sign the twins up for lessons." The pink words *I love my wife* circle a red heart on his white T-shirt.

When I'm caught reading it, Valentina gives me a playful smirk.

He drops off another plate with Willow before heading back to the grill.

"Eden might like piano too." Valentina nods toward a girl—thirteen, maybe fourteen—emerging from the stone house.

"I'll check my schedule. I think I only have Tuesdays left."

Russ cracks open a soda. "Ethan's kids gave you glowing reviews. Now my daughter wants in too."

"Mine as well." Liam bellows from the glow-stick basket.

"I don't have enough days for all the kids."

"They'd behave in a group." Ethan's voice slides in, close enough to snag every nerve. He steps between Willow and me. Heat radiates from him, and the plate trembles in my hands. "All the kids on the lane can join mine for group lessons if it doesn't make it too hard for you."

I look up, and it's just the two of us. "That should work if you're okay with it."

His gaze softens. A sheepish smile curves his lips as he reaches for my other hand. The touch lingers, hidden in plain sight. "So good to see you."

"Glad to be here." The words are thin for what I feel. "I didn't bring Greta. We drove Willow's."

"I know where you live." He winks before his focus shifts back to the group. "Ready to bless the food?"

Russ claps a girl's shoulder and tells her to gather the other kids.

Asher comes running, a marshmallow stuffed in his cheek. He barrels into me for a hug. "Miss Ruby!"

I crouch to wrap one arm around him, hamburger in the other. Sticky marshmallow smears my leggings, but it's worth it.

When the group circles to pray, Jason introduces his kids. Then Liam and Russ do as well. I try to remember names, but it's too many at once.

Silence settles for prayer. "Excuse me." One of the twins pipes up, his hand in the air, eyes glinting. "Are you going to be Asher and Poppy's new mom?"

Heat floods my cheeks. Laughter bursts from the adults.

Jason calls, "Atticus! Where did you hear that?"

"Val used to take care of us, and we watched movie nights together. Now she's our mom."

"You're onto something." Jason chuckles.

By the time laughter fades into prayer, Ethan's hand slides into my free one. He doesn't let go, and I don't want him to. No wonder the kids already suspect.

The rest of the night spins an easy rotation. Lanterns glow in the yard, laughter rises with the sparks, and promise floats in the air. We roast marshmallows, pass around brownies, talk about weekend games, the kids' school adventures, and what house in the church community needs fixing up next. Glow sticks streak through the dark like fireflies as the children chase each other. Every so often, they drag us from our seats into their games of flashlight tag, laughter connecting us all.

And through it all, Ethan's gaze finds mine across the way. No words are needed between us, but I sense it—he's daring me to imagine belonging here. And the Ruby he remembers never turned down a dare.

Ruby

The bonfire begins winding down, the embers glowing low. Now, the cold seeps through my jacket. I should've worn Ethan's hat, the one still buried in my purse in the car.

Yawns turn to whining, and Ethan pushes up from his seat three places down. Firelight catches on his face as he claps. "All right, Bishop crew, inside before somebody face-plants in the firepit."

Poppy darts around the circle, glow stick twirling in her mittened hand, and plants herself in front of me.

I rise to hug her good night, but she tips her face up, eyes bright. "Miss Ruby, are you coming in too?"

"Yes, Miss Poppy." Willow's elbow nudges my side. "I'm sure Miss Ruby can come."

"Can you read us a story?" Poppy's yarny grip curls around my hand, but it's her plea that holds me tight and ignites a desire to be a part of their family. "Just one, maybe?"

"Or two," Willow teases from the chair beside me. "I'll wait for you at Valentina and Jason's house. I need her insight on my work project anyway."

Across the fire, Ethan watches, face unreadable, as if waiting for Poppy to let go of my hand.

I lift our entwined hands. Surely, he can see it with the glow sticks' shifting colors over our wrists. "Is it okay?"

The firelight flickers over the softness in his smile now. "If you're up for it."

The other dads are gathering their little ones. Valentina stands off to the side, speaking to her stepdaughter, who looked moody earlier when she beckoned her.

Ethan clamps a hand on Russ's shoulder. "Don't forget you're on putting-out-the-fire duty."

The taller man rolls his eyes. "Like I'd forget."

Then I fall in step behind Ethan and the kids toward the house.

Which is how I end up on his sofa twenty minutes later—kids now in pajamas, Poppy curled against me, a picture book open across my lap. Asher leans heavily into my other side, drinking in every silly voice I give the characters.

"I'm small," Poppy declares, hugging Cloud when the mouse tells the owl he has a big heart. "But I have a big heart too."

"The biggest." I press a kiss into her curls, unable to help it, then squeeze Asher's shoulder. "And so do you."

We finish Poppy's book and dive into Asher's choice, an adventure about a boy and his dog who dig a hole to the center of the earth and find treasure guarded by a grumpy dragon. The kids giggle when I roar like the dragon, then howl when the boy distracts him with hot dogs.

"Do you think a dragon would give up gold for a hot dog?" I ask midstory.

"Yes!" Poppy shouts out.

"No way." Asher shakes his head. "He'd want pizza."

Their certainty pulls a belly laugh from me, and my stomach aches a tad.

By the time the stories end, they're pleading for another. My lips part. "Maybe—"

"That's enough for tonight." Ethan's gentle voice cuts into my offer for one more.

We turn.

He's leaning against the passageway where the kitchen meets the living room, arms crossed. The light catches his warm eyes. How long has he been there, listening?

"Miss Ruby has to head home."

I nod. "Miss Willow's still waiting for me. I'd better not keep her long."

Asher stifles a yawn. "But, Daddy, our goodnight song."

"And prayers too." Poppy clutches Cloud to her chest.

Ethan sighs. "Say good night to Miss Ruby first. Then songs and prayers."

Their arms wrap around me, clinging, begging me to stay. "Let me text Miss Willow."

I message her to explain the delay.

Willow: Take your time. I'll be another thirty minutes.

It takes less than ten minutes, Ethan strumming "This Little Light of Mine" while their small voices wobble and fade. It's Asher's turn to pray, and he bows his head. I close my eyes, just as Ethan does. "Lord, please keep Miss Ruby in our lives forever, even if she doesn't teach piano anymore."

His simple words nearly split my chest. By the time he finishes with amen, my throat aches, and I can barely croak an echo of the word.

Poppy yawns, hops off the sofa, and reaches for Cloud.

Asher rubs at his tired eyes.

"You two are already half asleep." I hug them tighter than I mean to. Poppy insists I follow her upstairs, so I trail her and linger as Ethan tucks her in. He kisses her forehead and whispers. "Sweet dreams, Peanut. I love you, and God loves you even more."

"I love you too, Daddy."

This sweetness between them is special torture.

"'Night, Poppy." I wave when Ethan steps back.

"Can I see you again tomorrow?" A yawn muffles her question.

"I'll be here on Wednesday. Okay?"

No response.

We slip into Asher's room next. He's already under the covers. Ethan ruffles his hair, kisses his cheek, and murmurs, "I love you, buddy."

"Love... you, Dad."

"And always remember that God loves you."

Something splinters inside me. Ethan as a father? Watching him take care of his kids is a lesson in love itself. He's a gentle and steady presence. Loving him now means loving this whole package, but his kids make it perfect.

"They're wiped out," I whisper as he eases the door shut.

His hand finds mine, fingers lacing with warmth. "Getting them up for school tomorrow will be the real challenge."

"I can only imagine."

"Is Willow waiting in the car?" he asks as we step onto the main floor.

"I've still got ten more minutes."

He turns to me, hallway light skimming his face. His dimple winks into sight, stealing my breath. "At least I've got a few minutes with you." He brushes a crumb from my sweater before sliding his arms around my waist. "Thank you. For being here. For reading to them."

"I had fun." My fingers lift and curl around his neck. "Your friends are wonderful."

"They think the same about you." His lips brush mine, and my body hums, weightless.

When he raises his head, I rise on tiptoe, melting into him, hungry for more. My lips graze his, maybe by accident or desperate need. Then he's kissing me again, slow and deep.

Soap. Cedar. And a faint bonfire smoke wraps around me like something new and achingly familiar. His mouth tastes of mint, and with every tender press of his lips, something in me cracks open. My heart aches with the same fierce, unstoppable love I once gave him. The love I never stopped feeling, no matter how much I tried.

We were here once before, and everything fell apart.

I ease back, my lips still hovering over his. "I don't want to pick up where we left off." My whisper shakes. "I want to start fresh. To give us the love we always deserved."

"What if I don't want to forget the past?" His forehead rests against mine, voice ragged. "How we got here. Despite everything."

"You're right." I shudder. "We need to remember. We weren't ready then. Maybe all this time apart was just preparing us for now."

And then his mouth claims mine with a kiss so heated, familiar, and new all at once. We're teenagers again, reckless, breathless, desperate to hold on. My hands fist his shirt. His grip at my waist tightens, drawing me closer until I'm dizzy.

Maybe some risks are worth it.

Ruby

They definitely are, or so I realize Monday morning when a vase of wildflowers—burnished golds, bejeweled burgundies, and crisp autumn whites—arrives at the coffee shop. In the center stands a single rose.

Tucked against the glass is a card. I don't remember what Ethan's handwriting looks like, but I know it's his before I read the note.

Ruby,

You are fearfully and wonderfully made according to Psalm 139:14.

I'm glad God has given me another chance with the one and only beautiful woman meant for me.

Will you go out with me Wednesday? All day. Give me your answer when I bring you lunch at the end of your shift.

The words blur as warmth spills through me, filling places I thought had been empty too long to ever be whole again. I press the card to my chest. For the first time in years, hope doesn't feel fragile—it's alive.

CHAPTER 22

Ruby

"Very good, Sarah! Now try the left hand with the melody." I lean closer and tap the spot where the notes shift.

Sarah's bangs slide across her forehead, and her pink-sparkle glasses slip down her nose. She pushes them back with a practiced motion before her fingers hover. Then she presses the keys with the thrust of someone desperate to get it right.

The early afternoon light slants through Sips and Scripts's wide windows, warming the worn piano bench. The shop is quieter at this hour. The only interruptions are a blender whirring at the counter or the hiss of the espresso machine. A few customers shuffle between bookshelves and the pastry case, their voices muffled like background music.

"You've got it, honey." I pat her back.

"That she does." Scott Jenkins rumbles from the chair he dragged closer. The paper he's been pretending to read crinkles in his hands. He already skimmed it earlier while killing time at his wife's book club, but I won't call him out. He gives me a look over the rim of his glasses. "Girl didn't leave school early just to waste her time."

Sarah flashes a smile, then fumbles through the change again.

"Like this?" she asks, hopeful.

"Exactly like that," I encourage, even though it's not flawless. "Piano's like trying to pat your head and rub your stomach at the same time. Awkward at first."

Her giggle bubbles out, and something inside me stirs. Not just pride, but purpose. Watching kids discover what they're capable of fills something in me I thought was void.

Scott clears his throat. "And I didn't hand over my Ram so you could slack on the lessons."

He paid me by bartering his old truck, insisting it had "more life in it than people gave it credit for." When I argued my schedule was already crammed, he found a way by pulling Sarah from school an hour early every Tuesday.

"Miss Ruby?" She tilts her head, catching me staring into space. "You looked far away."

"Sorry, sweetheart." I fiddle with the short hairs at my nape. "Just thinking about tomorrow."

Scott makes another sound low in his throat, not bothering to glance up from his paper. "Thinking about a certain pastor, more like. Man can't seem to leave this coffee shop when you're around. If you ask me, Bishop's gone head over heels."

Heat creeps up my neck, and I bite my lip to keep from smiling. They walked in earlier while Ethan was still hanging around after bringing me lunch, lingering like he had nowhere better to be.

"Are you marrying Pastor Bishop?" Sarah blurts.

"What? No." My laugh comes out sharp. "Definitely not."

"But he kissed you on the mouth like Pappi kisses Nana. And you were smiling... like a princess."

I choke on air. Nine-year-olds aren't supposed to notice kisses, are they? I press both hands to my cheeks to cool the burn. "Well... princesses still have to get through tricky passages. So let's try that section again, okay?"

Sarah dives back in, her brow furrowed. The notes emerge steady, smoother this time. The aroma of cinnamon muffins and espresso mingles with the musty scent of old sheet music, wrapping me in something dangerously like belonging.

Scott's car might have paid for these lessons, but Sarah's progress pays me in ways I never expected. And with Ethan... with tomorrow stretched out ahead of us, maybe I can believe in roots here. In purpose. In something steady enough to hold.

Ruby

I'm not sure when the snow usually starts for the season, but today's cloudy. Even without flurries, the chill in the air energizes me as I hurry down the narrow stairs and push open the coffee shop's back door. My bag hangs from one shoulder, weighted with my coat, hat, and gloves I won't need yet. For now, the soft sweater over my brown leggings keeps me comfortably warm.

The familiar scents of coffee, cinnamon, and baked bread cling to the air as I step inside. A few customers glance up—some dining in, others hunched over their laptops. I lift a quick hand to the ones who meet my gaze, then slip past the line Landon is tending to and head straight for Willow as she shuts the fridge door.

She wipes her hands on her apron. "Ruby, I love that yellow."

"Thank you." I lean in and hug her tight. My chest presses hard against hers, breath caught shallow, like my body can't decide whether to steady or stumble. My words scrape low against her shoulder. "I'm so nervous.

Willow scoots back enough to give me a knowing look, then flicks her gaze toward the counter. "I wonder who's responsible for that."

I follow her focus, and there he is—Ethan, grinning. He lifts the two cups he has in hand.

I fold my lips to hide my smile and turn to my colleague as he selects a muffin from beneath the glass. "Landon, thanks for covering my shift."

"Of course. Have fun."

"That's the plan." So I make my way to Ethan. Heat prickles the back of my neck under several curious gazes, particularly Doris and Shirley in their usual morning spot. Doris catches my glance and waves, her grin wide enough to split the room. Shirley doesn't hide her smugness as she mouths for me to read her lips, "Saw that coming."

"Ready to go?" Ethan offers a cup, his eyes steady and soft. "Turmeric tea blend?"

"Thank you."

We stride to the door. His hand settles on my lower back, warmth spreading through me as if it's a usual thing. Like we're just another couple in town. He calls out a cheerful goodbye to Doris and Shirley, then pushes the door open for me. Once he closes the door, he takes my free hand in his and laces our fingers together.

"People are looking," I whisper as we step on the sidewalk.

"That's because you're with the pastor." He smirks, just before someone walking past nods a greeting. Then he whispers in my ear. "Instant scandal."

"Or maybe they're just confused why their pastor's walking around with a birdbrain."

"I gotta say..." He shoots me a sideways glance and a sheepish grin. "I'm looking better than I feel. You're the one shaking."

"You are impossible." I lean in and bump his shoulder with mine.

"Takes one to know one."

"That's the best you've got?" I laugh. "Over a decade later, and you're still stuck in high school comebacks."

"Funny. You're the one making my heart race like I'm sixteen again."

I laugh too hard at that, the joy bubbling out of me, un-restrained. We cross to where he parked his SUV two shops down. He couldn't pick me up from the residents' lot, not with my truck taking his usual space.

He swings open the 4Runner's passenger door and, with one swift motion, plucks the bag from my hand. Then he leans in and brushes his lips over mine, and warmth jolts through me.

"I wanted to do that back there," he rasps, stepping back until I bask in the glow radiating from his brown eyes. "But I wasn't sure you wanted an audience."

I tap his chest, the blue plaid soft. "That didn't stop you yesterday after lunch."

"I wasn't going to see you the rest of the afternoon." He winks, and his unzipped plaid jacket displays his gray sweater beneath it as he stretches. "Had to do what I had to do."

I scoot past him into the seat. Once he closes my door, he circles to the back, tosses my bag inside, then jogs up front. The dashboard clock reads eight forty-five.

"Thought about bringing Greta." He starts the engine. "But if we hit bad weather, the SUV's safer."

"I'm not complaining." I snap the seat belt into place. "I get to spend a day with you."

"I'm honored you'd spend today with me." He buckles in, backs out, and eases us down Main Street. Traffic thins as we pass the last gas station, storefronts giving way to quiet stretches of road and half-bare maples, their remaining leaves clinging in dull gold.

"You talked about starting over." He stops at the next red light. "But we agreed not to lose our memories, right?"

"Right." I sip my tea, warming my hands on the paper cup.

"I was hoping we could start with something simple. Like you eating breakfast instead of skipping it." Of course, he remembers I admitted I didn't eat breakfast. "If you haven't eaten, we can stop, but—"

"Actually, I didn't want to take chances. I ate something."

His grin makes him look younger. "How about an early lunch, then?"

"Sounds perfect."

We're on a familiar road now, winding between hills.

"Are we going to Skypoint?"

"You were always the mysterious one." He throws me a look that carries too much meaning, then faces the road. "Guess it rubbed off on me. Speaking of which, I heard the residents requested your return for the Christmas concert."

The words warm me. "I got the email yesterday. Haven't had time to respond yet."

He slides me his phone, rattling off the passcode. "I was hoping we could practice the song we sang to the kids. Perhaps we can perform it that night."

"Is that so?" My finger hovers over the screen, a song already queued.

"I'm supposed to play a couple pieces. Figured one could be you and me. Starting new, right?"

I nod and press play. Music bursts from the dash. "You Are the Reason" swells through the SUV. His hand slides across the console, covering mine. Heat presses into my skin, steadying me even as the song soaks into my mind. It aches so beautifully that my vision blurs with a fog thicker than the mist streaking the windshield.

At a junction, the sign for Skypoint points left, but he steers us down the unmarked road, gravel popping beneath the tires.

The song ends, and I clear my throat to mask the emotion. "Weren't we supposed to sing along?"

"I liked just listening to it this time."

"I thought pastors only listened to Jesus songs." My voice edges on a whisper. Sometimes I wonder if I've sinned so far that I can't be repaired.

"Not every song has to say His name to point us toward Him." His hand squeezes mine before he grips the wheel again. "As long as it doesn't glorify what drags us from God, music can still stir hope, remind us of His truth. That's what matters."

Beyond the windshield, the hills climb upward. Leafless trees mingle with the evergreens, while others are still gold-tipped.

I toy with my sleeve. "As you know, I've sinned a lot. I prayed once to have a relationship with Jesus back then. But that was before... everything. Do I need to do that again?"

He's quiet, as if piecing together my statement. "Well, your relationship with God doesn't vanish because you drift." His gaze never strays from the narrowing road—just like he's never strayed from the straight and narrow. "When you surrendered to Him, He claimed you. You may wander, but He pursues His own, brings them back. That's His promise."

His confidence in his faith, his tenderness in his explanation, and his knowledge of the Bible prove he's a great pastor. "John chapter ten, verses twenty-seven and twenty-eight say, 'My sheep listen to my voice; I know them, and they follow me. I give them eternal life, and they shall never perish; no one can snatch them out of my hand.'"

My chest tightens, conviction breaking over me like dawn. All this time, through every reckless choice, every scar I gave myself, God was there. Watching. Protecting. Waiting. To bring me back to Him.

We turn off the unmarked gravel road into a narrow opening I never would've noticed. The SUV bounces over rutted dirt, weaving between bare-limbed maples while lacy evergreens shield the place.

At a small empty lot, he parks and cuts the engine. He winks at me. "We'll need coats, hats, and gloves. I brought extras."

A soft laugh slips free. "Always prepared."

He steps out. Before I can reach for the handle, he's already swinging my door wide. Then he rushes to open the back door.

Cool air whips at my face, biting against my cheeks and ears.

As we bundle up, Ethan's not content with my jean jacket, so he drapes a spare heavier jacket over my shoulders—cedar, soap, and a scent so him clings to the fabric. "Good thing I brought this extra."

"Still looking out for me?"

"Always." He tosses the spare hat to the back seat and grabs his guitar case like those days he used to haul it to the park to play and sing to me.

My chest tightens. "Music today?"

"As we start over"—he meets my gaze with a certainty that steals my thoughts—"I wanted to begin differently from last time."

I nod, anticipation rolling through as he leads me over slick stones, one step after another, until the valley unfurls wide before us. A river coils in the distant mist. Hills roll out in muted colors—burnt orange, russet red, and deep pine. A thin waterfall spills off the cliff, its steady roar softened by the morning hush. The hazy gold sun presses through gray clouds, adding ribbons of light to the mist.

"Wow." My throat knots. "So stunning. Why isn't anyone else here?"

"Too cold. And most people assume it's Skypoint's private land. Suits me fine." He takes my gloved hand, weaving his gloved fingers through mine. "This is my favorite place to talk to God. Whenever the kids are at a sleepover, I come for the sunrise."

"It looks like a perfect place to keep distractions at bay."

His breath fogs in the air. "Someday I'll bring you back at sunrise."

My chest swells so fierce that I almost can't inhale. He's bringing me to the place where he meets with God? That proves I'm no longer standing on the outside of his life. I lace my fingers tighter through his. "I'd love that."

Then he lets go to unclip the case and slide out the guitar. "Can you hold this, please?"

I cradle the guitar while he straightens the blanket he pulled from under the case.

He takes the instrument back, standing tall, shoulders squared. "God kept putting a song on my heart when I prayed for you... when I didn't know if you were even alive."

He strums low at first. But his voice rises, rough and steady as he sings Rascal Flatts's "Bless the Broken Road."

The sound tears me open. Every lyric drags me through my past, a reminder that, in every high and low, God placed the right people in my path to show His goodness. To keep me alive when I wanted to quit.

Then comes Bethel Music's "No Longer Slaves." Each word digs where I've buried regret and shame. It's true what it says about being a child of God.

My heart splinters. Tears burn my eyes and spill free. This song could've been written for me, for the nights I didn't think I'd see another sunrise.

Ethan's eyes close, lashes trembling, face tilting skyward like he's offering it all to God. A soft sob escapes me, and I can't help but sing through tears. Unbidden and free.

When the last chord fades, I swipe at my face and blow out a shaky stream of air.

He clears his throat. "This next song came to mind when you told me what you'd been through the last twelve years. I was so mad at myself. It was all my fault." A choked gasp trails the words.

I touch his arm. "We are here now, together. That's what matters."

His fingers shift on the guitar. It's a familiar tune, Danny Gokey's "Tell Your Heart to Beat Again."

I join in. My voice falters, then steadies, lifted into the cold air. By the end, I'm on my feet, each word scraping through a hitch in my breath.

"This next song is by Switchfoot, 'This Is Home.' God put it on my heart when you watched that movie with me and the kids. I felt... you belonged there with us." He strums a soft chord and another as he sings the first part.

The words wrap around me like arms I thought I'd lost forever.

Something inside me breaks wide open when he sings the chorus. I feel at home. I belong. I'm assured of what home really is—not a place, but where love lives and, most of all, where God is at the center.

"Do you know Colton Dixon's 'Through All of It'?" I ask when his song ends.

"Yeah."

"It carried me through the worst of it. Sing it with me?"

"Of course."

His strumming picks up, and our voices braid together, ragged and shaky, but whole. Worship pours out of me in a way I haven't felt in years—unfiltered, like I'm alone and free.

This song always reminds me of how God has been with me in every circumstance.

Song after song follows, Ethan knowing each one, until another slips out of me without thought. The chorus I sang over and over on Monday night as I thanked God for bringing Ethan back into my life.

The guitar stills. When I open my eyes, his tear-swollen gaze meets mine. "I don't know this one. Can I just listen to you?"

I sing through the chorus again, adding lines I'll never remember later. Shaky but sure, the words spill like confessions. When I can't make up the words anymore, I open my eyes to find Ethan's brimming with something like adoration, head tilted. My cheeks heat over him watching me. "Sorry."

"I'm glad you found your gift." He sets the guitar on the blanket and gathers my gloved hands in his.

We stand still. He closes his eyes, so I do the same. The song still thrums inside me.

"Dearest God..." His low voice breaks the stillness. His next words each carry reverence as he prays for healing and restoration. "We ask for the courage to follow You together, to trust You, that our love for each other never outgrows our love for You. We ask that we can ever draw closer, not just hand in hand, but heart to heart, in Your presence. That we learn to encourage and support, to forgive, to listen...."

When I whisper amen, I feel lighter than the air in my lungs. Free. Whatever comes next, I know one thing for certain. It's in God's hands.

Before we leave, he snaps a photo of us with the valley be-hind. I don't bother asking where we're headed. We ride with gospel music filling the SUV, a playlist of songs we listened to years ago.

At a gas station, Ethan insists on Slurpees.

"We can't forget the traditions." He hands me a cup.

I fill mine with berry. He pumps his full of Coke.

"Way to ruin our lunch appetite." As we step outside, I can't stop giggling like the child I used to be.

"Not good for us, but I'm trying to make up for what we missed."

His words slice through my chest. "I'm liking what we have now."

"I wish I could turn back the clock." He holds the door for me, his voice low and rough. "I'd make sure you never suffered again."

"That's why we have God to mend what we can't." I shove at his chest. I've been listening to replays on the church web-site. "Words from your sermons."

He beams and nods before closing the door and heading to his seat.

We stop in Hudson for lunch, then head Upstate. He parks on a familiar lane. And house? Rows of bare trees stretch wide, a place that carries more than fruit, but memories live here.

"I'm sorry again about your grandparents."

Ethan's gaze fixes on the property. The two-story farm-house is freshly painted. White siding with green shutters.

Potted plants line the front porch, proof that someone still calls it home. Beyond it, the yard rolls wide and open. Under the now-leafless oak tree, we once spread a blanket for a picnic. Golden grass sweeps toward the orchard, where rows of bare trees await spring's reawakening.

"Wish Dad hadn't sold it. Wouldn't accept a penny from Mom's parents to cover Grandpa's hospital bills."

"You'll always have these memories, at least."

"Because of you." His eyes meet mine, rimmed with gratitude and nostalgia. "You're the reason I saw Grandma one last time before she died."

"I still can't believe she had a stroke a week later."

"It was shocking for someone who'd always been so healthy."

We fall quiet, both caught up in the weight of that trip.

"We could've been kidnapped, you know," I tease, shaking my head.

He laughs. "The guy delivered flowers to your shop. Your aunt had his number. Your impulsiveness got us places we never would've reached if we'd played it safe."

"Reckless is what I was." I toss my head back, laughing at how I begged the driver to take us when I learned he was headed this way. "You said your grandma had an orchard and she'd love me. Couldn't pass that up. And she welcomed me like family. Her apple pie..." I close my eyes and taste the ghost of cinnamon, sweet and buttery, on my tongue. "She was wonderful."

"She was." He squeezes my hand. "Let's see if our initials are still there."

He tips his head, releases my hand, and slips out of the car. He jogs around to my side, opens the door, and takes my hand again. His grip stays firm as we hurry across the wide sprawl of the property, the farmhouse quiet behind us, no one in sight.

We duck beneath the shade of the old tree, the crisp November sharp around us. My fingers find the rough bark and brush over the faint carving etched years ago.

"Sure enough." He traces the grooves, then leans in against me to frame a shot. "One more picture."

The spontaneous drive afterward leads us to the high school track in my old neighborhood. My chest tightens over the family I've lost.

Then Ethan bumps my shoulder, and his grin resurrects the warmth. "Remember the nights we ran laps under the stars?"

How many times have I tried not to revisit those then-painful memories? Memories that can be sweet again now. I shiver. "Unforgettable."

"You need something to warm you up." He rubs my arm. "Let's swing by a coffee shop."

But he doesn't drive us to just any coffee shop. We go to *the* coffee shop, the place where everything shattered. The sight alone clamps my chest, old hurt pressing hard against the fragile edges of this new beginning.

Ethan says nothing, just steps to the counter and orders like it's routine—an apple turnover for him, a blueberry scone for me. He slides the bag into my hand, his fingers grazing mine long enough to seal our past.

I force a smile, though this place still smells like coffee and heartbreak.

Outside, cold air bites my cheeks.

He glances over, his eyes too knowing. "We have to erase the bad memories from here." He loops an arm over my shoulders and shelters me, daring me to believe. Then he gives me that smile full of promises unsaid. The pastry bag between us is less a reminder of what we lost, more a promise of what we might rebuild.

We drive again, just holding hands and letting melodies from the stereo rest between us. We end up at a small theater I used to sneak into. It's nearly empty inside. We sit in the back for a PG holiday film.

The buttery popcorn, the dim lights, his fingers laced with mine, it all pulls me into him more than any movie ever could. I barely register the plot—something about a snow globe and a Christmas wish—because all I can feel is the steady brush of his thumb against mine, the way his laugh at the corny jokes ripples straight through me. The flicker of the screen images washes his face in pale light, and that's when I notice he isn't watching the movie. His gaze lingers on me, eyes soft, the corner of his mouth lifting like he knows a secret. My smile stirs in answer, but before it can fully form, he leans closer. His hand comes up, warm against my cheek, and then his lips catch mine midbreath.

I lean in, my lips capturing his, and we make out as if we're teenagers again, tasting first love and the danger of being caught.

We break apart, gasping, but my hand still grips his sweater, holding him as if letting go might undo everything. I laugh at myself. "I didn't know pastors did this."

"I'm still Ethan. Still in love with Ruby." He rests his forehead against mine.

"This feels unreal," I whisper. Did he just say he's still in love with me?

"It's real." Each word carries the certainty I've ached to hear.

When we leave the theater, Ethan beams as he announces our next stop. We're driving all over Brooklyn, memory after memory fluttering through me like pages from a scrapbook I'd forgotten. Back then, we rode trains until he started driving. Today, it's just us in his SUV.

We stop at a recreation center with an indoor pool. "No ocean this time." He shrugs. "But today felt like the right time to revisit."

They sell swimsuits, as he clearly knew. With limited selection, I end up with a black one-piece, and he chooses navy trunks. We dive in, only five others swimming around.

"I love it," I say as we float side by side, hands brushing under the water until they stay linked. Every splash, every glance, assures me this isn't a dream.

We talk about the future, similar conversations to those in the past when we thought we'd start a family someday. It's not the place for such a conversation, but it's us. We've always done things differently. Today's date might've been unusual for many couples, but it's perfect for me. And I think for Ethan too.

"You probably don't want more kids." I push wet hair from my face.

"If God wants us to, I won't say no."

I smile.

Then he draws me into his arms. "Is it okay if I tell the kids about us? I know it's soon, and I didn't want to rush—"

"I'm not getting any younger." My whisper disappears against his mouth as he kisses me.

When we climb out, shivering and laughing, I feel fourteen again. Only stronger. Hopefully wiser.

At the car, he kisses me once more before opening my door. "One more stop. I hope we're not too late."

"What exactly is that?"

"This is Brooklyn." He grins. "Full of mysterious places."

CHAPTER 23

Ethan

My goodness. Pulling into the shelter's parking lot, I'm bowled over by adrenaline coursing through me. Oh, how I missed Ruby, how I love her! More now than I did back then. When I took her to the valley, I only intended to show her my special place, sing to her, then pray before our day started.

But we'd ended up having a worship service together. She sang with such conviction, her voice not as polished as at the Skypoint event, yet so captivating it drew me in. She gave herself to song so effortlessly and freely that I experienced the power of God's presence.

Then her genuine confession, her fear she'd lost her salvation. In that moment, I remembered why I'd fallen so hard for her in the first place. Ruby's never tried to be perfect—she's always been real. And now that I'm older, that's more than enough.

I ease into a space among cars likely belonging to volunteers. The dashboard displays five o'clock, but darkness already shadows the sky. I look back at her, smiling.

"What? Are you—?" Her eyes widen in the soft glow spilling from the shelter windows.

"Remember when you ate my pie at the first dinner we came to? Tonight, I'm getting two pieces."

"Excuse me?" Her voice carries laughter as she swats my wrist.

I can't help laughing, freer than I've felt in years.

"You, Ethan Bishop"—she narrows her eyes in mock outrage—"told me you didn't eat pumpkin pie. I convinced you to try my Cool Whip, and you polished off the whole slice."

The dramatic way she draws it out leaves me doubled over laughing. I circle around, open her door, and take her hand. My chest aches as our fingers thread together. No gloves. Her hand's still cool from our swim, mine warm from driving.

The air bites at my damp hair, but with Ruby walking beside me, I don't care. It feels good to laugh, to love, to pour myself out for someone other than my kids, friends, or congregation.

"You realize we'd need to register to volunteer, right?"

"I've been in touch with this shelter." I lift her hand and brush my lips across her knuckles.

"You have?"

"Our church helps fund them."

Her eyes widen, and her other hand presses against her chest. "Wow.'"

Inside, the dining hall exudes warmth. Guests waiting for plates line rows of tables. Volunteers in red shirts and aprons weave through with trays. Paper turkeys and hand-cut leaves are taped to the walls, and garlands drape across the serving tables. I spot Jared, our shelter coordinator, and wave him over.

"Ethan, welcome." He clasps my hand.

"This is Ruby." The words slip out naturally. "My girl-friend."

Jared's grin widens. "Nice to meet you, Ruby."

He leads us into the back room and hands out red T-shirts and aprons. We slip them over our clothes and take our place at the cider and hot chocolate station. Other volunteers scoop mashed potatoes, carve turkey, and ladle gravy. A faint hum of Christmas music floats through the speakers.

Ruby passes me the cups, chatting with the volunteers who check to see if we need help. This feels so natural, standing beside her and serving together.

She passes me another cup. "You're smiling too much."

"Can't help it." I brush her fingers as I take it.

Turkey and gravy steam from the serving tables, and the spiced bite of cider lingers in the air. But Ruby's presence has my cheeks hurting from smiling as we weave through the rows, handing out drinks. She greets familiar faces—kids she grew up with, now weathered by life—and my heart aches for them, even as it swells over the way she makes each one feel seen.

After dinner, the room shifts. Plates vanish, tables are pushed back, and volunteers string up more lights. Someone flips on a speaker, and the first notes of "What a Wonderful

World" roll across the room. Just like years ago, the floor is open and dancing begins.

I strip off my apron and T-shirt, and so does Ruby. We toss them into the bin in the back closet, and I put out my hand. "Dance with me?"

Her smile curves as she slips her hand into mine. I guide her to the center, weaving between dancers, and her head settles against my chest. I fold her close like I've been waiting years to do.

Wisps of her hair caress my neck as she sways with me. "You always did surprise me."

"With what?" I press my chin to her hair. The faint mint scent lingers.

"The first time we came here, you said I was your future wife. Today, you called me your girlfriend, no question asked."

"I had to assume. Can't a man dream?" I brush a kiss against her ear, and she gasps. "If you haven't noticed, I'm still clumsy out here."

Her laugh is soft, bright eyes tilting up to mine. "And here I thought pastors were supposed to have two left feet."

I huff a laugh and rock us in an overdone sway, almost spinning her off-balance. "Careful, Ruby. You'll ruin my reputation."

"Oh, don't worry," she whispers in my ear, her breath tickling and warm. "Your secret's safe with me."

I grin and spin her enough to earn her laugh again before pulling her back to me. "Brave words for someone whose toes I haven't stepped on yet."

She smirks, leaning back into my chest. "Yet."

The song carries us until it feels like it's only the two of us. Ruby is smiling, teasing me like old times, only sweeter now. The rest of the room fades, voices and movement smudging into a blur while she stays my central focus.

When we get back to Meadowbrook, I park halfway over the curb now that Ruby's truck occupies the space I used to park in. I won't be long. Still, I walk her all the way, fingers locked with hers, until we're standing at her door.

"Thank you for today." My hand lifts almost without thought, tilting her chin. The balcony light spills over her warm, flawless skin, and my fingers tremble against her cheek. How is it possible she's agreed to give us another chance?

"I really had a good day." Her smile still makes my heart stumble like I'm fourteen and seeing her for the first time.

"I wanted…" My throat tightens, but I push the words out. "If you don't already have plans, the kids and I would like you to join us for Thanksgiving."

Her lashes flick upward. "Won't you be getting together with your… parents?"

She hasn't asked about them yet. I hadn't dared volunteer.

"It's my house. They'll be there." I clear my throat. "We're starting over, Ruby. If my parents can't accept that, that's on them."

She presses her palm against my chest, her eyes searching mine. "I don't want to come between you and your family. You can't be stuck choosing."

"Please." I lean in and brush my lips to hers, trying to erase every memory of rejection she's carried. "If you come and feel uncomfortable, you can leave right away. But please, I want you there."

Her playful slap against my chest steals the tension. "Since when are you this relentless?"

"I'm not the boy you knew." I rest my forehead on hers. "Besides, aren't you the one singing 'One Life to Live'?"

She exhales, stirring my hair. "See you Friday for piano?"

"Who said anything about waiting until Friday?" I wrap her close, her cheek settling against my chest like I'm her anchor. My chin rests on her hair. "We missed the kids' Wednesday lesson today, so I'll be by tomorrow."

She tilts her face up, and I curl my hand around her waist before kissing her. Gentle at first, like a butterfly's touch. She takes it from there. Her hand clutches my sweater, and I sink my fingers into her short, soft hair, kneading her scalp until she melts against me. Her arms loop around my neck, chest presses to mine, and I'm breathing hard as if we're scaling mountains together.

When we break apart, I cup her face, smiling like a fool.

"What happens now?" Her breath trembles between us.

"Now?" I tuck a stray strand behind her ear. "We don't run. Not again."

Her smile blooms, fragile and fierce all at once, and my chest aches under the power of it.

"What should I bring tomorrow?" she whispers.

"Nothing." My thumb sweeps her cheek. "Just you. That's all I've wanted since the day I let you go."

Her eyes glisten, her smile holding all the love words can't carry. It hits me hard, stripping me bare.

"I love you, Ruby." My voice cracks under the weight of it. "Never stopped. Always will."

Her laugh trembles into a sob. "What am I going to do with you?"

"Let me love you."

She nods, her gaze searching mine with the unspoken truth. She's trusting me with her heart.

I steal one last lingering kiss, savoring the comfort of her presence. I'm not ready to let her go, yet I do. She slips inside, the door closing with a click, before I turn back to the curb.

I text Jason to check if the kids are awake. He says they're showered, pajamas on, still buzzing with energy.

As soon as I pick them up, they want to know about how my day with Ruby went. I tell them to wait until we get home and then convince them to stay still until after our night prayers in Poppy's room. That's when I share my day. "What do you guys think about her being my girlfriend?"

"I've never had a mommy before." Poppy beams, hugging Cloud tight.

"I already knew you were going to marry her," Asher pipes up.

"Oh, really?" I take his hand from where he's seated at my left. "And how did you know that?"

"I told Atticus and Felix you had her pictures before we met her. That you knew her in Brooklyn. They said that means you like her."

"You're very smart." I kiss his head.

Home feels like home again tonight. But even as my heart soars, my parents' upcoming visit fizzles the anticipation. I told Ruby it's my house, my choice, but what if they look at her the way they did all those years ago?

CHAPTER 24

Ethan

Thanksgiving morning arrives under a heavy gray sky, the kind that hints at snow even if the forecast insists otherwise. God has a way of overruling the meteorologists. Around here, the first snow might sweep in as early as late October or hold off until December. So far, we've only woken to frost once or twice.

It's barely eight, yet the kids are already darting from window to window like eager watchdogs.

"They're here!" Asher nearly wipes out on the hallway rug as he charges for the front door.

Poppy scurries behind him. "Nana is carrying a big box of pumpkin pie."

I laugh, ruffling her curls. "Probably two."

I swing open the door as Mom steps onto the porch, Dad trailing her.

"Happy Thanksgiving." I take the box from her. The scent of cinnamon drifts up, confirming Poppy's hunch.

Mom glances back at Dad, who trudges in with a foil-covered ham tilted dangerously in his hands. She shifts her purse higher on her shoulder. "Frank, hold it flat, for heaven's sake!"

"I cleared the fridge for everything." I step aside to let them in. "Though between what I cooked and the pies some church members dropped off, I could've fed the whole block."

"I cooked the turkey last night." Mom swoops Poppy into a hug before reaching for Asher. "We'll keep it warm in the oven. Come on, my little helpers. Nana needs extra hands."

She ushers them off, leaving me to greet Dad.

"Your mother had me working all night." He tugs at the shirt collar beneath his wool sweater. "I plan to collapse on your sofa for the rest of the day."

"I'll make sure of that." I chuckle and set the ham on the counter before heading back outside.

Harvey rolls into the driveway, his Jeep skidding to a stop beside my parents' sedan.

"Look who shows up after all the work's done," I call as he climbs out.

"If I'm staying the night, I've got to make an entrance." He pulls a duffel from the back.

The kids barrel toward him, and he drops the duffel onto the pavement. He scoops them up with ease, steering them toward his car. "I brought you something."

They squeal as he hands them each an inflatable turkey noisemaker that honks with every squeeze.

"Classic Harvey. Nothing says 'Happy Thanksgiving' like arming my kids with noisemakers before I've had my breakfast."

"Better them than me." He smirks and brushes past me toward the house.

We've butted heads plenty in the past, usually over Ruby. But most of it came from my insecurities, not him. He's the fun brother, the fun uncle. My kids adore him.

Mom reappears, all brisk efficiency. "I'm not trusting you two to get the timing right. Your father's already taken up residence on the sofa, and I've still got half the food in the car."

"Mom, we've got all day."

Harvey snorts and nods his agreement.

"Honestly, we don't need all this food."

"Didn't you say Maddie's family is coming?"

"Just Charlotte's family. Her kids wanted to play with mine."

Mom frowns. "And her mother?"

I toss my head back with a wince over Charlotte's text this morning. "Her mom decided to tag along. She hasn't seen the kids in a while." I force a smile, though a knot tightens low in my chest. Ruby's coming, and now my mother-in-law. Perfect.

"None of the guys on the lane are joining us?" Harvey asks.

"Jason's got his own big crew. Liam's off in Australia. Russ is out of town."

I'll wait until we're back in the house before saying anything about the extra guest. Dad's back in the kitchen, fridge open as he peers through it, probably looking for a drink.

I pat his shoulder. "I left all the drinks on the deck in the cooler." Then I clear my throat for my big announcement. "And... Ruby's coming over."

Mom's brows crease. Her hands freeze in the middle of tying her apron. "Ruby?"

"Our piano teacher. She and Daddy are getting married," Poppy chirps, swinging the coloring book Mom just handed her.

"It'll be nice to have a mommy," Asher adds, then blows through the noisemaker.

"Ruby," Mom repeats, nodding. "As in, *Ruby* Ruby?"

Dad doesn't say a word, but my chest tightens at the look he trades with Mom.

"You guys know Ruby. Come on." Harvey tears open a bag of chips, crunching through the silence. "God knows this family could use a genuine soul like hers."

Dad exhales. "Son, I'm not sure that's wise."

"You're a widower." Mom employs that usual edge of stern warning. "Maddie's sister will be here. People talk. You're the pastor. And the kids—"

"Are happy about it," I cut in. "Their opinion matters most. This is about Ruby and me, not the town."

"Ethan's a grown man." Harvey crosses his arms. "And a pastor. I'd say he's capable of discernment."

Mom's lips press thin before she returns to adjusting her apron.

A knock breaks the tension shortly later. I open the door to Charlotte, her husband, their two little girls, and Maddie's mom.

I scoop the girls into hugs, one at a time, holding them close. "I can't even tell who's older. You're growing like weeds." Their giggles spill out as I tickle their sides.

"Happy Thanksgiving!" Charlotte beams, her warmth unchanged. "I hope it's okay that we came early."

"The girls were restless." Her husband ushers them inside.

"Of course. Make yourselves at home."

Maddie's mom wraps me in a hug, her perfume achingly familiar—floral with a trace of lavender, just like Maddie's.

My kids shriek and launch themselves at her. "Grandma!"

The house swells with familial warmth and catching up. The girls race Poppy and Asher toward the playroom.

I keep my smile steady, though my gaze flicks to the clock more than I'd like.

The next hour blurs with Mom's coffee cake and scrambled eggs, the kids drinking eggnog between bursts of laughter. Poppy and Asher soon bundle up with Charlotte's girls, eager to play outside.

Dad, Harvey, and Charlotte's husband bicker over how to carve the ham, and I remind them that it's easier to buy a spiral-cut ham. The kitchen hums with voices and clinking dishes as Mom doles out tasks to Charlotte and her mom.

"You men can go watch your game now." She waves them off. In the living room, the TV is already on with low commentary drifting through.

I told Ruby she could come as early as she wanted. I wanted to spend today with her. But now, with the house packed, my parents watching, my in-laws in the kitchen, and Maddie's shadow in every corner, God help me, this feels doomed before it begins.

I should probably stay nearby, in case Ruby shows up soon.

The doorbell rings before I leave the kitchen. A chorus of "I'll get its" rises from the women.

"No, let me." In three strides, I'm at the door, swinging it open.

"Hi." Ruby's warm smile nearly steals the breath from my chest. Nervous, yes, but radiant all the same. She's stunning in a flowy navy jumpsuit tucked under a marigold peacoat, her pixie curls glossy in the midmorning light.

"You look"—I swallow hard and reach for her bag, a cinnamon-and-apple scent spilling out—"stunning." I lean in and brush a kiss against her cheek, wishing I could do more.

Her gaze flicks past me into the hallway, then down at her outfit. "Is this... okay?"

"You look perfect." Little wonder she'd worry about her attire with my father so critical of what people wear.

She exhales shakily. "I didn't realize your guests would be here so early."

"You're the guest of honor. Your timing is perfect."

Wincing, she gestures to the bag. "Store-bought pie counts?"

"It counts." I grin and step aside. "Come in."

I close the door behind us while she slides off her ankle boots. Then I help her ease off her coat and hang it on the hook.

She takes slow steps behind me in the hallway. The kitchen hums with women's voices, drowned out by the living room TV. The hallway opens up to the living room on the right and the kitchen on the left. Charlotte gives a polite smile, Mom nods, tight-lipped, and Maddie's mother just stares. Mom must've already filled her in on who my guest is.

Ruby gives me what looks like a silent plea. How do I make her feel like she belongs here when the air itself is hostile?

"Ruby! Welcome!" Harvey's voice booms as he strides out of the living room. "About time you showed up. This family's been in desperate need of class."

"Class?" Ruby scrunches her nose and matches Harvey's lightheartedness. "Unless you want piano classes, you've clearly got the wrong teacher."

As he keeps Ruby talking, I glance toward the living room. Dad's planted on the sofa, focused on the TV, pretending to be oblivious.

What's wrong with my parents? I snap back to the kitchen. The women are still standing as if waiting for direction. "Mom, you remember Ruby, right?"

"Of course." Mom's forced smile barely twitches. "Yes. Welcome."

"Dad." My voice rises over the TV. He barely flicks his gaze from the screen, deadpan, while my brother-in-law's words trail off. "Ruby's here."

He rises, slow and reluctant, but at least, he stands. His smile looks practiced, the nod stiff as he gestures with a piece of cutlery. "Nice to see you again."

"Thank you." Ruby's lips curve into a polite smile beneath her now-dim eyes. "It smells wonderful here."

If only my kids were inside. They'd come squealing and throw their arms around her and do what the rest of us are too stiff to manage—make her feel at home. Instead, it's just me standing between her and a room full of history somewhat repeating itself.

How naïve I was to invite her. I underestimated how hard today would be. If she gets through it, she'll be stronger than any of them ever gave her credit for.

CHAPTER 25

Ruby

Apparently, I'm the guest of honor. Or, more appropriately, the main course under their feasting stares. The thought gnaws as I lift my chin higher than my nerves allow.

Ethan's dad and Harvey wander back to the living room, football commentary filling the silence they leave behind. Charlotte's husband follows them, having introduced himself from a distance when he trailed over. I can't remember his name. At least Harvey filled me in with details of why Ethan's mother-in-law showed up last minute, while my poor Ethan tried to herd his family into behaving.

I knew Charlotte would be here. Ethan mentioned it when we picked up drinks and things to make his place look festive. Pumpkins on the porch, a new tablecloth, and lights strung above the dining table. He'd said Charlotte was kind, a buffer between him and his parents. But she didn't appear welcoming while her mom gawked like I'm a threat.

Where do I even begin?

"Come in, sweetheart." Ethan tips his chin toward the kitchen. I follow, wishing I still had the tote to give me something to do. My purse is out in the truck. I'd crammed everything, including the kids' gifts, into one tote with the pies. Easier to juggle one bag than many if I need to bolt. Valentina's house is just across the street. Two nights ago, when she tagged along at our girls' night with Willow, she promised I'd always be welcome there. So that might be my escape plan.

The kitchen hums with motion now that everyone's back is turned. Ethan's mom peels sweet potatoes. Charlotte tears open a salad bag. Her mother slices tomatoes, the knife thudding against the board.

"Thanks again for bringing this." Ethan plants the bag on the marble counter and starts unloading.

"That's for the kids." I reach for the other tote.

"You're spoiling them."

His radiant smile has tension slipping off my shoulders. "It's nothing big."

I crane past the kitchen doorway toward the playroom—empty. Where are the kids? Their chatter would be a welcome distraction.

"Care for anything to drink or something to eat?" Ethan asks.

"I'm fine." My grip tightens on the tote, fingers aching with the need to hold onto something steady.

He carries the pies to the fridge. The stove clock displays 9:33. So much for coming early to grab a quiet moment with my boyfriend and the kids before everyone arrived. The kids were so thrilled when they found out about us. In their eyes, a wedding might as well happen tomorrow.

A cabinet slams. I flinch. Ethan's mom closes it with force before turning toward him. "Do you still have Grandma's pan?"

"It's in the shed with all the spare stuff. I'll go get it."

Her fake smile slides my way.

"Can I help with anything?" I wouldn't mind doing something.

She shakes her head. "No, honey. We've got it under control." Her practiced sweetness grates down my spine. Then she tilts her chin toward Charlotte. "Why don't you start the guacamole for the chips?"

Sure, they need another set of hands. But the message is clear. I'm still Ruby, the stain on their perfect boy's reputation.

Ethan's hand lands on my arm. "You want to come with me to the shed?"

"Yes." I all but sigh in relief.

"You'll need shoes, though."

"Right." I clutch the bag to my side, almost grateful for its weight. "Where are the kids?"

"Outside with their cousins." His smile softens. "They'll be happy to see you."

At least someone will.

I slip back to the hallway for my coat and boots, wiggle my feet into them, hug the coat to my chest—I can put it on later—then follow Ethan through the sliding door. His hand warms the small of my back, a reminder to tune out the family static. Like before, only Ethan's opinion matters.

"You okay?" He squeezes my free hand, pausing with the door half shut.

"Never felt better." The crisp air nipping at my cheeks is less biting than the fake warmth suffocating me in that kitchen.

"I'm so glad you're here." His steady focus unravels my stomach knots. However long I last today, I'll be fine.

Laughter rings from the playset in the yard.

"Miss Ruby!" Poppy shrieks the second we step off the deck. She barrels into me, arms cinched so tight around my waist that my hand slips from Ethan's.

Asher bounds after her, arms flung wide. "Yay, Ruby's here!"

Their joy slams into me like sunlight breaking through clouds. I bend to hug Asher, his arms circling me with that all-in, wholehearted squeeze he rarely gives me. He's not into embracing much.

"Let's not knock her down now." Ethan's hand rubs my back. "I'll grab that pan for my mom, okay?"

I nod, and as soon as Asher's hug ends, I hold up my tote. "I brought you something."

Two girls, one with ash-blonde hair, the other with brown, bounce toward us. Charlotte's daughters, just about Asher and Poppy's ages. At least Ethan warned me about the cousins.

"With Christmas around the corner, I saw these and thought of you." I pull out a unicorn night-light for Poppy.

"When you turn this on, whether in a fort or just your room, you'll see unicorns dancing on the ceiling."

"Yay!" Poppy hugs me again, tighter. "Thank you!"

Next, I hand over the spaceship version to Asher, and he beams, hugging me so hard I nearly drop the bag. Then I fish out two fluffy novelty pens—pink and purple with little lights and silly toppers—for the girls. I click one on, showing them how the cartoon topper flashes. Their squeals nearly split the air.

"I also brought stickers and activity books." I point toward the wooden patio table. "We can work on them sometime—"

"Let's do it now!" one girl shouts, and the others race to the deck.

Soon, the table hums with chatter as we peel stickers and work through the hidden picture puzzles, page after page. Laughter bubbles around me at upside-down squirrels, turkey legs stuck where hats should go, and the kids' silly answers to the questions.

I hand Poppy a sticker when she spots the acorn. "What's your favorite thing about Thanksgiving?"

"Pumpkin pie!" one girl yells.

Asher chortles. "Turkey legs."

"Nanna and Papa come. Uncle Harvey too." Poppy presses her acorn into place.

Despite the chill in the air and their bare sweaters, no one complains. Their innocence and open hearts warm me from the inside out.

"Looks like you're having too much fun."

Ethan pauses by the door, a lopsided smile in place.

"We're having fun." I wave him off and turn to the kids. Not about to let him think I need entertainment because his family can't—or won't—welcome me.

Later, Poppy slips her hand into mine. "Can we put the lights up in my room now?"

"Mine too!" Asher bounces at my side.

"Of course."

Their little hands tug me through the patio door. The kitchen hums with low laughter, spoons clinking, the women bent over chopping and stirring, a circle I'm outside of. Story of my life. I was never part of the big group.

After a look at both rooms, we pick Poppy's. There's more space since Asher's Lego table hogs half of his floor.

The four kids tear into the boxes, drag over blankets, and shove Poppy's dresser and nightstand aside before tying up sheets they yank from the linen closet. A fort takes shape, crooked but glorious.

Swept up in it, I crouch under the sagging tent as they click on their new lights. Unicorns and spaceships scatter across the ceiling, flickering pink and blue, and the kids dissolve into giggles when I spin silly stories to match.

In one, Poppy's unicorn discovers cotton-candy clouds and sneezes rainbows whenever she laughs. Asher's spaceship zooms in, trying to lasso the unicorn with licorice ropes. The cousins add their own twists—marshmallow meteors, popcorn planets, black doughnut holes—and soon we're all laughing so hard my cheeks ache.

At some point, Ethan checks in. The kids haul him inside the tent too, and he folds himself down beside me, his knee brushing mine in the cramped space. Their chatter and laughter fill the room as his hand finds mine. The warmth of his fingers can carry me through whatever today brings.

Eventually, the fort comes down when we step out after Charlotte and her mom corral the kids for *A Charlie Brown Thanksgiving* downstairs.

I hover in the kitchen doorway, unsure where to plant myself. Ethan and Harvey are in the living room, hauling in chairs as his mom directs traffic. The knife whirls in the kitchen where Ethan's dad seems busy.

Maybe I should slip out to the truck, call Willow, and see if it's not too late to join her. And her family. Or I can wander next door to Valentina's. Her driveway was packed, laughter spilling out. They'd be friendlier, at least. I'm not stealing anyone's son.

"Ruby?"

The deep voice yanks me around. Ethan's dad stands by the counter, silver hair catching the overhead light.

"Do you need any help?" I tinker with my jumpsuit's loose belt.

He powers down the electric knife and nods toward a tray off to the side. "Can you hand me that, please?"

I step forward, hand it over.

With meat-stained fingers, he starts lining up neat slices of turkey. "How long do you plan to stay in Meadowbrook?"

"I live here now." My voice is calm, even as my pulse trips.

His gaze flicks up, then back to the meat. "And how did you know Ethan lived here?"

"I didn't." I shift on my feet, the question pressing down.

He nods, lining another row of turkey. "What is it you do again? Music, right?"

"Yes."

"And your family, do they live in town too?"

Each question comes before I can finish the last, like he's probing for cracks. His smile might look casual to anyone else, but I know better. I've been here before, his questions stacked like evidence, me on the stand.

Back then, I was younger, desperate for their approval. Not anymore. But still, even after the day Ethan and I just shared, doubt lingers. What if Ethan snaps out of this, decides our reunion was a mistake? It isn't just his parents this time. He's a pastor now with a whole reputation to protect.

All I can do is trust God with this moment—that I'm here for a reason, and I'll make it through the main meal at least.

CHAPTER 26

Ruby

By noon, lunch is ready. Ethan's table stretches longer with the extra leaf extended, chairs dragged in from the living room and study. The tablecloth matches the cranberry sauce, and tiny pumpkins and unlit candles line the center-piece. Dishes of food steam between us, displaying mashed potatoes crowned with butter, green bean casserole under crisp onions, sweet potatoes caramelized with marshmallows, glossy gravy, and his mom's pumpkin pies waiting their turn.

Chatter swells as plates fill. Harvey fields questions about his fiancée, why she isn't here, and whether they'll spend Christmas together. He grins, says she'll be there then, not today, which earns him teasing about wedding plans. Laughter bounces down the table, overlapping like clinking forks.

Beside me, Ethan stays quiet. My tension hums through him, and he carries it without a word. I manage a faint smile and act like I'm listening to the conversation, but my run-in with his dad still tangles up my thoughts.

I fork the broccoli and lift it to my mouth. Then stir through the sweet potatoes.

"So, Ruby, how did you and Ethan meet?" Charlotte asks.

The steam fogs my fork as I stall before my lips part. Everyone is looking at me for an answer. "I was singing at Skypoint about a month ago—"

"We met in freshman year," Ethan cuts in, his voice soft. His hand finds my leg under the table.

"I'm assuming you two reunited coincidentally, then?" Maddie's mom asks, expression unreadable. Perhaps just curious.

I nod.

"Nothing catches God off guard," Ethan adds, his palm pressing warmth and comfort into me.

"What have you been up to all these years?" his mom asks. Her makeup's smudged at the edges, evidence of her morning in the kitchen. "Married? Any children?"

"Never married." My throat feels dry. The moment hangs like I'm standing before judges on a stage, lights hot and unforgiving.

"Life happened." I clink my fork on the plate. "Mama passed. Then my aunt." The urge to reveal more tugs at me. I should expose myself before they ask Ethan why he'd tie himself to me again. But maybe now is not the time.

"I'm sorry for your losses," his mom says, the pastor's wife's required response.

"That's a lot to shoulder." Harvey leans in, brows drawn. "I'm sorry, Ruby."

I nod, throat tight at the weight of his sincerity.

"How old were you?" Ethan's dad presses.

I answer.

Giggles ripple from the kids' table beside us. It'd be nice to slip to their table, rather than sit and answer questions on a test I won't pass.

"Have you found your footing now?" Mr. Bishop asks again.

Ethan bristles. "Dad—"

"It's okay." Maybe he needs to hear the truth. People carry scars. God redeems anyway. "I've struggled with anxiety and depression. Therapy helped." I hope. Otherwise, I'd have had another episode by now.

Silence drops like a weight, broken only by forks scraping porcelain and the kids' chatter spilling over from their table. My shoulders lift, oddly relieved. At least it's out. Now they've got a real reason to dislike me.

"I'm sure glad you're back." Harvey scoops green beans, then nods at the centerpiece. "Looks like my brother's house finally has a woman's touch. He's less broody too. Guess you're the cure."

A smile curves my mouth. It's hard to stay mad at Harvey for long.

"You should all come to the tree lighting next week." Charlotte steers the conversation forward, tossing out questions her husband fields.

Ethan's mom chimes in now and then.

I cling to Ethan's presence beside me, and the way his eyes soften when they find mine promises he's okay with whatever I just said.

"Ethan, are the kids okay with you dating so soon?" Maddie's mom asks just when I thought we were done.

"Yep."

My gaze flicks to his parents. Mr. Bishop dabs his mouth with a napkin. Mrs. Bishop won't look at me.

"As long as Ruby goes to church." Mr. Bishop's posture stiffens, authority rolling off him as easily as breath. "The kids need a spiritual role model."

"Faith is more than attendance." Ethan tosses his napkin onto his plate. "I didn't realize Ruby and I would be the main topic at the table."

"Ruby, you, Ethan, Alyssa, and I should go skiing in the Catskills." Harvey grins, lightening the mood. "Snow'll be good this year."

I exhale, grateful for his ease.

Somehow, we get through the meal, thanks to Harvey steering conversations back to stories about work, football, and memories.

The kids scatter from their table, and Poppy runs straight to me and grasps my hand, begging me to join her in the playroom. What a relief!

"After I help clean up—"

"It's okay." Ethan's voice dips with understanding only he has. "Go with them."

And I do. The girls want Barbie fashion shows. Asher wants nothing to do with it. But he likes role-play, just not with dolls.

"I've got another idea." I squeeze into a chair too small for me. "Blocks. We'll build a school."

That perks them all up. Soon, jumbo blocks fill the room, toy cars lining up to "drop off" stuffed animals at class. Asher takes the teacher role. The rest of us and the stuffed animals become the students. He smacks a block like a chalkboard, and the girls dissolve into giggles when he makes the stuffies misbehave.

Their laughter swallows the hum of voices and clatter of dishes from the kitchen. Eventually, even that fades, replaced by soft holiday music.

Then hushed voices drift through the vent on the wall beside us.

"What happened to being a florist?" The deep timbre sounds like Ethan's dad.

I sit still, my hand clinging to the stuffed elephant.

A low voice in response is probably Ethan's, though I can't catch the words.

"Do you even know her testimony?" Mr. Bishop speaks again. "She only went to church back then because of you."

"You have no idea what she's been through!" Ethan's voice rises this time.

My chest tightens.

"Honey, what your dad is saying... She's broken. Do you even know why she was in rehab?" Concern carries in his mom's voice. "The children need someone stable. You have to think about them."

"Ruby is not broken," Ethan insists. "If anything, we broke her by expecting perfection, looking at her with disapproval, judgment. You were all cold toward her today. She sat through it and your questions like she was on trial."

"Ethan!" Mr. Bishop snaps. "You're blinded by nostalgia."

"No, sir. I'm not blinded. I see her more clearly than I ever have. And you? You're still judging her."

"Ethan, honey—"

"No!" He cuts off his mom. "I don't need your opinions. You either support me with Ruby or don't say anything."

"Someone's yelling!" one of the girls says, wide-eyed.

"Music class time." I scramble to my feet and snatch the toy piano, pressing keys at random. "Let's do school band!"

They take turns pounding the keys, the noise drowning out the argument.

It'll be awkward if I don't leave after this. Even if dessert hasn't been served yet, Thanksgiving dinner is over, and I've lingered long enough.

I did better than I expected. I'd prayed every day since Ethan's invitation, and each time I replayed his *God's Masterpiece* series on my phone, I felt more at peace about seeing his family.

Here I am—bruised, not broken. The messages repeat in my head, threading with the lyrics of "I Am," one of my new favorite songs. I'm reminded I belong to God. I'm His. No one can strip that away—not my past, not my circumstances, and not his parents.

"Hey, guys!" Ethan steps into the playroom. His smile, though it reveals his dimple, doesn't quite meet his eyes.

The kids invite him to join us, but he asks if they want dessert instead.

"Pumpkin pie!" shouts Poppy.

"Chocolate pie!" says one of the cousins, and they drop everything and scatter off.

I stand and cross to him. "You look like you've been hit by a truck."

He pulls me close, and I sink into his chest, feel the ragged rise and fall of his breathing.

"Are you okay?" I ask.

"I am now."

We hold each other in the quiet, music playing in the background. Then I scoot back. "Thank you for having me. I'm gonna head out, okay?"

"I'll go with you. I need air."

"Ethan." My gaze lifts to his. He seems serious about this. "You shouldn't leave your company."

"Harvey, as well as Charlotte's family, are staying the night. They'll keep an eye on the kids." He cups my face, his eyes softening, though sadness lingers. "You didn't have to stay this long. But you did. Thank you."

I shrug, and my lips press tight in something that might pass for a smile. "I loved spending time with you and the kids." Harvey, too, when he's himself, but his parents? That's another story.

After I say goodbye to everyone, I can almost feel their relief. Ethan tells them he'll be back soon, though he doesn't look at his parents when he says it. "If I come back when some of you are gone, I'll see you next time."

Minutes later, we're parked in my truck down the dirt road. I'd let him drive, preferring to let my nerves settle first. The heater hums low, and a half-open bag of candy corn rests on the console between us.

I pop a handful into my mouth, then laugh. "I can't believe you snuck out with a bag of candy corn."

"Best way to work off frustration without saying something I'd regret." All the candy in his mouth muffles his words.

"Not the worst idea."

Silence rests, broken only by the candy bag crinkling, our hands brushing as we reach for more.

"Sorry I was terrible company today." He shifts in his seat, and his pinkie hooks mine.

"You were the host. I didn't expect you to entertain me. I did just fine."

"I thought my parents would be better." His jaw hardens, and he tightens the link between our fingers in a pinkie-swear apology that takes me back decades. "Turns out, they're worse. I never should've put you through that. You barely ate."

"Your mom still makes a mean sweet potato casserole." I try for lightheartedness, not sure how to express that I'd choose him again, even here, even now. But... I free my finger to pluck another candy from the bag. "Your parents were right about one thing. I *am* unstable. And you do have to think about your kids."

His head jerks up, brows slashing together. "Ruby, you heard?"

"The playroom vent."

He buries his face in his palm. I reach over, pull his hand down, and thread my fingers through his. "Ethan, I didn't expect any less from your parents."

"You heard all that, and you still sat there, still entertained the kids?"

"I'm okay." I rub my thumb across the back of his hand. "After you assured me I didn't lose my salvation and God hadn't given up on me all those years while I shoved Him aside, I had a new hope and excitement to seek Him. Your sermons are good." My throat tightens, but I push through. "That *Masterpiece* message? It came to mind today. I don't have to worry about what they think. Not when God sees me differently. Not when you see me differently."

His dimple breaks loose, and his eyes glow with something fierce and tender. He reaches for me, and I lean over, meeting him in the middle. The console presses between us, but his arms draw me close anyway.

"Welcome home." He slides a hand to the back of my neck, our foreheads touching. The cab feels warmer, and I'm glad I shrugged out of my coat before we got in.

"We're in a truck on a dirt road, not home." My tease is a squeak.

"Wherever you are feels like home." His lips brush mine, his breath ragged. "I missed you so much."

The way he exhales it, like it's half a confession, half a prayer, makes my chest ache.

"I missed you too."

Now, the cab is ten degrees hotter, my blood heating my hammering heart.

"I love you, Ruby. And I won't let anything—or any-one—come between us again."

"I love you—" My words vanish when his mouth claims mine, slow and certain. A half sob breaks from me as I kiss him back with everything left in me. My wild heart might burst from being in his arms, from hearing the promise I long ached for.

I'm no outsider here. With Ethan, I'm home.

CHAPTER 27

Ethan

My favorite place to be is wherever Ruby is. Last night proved it again. We lingered on the dirt road to Chuck's house, talking about nothing and everything until she drove me back at eight and I kissed her good night. She followed me into my dreams, then into my waking thoughts this morning. I won't admit what kind of dream it was, but my prayers this morning had to be... thorough.

With our houseguests still present, I head downstairs to catch up with my brother, my sister-in-law, and her husband. Still, I can't stop wishing Ruby was with us.

The second Charlotte's family pulls away, Harvey claps me on the shoulder. "If it's okay, I'll stay another night. Gives me extra time with the kids. You and Ruby deserve a date after yesterday's disaster."

The warmth from his hand reaches right into my chest. "Afraid you don't have to twist my arm on that one."

So Ruby and I visit the Meadowbrook Bistro, then tuck ourselves into the theater's back row. Previews flicker across the screen, and popcorn scents the air. I squeeze her hand. "Sure you don't want popcorn?"

"Unless you want me rolling down the aisle like a buttered bowling ball, I'd better pass." Her shoulder nudges mine. "But since you've asked three times, maybe *you're* craving it."

"If you hit the floor, I promise I'll catch you. Though probably *after* I finish the bucket."

Her laugh rings out like a chord that loosens every tight string in me.

"Wait. I know that actor!" She points at the screen. She reaches for her bag tucked beside her, but I snag her hand back to me.

"Practice staying put before the movie starts."

"But I have to know." She wrinkles her nose, face luminous under the overhead lights. "I can't even remember what the commercial was about."

"Don't rewrite the story in your head. They've managed just fine without your edits for decades."

Her hand slips free. She wiggles her fingers into my side and laughs when I flinch at her tickling. "That's what you get for—"

"Bad mistake, Ruby Morrison." I haul her back against me and launch a counterattack. Far more ticklish than I am, she squeals and squirms, swatting at me between laughs.

"Stop! We're getting loud."

"You started it." My words choppy with laughter, I pull her close again. She's breathless, her hair soft against my lips when I kiss the top of her head. She smells like... Ruby.

"Pastor?"

We jerk apart so fast that my wrist smacks the armrest. Ruby fumbles her purse from the floor to her lap as I straighten in my seat. Of all people, Mary Beth is standing in the row before us, a soda cup in one hand, scarf wound thick around her neck. She arches a brow like she's caught us sneaking into an R-rated flick instead of *A Christmas Carol.*

"Mary Beth." My voice cracks, and I find a polite smile. "This is—"

"Ruby. How could I not know her?"

"Hi." Ruby waggles up a wave.

I lace my fingers to keep from fidgeting.

"Haven't seen you at church since your fall." Mary Beth's tone is cooler than the condensation gilding her cup. "But it seems your presence in town has been... growing."

"I gave up on the popcorn line." Another woman slides in beside Mary Beth. She falters midword when her gaze rises to mine. Recognition softens into a slow smile. "Hello, Pastor."

"Hi."

The lights dim and cloak us in merciful darkness, cutting off the small talk.

The movie rolls. Despite the women in front of us and the other moviegoers further down their row, ours stretches along nearly empty. At the far end on our right are two figures I take for strangers. Otherwise, it's only Ruby and me.

I pivot to her. The screen's glow paints her face in soft light. I reach for her hand and brush a kiss across her fingertips.

Her breath grazes my ear as she leans close, and her whisper sends warmth skittering through me. "You're going to be in trouble."

"With you, it's always worth getting caught."

My reply makes her shiver, and I grin.

A couple of heads turn in front of us, and we break apart, focusing on the screen like model moviegoers. But my peripheral catches Ruby's hand covering her mouth to hold in a laugh.

I shift on the armrest until my hand brushes hers. Then I let my fingers wander to thread with hers. Stealing touches in the dark feels reckless, yet thrilling. And we pull apart whenever one of the ladies shifts or glances back.

Halfway through, the film fades to background noise. I can't track the plot, not with Ruby's warmth seeping into me, her presence louder than the surround sound. And still, part of my mind spirals. How do I broach dating her again? Do I make a formal announcement at church? Or wait until we're engaged? With Maddie, it was all rushed—my parents eager, our ring chosen, our marriage more circumstance than choice. If I'd had to walk into a jewelry store myself, I'd have gotten cold feet.

The credits creep closer. I lean in to whisper. "Want to slip out before we're cornered?"

Her lips curve, eyes gleaming in the flickering light. "Lead the way, Pastor."

We rise just as the lights blaze on.

"That was so unexpected." Ruby bumps into me while we walk down the carpeted hall. Across the way, another theater plays the same movie to split the crowd.

"Life with you is always unexpected." I tuck her against my side and kiss the top of her head. Then we step out into the night, the evening brimming with possibilities.

Ethan

Thanksgiving weekend stretches lazily. With their basketball canceled for the holiday, the kids dart between houses on the lane this morning. Squealing and laughing, they chase one another.

Harvey left an hour ago, just before we walked over to Jason and Valentina's house. As the kids streak in and out of the back porch, the rest of us sink into Adirondack chairs and cradle mugs of coffee and spiced cider. The air is crisp, but heat radiates from the gas firepit at the table's center.

Normally, we'd be sweating through a two-on-two basketball game. But with Liam still away until tomorrow, it's just as well. I doubt I'd have kept my head in the game anyway. Not with Ruby here. Valentina invited her this time, which saved me from finding an excuse to visit her.

"Hope you guys are hungry." Valentina carries over a tray piled high with breakfast burritos. The smell hints at the green chili she's tucked inside. "Now that the kids are fed, the adults can eat in peace."

"That beats the turkey hangover." Russ salutes with his steaming cup.

Jason rises to take the tray, brushing a kiss against his wife's cheek. "Shouldn't you be feeding these yahoos leftover turkey? We should save this good food for after they're gone."

Valentina arches her brow. Lips curving up, she hands him the tray. "I won't because you're tired of turkey too."

Such love sparks between them. That kind of adoration makes the rest of us fade to the edges for a beat. The back door slides open. Ruby emerges, and morning sunlight tints her hair with a golden hue. I set my cup on the table and stand as she approaches carrying a bowl with peeled oranges, pomegranate seeds, and pear slices.

"Val thought we'd need something sweet." Her gaze collides with mine, and the air spikes twenty degrees hotter.

When I reach for the bowl, our hands brush. Heat streaks up my arm and burns into my cheeks. Then she smiles just for me, and my world tilts off its axis, dissolving any noise until there's only her.

"Thank you." My voice breaks the way it used to when I was sixteen and head over heels for her.

"Val did all the cooking." She crinkles her nose.

The women settle into chairs, and Ruby slips onto the seat beside me. Plates fill, and steam rises from the burritos we unwrap. At the first bite, my tongue tingles with chili heat, soothed by the sweet citrus Ruby brought.

Conversation flows as Russ shares his failed attempt to deep-fry the turkey at his parents' house.

"At least you didn't have to explain to your aunt why her entire kitchen smelled like burned pumpkin bread." Ruby wipes her mouth. "This sort of thing happens even when you're a pro at cooking. I nearly smoked us out one Thanksgiving in my attempt to be useful."

Valentina perks up. "That was you too? Brooklyn kitchens must be cursed. I set off the smoke alarm with rice I've made a dozen times. Never once burned it until then."

Ruby's eyes light. "Maybe it's a Brooklyn thing. We don't burn bridges, just food."

"Okay, let's not blame bad cooking skills on the kitchen, ladies." Jason lifts his burrito to take a bite, but Valentina snatches it away.

Laughter spills free from all of us, and Russ even has to spit cider back into his cup with a choke. Best of all? Ruby's shoulders relax as she beams. She might as well have sat in my friends' company a hundred times before.

Conversation drifts between bites, the fire crackling low between us. Russ groans about the box of tangled Christmas lights awaiting him at an elderly church member's house. "Your job was a breeze compared to the homes Jason and I tackled."

Ruby cranes past me. "I can help."

"Aha, someone who feels sorry about my dilemma!" Russ shoots me a look, glowering for effect.

When Ruby's hand brushes mine and she asks if I'll join too, I can't resist. Before long, we're all roped into helping Russ string Amber's lights.

Which sets the tone for the holidays as we head to the tree lighting ceremony on Tuesday.

The scent of kettle corn and roasted chestnuts drifts from the food stalls. Kids run past with candy canes, and hot cocoa sloshes in their mittened hands. A choir gathers on the courthouse steps, their voices carrying carols across the square.

Poppy slips her hand into Ruby's as we stand among the crowd. Beside me, Asher tears into his cotton candy. The choir pauses, and the giant tree blazes to life. I peek at my kids' reactions, and my chest pinches at how natural they look while Ruby bends to listen as Poppy points and Asher beams in the glow.

Catching my eye, Asher spreads his arms wide. "Can we get a tree this big?"

The artificial one at home is ten times smaller. I gave up on pine needles years ago.

"It's Pastor Ethan and the piano teacher." Whispers emerge from somewhere behind us, maybe to the side.

I don't care. Poppy longs for a mom. So does Asher. Besides, I'm just as gone on Ruby as they are.

Maybe it's only the holiday haze, but I can't picture the season without her wrapped up in it, big bow and all.

Ethan

The following week, our usual decorator strings up lights on the lane. Now, the place glows when the kids crowd into our living room for group piano lessons. My two are more interested in their friends than the scales, but I don't mind. The whole point of this is Ruby. The guys and I lounge around, cheering as the kids fumble through "Jingle Bells."

But the lesson time isn't enough time for my kids to see Ruby. So we begin stopping by Sips and Scripts after I get the kids from school.

Today, they talked her into helping us decorate a Christmas tree.

"You don't have to be passive like me," I whisper in her ear. "You can say no to them."

"But I want to decorate a Christmas tree—a *real* tree." Her brown eyes glow. She shrugs, her smile sweet. "I never had one before."

Yep, she genuinely wants to.

"A real tree, huh?" I'm in no position to say no. Apparently, my prelit and flocked beauty will stay boxed in the garage this year. I pull out my phone and bring up a search. "Seems I've heard of a tree farm around here."

After her shift, we pile into the 4Runner, drive to the tree farm, and come home with pine needles clinging to our coats. We string lights, hang ornaments, then eat pizza and drink hot cocoa as we end the night curled on the sofa watching *Rudolph*.

On Friday, music is again forgotten when my kids crowd around Ruby to champion baking cookies with friends instead. She ruffles Asher's hair, then straightens Poppy's pigtails. "I didn't bring any flour, guys."

"We have flour at the house!" Jason's twins chime in.

Minutes later, the kitchen is alive. Carols humming from the radio, counters dusted white, the air thick with sugar and cinnamon. Ruby and Valentina bake with the kids, while us guys lean against the counter, shameless taste-testers. Jason's teen daughter knows what she's doing, but the other kids turn gingerbread into comic disasters.

"Careful with that gingerbread man." Ruby guides one of the boys. "He's one broken leg away from being a snowman."

The kids roar with laughter, proud of their crooked creations as they settle around the table to eat what they baked.

Valentina lifts the lid on a box of gingerbread houses, and chaos bursts loose. Powdered sugar fogs the air. Candy bowls tip. Gumdrops disappear into mouths quicker than they stick to rooftops. Ruby and Valentina trade a look, laughter spilling between them.

Valentina wipes the twins' sticky fingers. "Who knew architecture required this much patience?"

"Good thing we're not building the town hall." Ruby rolls her eyes.

Standing there, laughing with Valentina, and making the kids shriek with joy... Yep, Ruby belongs here. *With us.*

When the last roof stands, the kids bolt for the basement, and the house quiets. Just six of us remain—Ruby and me, Jason and Valentina, Russ and Liam. We gather around the table, the evening's endeavors still sweetening the air.

Liam holds up a hand, green eyes gleaming. "You still have that game... Blurt?"

"Yeah." I nod toward the living room shelf stacked with board games and old books.

"There's enough of us to team up." He rubs his hands together in a let's-get-at-it gesture. "Teams of three. Me, Ethan, Ruby versus Jason, Valentina, Russ. Losers handle cleanup."

"Better get used to dish duty, buddy." Jason smirks.

The game kicks off. Ruby nails the first answer, slaps my palm, and shimmies a victory dance. "Great teamwork, Ethan."

"Not bad for a rookie," I fire back, and Russ groans like we've already clinched the game.

The round heats, answers fly, and ridiculous questions spark laughter.

When we tally the final scores, Ruby clears her throat, mock serious. "Team Jason, Valentina, Russ... winners. Team Ethan, Liam, Ruby..." She lets the pause drag. "Dish duty."

Jason throws his arms up in victory while Russ struts as if he won MVP.

Liam grunts. "Man, we had it."

I shake my head, stretching back. "So much for your game plan, Liam. Now we're stuck with cleanup."

Ruby bumps her shoulder into mine. "At least we'll make a good dishwashing team."

And honestly? I don't mind losing. Not when it means standing shoulder to shoulder with her at the sink, suds and laughter turning losing into the best part of the night. But with losing on my mind, all I can think of is whether or not my relationship with Ruby has at last ended its decade-plus losing streak.

CHAPTER 28

Ruby

December rushes past in a blur of piano lessons and rehearsals. Most of my days consist of preparing the kids for their concert at Skypoint. Group lessons take longer, but they've helped the kids learn familiar Christmas songs, alternating with them singing as I play. In between, Ethan and I steal moments to rehearse our song—or songs. When we get into music, we can't help but sing more. Sometimes with the kids as our eager audience, sometimes with their voices blending into ours if they recognize a tune.

Whether I'm teaching piano at his house or not, I haven't gone a single day without seeing Ethan and the kids. He stops by the shop before school, and I slip them pastries with hugs. Sometimes they drop by again after he gets them from school to say good night.

The concert falls on the day before Christmas break. Just one week left until Christmas. I used to enjoy white Christmases. But twelve years ago, snow lost its charm. This year, we've only gotten flurries and a hazy sky.

Tonight, the residents, their families, and some members from Ethan's church crowd Skypoint's clubroom. I line the kids on the stage's unlit section while the band closes their final song.

"Can I stand in the back?" Poppy whispers as I guide her to the front row, her small frame easy to tuck in the center. "I'm nervous."

"You'll do great, sweetheart." I squeeze her shoulder, my voice low against the blasting music. "Just look at your daddy. He's right in the front row with all his friends, your neighbors."

She nods, and I smile before slipping behind the curtain near the pianist whose hands glide across the keys.

The Skypoint clubroom glistens from the LED candles on the trim and the twinkling Christmas strands looped along the exposed beams. Garlands drape the windows, offering the clean scent of pine.

The final piano notes fade, the guitar trails off, and the drums fall quiet. Applause erupts, a wave that rattles my chest.

We're next. In a brief shuffle, the singers step off the stage, Ethan takes his place at the stand, and I slide onto the piano bench and smooth the song sheets across the stand.

"Isn't Christmas worship so uplifting?" His voice carries warmth through the room, and his dimple deepens, offset by dark hair glistening under the spotlight. He was cute as a teen and youth, but the man he's become is striking in his black blazer and gray shirt, no tie.

"Tonight is a reminder of what God has done for us." He speaks about Jesus's birth, the reason for the season. He thanks God for the Skypoint facility, calling it a place of rest and connection for those trying to get back on their feet. "If God lays it on your heart to give, your gift will be a blessing."

Reverent applause rises from soldiers in uniform. Veterans and some who are not lean on canes or rest in wheelchairs, scars, visible or invisible, etched into their faces. Families sit beside them, shoulders pressed together, combined with the community and church members here for this event.

"And now…" Ethan gestures toward the children, and the stage lights spill over them. "Let's enjoy the music Ruby Morrison prepared with our young stars."

My heart stutters at the way my name slips from his lips. Dozens of small eyes focus on me. I nod, then let my fingers brush the keys. The first note floats out, coaxing, steadily. I sing to guide them, and their voices rise through two verses of "Silent Night," just as we practiced. Then "Joy to the World," a stretch for them, but they push through, not perfect but beautiful.

My chest swells as the last chord fades into thunderous applause. I move to the stage's edge, clapping for the kids, bowing and curtsying so they follow my lead like in our rehearsal.

"Wow!" Ethan's voice booms over the mic, chasing the applause, and I usher the kids offstage.

Willow meets us and steers Asher and Poppy toward her seat while the others find their parents. She squeezes my hand and whispers, "You did amazing."

I mouth, "Thank you."

Then she soft claps for the kids as Ethan continues to talk. "You guys were incredible. So, folks, are you ready for this last session?"

I hover behind the curtain, my heel clicking against the tile, my heart pounding. Was it me singing first or him?

"I was asked to present two songs tonight." He flashes the grin that wins over any crowd. "But you're in for more than just my boring voice and guitar skills."

Laughter ripples through the room, followed by applause.

I freeze. Oops, the piano still has to be moved. I turn around, but Krish Mahato, acting tonight as one of the stage-hands, is already wheeling it into place and locking the pedals before he clips a mic on. Ethan adjusts the wireless mic hooked to his blazer collar, the slim black headset curving along his cheek.

"The last time Ruby sang here," he continues, "was back in October when we were reunited."

What is he going to say? My lungs tighten. I blow out a stream of air, bubbles of nerves bursting in my chest.

"If you haven't heard her sing"—his voice soft-ens—"tonight is your chance."

Applause erupts and draws me forward. My heels click against the stage. Ethan leans in and brushes a kiss to my cheek. His warmth and the faint spice of his cologne curl around me.

"Did I tell you how stunning you look tonight?" he breathes, almost stripping away every last nerve. He must've turned his mic off because the sound doesn't carry beyond us.

"You look handsome too," I whisper back, breathless. He knows I'm unraveling.

I smooth the velvet over my stomach, and my fingers brush the silk belt cinched at my waist. Willow insisted I leave the store with this dress. It hadn't cost a fortune, and I liked that the neckline didn't reveal too much. Plus, I looked good in burgundy. I felt confident.

As I slide onto the piano bench, Ethan bends close until his breath warms my ear. "Don't look at the crowd. Pretend it's just us, the kids, and Willow like before."

My gaze flicks to the front row where Willow and the kids sit. I can start by looking there and over the rest of the heads in the audience. I've done this before, but I always tremble before an audience. Then my hands find the keys.

The audience falls silent. I blow out a breath and glance at Ethan, standing beside me. His smile steadies me, and I'm ready.

I lower my gaze to the sheet. My fingers coax out the first notes.

His mic's audio feed is back on. His voice comes in deep, crisp, and reverent.

My heart wraps around the lyrics. When he finishes the verse, I echo it and focus on Willow and the kids in the front row, Valentina and Jason beside them, the rest of the Renewed Lane crew behind them.

I hardly need the music. I've memorized every line, determined not to stumble. Once I finish, Ethan slides into the chorus. We trade lines, then meet in harmony, our voices weaving together. The room blurs as the ache of each word seeps into me, renewing promises he's whispered in our quiet moments.

I flick my gaze to him, fingers moving along the keys. His voice wavers when his gaze finds mine, eyes glistening, and my own vision blurs. By the final verse, my chest aches from more than nerves.

I draw out the last chords and slow the keys until the notes fade. Ethan rests a hand on the piano. Holding my gaze, he repeats the chorus, this time with no instrumental accompaniment. I join him, harmonizing until the last word lingers between us.

Silence stretches. We stare into each other's eyes. We've said so much in the song that I can hardly breathe.

Then a single clap breaks the stillness, and the applause swells.

I stand, and Ethan sweeps me into his arms. His chest rises and falls against my trembling one. "Every word in that song is meant for you," he whispers.

The lump in my throat chokes off any reply. He eases back and clears his throat. Lights still bright, I blink toward the crowd, wet lashes sweeping away excess moisture. Tissues dab at faces, and people smile through tears, clapping.

"A treat, right?" Ethan says, voice rough.

Willow and Valentina flash thumbs-ups. Poppy and Asher wave wildly, their smiles wide.

"Bravo!" Liam stands, swinging his coat. "Again!"

Ethan grins at the room. "We'll have to save that for our Valentine's event. This next song wasn't part of my original plan. I realized you needed something better tonight."

I start to slip off the stage to give Ethan space for his next song, but his hand catches mine.

"Ruby and I have been practicing 'You Are the Reason,'" he tells the crowd. "But we've also sung so many worship songs together…"

My stomach twists. What is he doing? I need time to compose myself for the last two songs before he has me singing with him again.

"When Ruby sang this one with me, I knew she had to sing it again. If you've ever wanted to be uplifted through music"—he releases that mischievous grin—"she's the one you want leading you in 'Goodness of God.'"

"What?" The word scrapes out of me, half whisper, half growl. My glare says, "Don't you dare."

He only smiles, innocent as ever. "Yes, Ruby Morrison, please sing 'Goodness of God.'" With that, he releases my hand and steps back.

Sliding onto the piano bench, I close my eyes. I need to breathe, to remember what the song means to me. The first time I sang it for Ethan and the kids, his eyes brimmed with tears, his arms locked tight around the kids by the end. That memory steadies me.

By God's grace, the words flow. I don't deserve His goodness, yet He's given it anyway. Another chance to walk with

Him, to live for Him, and maybe, to step into Ethan's world as part of his family.

I'm no CeCe Winans, but I must've done something right before the final note faded. Sniffles now ripple through the crowd, and applause follows.

I move straight into "One Life to Live," weaving in the new lines I'd added about God's gift of life—how we have only one life to live for Him. He's created us for a purpose, and it's His. Then I close with the chorus and urge the audience to echo me. Their voices rise and fill the room.

To end on a joyous note, we all sing "We Wish You a Merry Christmas." Laughter and clapping carry us into the transition toward the dining room, where finger foods, fruit punch, hot cocoa, and the kind of warmth that makes this night a celebration await.

"Ruby, you're the bestest singer ever." Poppy throws her arms around me once Willow brings them into the dining area.

"So are you, sweetheart." I hug her tight.

"I've never heard a voice that beautiful." Asher pipes up through a mouthful of cookie.

"Thank you, Asher." Warmed clear through, I join the others.

Valentina hands out gifts to residents seated at the tables, while Ethan stands by the Christmas tree, deep in conversation with a small group.

"Oh, my darling Ruby." Nessa sets a bag on the table and enfolds me in her arms. "You are so talented."

"Thank you, Nessa." I don't feel as talented as she makes me sound, but her kindness buoys me. She touches my cheek with motherly affection. "And Ethan—his voice has never sounded better than alongside yours. What a duo." Her wink says she knows more than she lets on.

Willow and the kids chat with residents at the next table. Nessa hands me gift bags, and I make my way around the room, greeting people and passing them out. Each one contains a small Bible, a devotional, a scarf and gloves, and some homemade cookies from the church members.

Again and again, people voice their appreciation. "That duet was beautiful."

"'Goodness of God' gave me chills."

"Don't stop singing together."

I'm not sure what to do with such undeserved praise, but their joyful expressions bless me.

"You two sounded like you've been singing together forever," says a veteran leaning on a prosthetic leg. I'd heard his story earlier. He'd lost it in service. His smile widens as he clasps my hand. "He made the song sound better."

"The way he looked at you..." A young woman sighs at the same table, her eyes shadowed. "It's obvious he's not single anymore."

At her bluntness, heat rushes to my face. I don't know her story, but I'm glad she's here, surrounded by support tonight.

When I circle back to Ethan, he's fielding the question from several people—what exactly we are.

"Ruby and I have known each other a long time." He catches my hand and squeezes it as his gaze finds mine. "I'm so glad she's back in my life."

He says it with such certainty and smiles at me like the rest of the room has vanished. He doesn't need to elaborate. The songs—"You Are the Reason," "Goodness of God," and "One Life to Live"—twine around my heart. All three voice everything I hope to believe in for our future. Dare I?

CHAPTER 29

Ruby

Two days after the concert, life should feel normal again, but Willow insisted on giving me the day off so I could take the kids Christmas shopping for their dad. With school on break and everyone distracted, I also suspended piano lessons until the new year.

"How do I look?" I lift my hands, earrings brushing my cheeks as I turn in front of Willow at the counter.

"Overdressed for shopping with kids," she teases.

"Leggings and a sweater, seriously?"

She slides over the box of treats I packed for Ethan and the kids. "You could've skipped the lip gloss. Ethan will love you either way."

"I didn't dress for Ethan." I wave the box of treats at her, unable to contain my smile. The shop is quiet this morning, though Christmas hums in the air. Lights dress the windows, carols play, and we even squeezed in a tree after moving the kids' play table aside.

"You'd better go before I change my mind." Willow waves me off.

"Thank you again."

At Ethan's, the front door bursts open before I step out of my vehicle.

"They've been counting the minutes," Ethan calls as Poppy and Asher barrel into me. Their arms nearly knock me off-balance.

"I brought you some treats in the truck." I squeeze them tight in a group embrace. "But your daddy needs some too."

They scramble for the truck, Asher dashing to the passenger seat, but when I lean into Ethan, he calls Asher back. "We gotta get your booster seats set up, buddy." Then he grips my upper arms. "Thanks for hanging out with them today."

"Sorry we left you out." I wink.

"They wanted you all to themselves. There's a spare house key in the birdbath's base, in case you return while I'm visiting the church members in the hospital."

I already wrapped presents for him and the kids, now under the apartment tree. Thankfully, Asher dropped hints about what his dad wanted. I can only hope he'll like it.

After pastries and cocoa at the kitchen table, we pile into my vehicle. Instead of a specialty store in town, we head to the country store where rows of shelves offer affordable, quirky gifts. The perfect place for kids to hunt for treasures.

The kids clutch their dollar bills, eyes dimming each time a price tag is too high. I promise to cover the rest, but before long, Poppy's dragging her feet.

Once the salesclerk tucks our purchases into cloth totes, I toggle Poppy's droopy pigtails. "Let's get some ice cream."

That perks her up, so we make a stop at the ice-cream shop. We laugh over stories of our best Christmases while we eat. Halfway through her cone, Poppy presses a hand to her stomach.

"Too much sugar?" I tease and suggest she tries to use the bathroom. I hope she's not getting diarrhea.

She comes back shaking her head. "I don't need to go."

"I think she ate too fast." Asher chomps his cone as if demonstrating how to eat too fast.

Poppy lays her head on the table, and ice cream drips down the side of her cone.

I touch her forehead. No fever. "You okay, sweetheart?"

"I don't feel so good."

I'd best get them back home, so I usher them along.

After knocking on Ethan's front door several times to no answer, I unlock it with the spare key. Asher begs to play outside, but I shake my head. "Why don't you stay nearby until we're sure your sister is all right?"

Poppy wants to lie down, but with her skin slightly pale, I don't dare send her off to her room. "How about you sleep on the sofa where I can keep an eye on you?" Once Poppy nestles under a throw on the sofa, her small body curled into a ball and unsettling my heart, Asher and I stow away the gifts.

Then he bounces from foot to foot in front of me. "Would you play UNO?"

I nod. "What a perfect idea." Soon, he returns with the cards from the bookshelf. About to sit with him, I pause. "Do you know where I can find a bucket?"

His tongue sneaks between his lips while he attempts to shuffle, the stack of cards massive in his small hands. "Um, there's one in the garage."

"I'll shuffle after I grab it." I start for the garage. It's just a matter of precaution since stomachaches can lead to throwing up.

"Ruby..." Poppy's weak voice snaps my head up as I return, bucket in hand. She clutches her stomach, her face even paler. I rush to her just in time, and she leans over and retches into the bucket. The stench replaces the room's crisp pine scent.

"Asher, water, please." My heart clenches as I hold her pigtails, murmuring apologies while her small body heaves again. When she's done, trembling, I give her the water to rinse and place the back of my hand on her forehead. She doesn't feel hot, so I tilt her back to lie down. "It's okay, sweetheart. I've got you."

"Is Poppy going to be okay?" Asher's brows knot.

"She will." I wipe her tears, then spread the throw blanket up to her chin.

"Daddy prays for us when we're sick." Asher crowds in beside us. "Can you pray for her?"

"Of course."

He lowers himself by the sofa and slips his hand into mine, the other resting on his sister's knee. I pray for words I hope can reach God's heart.

"Amen," Asher echoes.

I carry the bucket and toss the vomit into the toilet, but I barely make it back before she's gagging. She slides off the sofa, her timing impeccable.

"I want Daddy," she whimpers after throwing up again.

"I know, love." I wipe her mouth with a tissue. I've barely had a moment to call her dad.

Once I ease her back on the sofa, I snag my phone from the purse I tossed on the floor and dial Ethan.

He answers on the third ring.

"Sorry, Stacey's infusion ran long—"

"It's Poppy."

He gasps. "Is she okay?"

"She's been throwing up. No fever."

"Probably a stomach bug. I'll be home right away."

She vomits again. I just hold her, letting her cling to my neck the way I'd want to if I were a child. Then I notice—

"She's warm." I send Asher for a thermometer. Soon, I'm frowning at the reading—99.7. "Sorry, Asher. Any chance you can help me with a wet washcloth?"

He scampers off and returns with one dripping. I have to squeeze out more water. "Thanks, bud."

I press the cool cloth to her forehead, whispering reassurances, braver than I feel.

To distract Asher, I ask him to pick a cartoon. We kneel by the sofa, the screen flickering while I keep one hand on Poppy.

The door jerks open and slams closed.

Ethan's steps thunder across the floor, and he rushes to kneel beside us. Lines crinkle his forehead. "Oh, Peanut." He brushes her hair back. "What's wrong, honey?"

"I don't feel so good," she whispers against me.

"I took her temp," I tell him. "I've kept a cool cloth on her."

"Ruby and I prayed," Asher adds.

Ethan ruffles the boy's hair. "Thanks, buddy." His gaze meets mine over Asher's head. "Thank you for being here. I'm sorry I wasn't sooner."

"Asher's been very helpful."

Poppy shifts on my lap, her weight pressing into me.

Ethan gives her the kids' acetaminophen, but she throws it right back up. He runs a bath and then carries her upstairs.

I stay with Asher and play the card game until Ethan returns, relaxed now. "She's asking for you."

Pale but waiting upstairs, Poppy is tucked under her girlie bedding. Smiley elephants and unicorns—all in frilly circus attire—appear too chipper around her wan face. I slide a unicorn book from her shelf, settle beside her, and read aloud until her breathing evens and her little body relaxes.

The afternoon slips by as Ethan and I trade off—one of us tending Poppy, the other hanging out with Asher. Dinner comes and goes. Somehow, I'm still here, saying goodnight prayers with the kids before Ethan takes Asher to his room. I'm saying good night to Poppy when Ethan returns.

"Can you stay the night?" Her hot hand clings to mine.

How can I say no to a sick child? I glance at Ethan.

His jaw works, lips parting. "Peanut..." He pets the top of her head, her curls released from their pigtails since her bath. "She'll stay a little longer, but not all night."

Her lips tremble into a pout, but she doesn't argue.

Still, she doesn't sleep. She throws up again, this time in her bed, and Ethan and I strip the sheets and remake it. Every time I inch toward the door, she pleads with tearful eyes for me to stay.

"You go to bed," I tell Ethan. "I'll sit with her."

He shakes his head. "I'll stay too, in case she asks for me."

Later, I run a load of laundry. When I return, he's asleep on the shaggy unicorn rug. Smiling, I fetch a blanket from the linen closet and drape it over him. At last, Poppy's sleeping too. I press my hands on her forehead. Good, it's cool beneath my hand.

Something loosens in my chest. If I leave and she wakes, she'll only rouse Ethan. So I lower myself on the rug, lean my head against the bed, and stifle a yawn. A catnap should be enough to get me on the road.

When I open my eyes, light streams through the dreamy-lavender dotted swiss curtains, and a blanket's draped over me.

Ethan's gone.

I hurry downstairs, drawn to the scent of coffee, bacon, and eggs.

"Morning." Ethan lifts his mug, smiling like this is a normal way to wake up. It's cute. But I'm supposed to be at the coffee shop working in—what? I rub my eyes. The stove displays 7:28, and my pulse races like I've been caught.

"I should go." Still, I hover between the hallway and the kitchen.

He sets the mug down. "Eat first."

"I don't eat breakfast."

"Please."

His tone softens me, and I almost smile. Then a knock rattles the door. Ethan crinkles his face before he strides over. Cool air rushes in as he opens it.

"We need your signature," a gravelly voice says. "Been calling since yesterday. No answer."

"My daughter's sick—"

"It's freezing. You gonna let me in?"

My gut twists. Not one of the Renewed Lane crew.

"Uh, sure." Ethan steps aside.

Mary Beth Moore sweeps in. Her gaze darts from him to me, and her eyes widen. She spins, head shaking. "Oh my!"

"Ethan's daughter is sick. I was—helping," I stammer.

Ethan only grips the back of his neck. With his hunched stance projecting guilt, his silence isn't helping.

"Explains why you didn't answer my calls."

Heat crawls up my neck. I can't make this less awkward. Brushing past her, I whisper to Ethan. "I'll pray Poppy feels better."

"Thanks," he murmurs.

"Prayer... *right*," the older woman mumbles under her breath while I open the door.

The cold air slaps me. I step out and close the door behind me.

Ethan's problems just got bigger. Mine too because unease settles deep in my stomach. His reputation is the one at stake. Could this pressure sabotage our relationship?

CHAPTER 30

Ethan

The year always ends faster than I want it to. Emails load my inbox, and half-finished notes for next year's schedule litter my desk. But my mind keeps drifting. I promised I'd meet Ruby for lunch even after Friday's mess with Mary Beth.

Thankfully, before I could sign a thing, Poppy called out, and I went running. Asher had woken up too, and in his blunt way, he told Mary Beth about his sister's illness and Ruby stepping in. Good thing it turned out to be nothing more than a twenty-four-hour bug. Poppy's back to herself, and neither Asher, Ruby, nor I caught it.

Now, I may have to see Ruby on my way home. The kids are hanging out at Liam's house today. I sigh, pull out my phone, and type.

Me: Sorry won't make it in time for lunch. Wish I could.

Her reply buzzes back within seconds.

Ruby: I'll forgive you... if you buy me pie later.

I can't help smiling. That's Ruby, playful when she should be disappointed. I tuck the phone aside, her warm response making the office work less daunting.

From outside my open door, my secretary, Diane, answers the phone. Another line rings before the first one ends.

A soft knock follows, and Valentina peeks her head in. "I'm heading out before Liam and Eden get burned out with all the kids." Her immaculate makeup doesn't obscure her inner glow as she beams. "Seems we're getting a white Christmas after all."

"Don't trust the forecast." I roll my chair sideways to face her. "Tonight's flurries will vanish before Christmas." Yes, it's three days before Christmas, but the forecast indicates mild snow tonight.

"Where's the faith, Pastor?" She wags an accusing finger. "Anything else you need me to tackle before I go?"

"You're watching my kids soon. That's enough help." I sink back in my chair, clicking my pen. "How did counseling go today?"

She slips in just far enough to lean against the doorframe. "Not bad. People struggle more around the holidays. Loneliness hits harder. But sometimes talking it out helps them remember they're not forgotten."

I nod. "We're blessed to have you here."

She smiles, then waves off my gratitude. "See you soon."

When she's gone, I drag my chair back to the screen. Calls to return, emails stacked still unopened, a January agenda glaring from a page. The board of trustees will want numbers—budget reports, outreach plans, a full year of ministries mapped out. Recovery programs, youth nights, mission calendars, and whatnot.

I rub my eyes and dive in, dialing one number while typing notes from the last call, answering emails between rings. The keyboard clatters, and windows stack across my screen as I update the report. Even pushing hard, several minutes vanish before I look up at the clock. I'm still behind. If I'm not careful, dropping by Ruby's is going to make me late picking up the kids. At least, Valentina will understand.

"Well…" Low voices outside snag my attention. Diane again. "He's busy right now."

Good at her job, she fields calls and wards off people when I'm swamped.

"I know. I just wanted to bring—"

That unmistakable voice jolts me out of my chair. I step around the desk and out the door.

"Ruby." Her name slips out like light breaking through.

She jiggles a paper bag. "Brought you lunch."

"Come in." I reach for the bag and inhale the delicious smell wafting my way. Then I beckon her inside. "After you."

I set the bag on the desk, half close the door, and draw her straight into my arms.

"What a sweet surprise." I greet her with a kiss meant to be precise. But the cherry taste of her lip balm lingers, and I can't help kissing her again.

Her arms loop around my neck, pulling me closer, and my composure crashes loose.

A throat clears. A knock rattles the doorframe, and we jolt apart.

"Oh... Diane." I clear my throat.

Just like her mother's would, Diane's eyes widen. But, instead of pure shock, hurt flares their edges. Mary Beth's eyes would be hardening into something more intense. "Wow, Pastor."

I drag a hand over the back of my neck.

Beside me, Ruby covers her mouth.

Diane's shoulders slump. "I see what Mom meant."

"Ruby was just—" I stop when the words register. I shouldn't be surprised that her mom twisted the narrative of what she saw at my house.

The paper bag crumples in Ruby's hands as she busies herself unpacking the food she brought. The scent drifts through the room.

I could tell Diane I'm dating Ruby, but I don't owe her an explanation.

"Anyway..." The word wobbles. I'd better steady my voice. "Did you need something?"

Her lips purse. "The families you'll be praying for on Christmas Eve—thought you'd need the names now."

Seriously? She could've left the folder on my desk anytime. But she waited until Ruby was here?

I bite down on everything I want to say about her coming in to snoop. "You can put them on my desk."

Diane's gaze flicks to Ruby before she retreats. The door clicks shut behind her.

Ruby exhales, then grimaces. "I'm causing you a lot of trouble."

I don't want her worrying about us, so I gather her in my arms. "Come the new year, I'll let everyone know we're together."

"I kind of like sneaking around." She quirks that mischievous grin.

"I'm not sure we're *sneaking*. Half the town knows our little secret."

She smiles, and I'm so undone that I can hardly wait for the world to know we belong together.

Ethan

Hours later, the first snow of the season soon becomes more than flurries as I go over my sermon notes for Christmas Eve in two days.

The kids are already asleep, exhausted after a long day of playing. I move to my office window. Thick flurries plop on the ground. Bedazzling, they dance and drift past the house lights. Two inches pad the ground already. This "gentle snowfall" is shaping into the blizzard of the century.

I should've insisted Ruby stay when she stopped by Valentina's to hang out with the kids. Instead, she drove off as the flurries started.

The wind howls, rattles the panes, and whips the snow into frantic spirals against the glass. Each rioting ice crystal tings or pings the window. Two hours ago, the weather service issued a blizzard warning, including eight to twelve inches, winds up to fifty miles per hour, and near-zero visibility.

Unease taking residence in my heart, I return to my desk and the sermon notes. Ruby's alone in the apartment, the storm raging outside, while Willow's off at a Christmas event in the city.

One of the first things Ruby told me when she opened up about our years apart started haunting me after I sent the kids to bed. Her mom's accident followed the end of our relationship during that long-ago blizzard. The pain in her eyes and her shiver as she spoke won't let me go now.

I lift my head upward. "What do I do, Lord?"

The silence presses back. I rub my jaw, the beard coarse beneath my fingers, as I shape a plan I trust God will honor. If I text and she answers, that will be my cue.

I reach for my phone, pull up her name, and type.

Me: Thinking of you.

Ruby: Hi.

Me: Are you doing okay?

Ruby: Yeah... Why?

Me: Just checking.

Dots appear. Disappear. Then finally—

Ruby: Actually... I'm thinking of calling Brenda. But it's late.

Brenda. Her counselor. Which can only mean one thing. She's terrified and perhaps on the brink of another panic attack. I shiver at the possibility of her being alone when that happens. I type.

Me: Kids and I are coming over.

Ruby: No, Ethan. Don't. Roads are bad.

Me: That's why I have the right car.

When her typing bubble vanishes, I glance at my abandoned sermon notes, then at the window. The snow falls so thick that I struggle to discern the shadowy trees.

I start with Poppy's room. The unicorn night-light Ruby gave her throws soft stars and prancing fantasy horses across the ceiling. Her small chest rises and falls under the covers. I sit on her bed and touch her shoulder.

She stirs, rubbing her eyes, and winces. "Daddy?"

"Yes, Peanut." I brush hair from her forehead. "Grab your pillow and Cloud. We're going out."

"Why?" Her voice is thick with sleep.

"We're having a sleepover with Ruby."

She yawns but nods, clutching her stuffie.

Next, I head for Asher. A light sleeper, he pops his eyes open before I speak. He doesn't ask questions when I tell him where we're headed, just swings his legs out of bed.

With the kids bundled in jackets, hats, and boots, I grab three extra blankets from the closet and tuck them under my arm. We'll need them for the floor. As I let the kids into the car in the garage, the storm rages, but it can't rattle my decision. Ruby's not facing this night alone.

Ethan

About an hour later, the kids are already back asleep. Poppy was curled up in Ruby's bed with Cloud clutched under her chin when I last checked. Asher snuggled into Willow's bed after I layered it with our spare blankets so he wouldn't disturb the sheets.

The drive, usually ten minutes, took twenty-five. Snow blanketed the roads, and the SUV slid once on a hidden patch of ice while the wind shoved against the vehicle like it wanted us back home.

Now, at last, Ruby and I are each wrapped in a blanket on her sofa. The room glows with LED candles flickering on the coffee table, and Christmas lights twinkling on the tree. Their holiday cheer softens the storm's harsh howls outside.

"You brought the kids out in a blizzard..." Ruby studies me, her expression tender. "Because you were worried about me?"

"Probably an adventure for the kids." Her shock undoes me, but I mask it. "When they wake up, they'll be thrilled to be in a new place."

"You didn't have to do that."

I shake my head, rest my hands on my thighs over the blanket. "I kept imagining you here, stuck in that memory."

She leans in and presses a fleeting kiss to my lips. "Thank you. I was trying to be brave, but—"

"Storms are hard."

"Storms are hard," she repeats. Her eyes glisten in the dim light. I fight the urge to pull her into my arms. That will lead to kissing and then what? So, I shift to face the table.

A white book gleams there, its bold title easy to read in the twinkling lights and flickering candles—*Anxiety Shadows: Finding Peace in God's Presence*. Colorful bookmarks bristle from its pages.

I reach for it, flipping a few. "This is the one you quote from?"

She nods. "It's been helpful. I still go back through it. Tonight, I thought I'd revisit a page that..." A sigh interrupts. "Do you ever have days that replay? Moments that come back with Maddie's death?"

My gaze meets hers. She sees right through me, doesn't she? "Regrets, you mean?"

She nods, and I set the book back down, heavier than I picked it up.

"The helplessness. And everything with it." No need to rehash how, during the first three years after Maddie passed, I wore guilt like a second skin.

"Why I'm terrified of storms isn't the storm itself." She hugs her blanket tight around her legs as if she can hold herself together. "It's the guilt. Always questioning if I could've prevented it if she hadn't been on the phone trying to reach me. And then it replays. Over and over. Until I might as well be right back there again."

My chest aches. I steal her hand from her lap and cover it with mine. The scent of mint drifts from her hair as I press a kiss to the crown of her head.

"It's hard for me to go near a lake and see it as another part of God's creation... see beauty." Just because I'm a pastor doesn't mean I'm not prone to struggles. "All I can think of is what happened at one of the many lakes. I had counseling too, but I can't say it took away all the guilt."

"I'm sorry." Her fingers now stroke the back of my hand.

The flickering LED candles and string lights mesmerize me. "Everyone knows Maddie drowned. Except... No one knows it was suicide. Charlotte knew Maddie best. She saw the signs. Of course, she didn't warn me. Maddie's death was ruled an accident, but it wasn't. You see, Maddie already arranged everything with her sister—burial plans and all—like she knew she was going to die."

With the confession stifling, I push out a heavy breath.

Ruby takes my other hand too as I share what I've carried for years. How rarely Maddie and I were home together at the same time. How I let her slip away to her "getaways" without asking what she really needed. How I only recognized the signs after it was too late.

"The worst guilt is our marriage. There were so many gaps, times when the intimacy was gone, and my mind... wandered to you. I wonder if I ever showed her enough love."

Ruby squeezes my hand. "It must have been hard if she wasn't showing you love either. Love has to go both ways."

"Being a pastor, a Christian, I should've known better. I should've gone above and beyond."

"Don't look at what you can't change." She releases my hands and shifts, then cups my face until I turn to her. Her eyes, now fierce in her conviction, blaze with warm golden light that's not mere reflection from the candles. "You're a loving, caring man, Ethan Bishop. I've seen it in the way you express your love for your kids, the way you protect them, the way you"—her voice trembles, sincerity steeped into every word—"the way you love me. Like tonight. You showed up despite the storm, regardless of the hurdles to get the kids here. You showed up for me."

My lips part, but her glassy eyes have me gulping and my throat catching. I can't remember what I was about to say. A silence passes, the storm's howl muffled by the walls, the weight between us easing.

"I love you, Ruby," I whisper. At least, that I can say.

Her candlelit gaze—no, it's a Spirit-lit gaze—seeps into mine, brimming. "I love you... so much." She trails her fingers along my jaw, and my insides melt as the love she looks at me with goes beyond words. "You're here with me in the middle of the storm, and that's what love is—showing up when it matters most."

The words settle deep in my chest, my head almost leaning in, in my gravity, but now, when we are so alone, kissing could lead things astray. So I focus on her words, a sermon series I could start writing next year on love.

Awareness swims between us, and neither of us dares to speak. Then Ruby's hand drops from my face, and I already miss the warmth. She slaps my shoulder, her smile more radiant than the Christmas tree. "Movie marathon?"

I let out a breath, relieved by her lightness. "Your pick."

She reaches for the remote from the basket under the table, flips through a stack of cliché modern Christmas movies, the kind I wouldn't normally endure. But with her beside me, I don't mind. We start watching, and I smile as she scrolls her phone between scenes, looking up the actors. "She's good. Let's add her to our watchlist. Oh, and him too."

We laugh, building a playlist we'll never finish, but the joy is in making it together. My chest expands until my emotions brim too full to hold in.

By the third movie, I'm stifling yawn after yawn. Our hands are clasped. I don't even remember when that happened, and our heads are dipped together, side by side. With her warmth pressed against me, closing my eyes is inevitable.

I flick my gaze open now and then. The TV glows, shadows drifting across my heavy lids. At some point, I rub my eyes. Ruby's weight has settled against my shoulder, her breathing slow and deep. Careful not to wake her, I ease the remote from her lap and click the TV off.

With nowhere else to sleep, I close my eyes. I wake up to morning rays spilling through the slanted blinds. I blink at

Ruby beside me, hair mussed, her face soft and vulnerable in sleep. My smile breaks wide, my heart warm.

I shift, and she stirs, opening her eyes. Recognition warms her features, and she snuggles closer.

"Go back to sleep, sweetheart." I ease her head into the space I vacated, tucking a cushion behind her. "I'm just headed to the bathroom."

"All right." Her voice, husky from the night, rasps. She rubs her eyes. "Maybe we can bake cookies with the kids today."

"I'm sure they won't argue."

I stand and stretch stiff muscles. Beyond the kitchen window, the world lies blanketed in fresh snow, bright and unbroken. A white Christmas, that's what we're getting this year. But Ruby's the best gift the kids and I could have wrapped up in our lives.

That knowledge only grows stronger over the holidays. On Christmas Eve, we drive Ruby back to the house and join our friends on the lane to play in the snow. Up on the hill by Chuck's land, we sled, and Ruby's squeal carries far in the cold air.

The gathering flows into our house—cookies in the oven, group games, Christmas music cheerful in the background. Later, we head to Jason and Valentina's for dinner before the evening service. For the first time since her panic attack at church, Ruby comes with us for the quiet candlelight service. Seeing her seated with my kids and friends, a candle illuminating her soft brown face moves me again in a way I can't describe.

We spend another night curled up with Christmas movies after the service, and I read *The Night before Christmas* to the kids. With the snow still heavy, my parents and brother decide we'll gather sometime before the new year instead. The kids light up when we say good night to Ruby and hear she'll be back in the morning.

More than ever, I'm certain this is where we begin again.

CHAPTER 31

Ethan

Mondays are hard enough for pastors—second-guessing whether Sunday's message landed or something came across awry. Add to that the first Monday of the new year and being summoned by the church elders for an emergency meeting.

I shift in my chair at the head of the table, not the seat I'd have chosen, but when I walked in five minutes before the meeting, it was the only one left. The January wind rattles the windows, an echo of the chill inside as seven elders appraise me like a jury.

Three stern faces suggest I'm the subject of today's agenda. No, four. At least two look friendly. One remains unreadable.

"Thank you for meeting us on such short notice." Helena, sitting at the table's far end, offers a sympathetic smile. Her manner's a warm contrast to some of the others.

"Sure." Not that I had much choice.

"We won't waste time, Pastor." Mary Beth tilts her chin high as though she's chairing a trial instead of a church council. With the folder open in front of her, she has her own agenda written down. "We need to address a matter affecting this congregation's stability."

I fold my hands on the scarred oak table. "I'm listening."

"I'm sure you know what this is about, Ethan." Robert reclines, gray hair shining under the fluorescent lights. He drags his fingers over his beard. Founding families like his carry weight here, and he knows it. "Word travels fast in a town like ours."

My stomach tightens, confirming my suspicion since Mary Beth called about this meeting last night. "If this is about Ruby Morrison—"

"It is." Patricia Doyle, a part-time accountant alongside Mary Beth, flips a page in her notes. They must've had a meeting before summoning me. "I'm obligated to bring up trends. Giving is down. Families are unsettled."

"Three households have said they'll withdraw support if certain... appearances aren't dealt with." Mary Beth jabs a finger into her open folder.

"Appearances," I repeat. The four syllables hang cold between us.

Helena clears her throat. "Pastor, I don't think the issue is you dating." Her tone is softer, sympathetic. "A remarried pastor could ease a lot of pressures, especially from our single women in church competing for your attention."

"But it's *who* you're dating," Robert speaks up.

My hands clench on the tabletop. "What *exactly* is wrong with Ruby?"

"She's not a church member." Mary Beth speaks as if she's in charge of the meeting. "How can a pastor date someone who doesn't even worship with us weekly? She could very well not be a Christian as we know—"

"That's why we have live stream services," Nessa interjects. She's the only one who's been smiling at me all morning. "Most of us saw her music impact those at the Christmas event. One resident told me he felt God's presence in the room when Ruby sang. Another asked for the lyrics to 'Goodness of God' and said it drew her closer to Him and moved her to tears. Ruby loves the Lord. We should trust Ethan's judgment where she's concerned. In fact, we ought to be thanking God that our pastor has found a woman who can share his burdens."

"My daughter witnessed you and this Miss Morrison smothering each other in your office."

"Hold up." I raise a finger to make my point. "It was a kiss with the woman I love. It's called dating."

"Huh!" Mary Beth smirks, enjoying her dominance of the meeting. "You want to tell everyone about the morning I showed up at your house? When she stayed the night?"

"My daughter was sick!" Heat climbs my cheeks. I draw out a breath to compose myself. "Poppy begged her not to leave. She slept in my child's room on the rug."

"Still looks bad," Patricia says. "The Crawley, Henderson, and Thompson families—whom, I might add, together contribute nearly thirty percent of our budget—are threatening to leave."

"So we're equating tithes with truth now?" I shift in my seat. If Mary Beth and Patricia aren't exaggerating, 30 percent could gut programs and salaries. However, my three friends bring in another thirty. Even if Russ isn't consistent in church attendance, he's consistent in giving money.

"Pastor." Robert taps a finger on the table. "We're equating leadership with perception. Where is this Ruby on Sundays? How do we know she's not going around tempting pastors to distract their ministry?"

My chair screeches as I leap to my feet. The urge to rip into someone claws so hard I curl my fists tight. "Ruby has more faith and integrity than half the people gossiping about her."

The room goes dead silent. But my fists hold my attention. I rarely lose my temper. I can't even remember the last time. Except with Harvey. The day he confessed what he'd done to Ruby.

Mary Beth's jaw hangs open. Even the elder who's kept silent all morning looks startled. Across the table, Nessa's kind eyes steady me, and Helena's small nod suggests my outburst is understood.

I drag in a breath, the tension loosening its grip, and my hands go lax at my sides.

"I'm sorry." I exhale. "But I won't sit here while she is maligned. She's cared for my children, filled our home with music, and brought joy back into our lives."

Helena holds up a hand. "He's right. We have no business calling accusations without proof."

I drop back into my chair.

"What happens if more families walk out?" Mary Beth presses. "A pastor's first duty is to protect the flock."

"My duty"—the words drag out from deep inside—"is to shepherd with honesty and love, not to cave to fear."

"Ethan, no one doubts you're a good pastor." John finds his voice, as if he'd been soaking in the arguments. "But unity matters. Can you see why people are uncomfortable?"

"I can see it, especially with all the rumors already circling in the church. But do you think I'd pursue someone who'd sabotage my faith in God?"

Nos and maybes respond.

"Do you believe I love this congregation?"

Agreeable murmurs and nods.

"Then trust me when I say Ruby is not a threat to my ministry. But if you can't trust my judgment or if you believe I'm unfit because of who I love, then maybe you need another pastor."

I hadn't seen that coming, but the words are out there now.

"You're threatening to resign?" Robert's nostrils flare.

"I'm saying I won't be bullied into ending my relationship with Ruby." I press my palms on the table. "But I also don't want to act out of pride. So here's what I'll do. I'll take two weeks away from the pulpit to pray." And fast. "The assistant pastor can step up. If, during those two weeks, you conclude I should step aside, I won't stand in the way."

"You'd risk it all?" Patricia asks, eyes wide and voice shaky.

"I'd risk everything except the truth."

Silence hangs like a storm cloud.

Then Nessa's brown face brightens. She leans forward, lips parting. "That sounds like a man who fears God more than men."

"We'll see how the congregation responds to your absence." Mary Beth snaps her folder shut.

I stand, pushing back my chair. My shaky heart hammers, but my resolve holds steady. "I know God brought Ruby back into my life. I just need to find out why."

Usually, conviction strikes when I've crossed a line. But as I leave the conference room, peace settles over my heart. I don't believe pursuing Ruby is wrong, yet should I fear my love for her has begun to outweigh every voice in opposition, even God's?

Time to fast and seek God's clarity. But that also means stepping back from Ruby, at least for a while. The thought terrifies me, and "God's will be done" feels dangerous. What if His will means Ruby and I aren't meant to be?

Still, God's way is always best. I have to trust Him.

My first stop is Sips and Scripts. Ruby stands behind the counter. Laughing, she hands a customer their drink. Willow's there too, counting bills at the register.

When Ruby notices me, her smile lights up, and my heart sinks over what I need to tell her. I glance toward the book nook. With the holiday lull, the seats are empty.

"You're okay?" Ruby slips her hand into mine before I even realize she's come around the counter.

"Can we talk?" I entwine our fingers, grounding myself.

"Are the kids okay?"

"They're fine. Amber is with them this morning." Ruby met Amber when we helped her hang Christmas lights.

I lead her to the sofa in the sitting area. A single carnation rests in a vase on the table, fragile against the weight of what I'm about to say.

"Are *we* okay?" she asks. Wide eyes search mine.

I exhale. "I had an urgent church meeting this morning."

"Oh no." She bites her lower lip, obviously piecing it together. "I knew that was coming ever since... Mary Beth caught me at your house."

I almost smile. How spot-on she is. "You're right."

"How did it go? Did you... get fired?" Her voice cracks. "Oh, Ethan, I'm so sorry."

"It's okay, sweetheart." I keep my voice steady, careful not to let her spiral. The last thing I want is for her to think this means I'm letting her go.

She nods, but her shoulders stay tense. "What happened?"

"I'm taking a break from teaching at church for a couple of weeks."

"What?" Her head jerks up. "Ethan, I can't be the reason you're not in the pulpit. Your calling—the community needs to hear from you."

"Yes, they do. But I need to hear from God." I lean forward, elbows on my knees. "Even pastors need time to stop and pray. I don't do it often enough. These upcoming two weeks, I want to seek Him without distraction. I'll still be with the kids, but while they're at school, I'll spend that time with the Lord."

She presses her lips together, and her vibrant eyes dim.

"And we'll take a break from piano lessons if that's okay."

"Okay." Her alarmed expression speaks louder than words.

"You and I..." Her shoulders stiffen, and her head ducks as she angles herself further away. She's already bracing for goodbye. "It was all too much. Too fast. Too good to be true."

"Ruby." I cup her face, drawing her eyes to meet mine. "Honey, look at me. I'm not ending things between us."

She nods, but doubt lingers.

"We just need a couple of weeks. A pause to pray and ask God what He wants for us."

Her hands fold together in her lap. "I can understand that. Whatever God decides, I guess... What other choice do I have?"

I brush my thumb over her cheek, her luxuriant skin soft as silk. "I hope what He decides is that I get to keep you. But either way, Ruby, He's the one writing our story. We're going to be okay even if we—"

"Okay." The word breaks from her on a gasp. She blinks, probably pushing back tears, then rises, and slips from my touch.

I stand too, reach for her, and guide her into my arms.

"I don't want to... Why does it feel like a final goodbye?" Her heart pounds hard against mine, but her arms stay stiff before she steps back, carving space between us.

My chest hollows. I stop short of taking her hand, dropping mine to the back of my neck instead.

Lord, the look on her face... It's like I've shattered her all over again. I can't do this.

The same cut slices through me for making her feel the way she does.

"Have a good day." She forces a small smile. "Say hi to the kids for me."

"I will." My throat tightens as she leaves.

Lord, help her believe me that this isn't the end.

Chills course through me.

Please don't confirm otherwise.

CHAPTER 32

Ruby

True to his word, Ethan doesn't contact me over the next week and a half. That's gotta be long enough now that it's Wednesday. Or will he wait until Monday, two *full* weeks, to tell me if he's heard any confirmation from God about us? I wasn't sure if keeping our distance would include texting. Still, out of respect, I haven't reached out, even when everything in me aches whenever my phone lights up with a call or text that isn't his.

I miss him, and I miss the kids. The way they beam and run to me for hugs every time Ethan brings them by. I miss their smiles and innocent yet blunt questions. At least, Valentina keeps me in the loop by dropping in.

On the bright side, this time apart has forced me to stop wallowing and drawn me to lean on God more than anything else.

Besides a few people from church, I've made new friends in town beyond the regular customers who come to the shop.

Amber, though technically Ethan's friend, has become mine too. She's shown up with pies more than once, claiming she "baked too many." Of course, I know better. Then there's her neighbor, Martha. She heard I play piano, and the next thing I know, I'm on the city's payroll for the council chorale. Saturday morning rehearsals work out for my schedule, and the little extra money is enough to get health insurance. My truck insurance will have to wait until March, when things even out, but for the first time in years, I feel steady.

The steadiness motivates me to plug into things like a Bible study with my two friends.

Today, we're in the sitting area for our second Bible study of the year.

"'So do not fear, for I am with you; do not be dismayed'..." Valentina's voice pulls me out of my thoughts as she reads Isaiah 41:10. "'I will strengthen you and help you; I will uphold you with my righteous right hand.'"

"I always need reminders of that verse." Willow shifts on the sofa beside Valentina, her Bible balanced on her lap, palm pressed between the pages to hold her place. She lifts her gaze to me. "Am I reading next?"

I reach for my Bible—Ethan's Christmas gift, along with the citrus perfume I used to wear back then and a necklace with the ring he once bought me, now remade into a pendant for the sterling silver chain. He said a heavy Bible in hand beats scrolling on a phone app. The leather is soft, the smell new, and the pages crisp beneath my fingertips as I flip them. "What was I supposed to read again?"

Valentina checks her study guide. "From Psalm 56."

"Right, verses three and four." I find the page and scan the words I need to hear at the moment. The overhead light illuminates the lines as I read aloud. "'When I am afraid, I put my trust in you'…"

Willow follows with the verse in Philippians about not being anxious. Her voice is steady, almost like she's reading it straight into my heart. While the words sink in, my gaze drops to the table and our untouched platter of cookies. We started right after dinner, and no one's reached for dessert. Outside the window, snow drifts under the streetlamps, and more flurries dance in the air.

"'What does it mean to trust God?'" Valentina reads from the discussion guide.

Tonight's study, "Trusting God when Life Doesn't Make Sense," had to have been the best choice.

"Trust means complete surrender." Willow crosses her ankles and sets her Bible on the table. "But that's hard when life feels upside down." She looks at me across the table and back to Valentina beside her. "That's the point, though, isn't it? Letting go of needing answers."

"Amen to that." I nod, though my chest tightens since Ethan and I are taking a break.

I've yet to know how God speaks to people. I'd probably miss His voice. Especially since I've been so busy dodging the hushed coffee-shop whisperers, the women gossiping about me spending the night at the pastor's house when we weren't married, hinting I might be the reason he stepped down.

Willow confronted a group once. "You're gonna need to find a different place to discuss your book if you're coming here to spread false rumors."

The women had stammered. One muttered an apology. Another fumbled with her book. Their eyes wouldn't meet hers.

I'd wanted to disappear where I stood behind the counter.

"I'm living that test." I now admit my struggle to discern God's voice from all the others. "I can't control what Ethan decides, and I'm trying to trust God and not text Ethan to ask if God's told him anything. I'm hoping God will hold my heart regardless of where Ethan and I end up."

"Exactly." Valentina leans back, her blue sweater simple, but her lips a bold red. She's not the type to step outside without some polish. Her eyes gleam, dancing with amusement. "But you shouldn't worry where you and Ethan are concerned."

"Did he say anything?" I grip my Bible tight enough to make my fingertips slip.

She lets out a soft laugh. "I was wondering when you'd ask about Ethan again."

Heat rushes into my cheeks. "I only wanted to know if he's okay." Maybe what he's thinking too.

"He's out of town."

"Oh." I reopen my Bible in an attempt to hide my disappointment or to remind myself where I'm supposed to be focusing.

"He's taking this prayer break seriously, Ruby," Valentina adds. "He's at the Long Island house. His kids have been with us for the last two days."

"That's good." My voice wobbles free. I wince at the shaky sound, then straighten my shoulders. When I raise my head, Willow is watching me, her knowing smile says she's reading every thought.

Interesting how Valentina didn't call the Long Island house hers and Jason's, like Ethan once did. He said all the families on Renewed Lane use it as a retreat for shared group getaways or private personal time.

"Like Ethan said…" Willow arches a brow, all understanding. "He's praying. You've been praying. That's good for both of you. Your health and your relationship with God come first. If Ethan comes back and decides love isn't an option, you'll make it through because you're grounded in God."

"Willow's right." Valentina's voice softens. She reaches across the table to touch my knee. "We want to ensure you don't spiral into another panic attack."

A laugh bursts out before I can stop it, the sound too loud, too raw. "I can't believe I'm sitting across from two shrinks. My two best friends, no less. How odd is that?"

"See what I mean?" Valentina tosses her chin higher, her ponytail swinging as she shakes it. "God doesn't make mistakes."

"Meaning giving you friends who are shrinks." Willow smirks.

We conclude the night with prayer. Carrying God's peace with me, I get through the rest of the week. With no piano lessons on Wednesdays and Fridays—Ethan's neighbors all paused theirs since he stepped back and they want their kids to stay on the same level—the break has given me space to organize my calendar so nothing slips through.

Now, leaving Saturday's council chorale rehearsal at City Hall, I step into the freezing air with music still buzzing in my blood. The chill bites through my coat, and I hurry to cross the road. My breath fogs white, leaving me relieved to climb into my truck.

I fire the engine and crank up the heat. My phone buzzes against the dash. "Probably forgot my scarf inside." Did I even bring a scarf today?

As I reach for the phone, *his* name sends warmth radiating through me. My fingers tremble to swipe the message open.

Ethan: I miss you.

A sharp ache jabs my chest. I type too fast.

Me: I mis u 2.

I hit send before seeing the typo I can't fix. The dots appear again, and the slipup no longer matters. Then a message dings.

Ethan: I know you still have reservations about coming to church since the last episode. But any chance you can come tomorrow?

I type the words *Is everything okay?* I delete them and type again.

Me: Okay. Just be prepared if I pass out.

A smiley face pops up.

I stare at the screen, waiting, needing more. Something. Anything. My hands itch to type the needy words: *Do you love me?* Somehow, I hold back.

Me: Are you teaching tomorrow?

Ethan: I know I left you hanging with that last emoji. This time, it's not a series, just a one-off message before we start the new one next month.

My breath whooshes out, and my whole body slumps into my seat. He's not fired!

Ethan: They asked me back this Sunday to teach, so I had to prepare a lesson.

Me: Okay. See you tomorrow.

Ethan: I can't wait.

Dare I send the words *I love you*? Too much? Too soon? Why hasn't he said it? Why'd he text instead of call? Has he not missed me like I've missed him? Is he easing me into the friend zone? Did God tell him something I don't know yet?

My thoughts spiral as I leave the lot. But my chest doesn't lock up the way it used to. No racing heart. No need for breathing exercises. That has to mean something.

Still, my stomach knots. Tomorrow's gonna be a storm I can't predict.

I shove the worry deep as I turn into the apartment lot. The last thing I need is another episode in church.

Ruby

Who am I? A child of God. A servant of the Most High. No matter what today brings, His love won't waver, and His arms will carry me through. I remind myself of that truth while dressing—wide-leg lounge pants, burnt orange, knotted high at the waist. The cream silk blouse I tuck in shimmers beneath the bathroom light, threads stitched into a subtle vine design across the bodice. Modest.

I turn in front of the bathroom mirror. It doesn't scream attention, but that's the point. Last night, I rummaged through my closet with no intention of checking boxes about church dress codes. In the end, conviction confirmed my decision. Frank Bishop's delivery may have been harsh, but I understand the heart behind his insistence on how one should dress for church. I had my ripped-jeans, bare-midriff season. Now I'm older in a different season of life.

The church lobby buzzes, the air warm as voices stack on voices. Willow and I slip through, greeting and smiling at familiar faces, but my heart stutters when we pass Ethan. Too many people circle him, so he can't see me. And that's for the best.

With so many empty seats inside the sanctuary, no wonder Valentina sees us the moment we walk in. She waves from the middle row, center aisle, Jason beside her. Unlike my first Sunday here, with my pulse racing as we sat in the back row, I don't feel nervous. We hug and swap greetings.

A tap on my shoulder pulls me around. Liam's green eyes meet mine, bright as ever. "Good to see you again, Ruby."

"Thanks."

He winks, and I follow his gaze to Willow beside me. Crimson blooms in her cheeks under the overhead lights. Russ grins as he slides in next to Liam and lifts his thumb at me in greeting before Jason and Valentina turn to greet their friends.

People continue filing in, and the sanctuary fills, chatter rising until the music cuts through and worship begins. I close my eyes, letting the lyrics clear the noise in my head.

When I open them, my gaze strays across the aisle. Front row, left side is Ethan. White button-down, dark pants, blazer smooth across his broad shoulders. Is that Harvey? And beside him, a girl. Maybe his girlfriend now. She leans in and whispers in his ear, and he smiles.

Perhaps he's here for the weekend. Unless he came to play buffer so my tears won't tempt Ethan into changing his mind from doing what he's decided God told him to do—end this, us.

I ignore the knot in my stomach and refocus on the lyrics.

After the singing, Ethan steps onto the pulpit, and the congregation erupts in cheers.

"Hello, everyone." His dimple presses into the fresh stubble along his jaw, the trim shave only making it stand out more. "It's great to see you too."

The applause swells louder this time. Cheers even carry from the back rows. He waves for everyone to sit, then rolls into announcements—February outreaches, March events, small groups.

"I hope you can connect with one of the groups or start one if we don't have the right group for you."

His gaze sweeps the room, then snags on mine. For a heartbeat, the corners of his mouth lift in a teensy smile meant just for me. Heat rushes through my chest, and I draw in a breath when his gaze resumes its trek along the congregation.

"My last sermon was about prayer." He bows his head. "Let's take a moment to pray before I share what God has put on my heart."

The sanctuary hushes, silence rippling through the room as he prays until his low amen stirs the same response from the rest of us.

"'Beauty in the Broken.'" His right hand rests on the pulpit, the other hanging loose at his side, his shoulders relaxed. "How many of you have a rose garden?"

Hands rise. He asks how many know a rose flower. Every hand lifts, including mine.

From the pulpit, he retrieves a single rose. Displays it for all to see. "You see this rose?"

Murmurs and nods.

"Beautiful, right? But watch."

He curls the bloom into his fist. When he opens it, crushed petals scatter to the floor. He then drops the stem.

"The rose was perfect. Now it's bruised. But tell me—has it stopped being a rose?"

"No," the congregation answers.

My heart stumbles. Why a rose? It's always been our flower. Always him.

"It's still fragrant, still valuable." His deep voice carries over us with the confidence he always had, even as a teenager. "This was one flower cut from a bush of many. Storms batter my rosebush every winter. But come summer, it blooms again. Roots still hold, storm or not."

He shifts behind the pulpit and opens the Bible on the stand. "Let's open our Bibles to Isaiah 43:19."

I reach into my bag, fingers brushing the soft leather, and join the rustle of pages opening.

He reads the verse, then closes the Bible. "Sometimes, the new thing God is doing doesn't look shiny or perfect at first. Sometimes, it looks like a life pressed down, akin to this rose. You look at it and think: 'It's ruined.' But if you lean in, it still carries a fragrance. Its beauty isn't erased."

His words take root as he weaves in Scripture through themes of identity in Christ, value that never fades, and steadiness under pressure. Voices rise with amens. Hands clap in conviction.

I'm caught between wanting to clap and shouting my agreement to what he's teaching. I remain silent. No need to cause a distraction during his beautiful sermon.

Then his gaze rests on me again. That smile, that small nod, feels like a wordless prayer meant only for me, reminding me I'm part of his story somehow.

Muffled sniffles ripple across the audience, people moved by his words.

He continues. "As we wind down the last week of the new year's first month, if you haven't already taken time to rest, to pray, I want to encourage you to do so. This year isn't just another page on the calendar. It's also a chance to step into what God has already prepared."

He bows his head, and my eyes slip shut. Willow's hand finds mine. Ethan's voice rises again, inviting those who need a personal relationship with the Lord to raise their hands. Curiosity pulls my eyes open long enough to see a few lift. I close them again and listen as he prays over them.

When he finishes with an amen, the room bursts into clapping. I join in, palms stinging with the force.

After he encourages those who prayed to stop by the coffee shop for a welcome-home gift, his gaze sweeps the crowd. A smile curves his mouth. "I know most of you are eager to hear about the special announcement I mentioned in the email."

Heat crawls beneath my coat. An email? No wonder the church is packed. I close my Bible and slip it back into my purse.

"This year, I want to challenge all of us to seek Him first. Before we make our own plans, let's ask, 'Lord, what are You already doing? Where are You leading me?' Because when we align ourselves with God's vision, even the wilderness becomes a pathway and the driest wasteland can bloom with streams of Living Water."

He steps down from the pulpit, moves closer to the edge of the stage, and scans the congregation. For a heartbeat, his focus lands on me. Then his lips part. "These last thirteen days, I've spent time in prayer and fasting, asking God for clarity, not just for this church but also for my walk with Him. My personal life. Specifically, my relationship with Ruby Morrison."

Murmurs ripple through the sanctuary.

Blood drains from my face, and I duck my head. Every instinct screams, "Bolt!"

But Willow squeezes my hand, and Valentina taps my shoulder. Did they know what he was going to say today?

"I'm sorry for not being forthcoming right away." Ethan's voice projects in crisp clarity. "My favorite place to be is with Ruby and my kids."

My eyes widen, and my head jerks up. Am I hearing right? Is this a dream? He's looking at me, smiling, and his expression is one of awe. My throat runs dry. I see nothing but the love, oh so sincere, in his warm eyes. He doesn't have to say anything more for me to know.

"I'm deeply, completely in love with Ruby. And after seeking God's heart on this, I don't feel Him calling me to step back from that love."

Willow lets go of my hand, and Valentina's touch slips from my shoulder. To my left and right, some clap, while others sit in stunned silence. A few shake their heads, disapproval evident, but Ethan's voice draws me back from such distractions.

"Ruby and I are dating." He locks his gaze on mine. "I hope this puts an end to the rumors and gossip because anything said against Ruby, my kids, or my family is an attack on me."

"Yes, Pastor!" booms a voice from the back.

I twist and see Liam standing. Russ rises too. Then Jason and Valentina. Willow. A ripple follows. More people stand and clap.

Then Ethan is moving down our row and passing Jason and Valentina. I'm on my feet before his arms close around me and secure me in an embrace so fierce it nearly knocks me back into my seat.

"I missed you." My voice breaks, swallowed by the noise around us. I curl my arms around his broad back. "The last two weeks without you have been the longest."

His lips brush my cheek, then my neck, and goose bumps scatter across my body. He then squeezes me tight. His heartbeat hammers against mine or the other way around.

When we draw apart, the aisle is empty. Our friends and most people have drifted out, giving us space or chasing their kids. Willow is gone too. Ethan's hand trails my cheek, now sore from smiling.

"Is it okay if you join me at the after-party?"

"After-party?"

"We've got a lot of catching up to do. Willow knows where you should come for lunch."

Willow owes me an explanation, hiding all this while I fretted about how today would unfold.

The sanctuary hums with scattered conversations. Then a throat clears. Harvey approaches with a short woman at his side. Her wavy brown hair frames a soft smile.

"Can I have my turn with Ruby now?" He winks with familiar mischief.

"You'll get your turn soon." Ethan's arm loops over me.

"So much for preaching self-control," Harvey mutters. "You're staring at Ruby like she's communion bread."

A laugh bursts out of me, and I clutch my stomach to keep from doubling over. Ethan beams, then slips his hand into mine.

We slide out of the row and into the aisle. Harvey hugs me and introduces the woman—Alyssa. She has kind eyes, and she seems quiet, a calm counter to his energy. They make a great couple for sure.

Ethan takes me with him to the lobby, where we stand side by side before the line of people waiting to greet him. Congratulations, warm wishes, and hugs pass one after another. When Nessa wraps me in her arms, her welcoming embrace reminds me why I should be here. She's the heart of this place, always faithful and loving to anyone who walks through these doors.

Diane isn't here today. Usually, she's beside Ethan, managing the line and handling baked goods. Church members crowd forward with pies and loaves, pressing them into Ethan's hands, saying how much they missed him.

By the time the greetings taper off, a small mountain of food tops the cart, and Nessa organizes the different baked goodies.

So. Much. Food. I can't help fretting over it. "I hope there's plenty more people who could benefit from all this food."

"The list never ends." Nessa offers her kind smile.

Minutes later, my anticipation spills over as I drive the familiar road with Willow guiding me. We pass Renewed Lane and continue along the muddy and bumpy road to the property where we went sledding with Ethan and his friends.

I pull up to another farmhouse, its paint chipped, land sprawling, animals roaming the fields. "You and Ethan could've just told me we're having lunch at Chuck's house."

"What's the fun if I told you all the details?" Willow smirks, clearly enjoying every second of watching me squirm.

I shake my head, but yeah, there's something exciting in not knowing everything. Especially now that Ethan and I are back in a good place. Who knows what's coming next?

CHAPTER 33

Ruby

For a surprisingly formal after-party, we gather inside Chuck's barn. Just off Renewed Lane, his property is an oasis for his animals and would make a great wedding venue. I met him when he offered extra sleds from his shed the day we came sledding.

String lights, soft and golden, loop across the rafters. Others dangle down, a blizzard of illuminated snowflakes, throwing everything into a magical wintery haze. Snow-white tablecloths drape the round tables, each with a mason jar of wildflowers. Food crowds the long buffet-style tables against the north wall. Laughter from church members and friends hums along the floor and echoes through the rafters.

"Look who's coming."

Willow's voice jolts me from my thoughts. I follow her gaze. Ethan's parents approach our table.

My slight discomfort vanishes when Poppy and Asher barrel past them toward me, their smiles warming my heart. I push to my feet. The metal chair wobbles behind me as I step out and stretch my arms wide. Asher reaches me first, and I pull him in, then Poppy as they press against me. "I missed you, my sweeties."

"Why didn't you call us?" Asher asks.

Unsure what Ethan told them, I stall my answer.

"I practiced piano every day." Poppy's chin tips up high, and her grin reveals a new missing tooth.

I ache over missing out on that.

"I tried to practice." Asher squints. "But the fort-building kit you gave me at Christmas kept me busy." His little brow furrows, bashful yet proud.

I laugh, smoothing his hair. "I'm glad you've been busy."

Willow's voice drifts from behind me, light and easy as she chats with Ethan's parents. The kids continue chattering about what they've been up to. Then their friends tumble in, voices colliding with news about the baby goats outside.

"Hi, Mr. Bishop." I stop short of extending my hand, but he reaches out and clasps mine in a firm shake. I do the same with his wife, and she accepts it.

"This is quite a Sunday picnic you all have here." A ghost of a smile curves Ethan's mom's mouth.

"It's definitely fancy."

People cluster in groups or lean around their tables. Trays clatter as servers load more offerings onto the buffet.

Ethan stands at the serving tables. Head tipped back in laughter, shoulders shaking, he trades stories with Chuck, Valentina, and the guys from Renewed Lane. The ease with which he interacts with his friends or just anybody makes it hard to look away.

"So…"

I turn back to where Willow is already talking about the weather, filling the silence for me. "I just hope it doesn't decide to snow the entire month of February."

The microphone cracks to rescue us from stilted small talk. Jason's voice booms through the barn. "Let's give a clap for Chuck hosting our get-together today."

Everyone claps. I join in, palms stinging. I might be cheering for the distraction as much as I am for our host.

Jason motions for quiet. "We're going to pray, enjoy some good food, and connect. But first, if it weren't for Ruby being part of Ethan's life, we wouldn't be gathered for this lunch today."

Heat crawls up my cheeks. Again, the barn erupts with applause, louder than I expect, and seated beside me, Willow hollers like she's at a football game, clapping so hard her elbow bumps the water glass. It wobbles, and she snatches it just in time.

I sneak a glance toward Ethan's parents. Still standing, hands moving, faces tight. My stomach dips. Had Ethan told them I was even going to be at this gathering, let alone part of its reason, like Jason just announced?

After prayers, Ethan's parents find their seats. Soft music drifts through the speakers as we line up at the buffet. Platters of roasted chicken, beef and pulled pork stand in between bowls of baked beans, potato salad and baskets stacked high with rolls. At the dessert spread, apple, peach, or glossy pecan pies ooze goodness while platters of crackle-topped brownies or chewy cookies gleam under string lights. Bowls of candy corn dot the gaps, and a tiered cake rises like a showpiece.

Back at our table, Ethan and the kids slide in beside me. I focus on my plate, schooling my features so his kids don't catch the way his playful smile unravels me. My gaze strays a few tables over. There, his parents laugh with Harvey and Alyssa. A twinge slices through my chest. They smile so easily with her, not me. But again, Ethan's the one I'm dating. Their approval shouldn't matter, or so I keep telling myself.

I lean into him, whispering for his ears alone. "Thank you for coming back to me."

His left hand slips under the table, warm on my leg. Then he mouths, only for me, "I'm so glad God didn't say otherwise."

Same.

"Why can't Mr. Chuck have airplanes hanging in this barn?" Asher pipes up.

"That would be so boring," Poppy counters. "The lights are like stars. Cloud loves them."

"You kids have the best ideas." Willow waves her fork between them.

I crane past Ethan to smile at Asher. "How would you transform this place?"

"I'd start with airplanes—"

"No more lights," Poppy cuts in. "And posters of animals 'cause it's a farm. And then the string lights would have unicorns flying on them."

Between the kids' chatter and forks scraping, we adults have little to say. Soon, a trio of young servers in matching aprons whisk away our plates. Poppy and Asher dart off to sit with their friends.

I sink back in my chair. "Who catered this?"

"Brooks Diner."

My gaze flicks between him and Willow. "When did you even have time to plan this?"

She raises both hands. "Don't look at me."

"That's what friends are for." Ethan scrunches his face into a mock scowl. "I just came by yesterday to touch up and ensure everything was as I'd hoped. Of course, I'm no decorator."

Everything is simple yet elegant. Oops, I didn't intend to glance at the Bishops' table. Great, Ethan's mom is looking at our table, expression unreadable. When our gazes collide, I look away.

My stomach knots with that familiar sinking anxiety.

"Did you force your parents to come?" I rock my glass side to side. Water sloshes toward one rim, then the other.

Ethan reaches for my free hand under the table and squeezes it. His thumb traces a slow circle on my wrist and sends shivers racing up my arm. "I don't need their opinions, Ruby. I invited them. And while they're not throwing confetti, they showed up. I'll take that as a start."

The microphone crackles, and all heads turn toward Liam. He grins, broad and mischievous. "All right. Where do I start? There's no better way to enjoy food than with comrades. Who can agree?"

Whispers and chants.

"Right, yeah? If you don't agree, just nod along and pretend."

Laughter ripples through the barn, the easy kind that loosens my shoulders.

Then his expression shifts as his gaze focuses on our table. "Ethan, Poppy, and Asher, up to the front, please!"

"We'll be back in a sec." Ethan whispers in my ear. Then he brushes a kiss against my earlobe that leaves my whole body tingling. His jacket hangs over the chair he vacated. In a crisp white shirt tucked into dark slacks, his broad shoulders and lean build stand out, strength and grace in every movement.

Willow scoots closer to the table, smiling like she's in on a secret.

"What are they up to now?"

She winks. "Seems I'm in for a surprise today, same as you."

"Could it be I'm asking because you already knew where this so-called after-party was going to be?"

Her smirk says everything. "I'll tell you all about it tonight."

Maybe Ethan and the kids have a song to play for me. They emerge from the kitchen door by the food tables, and yep, "You Are the Reason" starts to play faintly from the speakers.

Ethan weaves between tables with the kids, and the barn hushes as if we're in a chapel waiting for the bride to appear. My eyes widen. Poppy walks solemnly at his side, clutching something like a candle in a procession—only it's a red rose, held straight and careful. The sight undoes me.

But why does a single rose warrant this hush? Why does everyone's focus follow as the trio reaches our table and stops in front of me?

Ethan nudges the chairs aside, clearing space.

Asher struts forward, chest puffed beneath his untucked plaid shirt. "Daddy says you love roses and you remind him of roses."

My hand presses to my thrumming heart, and my broad smile stretches so wide it hurts.

Then Poppy steps forward, cradling the single red rose. Its petals are thick, a deep-velvet red that seems brushed with firelight. And something glints inside—a heart-shaped ruby circled by a halo of shimmery diamonds. The gem flickers like flame, making the rose itself a jewel.

"Only one rose stands out," Poppy says.

"And only one Ruby deserves this treasure in the rose," Ethan adds, his voice shaky.

Air knots tight in my chest as Ethan kneels. I face him fully. The petals tremble loose as he extracts the ruby from the flower's center. Then they drop around him like confetti.

"Ruby Morrison…" His eyes glow so entrancingly that the world around me narrows to him alone. "You reappeared in my life like grace made visible. You gave my children more laughter. You gave me songs I thought I'd lost. You gave me hope." His voice catches as if caught between courage and awe.

The ruby heart gleams, rich and red and true, as he raises it. "I give you this as a symbol of my heart forever. Whether you take it or not, it's yours and lost to me when you aren't near. I never want to be without you or it again. Please, Ruby, be my wife, promise you'll stay with me forever."

With my chest squeezed so tight, I can barely breathe. My hands fly to my mouth, and tears sting my eyes.

"I was your first love," he continues. "Life happened, but it turns out we were just waiting for the right time to begin again. God has given us a second chance. Please, let me be your last."

My lips part to say there was no one before nor after him. He was always going to be my first and my last anyway. I clear my throat to remove the lump, but his children bounce on either side of him.

"Say yes!" Poppy clasps her hands together as if in prayer. "Then we'll be even, two girls and two boys."

"Is it okay if you can be our mom?" Asher asks so earnestly that, if I hadn't already made up my mind, I'd be certain now.

Then I look at Ethan with blurry eyes, and the emotion between us is too much to hold back. *Ethan...*

"Yes." I choke out through tears before throwing myself into his arms. "Of course, yes!"

The barn erupts in cheers. When I draw back from his embrace, he slips the ring onto my finger, lifts my hand, and brushes a kiss across it. Then he rises, eases me up with him, and seals it all with a soft kiss that melts every fear frozen into my being.

Little arms wrap around us, enclosing us in a group hug of four. My laugh tangles with Ethan's as I press my face to his shoulder, breathing him in—comfort, home, everything I never knew I needed. He's a package deal, and the best one I could ever hope for.

After that, the evening blurs with congratulations, music, and laughter. When we reach his family's table, his mom rises. She extends her hand, not a hug, not warmth, but a steady hold.

"I may not understand it all," she says, "but I can see how much you love each other."

"Thank you." My voice breaks around the tears.

Mr. Bishop offers his congratulations, standing to hug Ethan before accepting me with a firm handshake. Alyssa and Harvey follow with warm embraces, filling the gap Ethan's parents create.

Much later, we gather in the living room. Perched on the edge of the coffee table, Ethan strums "Goodness of God." Poppy snuggles into my left side, my arm curled around her, while Asher settles to my right, the lamplight soft across their sleepy faces. The glow catches the gleam of the ruby on my hand, diamonds flickering with every shift of light.

Ethan grins at me and the kids. This man, a pastor who chose a prodigal, and his children who have welcomed me with trust and open arms—this is home.

A year ago, I was alone, teaching piano at a studio, piecing my life back together. Tonight, I am wrapped in more love than I ever dreamed possible. Sometimes God's masterpieces really are born out of the most broken places.

CHAPTER 34

Ruby

"Thank you, dear." Priscilla's voice trembles as Mike takes the plastic-wrapped gift basket from my hands. They've lived at Skypoint for a year now, waiting to move into their new place in a few months.

"I was hoping to hear you sing today." In her recliner, she stifles a yawn with her hand. Gray strands of rumpled hair dangle loose around her face, and a blanket covers her legs.

Mike gestures for me to sit at the small dining table, and I slip into a chair while he settles beside his wife. Their apartment, like all the others in the facility, is one bedroom. The warm gold walls in its main room make it inviting.

"It's not my voice." I point to the sleek digital player in the basket. "But every resident now has one, loaded with uplifting music from generous donors."

"Too bad Ethan doesn't get paid for running this place." Priscilla curls her feet up under her blanket.

"He's on God's payroll." I smooth the folds of my knee-length dress, the fabric stretching when I shift. "Have they brought you dinner yet?"

"Priscilla doesn't have much of an appetite." The creases on Mike's face sink deeper. "I hope they didn't forget about me."

"I'll remind them when I head down." It's nearly seven. Ethan should be home from the wedding by now. I push to my feet and give a quick twirl. "I'll let you rest. Ethan's taking me dancing tonight."

"Valentine's dances are the best." Her eyes softening, she rests a hand on her husband's arm. "Every year reminds me of our first."

Mike chuckles. "I stepped all over her toes. She still danced with me."

Their tenderness stirs something deep in me.

"You two are Skypoint's power couple." I move to hug each in turn. I met the Carters on Christmas Eve. Since then, I've often seen them together—walking by the pool, laughing over meals, or teasing at a board game. Always together.

"Soon you and Ethan will be the shining couple." Priscilla tilts my hand to admire my ring, the forever valentine agleam in the light. "They didn't make them like this when Mike and I married."

"You're only in your sixties." I tug my hand free and swat at hers. "You're not as far behind the new generation as you think." Then I wink, wish them good night, and close the door behind me.

It's been a good evening so far, but it's only starting. Valentina already left with Poppy and Asher. They're babysitting tonight. Ethan and I watched their kids yesterday so Valentina and Jason could celebrate a day early.

Down the hallway, I stop at the elevator and press the button. Tonight's Valentine's program was beautiful. Children sang while I played the piano before I shared three of my own songs. Then other artists showcased their talent. Afterward, the event continued in the dining room, where food beckoned and laughter soon resounded. Some of the residents even danced, their smiles beaming brighter than the recessed lights. When Priscilla and Mike didn't join everyone in the dining room, I asked around and learned her headache hindered their coming down. So I brought their basket up.

A woman with a walker shuffles past, and the elevator's slow crawl saps my patience. Two flights of stairs will be faster. I stride along the carpeted floor toward the end of the hall and push the stair door open. Cold air whips at me, and I hug my arms to my chest. Long sleeves do nothing for the chill.

My heels click on the first step, and adrenaline spikes. Dancing tonight, finally. It's been so long since I let go on a floor. The last time was with Ethan after graduation. My fingers curl around the old ring almost touching the V on my dress. How nice to wear this ring as a necklace rather than leaving it in his box full of old memories.

I lift my hand to look at my engagement ring, imagining our wedding once the kids are out of school for the summer. By mid-June, I'll be Mrs. Ethan Bishop, pastor's wife.

What an absurd, yet intoxicating thought!

I gasp when my foot misses the next step. My heel scrapes the edge, and my ankle rolls. Instinct has me reaching for the rail. I should've grabbed it sooner.

Momentum pushes me forward. I fall, my head slamming into concrete.

The *thwunk* ricochets through my skull.

Then I'm rolling, rolling, and tumbling down the entire flight or however many flights. I'm only aware of the intense pain, the salty blood on my tongue, then darkness... and silence.

Ethan

Ruby's heartbeat monitor keeps time in the dim ICU room. Steady, indifferent to the way mine skips and stutters. If I were wired to one of these machines, the screen would betray the mess I am inside.

I hate seeing her like this. Tubes and wires invade her body. A bulky splint imprisons her wrist, and a pillow cushions her bandaged ankle. The vent tube taped at her mouth rises and falls with each forced breath, the machine breathing for her. Bruises mar her face, dark purples and deep blues against her soft brown skin. Still, she's the most beautiful thing in this sterile place where everything reeks of antiseptic.

They've run the scans—CT, EEG, and whatnot. I sent them to Jason and Liam when they asked. The guys passed them to their neurosurgeon friends. The good news matches what the doctor here already said—no bleeding, no fracture in her skull, normal brain activity.

"Why the coma again?" My voice rasps like a scrape of sandpaper as I raise my gaze to the nurse adjusting her IV. They told me earlier, but I can't seem to remember anything. Not now, when Ruby's life hangs in the balance.

The nurse's expression softens. "The swelling put too much pressure on her brain. If she tried to wake, seizures could've started. The induced coma keeps her safe and gives her brain the rest it needs as swelling goes down." Her hand brushes the tubing once more. "If all looks good, we'll begin easing her medication in about four hours to see if she's ready."

I nod, trying to fix the words in my head. Exhaustion fogs everything. When the nurse leaves, I drag my chair closer to the bed and reach out. My hand shakes as I push damp strands of hair off Ruby's battered forehead.

"Please, sweet Ruby..." My chest caves in. Bricks might as well be crushing me from the inside. "Stay with me."

Prayers usually flow naturally. Now, after thirty-six hours of crying out to God, my anxiety mounting with each passing hour, I'm not sure what else to say.

They only allow one visitor at a time. I've stepped out to let our friends see her, but I haven't left her side otherwise. Since I received the call that she fell—twenty-five concrete steps at Skypoint—I've stuck around, in case she wakes up.

My friends have taken turns with the kids, even brought them by to eat with me in the cafeteria. I haven't let them see her like this. Not with the tubes. Not while she looks like she won't be waking up.

"Oh, Ruby, why didn't you just take the elevator?" My mind drags me to the edge of a thought I hate to rethink. Could she have done this on purpose?

No. She sounded happy when we spoke on the phone, making plans for the evening. But... what if...?

I squeeze her hand tighter, pushing the darkness away. "I love you... so much..." My chest rises and falls, every breath heavy with agony. "I've been thinking about the day you reappeared in my life." A rough laugh scrapes out of me. "I was so stunned. Only you, Ruby Morrison, could make a man fall into a pool and still feel like he's flying."

I whisper of all the memories we've shared and what she means to me and my kids. I keep talking until I'm yawning through my words and blinking weary eyes.

Beyond the window, darkness has swallowed the dim evening light that once seeped through. It must be night, maybe late. I've lost track of the hours, but I don't have the strength to lift my wrist and check the time. My chin sinks to the mattress beside her undamaged left hand. Here, I can still see her face, and the deep, true red of her engagement ring glows in my peripheral vision. With my eyes so heavy, I can't hold them open. They slide shut, and I drift into uneasy sleep, tethered to the steady rhythm of her heart monitor.

Beep... beep... beep...

The sound sharpens in my ears. I jolt awake rubbing my groggy eyes. Ouch. My neck is too stiff from how it was wedged against the mattress. Blinking against the harsh overhead lights, I drag both hands over my face to chase away the fog.

Morning light streams through the window.

"Ethan?"

The groan is such a quiet rasp that I might have dreamed it. My head snaps up, and my gaze drifts to the bed.

"Ruby?" My chair scrapes backward and topples as I lurch to my feet. "You're awake?"

Her brows pinch together, her eyes clouding as she blinks at me. Does she... not know me?

Then her gaze settles, and a crooked smile tugs at her lips. "The beard," she whispers. "You're going for the mountain-man look?"

A choked laugh shakes out of me, and a dizzying relief surges from my brain to my limbs. "You're awake." The words tumble free like a prayer I've repeated too many times in the dark.

"My hand hurts..."

"Sweetheart." I catch her fingers, careful not to jostle the splint. My throat tightens. "You're awake. You're *really* awake."

I fumble for the call button, smashing it with my palm like it's the only thing tethering me to sanity. The red light flickers on above the door.

"I was so terrified." I brush damp strands of hair from her temple. My thumb grazes the bruise on her jaw, and my palm rests there, soaking in her warmth, a confirmation I'm not dreaming.

"The kids..." Her voice is softer now. "Where are they?"

"They're okay." I lean down, kiss her cheek, breathe her in. "I'm just... so glad you're still with me." My lips find her hair, and for the first time in days, the crushing weight in my chest lets up.

The door clicks open, and the nurse slips in. Her face lights up when she sights Ruby's open eyes.

I step back, letting her work.

She checks the monitors, takes Ruby's vitals, and shines a light across her pupils. "Do you remember how you fell, Ruby?"

"Uh, I... yeah."

While the nurse works, I grab my phone and move to the sink. First, I call Willow, who's been just as frantic. Then I fire a text in our group chat with Jason, Liam, and Valentina.

Me: She's awake.

When I turn back, Ruby is groaning under the nurse's explanation.

"Your right wrist is broken. It'll need surgery once the swelling goes down. We'll take more X-rays of your ankle and another scan of your head to be sure everything is clear."

Ruby clamps her eyes shut. Still, a strangled whimper tears out of her. "My head hurts so much."

"I'll bring something for the pain," the nurse promises. "And once we get your tests back and you're cleared, you'll be free to have something to eat and drink. How does that sound?"

Ruby sighs, her lips parting. "Good."

I cover my eyes with my hands and whisper a prayer through trembling lips. Never have I known gratitude deeper than this, for the gift of her life.

She's still here. She's stayed with me.

Now, June feels too far away for a wedding. I want forever with Ruby to start now.

***

Ruby

I battle to open my eyes. The pain meds do their job, softening the edges, but also leave my body under a lead blanket, thick and slow. Maybe Willow came by, or I dreamed her telling me I should never wear heels again. Maybe Ethan spoon-fed me chicken soup, or I dreamed that too. My heavy eyelids resist my attempts to pry them apart. At last, they give in.

Ethan sits hunched in the corner chair, elbows braced on his knees, hands pressed together as if clinging to a prayer. He's shaved his beard down to a rough shadow, his sharp jawline more visible in the bright light. After the nurse confessed he never left, I told him to go home. Still, he's here, his constant presence eroding my doubts. However, I'm not the only one who needs him.

"You should go to the kids," I rasp.

"They're still in school." He tilts his head toward me. "I'll bring them by tomorrow when they move you to a regular room. They've been eager to see you."

My chest loosens. "I can't wait to see them."

He rises and comes to sit on the edge of the bed. His gaze holds mine, saying everything he won't put into words. His hand finds my cheek, and his warmth seeps into my skin. I let my face rest against his palm before the heaviness drags me under again.

Noise draws me back—low voices overlapping, wheels squeaking against tile, and those machines beeping the metronome of life. I blink at the light leaking past the curtains. The room looks different, less confined. They must have moved me out of the ICU. On the bedside table, a valentine of red roses and baby's breath rises from a glass vase. Their scent cuts through the antiseptic until the air tastes like summer, and their image reminds me of my ring. My good fingers twitch as I rub the pinkie against the stones.

"Hello." The voice draws my attention to the doorway, to Willow, Ethan, and the kids. Then two small bodies break free and race toward me. Their squeals bubble through the room like my favorite song before Ethan reminds them that this is a hospital and they need to be quieter.

"Ruby!" Poppy's voice still rings as bright as a bell while she presses a single thornless red rose into my palm.

Asher lumbers up with a slightly crushed bouquet, florist paper crumpled from his grip. "Willow helped us get these. I thought a small bouquet wouldn't hurt your hand."

A weak laugh rattles out of me as I reach for them, chest aching in the best way. "You two are all the medicine I need."

Ethan warns them not to squeeze me too tight, and they ease back, wide-eyed, as if I might break.

"I'm fine," I reassure them now that I'm taking pain meds. "This summer, we'll find a field of flowers and pick until our arms can't hold any more." The image blooms in my mind—wild sun, bare feet, laughter tangled with petals.

"Will you be better by the time you and Daddy marry?" Asher asks, solemn as a judge.

"Yes." I sure hope so.

Poppy's small fingers brush my blanket. "Does it still hurt?"

"Sometimes." I reach my left hand and touch her wrist. "But it hurts less when you're here."

That earns me her shy smile, displaying the gap of missing teeth.

Ethan clears his throat. "All right, troops. Let's go get some cocoa, and we'll be back."

Poppy whispers a vow to sneak me hot chocolate. Asher grins and promises to bring me a chocolate croissant.

Once Ethan guides them out, Willow leans in and kisses my cheek. "You look so much better. It makes me glad."

As she draws away, her gaze flicks from my wrist in its splint to my ankle strapped in a soft brace, propped on a pillow.

"How are you feeling?" Willow eases onto the edge of the bed.

I can't feel much in my right hand—the splint and meds dull everything—so the real damage will stay a mystery until the X-ray results are back. But the nurse warned that surgery is likely once things settle. For now, pins and padding hold me together, keeping the pain muted behind the fog.

"Not bad if I wasn't trapped in here." I stifle a yawn. "What did I miss?" The world tugs at the edges again, sleep a slow tide pulling me under.

"The book club is wondering if you can host next month," Willow teases, her grin soft. Her voice washes over me, ebbing with that tide.

Whatever else she's saying will have to wait. She better not quiz me later, though, because my eyes won't fight anymore. The room blurs, roses lingering like a promise, and I sink back into the dark.

CHAPTER 35

Ruby

"I'm always excited about food until I remember my hand," I mutter as Ethan slides an arm behind me to adjust pillows until I'm propped upright. He pulls the rolling tray across the bed so it hovers over my lap. The savory scent of sausage, muffins, and the rest of breakfast overpowers the antiseptics.

"That's why I'm here." He nudges it closer. "I can help if needed."

"I won't need you feeding me today." My stomach growls, and my mouth waters. "My left hand can manage sausages and a muffin." Unlike the scrambled eggs he had to feed me yesterday. "I don't even eat breakfast."

"With all the meds they're pumping into you, food isn't optional." He settles into the chair across from me and uncovers his own tray of scrambled eggs and toast, coffee steaming at its side. He slides the fruit bowl onto my tray.

The room feels brighter this morning, sunlight streaming through the window. With the sun's pale gold blurred by a layer of fog, the air outside looks colder than it should.

"Is it all right if I bless our food?" His voice snags my attention.

"Of course."

Steam curls from his mug as he bows his head. I whisper my amen when he finishes, soaking in the reminder that I'm home with him and at peace with God.

He sips his coffee. "The kids want to skip basketball practice so they can hang out here tonight."

I shake my head. "Tell them no. I'll be out of here soon enough, watching them play."

The fruit looks so good. Instinct has me reaching with my right hand, but a sharp sting races up my wrist. I flinch and pull back with a hiss. Habits are hard to break.

"Honey." Ethan's eyes soften. "That hand's out of commission. Let me help."

"Ugh." I flop against the pillows. "I'll figure it out. I can use my left."

And I do just that. My grip is awkward, like a toddler learning to use silverware, but I can manage the diced fruit. I spear a chunk of melon, then work through a sausage and a muffin after Ethan peels the paper off it.

A knock sounds, and we both look to the door before he calls out to come in.

The doctor steps through, his smile kind, but his clipboard still makes my stomach tighten.

"Ruby." His eyes meet mine over the rim of his glasses. "We've scheduled your wrist surgery for tomorrow morning. Good news, though. Your ankle is only a moderate sprain with a partial ligament tear. It could've been worse. The orthopedic surgeon will come by tonight to explain the procedure."

"Okay." I exhale. The sooner it's done, the sooner I can get out of here.

"No food or drink after midnight."

"Got it."

"Any questions?"

A dozen circle in my head, but only one makes it out. "How long before I'm back to normal? Walking without looking like a penguin?"

Ethan stifles a chuckle.

"You'll need another five days here," the doctor says. "After that, physical therapy. As for your ankle, avoid stairs for at least three weeks. You'll get there, but it'll take time."

He lists local PT options, promises referrals if I need more, but my mind drifts. I already knew this wouldn't be quick. Still, hearing it aloud makes the walls feel smaller. The recovery road will be longer than I want it to be.

"How am I supposed to teach piano with a broken wrist?" I blurt once the doctor leaves. Yes, it's good my ribs are only bruised, not broken, but I still have a mountain of recovery to climb. "If I can't walk up and down the stairs, where am I going to find a new place?"

And the money, since I added health insurance to my monthly bills.

Ethan moves the tray aside and lowers himself onto the edge of the bed. He takes my good hand in both of his, warm and wrapping me in comfort.

"Don't worry. You're going to be okay. I promise."

His tenderness is enough to quiet my worries. The last time I woke up in a hospital, I was alone with fear as my only companion, despair the presence at my bedside. This time, people come and go to check on me. Friends, becoming family. Him. His kids. And that, in itself, is hope.

"I've already arranged to step back from work next month," he adds. "I can do most of it from home."

"You don't have to, Ethan."

"I know." He cups a hand to my forehead, brushing my hair back. "But I want to."

His words and touch wrap me in warmth. I keep quiet about the worry pressing at me. The apartment with its steep stairs won't be home anytime soon.

Unease creeps in anyway when I think of my students. I won't be teaching for a while, either. How am I supposed to pay for insurance with no work?

Ethan comes every day, bringing the kids after school. Each time, they have new drawings to press into my hands, and their laughter chases away the shadows of discouragement. I insist he spend nights at home with them now that I'm stronger, but they never leave until we've had dinner together. Sometimes, he wheels me through the hall since the nurses don't want me walking in the boot unless the PT is beside me. He always ends the evening with a kiss on my temple and a promise to be back in the morning.

Visitors fill the quietness. Nessa from church. Parents of my piano kids with flowers and get-well-soon cards. Even those I met at Skypoint, among many others. After surgery this morning, the countdown has begun. Four more days until discharge.

Willow and Valentina come in together as the nurse settles me back on the bed after a bathroom break. When she leaves, Valentina claims the spot beside me, Willow slipping into the chair across from us.

"By the way, we have the guest cottage ready for when you come out of the hospital."

"Oh..." My throat closes, and Valentina lays a hand on my leg. "It'll be easier for Ethan—and all of us—to keep an eye on you."

"Ethan's already lined up physical therapy." Willow sinks back in her seat, crossing one foot over the other. "Your students' parents want to keep their kids enrolled until you can teach."

Something inside me unknots.

Then Valentina sets a manila envelope on the table by the flowers. "Money Nessa and other church members collected. Also, families of your piano students wanted to help with your recovery."

"This means... so much to me." I swallow down grateful tears.

"Brought you some clothes too, in case you're tired of hospital gowns." Willow nods to the bathroom door. "Bag's in there."

"Thank you."

Willow crosses her arms. "Don't you want to know why I left it in the bathroom?"

Valentina's smirk quirks up her lipsticked mouth. "She got you a maternity dress for ease of slipping it on."

She must be joking. But she's not, as I discover the next morning when the PT helps me shower and change into the sage-green dress. Practical with short sleeves, it slides over the splint on my right wrist and my wrapped ribs, a concession to comfort. The waist hangs loose. If I'd been hoping for fitted, this is nowhere close.

Ethan has a church meeting this morning, one more before his month-long break. So, I take advantage of the nurse's presence and ask her to escort me to the café instead of having breakfast delivered.

"Great change of scenery." She wheels me through the quiet halls. At the window, she settles me in and hands me a call button to press when I'm ready for her to fetch me. Before leaving, she waves over a server to take my order.

"Muffin and sausage." I don't bother glancing at the menu. "And tea, please."

"Which kind?"

"Chamomile."

When the food arrives, I take my time eating, just soaking up the social atmosphere as people come in and out, most of them medical staff, ordering a hot beverage or walking away with food trays.

By the time they wheel me back, exhaustion has folded my limbs like limp sheets. The nurse helps me into bed, and when I open my eyes again, Ethan is sitting there. It's the simplest thing in the world to smile back.

"Sleep okay?"

"Yeah." I rub my eyes clear. "How was the meeting?"

"Not bad."

He studies me, his smile fading, and a cold knot twists in my stomach. The last time he looked this serious was when the emergency meeting ended with us taking a two-week break. "You'll be leaving the hospital in a few days."

"What is it?" The question leaves my lips before I can dance around it.

"Ruby..." He breathes slowly, like he's pulling in something heavy. "I... need to ask you something."

My pulse quickens. What did they tell him at church this time? "Okay."

"Don't take it the wrong way." He rubs a hand over his face, dragging his eyelids down while maintaining eye contact. "I have to know. Did you fall down those stairs on purpose?"

"What?" His question hits like a fist to the chest. My tongue tastes metallic. Surely, he can't be saying... "You mean to tell me you think I *threw* myself down a flight of stairs—on purpose?"

"Two flights." His voice grits. "I don't know what to think. You've been under so much pressure—the engagement, the church politics, the move... and everything in your past." His hands twist in his lap. "Sometimes people who've struggled with depression... hurt themselves. I had to ask."

He *is* saying it. He *has* been thinking it.

Air rushes out. The room tilts. I'm outside myself, staring at him—he looks earnest, terrified, desperate to make sense of what he can't control. Then everything snaps back into focus. Hospital lights so bright, the splint holding my hand captive from playing the piano, the new pressure in my head... "You think I'm unstable?"

"You're one of the strongest people I know." His lips press tight.

I sense the *but* he swallows back. I shift on the bed, hoping the truth might ease his doubts.

"I took a gift basket to the Carters." I skip ahead. "I was excited about the dance. I was thinking about our wedding." That happiness, compared to where I've landed, fuels my anger. "How could you even think that?"

Tears pool, spill, and blur his image. He rises from the chair, the mattress dipping as he sits beside me. His hand covers mine, trembling. He's terrified, and my almost death jarred him.

"I wasn't good at communicating with Maddie." His voice cracks. "I could've seen things coming. I—" He stops like the rest will make it worse. "I just need clarity. I can't lose you."

Of course. Now I'm Maddie. Will he doubt me every time my name comes up in a church meeting?

I draw out a shaky breath. "I appreciate what you've done." I pull my hand away from him. "But I can't be the person you're always watching for a crack. I can't be on trial the rest of my life."

"Ruby—"

"No." The single syllable rips out of me, painful, but for the best. "I need space. We... we need a break." Saying it is like tearing a bandage off slowly, and my rib cage now aches in a new way.

His hand brushes over my wrist, and his index finger trails to the ring.

I turn my face to the wall. "Go. Please, leave."

"Ruby."

"Leave. Me. Alone." The words scrape past my raw throat. I swallow down the desire to beg him to stay with me, to believe in me.

The silence feels endless, broken only by the bed's creak as his weight lifts. His footsteps fade, every one pulling him further from me, until my heart sinks with the emptiness he leaves behind. Then he says an I love you muffled at the door, and the words twist through me, wrenching open the freshly unbandaged wound.

When the door clicks shut, I crumble. The first sob slips out small. I'm still telling myself to hold it together. But who am I kidding? A ragged sound tears free, choking my throat. Tears spill until my head throbs with a pain that isn't from the fall.

I thought Ethan saw me whole. Instead, he's terrified, waiting for me to fall apart.

The truth? He's right.

Look at me now, falling to pieces. I have to get my act together. I'm not there yet, but I'll do whatever it takes not to sink back into that hole of darkness, not to seclude myself and die a little each day alone.

I cradle my broken wrist like a barometer, waiting for the ache to ease. "Dear God, help me lean on You this time. I've heard—ignored—the warnings from preachers, even from Ethan, that people let us down. God, You'll always be there. Always stay with me."

At some point, when I need to use the bathroom, I press the nurse call button. The last thing I need is another fall. My puffy eyes still sting, my vision still blurry. After emptying my bladder, I sprinkle water on my eyes using my left hand.

The nurse helps me back and steadies me onto the chair beside my bed. It's different from the bed, at least. She then rests a hand on my elbow. "Are you all right?"

"Yeah." There's nothing she can do to help with this ache. I reach for the remote clipped to the bed alongside all the other buttons and flick on the TV.

"Would you like your lunch delivered?"

I shake my head. Nothing sounds good.

After my evening meds, I force down a couple mini quiches. I use my hand, no fork needed, before the meds pull the edges of the world soft again.

Willow slips in after work. Her face folds with concern the second she sees me. She drops into the chair across from mine.

"Ethan kept texting me at work, said it was a must that I check on you tonight." Her brows knot. "You've been crying. Are you two okay?"

"He thinks I hurt myself on purpose." I groan into my pillow.

Willow nods, and her lips flatten like she understands where Ethan is coming from.

I stiffen. "Please don't tell me you think I did this"—I gesture to my broken body—"on purpose."

"No..." Her voice comes out low. "Of course not. Just try to put yourself in Ethan's place."

"But Ethan... Why would he think...?" The rest of the sentence dies, buried under what I said to him. I can still feel the pressure of his hand trembling when he held mine. The memory twists into guilt. I didn't try to see his perspective. I only saw the way he looked at me and the fear in his eyes. He lost Maddie and then my shaky past...

Willow's mouth presses into a thin line. "He's scared. Your history... He probably didn't know how to reconcile that with nearly losing you again. He asked because he's terrified and because he wants to be sure you have support."

The awakened guilt gnaws over the words I fired back, how I shoved him away when all he'd done was take care of me. The ache under my ribs is rawer than the bruise, and now, this churning assault of hurt, fear, and anger won't go away.

Willow rises and comes to the bed. The mattress dips when she sits, and her hand finds my good one. She curls my fingers against her palm. "You know I'm here for you. Everything's going to be okay."

Her certainty is a balm to my battered heart.

In three days, they'll discharge me for PT. I'm off the big monitors now, though my right wrist is snug in a splint and my ankle braced on pillows. The logistics of moving next door to Ethan offer a practical worry.

But the real one? I just broke up with the man I've wanted my whole life. In five brutal minutes, I snapped. Now, I can't take back the words. The thought batters me worse than any fall. What have I done?

Chapter 36

Ethan

“I don’t know if I should give her space or try to talk to her.” I pace around Jason and Valentina’s kitchen island, stopping only to search the couple’s faces as if they hold the answer. They sit side by side, hands resting on the marbled counter. My waist aches from leaning into it too long.

“She told me she needed time alone.” I wave in the air. “But what if that makes things worse?”

“Start from the beginning.” Jason narrows his eyes. “What made Ruby ask for space?”

I’d tried explaining to the guys earlier, but I clipped the truth short. Too many parents hovered at the gym during the kids’ practice for me to unload everything. Now the words scrape out. “I asked her if she fell on purpose.”

Silence settles.

Valentina’s gaze drifts to the chore charts tacked on their fridge.

Jason chews his lower lip. Then his lips part. "That's a sensitive question coming from you." He looks at his wife with the kind of warmth that says her opinion matters most. "What do you think, honey?"

She faces me, her appraisal kind but assessing. "What made you think she threw herself down the stairs?"

"The engagement stress, the church politics, the gossip..." I utter an endless list of what could've stressed her in ways I hadn't seen before. "With her history—"

"So you thought she tried to take her own life?" Jason's conclusion makes the statement more intense than the tone I'd intended when I asked Ruby.

Her words about throwing herself over the balcony railing to avoid going to church have haunted me. I hadn't gone as far as to think she'd take her own life, though. Right?

I let air out, panic snaking under my ribs over how the whole thing sounds. The kids' happy voices ring down the hall. We stopped over here after practice. "I want her to get help if..." I scrub a hand over my face. "I've been down this road before. Maybe it's automatic to think—"

"Ethan." Valentina's soft voice snags my attention. Her knowing gaze silences my excuses. "Ruby couldn't wait to start life with you. If she didn't see me, she texted me more times than I could count, asking about how your kids were doing during the two weeks you spent praying. Every minute she remained eager to know if you'd heard God's response." She leans forward. "She wants you in her life. That means she wants life, not death."

I sag against the island, forearms on cool marble. The edge bites into my ribs. "I thought—"

"Ruby has a lot going for her." Jason ticks off things I know but ignored when the odd thought snuck into my mind. "Singing at Skypoint, giving piano lessons, joining the city choir. She loves you. Does that sound like someone who wants to end her life?"

Heat churns in the pit of my stomach, and I begin to perspire. Why didn't I think about all these things? "She's been... happy. More like herself than I've seen in a long time."

"Do you think you might have projected your trauma with Maddie onto Ruby's situation?"

Valentina's question stops me cold. "What do you mean?"

She taps a knuckle against the counter. "You missed warning signs with Maddie. That experience now shapes how you read everything that resembles... you know. Naturally, you'll be hypervigilant." Her hand covers mine. "But right now, Ruby needs you to trust her, to believe she's not living in her past."

"Your instinct to protect is a good thing," Jason adds, his tone softer. "But protecting doesn't mean living in fear. Forgetting the past and moving forward—that's one of your sermons. It applies to you too."

I slipped into old habits, let fear lead where faith should.

Valentina pulls her hand away, and the room tilts, skewed by what I've done. Ruby isn't Maddie. She's been honest about her past, she's had therapy, and she's willing to call any time she senses panic. More importantly, she loves me for who I am, not because there's a condition to fulfill.

Jason's phone vibrates on the island, and Liam's name flashes on the screen. Jason taps the speaker. "What'd you forget?"

"Just checking." Liam's voice fills the kitchen. "Did you and Val solve Ethan and Ruby's feud yet?"

Valentina lets out a soft laugh. "We're working on it."

Some tension slips from my shoulders. "I'm still here, and I can hear you, by the way."

"My little rippers are supposed to take her cards to the hospital tomorrow. I don't want things to be awkward."

"They'll see her in a few days."

"And I don't want you brooding for—oh, I don't know—the next decade, mate."

"That's not going to happen." Jason smirks. "And the kids can take her cards tomorrow, of course. Ethan will text first and let you know everything is okay. Because"—he gives me a serious look— "everything will be okay."

"Perfect," Liam says, then shouts, "Good luck, Ethan."

"I don't need it." But I need all the prayers.

When the call ends, Valentina turns back to me. "You had a misunderstanding. You're obviously not getting any sleep tonight anyway. Go back to the hospital. The kids are still having fun and are welcome to stay."

For which I'm grateful, but the truth slides out before I can stop it. "I don't think she'll talk to me." I taste the raw edge of my question, see the recoil on her face. "She's never sent me away before."

"It's a hospital." Jason waves. "Are you expecting her to go all kung fu on you with a splinted hand and a braced ankle?"

The quip breaks something in me, and I snort, which loosens my chest.

"We all say things we can't take back." Valentina shrugs. "You did then. She did now. But she forgave you before. She's not the type to hold grudges. That's why we're sitting here."

Her words hit me, and I choke down a swallow. "I can't let her go."

"I know." Valentina nods.

If anything, Ruby's probably more terrified than angry. After all, the one person she trusted most doesn't trust her.

"Go already." Jason pushes to his feet. "Tell her what you promised when you reconciled. Tell her you'll take care of her. Liam said he heard you make lots of promises when Ruby passed out at church."

I meant it then. I mean it now.

Valentina crosses to the sink and fills a water glass. "With the recovery being a long haul ahead, so much will change if you're there for her." She passes the glass to me. "Show up. Don't fix everything all at once. Just be there."

Their words spin into plans in my head as the water cools my dry throat. Before the kids' bedtime, I want to tell them we're bringing Ruby home. I'll talk to them after I solve things with Ruby. Tonight, their basketball meet saved me from explaining our dilemma. Tomorrow, I'll have no excuse to give when they want to go to see her.

Driving over, I force myself to stay five under the speed limit. The last thing I need is a ticket or any delay. The slow drive gives me time to go over my words. Red lights drag, and every stop feels like a sermon in patience while I rehearse and re-rehearse lines.

I'm sorry.

I was scared.

I didn't mean it.

I should have trusted you.

Each time I start, the next thought pulls the sentence apart, and I have to start over. The words tumble and fumble in my head, but the fact is, I never need to memorize anything with Ruby. The moment I see her, I'll know what to say.

The hospital hallways blur as I push through. Speakers murmur overhead, nurses in scrubs drift past, and antiseptic and coffee scents hang in the air. At Ruby's half-open door, I peek in.

She's awake, eyes distant, lost in a place I can't reach. I rap my knuckles on the frame.

"Come in," she responds without looking.

"Ruby." I cross the room in two strides.

Her gaze flicks to me, her face crumples, and her lips part like she's about to ask me to leave.

"I know." I hold up a hand. I have to say what I need to before she kicks me out. "Before you send me away, hear me out."

Her lips press tight, but she nods against the pillow.

So I step closer and stop at her bedside, leaving a space so she can see me. My pulse thuds hot in my throat. "I promised I'd take care of you. Remember the day you fell at church? Everything I said that day and every day since you crashed back into my life, I've meant." I swallow the clog threatening to slow my words. "I meant it when I said I wanted to be better for you. Asking about the stairs wasn't judgment. It was an honest desire to understand so I could bear it with you. If that means getting help, I want to stand in that with you. While I want to hear your joy so I can share it, I also want to hear your pain so I can help bear it and hold you when it hurts."

Is she listening to the heart behind my speech? I almost pause to see, but I rush on instead. I can't let her interrupt and push me away.

"When I say I love you, I mean every piece of you. You make ordinary days extraordinary and worth remembering. When you're around, our family's whole. Your voice comforts me, your hand fits in mine, and you see me as Ethan, not just the pastor. And saying I love you is also making a promise to myself to put your needs before mine."

"Ethan…" Her voice quivers, eyes shimmering. She stirs, but a wince betrays the effort of trying to rise.

I sink to one knee beside the bed and grasp her good hand. My ring—blessedly still on her finger—presses against my palm. "Ruby Morrison, this hospital room isn't where I pictured you'd be." I cradle her hand, my thumb gliding over her knuckles. "But wherever you are, I want to be the one taking care of you. I want to help with showers, carry you up or down the stairs at our house, and make your recovery as seamless as possible."

A choked sound breaks from her. "I'm sorry. I... I didn't mean to say..."

"Shh." I thumb away her tears. "It's okay, baby. You have every right to be mad, to lash out, to feel everything. We'll argue and disagree. We'll fight. So what? In the end, that's what makes us... unbreakable."

I frame her face between my palms, her smooth skin bruised under my fingertips. "Which is why I have to ask. Will you marry me sooner? Like tomorrow or the day after?"

She shakes her head. Sobs rattle through her. She gestures to her splinted wrist, then her braced foot. "Ethan Bishop, look at me. I'm a mess. What kind of wedding would that be?"

I press her hand to my chest. My heart thrums beneath it. "You said it yourself when we picked the date. We've known each other for more than half our lives. Why waste another minute apart?"

"I should be presentable... the dress—"

"Happily for me, you already picked it out, right here in town." My lips tug into a smile. "I'll get it as soon as the shop opens tomorrow."

Her tears soften into a watery laugh. Her smile blooms bright enough to light the room.

"Are you sure you want to marry me so soon?"

"See, when you wait your whole life for the right person and you know you've found her, you don't want to wait a moment longer. When you were in that coma, all I could think was—what if I'd married you the moment I proposed? I'd have had even three blessed weeks with you... before you..." My voice splinters, and my throat tightens. I can't go on.

She squeezes my hand. "This wedding isn't for anyone else," she says. "It's for us. People or no people, I want you as my husband."

"And I want you as my wife." Warmth surges through me. I don't know any details about planning a last-minute wedding, but none of that matters. I've made up my mind. "I'll love you. I'll cherish you, in sickness and in health, starting right now. No pushing me away."

"Stay with me." She laughs through tears. "Don't ever let me push you away."

Her raw honesty drags me under, a pull I can't resist.

"Good." I release her hand only to lean in and slide my palm behind her neck, careful with the pillows so I don't crush her ribs. The second her lips touch mine, everything else is gone save for the pounding of my heart and the soft feel of her hair like silk in my fingers. I kiss her soundly, almost too fierce, too greedy.

Slow down! the warning brushes my mind.

I force myself back. My gaze falls into hers.

Her lashes flutter open, her expression one of wonder. Her left hand clutches my polo collar, keeping me close to her face as if letting go isn't an option.

"Is that why"—her voice rasps between our mingled breaths—"you talked me into getting the marriage license so soon? So you could marry me whenever your mind snapped?"

"If I remember, getting the license right away was your idea."

She tugs me down again and kisses me this time, slowly at first, sweet, yet possessive all at once. When she pulls back, I rest my forehead against hers. My legs have gone numb from the way I'm braced over, but I don't dare move. Not ready to let go of this moment.

"Could also be that God knew what was coming." My voice strains with everything I can't say. "He made sure we were ready ahead of time."

"I like"—her sob trembles against me, but it's a sob of joy—"how God thinks."

"Exactly." I ease back enough to cup her face in one hand, drinking her in. "I'm grateful He gave me forever with the girl who once made me believe in it. Now, she's the woman I get to have stay with me and share my life."

EPILOGUE

Ruby

"**G**ood morning, everyone." Ethan's voice booms from the pulpit, and his gaze finds mine in the front row where he sat beside me moments before. He's so effortlessly handsome in jeans, a white shirt, and a navy blazer with white sneakers.

Applause and cheers ripple through the sanctuary, the energy of worship still vibrating in the air. When he asks who's excited to be in church today, hands shoot up across the room.

"Before we dive into today's teaching, I'd like to invite my lovely wife, Ruby Bishop, to share the announcements and lead us in prayer."

The applause that follows is warm and genuine.

Almost four months into our marriage, I walk to the front. No reason for the nerves racking my stomach. The kindness with which the congregation has embraced me as their pastor's wife still takes my breath away. Nessa beams from her usual spot, and Helena gives me a thumbs-up.

Willow never had a permanent seating spot like many seasoned members, which made it easier when I encouraged her to move to the center row. She only agreed as long as she could sit behind me rather than in the front row.

I climb the final step to the pulpit, where my wedding ring gleams under the overhead lights.

Ethan gives me a warm hug. Then he hands me the microphone from the stand, unlike the wireless mic hooked behind his ear. He mouths, "I love you."

"I love you too," I mouth back before facing our audience as the applause fades.

These brothers and sisters have become true family. Overenthusiastic clapping has me glancing at where Willow stands. Two rows behind her, Valentina and Jason sit with their teen daughter, Eden.

I raise the mic. "Let's pray together for our community and the week ahead before we move to announcements."

The silence settles as I bow my head, praying God can use Ethan's message to touch someone's heart today. I pray for guidance, protection, and unity for our church family in the days to come.

After the prayer, I step behind the podium and slide over the iPad with the notes Ethan set up for me. "There's still another week to register for Vacation Bible School before it starts. This year's theme is 'Ocean Adventures with Jesus.'" I scan the congregation as confidence takes over. "We could use more volunteers for crafts and for snack prep."

Two weeks ago, I stood to share my testimony in front of everyone. The moment I told Ethan about my conviction to open up about my past, he set aside that Sunday's sermon for testimonies instead. After I shared mine—which left some people like Mary Beth with their jaws hanging in shock—sniffles and tears whispered throughout the sanctuary. Then Ethan extended the platform for anyone else who wanted to share, and people stepped up with stories of how God delivered them from addiction, financial struggles, and family reconciliation. That powerful service of prayer and encouragement offered a reminder that God continues to use the broken and restore them.

"Our youth summer camp is scheduled for July 15 through 22 at Pine Mountain Retreat." I scroll down when the screen dims. "Don't forget about our community outreach dinner this Friday at Skypoint. We're partnering with the food bank to serve families in need, and we could still use extra hands for setup and serving."

I finish with the last announcement and wish everyone a happy service.

"Now, let's welcome Pastor Ethan back to share what God has put on his heart." I click the mic into its stand.

More applause swells as he approaches. My pulse stutters when he leans in and brushes a chaste kiss against my cheek. "You did wonderfully, Mrs. Bishop." His breath warms my ear, and heat shivers through me.

"Thank you."

His face breaks into a smile so warm it steals my breath. That dimple will undo me every time.

My legs are shaky by the time I lower into the seat. I fan myself with one hand, heat rising in waves. Too warm for early June. Maybe they ought to switch on the air-conditioning before July.

Ethan begins his final sermon in a series about new beginnings and God's faithfulness, and my mind drifts to our new beginning.

We married two days after I left the hospital. Chuck hadn't dismantled the twinkling lights and decorations from the engagement party yet. After a few extra touches, including white roses everywhere with a single red tucked into each vase on the tables, the barn became a spring wonderland. Liam added a tent with coverings and space heaters, in case we had more guests. And, yes, almost half the church members showed up, as did the chorale choir members and most of our regulars at the coffee shop who knew about the wedding. Many of those same people loaned and helped us set up the extra furniture we needed as well.

Ethan's dad married us and surprised me the night before when he and his wife sat down with us and apologized for how they handled my past. I told them my choices and mistakes were mine alone and surely God had a lot to say in writing my story. I thanked them for raising a godly man I admire, the one whose faith helped me believe in a God I'd never known.

Even Harvey's eyes brimmed when he confessed. "I came between you two once. I couldn't marry Alyssa until I knew

Ethan was happily married, so you cannot imagine how blessed I feel since he's marrying you, Ruby."

Our first two months of marriage blurred with my recovery and long grueling physical therapy sessions—grueling because I was impatient, eager to do things on my own. However, I savored the process with Ethan at my side. He carried me upstairs, helped me dress, and even washed my hair. I might have stretched my helplessness longer than needed, just to feel his tenderness pour out on me. My favorite place in our room has become the book nook by the fire. There, I read and pray each morning while he drops the kids off at school.

"In closing"—Ethan's voice draws me back to the present—"I want you to remember God's love meets us where we are. Not where we think we should be, not where others expect us to be. But right here, right now, in our messy, perfectly imperfect lives."

His gaze locks on mine, his love in its depths, and my chest can't hold the rush of it. Love hasn't come easy, but we've learned that trust and patience are the core to a strong relationship. And with God at the center, it becomes long-lasting.

When he opens a time of prayer for those needing connection, I bow my head. Once he finishes, he invites everyone to meet us in the lobby, as he always does.

I'm still learning what this life looks like beyond Sundays. That's why I signed up for a pastor's wife conference in October, to delve into the role's ins and outs. For now, I've gone back to teaching private piano students, though I'll soon shift them into group lessons at Chuck's barn, which he's letting me rent. This consolidation gives me the freedom to help at Skypoint whenever they need music or entertainment.

The worship singer takes the stage for the closing song. A hand slides behind me, and my body warms as I turn to my husband. I touch his cheek and lean my head against him as we finish the song together.

Then the final notes fade. Ethan laces his fingers through mine and leads me toward the door. We've made a habit of slipping out before the crowd. Otherwise, he'd get cornered while visitors waited outside. Only the day of my panic attack broke that pattern.

"Hey." A voice catches us from behind. Liam. "I'm rounding up the kids so we can set up for tonight."

"Of course." Still holding my hand, Ethan checks his watch. "The Skypoint meeting won't take more than two hours."

"Thanks, Liam," I say. "Is that too many kids for you to handle alone?"

"Ouch." He clutches his chest. "Where's your faith in me?"

I wave him off. "We won't be long."

Still, I'll have Willow help him. His boys alone are a handful. Add Jason's twins, and roughhousing is guaranteed. Poor Poppy will end up hurt. With Russ out of town, she won't have another girl around to play with. After all, Eden is much older and often chooses to stay behind with Valentina and Jason.

We stand side by side as the line forms. People greet us, some with hugs, others with prayer requests. I'm still humbled when women step out of line to ask me to pray with them too.

I haven't had another panic attack since the one in this very church in October. That doesn't mean I'm healed and past it all. Knowing I'm not whole yet forces me to depend more on Him, even as I bow my head to pray with women whispering their urgent prayer requests.

I've come to see how hard Ethan works as a pastor. One moment, it's the middle of dinner and the phone rings with someone needing prayer. The next, it's a late-night drive to the hospital or an early morning visit to a grieving home.

No wonder the congregation adores him. Casseroles and pies still show up at our door, even months after I came home from the hospital. During my recovery, we couldn't eat half of it, but with the new food bank, nothing goes to waste. Each Sunday, after Nessa sets aside portions for families in need, someone collects the rest and serves it during their Sunday dinners.

Diana used to help handle food delivery, but she stepped down while Ethan was on leave. By the time he returned, he needed a new assistant. This time, he got to choose someone who wouldn't be jealous of his wife. I told him Diana quit because she realized he wasn't single anymore. He'd been clueless that she ever had a crush on him. He even claimed his cluelessness might've been because I'd always blinded him to the rest of the world.

Willow stops before me. "Where are the kids?"

"Liam already took them." I pull her into a tight embrace, so grateful God used her in reuniting me with Ethan. Where would I be now if she hadn't urged me to move in with her in Meadowbrook? "Figured it'd be easier to get them settled while he sets up for the bonfire."

"Do I sense heartbreak over missing out on the chaos?" Willow squeezes me tight, then steps back.

My throat tightens. I blink the sting away. "Can't I just give my best friend a hug for no reason?"

"Any time." She smiles. "You don't need me to watch them during your meeting?"

"Liam's fun with the kids. He lets them run wild, though. Having all of them alone—"

"Aren't Jason and Valentina helping?"

I smile at her wide-eyed look. "Valentina still needs naps, first trimester or not. And Jason, of course, insists on staying with her."

Their good news, Valentina's expecting, carried me through recovery. Her first pregnancy, Jason's fourth child.

"If I phone the diner, would you mind picking up chicken nuggets and fries and taking them over to Liam's?"

"Wait. You're sending me alone to Liam's?" Her hand flies to her chest. Her neck wobbles with her gulp. "Just the two of us... at his place?"

"And the kids. Look at you, red-faced." I cuff her shoulder and lean close, lowering my voice. "Don't act like you haven't imagined being alone with him when no one's watching."

"Shut up." She swats back at me, but the dark crimson blooming across her cheeks gives her away.

"You'll be fine. It's only for a couple of hours."

Ethan's counseling a couple at Skypoint and invited me along, in case the wife needs a woman's perspective. The simple gesture means everything to me. He's drawing me into his world, into his ministry. With him, I'm not just a bystander. I'm trusted. Valued. Seen as his partner in every way.

"Guess I might as well get warmed up to the street." Her lips twitch. "If I'm staying there for all ten days."

"Now you're talking."

Willow's staying with our kids while Ethan and I take our honeymoon to the Virgin Islands next week. She'll handle VBS drop-offs and nighttime routines. Ethan's parents will help out whenever Willow's at work and give her overnight breaks when they stay the night.

As she slips away, Ethan's arm curls around my waist, and his warmth seeps through my silk dress. I glance up. He looks so at ease, laughing with the last family in line, and I find myself smiling. As if aware, he looks at me sideways and winks. The swell in my chest nearly unravels me. I just might explode from love for this man.

I used to think forever had slipped through my fingers, but what once felt like an end between us became merely the middle of our story. Standing beside Ethan now, I know God gave us more than we lost. He gave us a new beginning, a second chance—with each other and with Him. And He'll stay with Ethan and me throughout whatever comes during our unending story.

Join my Insider group and download the exclusive Novella The Therapist's NeighborI send out short newsletters weekly with book deals and releases from me and other authors in my genre.

Willow and Liam's story is coming next.

Connect with me through social!

@rosefresquezauthor (Instagram)

Connect with me through my Facebook Group

Tiktok

Listen to my books for free on <u>YOUTUBE</u>

Follow me on <u>Goodreads</u> and <u>Book Bub</u>.

For E-books, keep reading for a free 31 day God's Masterpiece Devotional. (Soon I'll have an expanded devotionadevotional book launched for you to check out)

-THE END-

MORE BOOKS BY ROSE FRESQUEZ

Checkout the Rest of **THE BUCHANAN SERIES**

1 *First Site*

2. *Something right*

3. *Bright Side*

4. *Short Sighted*

5. *New Light (A Christmas Novella)*

ROMANCE IN THE ROCKIES SERIES

1. *Complex*

2. *Choices*

3. *Beyond Repair*

4. *Stand Out*

5. *Crystal Clear*

THE CAREGIVER SERIES

1. *The Doctor's Nanny*

2. *The Entrepreneur's Nurse*

3. *The Physician's Helper*

4. *The CEO's Companion*

5. *The Investor's Wife*

6. *The Soldier's Trainer*

7. *The Realtor's Attendant*

THE BILLIONAIRE REUNION SERIES

1. *A legitimate Date*

2. *A Sudden Romance*

3. *A Necessary Compromise*

4. *A Genuine Disguise*

5. *A Convenient Marriage*

THE OFFICE HEARTTHROBS

1. *Yours Temporarily*

2. *Yours Blindly*

3. *Yours Forever*

4. *Yours Faithfully*

SINGLE DADS OF MEADOWBROOK

1. *Where I Belong*

2. *Stay With Me*

3. *Anything For Love*

4. *Before You Go*

A NOTE FROM THE AUTHOR

Thank you so much for reading! It means the world to me that you chose my book out of the many other stories you could've been reading.

You can always Listen to some of my books for free on YOUTUBE

Stay connected with Rose Fresquez

Bookbub

Goodreads

@rosefresquezauthor (Instagram)

Connect with me through my Facebook Group

Tiktok